"Crisp, smart prose. Vivid, intelligent, and relatable characters. A story with verve and social urgency... First-rate storytelling."
—Kelly Parsons, author of *Doing Harm* and *Under the Knife*

"A violent thriller that pits integrity against corruption and expedience in an arid, pitiless landscape...*Memo from Turner* ticks all the boxes for righteous machismo."
—*Guardian* (London)

"This is an interesting story in an interesting setting, and the dialogue is first-rate. I look forward to more Turner stories."
—Nicholas Guild, author of *Blood Ties*

"An exuberant ride through violence in the human heart and the conditions that allow vice to flourish over decency...A gritty, hard-hitting moral novel."
—Soniah Kamal, award-winning author of *Unmarriageable: Pride and Prejudice in Pakistan*

MEMO FROM TURNER

MEMO FROM TURNER

TIM WILLOCKS

BLACKSTONE
PUBLISHING

Printed in the United States of America
Originally published in hardcover by Blackstone Publishing in 2019

First paperback edition: 2020
ISBN 978-1-09-409107-5
Fiction / Thrillers / Suspense

1 3 5 7 9 10 8 6 4 2

CIP data for this book is available
from the Library of Congress

Blackstone Publishing
31 Mistletoe Rd.
Ashland, OR 97520

www.BlackstonePublishing.com

To my love and inspiration:
Valentina

TUESDAY MORNING

LANGKOPF, NORTHERN CAPE,
SOUTH AFRICA

Turner's vision felt gritty, sometimes blurred, his eyeballs too small for their sockets. His head ached with a dull beat, interrupted by sudden shards whenever the tires hit a bump. He could feel his brain move inside his skull, tugging against the blood vessels as if they were cheese wires. The pain seemed worse than before. The same was true for the rest of his body: his kidneys, his spine, his ankles. Maybe it was because he was recovering, his nerves reawakening to work out how much damage had been done. Maybe he'd drunk too much water, maybe not enough. He had water but he didn't trust it. He couldn't remember the science and he couldn't risk an experiment. He had settled on the idea of eggs. He trusted eggs. If he didn't get eggs he was afraid his brain would explode before someone put a bullet in it. The one thing he knew for sure was that someone was going to try.

He glanced at the speedometer. One hundred forty kmh. He was going too fast for his blunted, depleted senses; much faster than it seemed, even on this run-down dead-end country road to nowhere. Easy enough in two tons of luxury technology with a five liter supercharged Jaguar engine under the lid. The irony was not lost on him. If the engine had been less potent and the car less than huge, a lesser monument to its owner's unslakable vanity, the event that had brought him here, to the back of beyond and beyond the bounds of his humanity, would never have occurred, and he wouldn't be driving as if the future were something he didn't expect to see.

The sun was behind him to the east. For the moment no one else was. Before he knew it the gate to the farm appeared just ahead and he stomped on the brake. The algorithms of the onboard computers raced to prevent catastrophe. The pain in his skull intensified. The red Range Rover slowed with contemptuous ease and Turner braced his hands against the steering wheel as his chest rammed the seat belt.

The dead man in the passenger seat beside him wasn't strapped in and lurched forward from the waist. His eyebrows bounced off the dashboard and his head flopped down toward his knees. Fresh rivulets of blood pumped from the bullet holes in his back to further stain the cream leather upholstery.

Turner was more familiar with corpses than most. Less so than a coroner, an undertaker, or a geriatric oncologist—and he wasn't used to ferrying them around, as an ambulance driver might be— but he was responsible for this one being dead. More precisely, he had fired three 9×19 Parabellum slugs through his belly.

The rusty iron gate was open. He swung a hard right off the tarmac and accelerated up the mild incline of a rough dirt track. The dead man flopped upright again and shunted sideways into the passenger door, his face flattened against the window. Half a kilometer ahead the blades of the wind pump turned on top of its slender steel pylon. Outbuildings and a rusting tractor, an old pickup truck; silage bales; the single-story farmhouse with its old-style red stone stoop. In the rearview mirror: the plume of his own dust.

Turner made a U-turn in the farmyard and parked. He left the engine on and opened the door to get out. A searing wall of hot air almost drove him back inside. His every joint complained as he levered himself upright and staggered through it toward the house.

The stoop was half laminated by an almost-black veneer of sunbaked gore. The smooth surface had crazed as it shrank in the heat and was blemished by the tracks of wildlife—birds, a jackal, and a business of flies, stranded and doomed as the wide pool of blood had congealed. An Olympic barbell loaded with eight twenty-kilo plates sat mired in the middle, as if in the aftermath of some bizarre contest of strength. On a small table stood a two-liter plastic jug from a blender. The inside was coated yellow with dried smoothie. More dead flies, glutted and drowned, floated in the rancid remnant in the bottom. Turner grabbed the jug. He ducked through the open front door and stumbled across the living room.

He stopped as he saw himself in an antique mirror on the wall. His black skin was gray with salt and dust. His features were unnaturally gaunt, his lips creviced and peeling. He did not recognize his own eyes. They were tunnels drilled into the darkness that now lay behind them. There were pictures in the darkness he didn't want to see; memories, revelations, that he dreaded to revisit yet would have to. He turned away from what he realized, with shock, was himself and continued to the kitchen and survival.

He tore the fridge open. There they were: two boxes of eggs. He opened them: eight left. He rinsed out the jug at the sink, the sound of the water grating on his mind. Still encrusted but the dead flies were gone; clean enough. He cracked all eight eggs into the jug, one in each hand, two at a time, unconcerned by the fragments of shell. Back to the fridge. Coconut milk, cow's milk, a banana, two oranges, celery, a tomato, a lump of cheese. He piled the jug to the brim, peeling the banana, ripping the whole oranges apart and cramming them in. He found the blender and the lid and liquidized the concoction for as long as his craving permitted.

He took the lid off and drank.

His eyelids clenched. If he had had any tears he would have cried with something more than pleasure or relief. His gullet convulsed in its haste to suck down the liquid. His whole being affirmed the rightness of the eggs. The contents of an egg could create a living creature strong enough to break through the shell and sing. They had to be perfectly balanced. They wouldn't explode his brain. Half a liter. His stomach cramped at the sudden assault. He lowered the jug and breathed. Enough for now. The cramp passed.

He took the jug back to the car and sealed himself inside with the dead man and the air con. He watched the empty road in the distance as it quavered in the harsh white sunlight. A flat, featureless terrain of grass and scrub. The Range Rover had a GPS tracker inside it. They knew exactly where he was. He wondered how much time he had before they got here. Not much. But time enough to make sure that when they buried him, they wouldn't be able to bury him under another mountain of lies.

He took out his smartphone and tapped and scrolled through the app he needed to send a voice memo. He took another swallow of the concoction, chewing on pieces of orange peel, his tongue reviving to the bitter tang, and set the jug on the seat between his thighs. He started to record.

"Memo from Turner.

"To Captain Eric Venter; cc Mohandas Anand; Colonel Nyathi; Pieter Meyer at the *Times*; myself; the cloud.

"Dear Captain Venter,

"You told me to keep you up to speed on the hit-and-run.

"The unknown girl. Culpable homicide, failure to render.

"I said I'd push it hard and close it fast. That was just two days ago. It seems a lot longer to me, but I've been in the slowness. The slowness is hard to explain. You have to be in it to know it. To know it, you have to go mad.

"I haven't closed. Not all the way, not yet.

"But I want you to know I'm still pushing.

"Maybe from beyond the grave.

"Things got out of hand, as things will. Chaos never sleeps. A good man meets chaos with composure. He does what's right because that's the way to cause the least pain and to die with the fewest regrets. That's what I thought I was. A good man.

"Now I'm not sure. I'll never be sure again.

"You told me it was a different world up here. You were right. You told me all this space would alter my mind. You were right. You told me you would worry about me and I believe that, in a way, you did. But not in the way I understood it.

"I wonder if you're worried now.

"It shouldn't have been my case. It was my first weekend off in three. But Saturday night in Cape Town left bodies all over the city, and you couldn't even find a pair of uniforms to spare so you called me in. I wasn't sleeping. I was up on Devil's Peak, practicing my long notes and waiting for the sun to rise. But you can't be in Heaven and on Earth at the same time.

"It was 6:00 a.m. on Sunday morning …"

PART ONE: SUNDAY

THIRSTLAND

ONE

The girl had no more reason to turn down this street than any other. In the humid labyrinth of Nyanga township all streets looked alike. They weren't even streets, just strips of baked dirt between rows of shanties and rusted shipping containers turned into homes.

If she had been here before she didn't remember. She didn't even try. She had no use for memory. The less she allowed to go in there, the emptier it got, and the more the monsters that lurked within the emptiness seemed inclined to sleep.

She didn't know what time it was. She had no use for time. The dogs had long since howled and gone to sleep. It was enough to know that the world was quiet and dark and that people would be few.

She had no use for people, for their company, their feelings, their help, their concern, their lies. She only had use for the things they had thrown away and which kept her alive. Even here there was surplus enough to survive on, as a rat survives. She could have bargained for more but she had learned that what little that more might be wasn't worth the cost in humiliation. And sometimes danger.

The rats were doing fine and so was she.

She walked the maze without destination. Without ambition, intention, or anything so grand as desire. Even need, she had found, could be negotiated downward. At some point fatigue would overcome her and she'd crawl into some hole to join the dogs in their dreams. When she awoke, she'd start walking again.

She had no use for self-pity. Animals felt no self-pity, they only felt pain. Children felt no self-pity. They only felt pain and sorrow and bewilderment. Self-pity was something you learned in a place of safety and the girl had never had the chance.

She saw the cars up ahead and stopped. There were two of them, one white, the other bloodred, parked side by side, noses out, in a vacant dirt lot by a shebeen, one of the city's many unlicensed pubs.

They were beautiful.

Stranded among the hovels and rusted containers, they shone as if with their own inner light. The single distant streetlamp, the pale half-moon, the waste glow from the bar, could not account for their radiance. They shone with dominance, ingenuity, wealth; with a fanatic and extravagant commitment to a way of being as remote from her own as the constellations wheeling above her head. She was moved simply by their perfection.

She smiled as a child might smile at some newfound wonder.

She looked about and saw no observers. She ran toward the cars.

Up close they seemed to squat there, huge-shouldered and silent. Something in their dormant power made her scalp shiver. Silver letters gleamed on their hoods. Toyota. Range Rover. She circled the white one and peered in the windows. The glass was too dark to see anything inside. She reached for a door handle, hesitated, drew her hand back. The cars would give her nothing that she needed. They had given her a moment of wonder and that was enough. She turned and ducked between the two great machines as a draft of sound gusted from the shebeen.

Voices. Music. A gust of coarse laughter. The sound faded down again.

She looked toward the shebeen. A long narrow shack half-reclaimed by weeds, built from planks of diverse origin and roofed in corrugated iron.

A tall black African stood outside the door. He wore a black suit and a white shirt that somehow conveyed an alien beauty similar to that of the cars. She knew at once that he was a dangerous man. A man who had killed and was ready to do so again. He wore this power of killing as he wore his suit, with the understated confidence that came from having earned it. She knew also that he'd never stoop to hurting her. At worst he would chase her away but she wanted to look at him. He was beautiful, too. He glanced at the two big cars.

She ducked. The cars were his, or in his charge. She crept around the back of the bloodred car, the Range Rover, and edged out one eye to watch him again. He hadn't seen her.

He lifted his right hand toward his face holding a burger half-wrapped in a paper napkin. The girl felt her stomach clench with hunger. He studied the burger without enthusiasm, then took a bite. He chewed and his face contorted with disgust. He bent forward and spit the mouthful out at his feet.

"Mother fuck."

He spat again, looked at the burger in his hand. He could have thrown it into the street, where it would have gone unnoticed amongst the drifts of trash, but he was not that kind of man. He looked beyond the Range Rover. The girl turned to look too.

A few steps behind the cars, shoved against the cinder-block wall of the building at the rear of the lot, stood three black metal garbage dumpsters. For the first time she noticed their stench. The man walked toward the cars and passed between them. The girl retreated on her haunches. The man used the paper napkin to raise the lid of the dumpster and tossed the burger inside. As he walked back to stand outside the bar he pulled a bottle of water from the pocket of his pants and opened it. He rinsed his mouth and spat and drank again.

The girl had a handbag slung around her neck, cheap striped cloth. She reached in and found a plastic cigarette lighter. She checked the flame. She shuffled back around the bloodred car and looked back at the dumpster. She risked a glance at the man. Could she get into the dumpster without him seeing her? She thought about it.

A gunshot slammed.

Dust and splinters exploded from the wall of the shebeen.

Before the splinters reached the ground, the tall man had dropped the bottle and drawn a gun from under his jacket. He opened the bar door and vanished inside.

The girl dashed to the dumpster and threw back the lid. It hit the wall and dropped back. She threw it up again and slid around the side and steadied it in place. She turned her face away from an eruption of acrid vapor. The lid held. The top of the dumpster was level with her shoulders. She peered over the rim into absolute darkness. She stretched her arm over the edge and clicked the lighter. The light of the flame fell across an uneven mass of every kind of waste, much of it organic and seething with tiny life. The dumpster looked three-quarters full. She scanned the filth and waved the small flame but she couldn't see the burger within range of the light.

She staggered away and doubled over and retched. She leaned her hands on her knees until she'd recovered. She wiped tears from her eyes, took three deep breaths and held the last, and straightened. She stepped back to the dumpster and shoved her head over the front rim. She stood on her toes and reached over with the lighter and clicked the wheel until she got a flame.

Voices rose some distance behind her as the bar door opened, one voice dominant.

"Simon, take Mark and Chris straight to the hotel. I'll bring these two clowns."

Locks clunked open. Lights flashed. She glanced over her shoulder. The tall African herded two young white men toward the white Toyota. They were both unsteady on their feet. If they'd seen her rooting in the dumpster, they didn't care. She turned back to her search.

"Dirk? Give me the bloody keys." The dominant voice again. A foreign accent.

"It's my bloody car." This voice slurred, younger.

"It's your mother's. Give me the keys, now."

Car doors slammed. An engine started up.

"What do you buggers want?" The foreigner. Then two new voices shouting together, the words indistinct. The foreign voice rode over them. "Shut up and calm down. Here, take this. Take it. Buy a new poster. Buy a new bar. Now fuck off before you get hurt."

More clunks. Lights flared right behind her.

"I said: fuck off, Dirk!"

"You didn't have to bitch-slap him."

"Get behind that wheel and I'll slap you."

"You wouldn't dare."

She sensed the car to her left, the white one, drive away.

She saw the burger.

Her lighter went out. She relit it. She was in luck. The burger had landed on a plastic bag but it was out of reach. She crouched, grabbed the edge of the dumpster with both hands, and jumped, boosting herself up so that she lay doubled over the rim. The metal dug into her belly just beneath her ribs but it wasn't something she hadn't done before. The burger was invisible again, She clicked the lighter. Again. Again. A car door slammed, then another. The lighter caught. An engine started. She saw the burger.

She reached out and grabbed it. Heard more shouts of contention. As she levered her body backward a flood of white light threw her shadow at the raised lid. The engine revs rose to a whine. The girl jumped down and twisted to land sideways. She blinked as white lights hurtled toward her.

Her bones collapsed.

Her guts popped inside her.

Her face bounced on glass.

Her awareness was swamped. She was blind. Dazzled by bright colors. She was pinned above the earth. She was falling. Couldn't breathe to scream. She saw the night sky.

For a moment she felt nothing, heard nothing. She stared up at the stars. Her body warned her. It was gathering itself, preparing itself, to devote everything it was and everything it had to the experience of intolerable pain. The pain was as yet a ghost, shimmering just beyond the veil of reality, waiting for the energy to become material. She sensed that ghost. It was coming. And it was her own flesh. Terror saturated her mind. Terror so intense that for a moment it kept the ghost at bay. Red lights glared into her face.

"Turn the engine off! DIRK! Turn the fucking engine OFF!"

The engine cut out.

The girl turned her head toward the voices. She looked down the shining red length of the car. A big white man opened the driver's door and jutted his bearded chin toward the interior.

"Satisfied?"

"It's my car."

"You're weak. You're stupid. And you're pissed. Now move over and put your seat belt on."

The big man cocked his fist.

"Alright, alright! I'm sorry."

The girl wanted to speak but was afraid it would invite the ghost. She turned her head. Another man's face stared down at her from the open rear window. Young, white, a huge muscular neck. He appeared to be horrified. She opened her mouth and a low moan came out and her insides started to scream and she choked the moan off. The young man called to the elder.

"Hennie, I can't find my phone. Give me yours."

"What do you need a phone for, dickhead?"

The big man turned and looked straight down at her. He frowned but without horror, as if he'd spotted nothing worse than a flat tire. "Bollocks," he said.

The girl tried to speak to him with her eyes. The big man got the message. He scratched his beard with a thumb. Grimaced. He didn't otherwise move.

"Hennie, the phone, Jesus!"

"Keep your fucking mouth shut."

The young man in the back opened the door and the big man, Hennie, took a step and slammed the door in his face. He looked down at the girl. Tiny points of light in dark sockets were all she could see of his eyes.

The drunken voice from the front seat: "What's wrong now?"

Hennie looked at her a moment longer. She raised her arm toward him. She heard and felt the grinding of bones, the bursting of membranes somewhere deep inside her.

"Nothing's wrong," said Hennie. He turned away from her. "Time to hit the road to dreamland."

The girl watched him get in the car and close the door. The

engine started. The young face appeared at the open rear window and peered down at her. He was crying.

The girl watched the bloodred car drive away between the shanties.

Brake lights flared. The lights disappeared.

And the ghost took possession of her body.

TWO

Hennie had been driving for seven hours. They were six hundred clicks from Cape Town and thirty minutes from home. He'd been glad to see the dawn, and its eerie splendor had not been lost on him, but in broad daylight the Northern Cape was something to be crossed not appreciated. The province was larger than Germany. Flat scrub desert stretched to the horizon in every direction. The sky was a hard, bright blue. It was always blue. There were days when Hennie would have danced with joy to see a single cloud.

He'd never been much of a sightseer, or a tourist, though he'd seen his share of the world and more. Maybe it's because he was a Londoner. In his view grand landscapes were best enjoyed on a cinema screen—deserts, jungles, canyons, waves pounding the rocks, forests in the snow, so forth. But then you were only looking at them for a few seconds at a time, and you knew that shortly someone would appear on a horse or driving a fast car, and that they'd shoot someone or meet a long-legged woman or find a suitcase full of cash. He'd hiked through all such terrains in his time, carrying a sixty-pound pack and a rifle. They were impressive for about five minutes, then they were just something to be crossed. He'd shot a good number of people, too, but he'd never met the woman or found the suitcase, or at least not in a landscape. The woman he had met at her husband's funeral. The cash was a sequence of digits in Switzerland.

His mind had roamed from one random thought to another since they'd left Cape Town and some had seemed profound and even important, yet now he couldn't remember a single one. He wondered how many thoughts he had had in his life. Probably millions, if you included things like deciding to cut his toenails or how many sugars to put in his tea. Most of them, too—in retrospect, almost all of them—had been a complete waste of time. Gone forever, and no more significant than the thoughts of a dog. The toenail stuff was probably the best of it. At least that had been useful. He'd seen men killed by neglected toenails.

He rubbed his face with one hand to improve the blood supply to his brain.

Time was catching up with him. He felt that he was in the best shape of this life but objectively that wasn't possible. Fifty-five-year-olds didn't win gold medals. But he believed he could take his twenty-three-year-old self on the grounds of stubbornness, meanness, and experience. He'd been harder on the outside but softer on the inside. The softness of youth was built into the machine. No matter how brutal your own life had been, you could always put that down to sheer bad luck. Wrong place, wrong time, wrong parents. You still had hope. It took another couple of decades to realize that there was no better world somewhere. A better life, maybe, but not a better world. Man was a vicious bastard, pure and simple, and mad into the bargain.

He turned from the tarmac unspooling across the veld and looked at Dirk.

Dirk lay slumped against the passenger door. Drool seeped

from the corner of his mouth to soak his Versace T-shirt. A handsome lad. Hennie felt a pang of love stab him in the chest.

Dirk would be twenty-four next month. Since the age of nine he had been Hennie's stepson. If he'd been Hennie's real son, Hennie would have made his life a misery and most likely would have driven him away. As his stepfather Hennie didn't feel a genetic responsibility for who Dirk was. Didn't feel obliged to mold him or feel embarrassed by him. All that was Margot's business. Hennie's was to keep Margot happy. Keeping Margot happy was the purpose of his life. No easy chore but he felt glad to have found any purpose at all. When necessary, it meant protecting Dirk. He had protected Dirk from the law. Question was, did he need to protect him from Margot?

"What a fucking cock-up."

He realized he'd muttered out loud. A grunt came from the back seat. He glanced up into the mirror. He saw Simon's white Toyota 4Runner, some hundred meters behind them. Simon was their head of security. He was Zulu, as solid as Table Mountain, and as close to a true friend as Hennie had. Hennie adjusted his angle on the mirror and saw Jason blinking and clutching his throat in the rear.

"Jesus." Jason's voice sounded like a cheese grater on a rusty pipe.

Jason Britz was of no more than average height but his shoulders half-filled the rear of the car. His primary occupation was lifting weights and injecting steroids. In theory, he was a farmer. For two centuries his forefathers had sweated, coaxed, and bullied a living from this godforsaken terrain, a land shunned by all flora and fauna edible to Europeans and even to the vast majority of Africans. No soil, no grass, no trees, no fruit, no mammals. In the four years since Jason had inherited his family's farm, the desert had reclaimed itself almost entirely. In practice he made a living supplying weed and meth to local dealers whose main clientele worked in Margot's mine. He wasn't in prison, or buried under the sand, because his uncle, Rudy Britz, was a police sergeant.

Hennie pulled a bottle of water from the holder and drank and put it back.

"Can I have some of that?" asked Jason.

"Get your own."

"The other bottles are in the trunk."

Hennie managed not to respond.

Jason said, "You think it's all my fault."

"I was enjoying the silence. Why don't you try it?"

Jason didn't speak again for all of thirty seconds.

"I wonder if she's still alive. I mean, well, you know who I mean."

"Shut up. You'll wake Dirk."

"I'll never forget that look on her face. It's bad juju, Hennie."

"Did you know that farmers are the root of all man's woes?"

"Man's?" said Jason.

"Mankind. The human race. Us."

"Ag, no man, we'd all starve without farmers."

"You've hit the nail right on the head."

Jason said, "I don't know what you're talking about."

"Crime, war, slavery, tyranny. Greed and murder for greed. Capitalism. Sexually transmitted disease. It's all down to the farmers."

Jason laughed. Hennie laughed too.

"You're trying to wind me up."

"Not at all," said Hennie. "Before farmers came along we had none of those things. Everyone was too busy, hunting antelope, buffalo, reindeer, seals. Fishing. They were always on the move and the men were all tooled up and fit with it, so there was a limit to how much bullshit any one man could get away with. But a farmer has to stay put, he has a shovel not a spear, and the good farmer, who breaks his back pulling weeds and digging irrigation—such as your father was—grows more produce than he and his family can eat. So the family gets bigger and your population booms and you grow even more food, and the surplus just keeps getting bigger too. So what do you do with that surplus?"

"You sell it," said Jason. "Or barter it. Or save it for a drought."

"Very good. But to do all that you have to store it, right? And if you store it, sooner or later some evil bastard is going to come along and steal it. So some local gangster gets a bunch of his own villains together and says to the farmers thereabouts, 'Look, we'll store it for you and keep it safe for when you need it. For a reasonable commission, of course.' Are you following me?"

"Sounds a bit like the drug trade."

"Very much so. Before you know it that gangster is calling himself the king, and the surplus isn't yours anymore, it's his, all of it, every grain, every goat, every egg. And if your farmer complains, the king sends his boys to kneecap your oxen, or peel the bark from your olive trees and rape your daughters. Now all the farmers are working full time for the king for no pay, not a red cent, and the king is in his castle, which the farmers built and paid for, and his boys have become an army but it's not enough because money's tight and you farmers can't be squeezed any harder without dropping dead even sooner than you already do, and somewhere over far yonder hills some other king is working the same scam. So what does our king do, if he's got the balls?"

"He muscles in on the new king's territory."

"Right," said Hennie. "War. War means slaves to work the new fields and give the king his foot baths and build temples for his gods and mine the gold for his crown. Prostitutes for the troops. More people. More surplus. More war. And basically there you have it. Civilization as we know it. Thanks to the bloody farmers. And, as Oscar Wilde said, the downtrodden masses have sold themselves for a very bad pottage indeed."

"What's a pottage?" asked Jason.

"A kind of thick soup."

"Yeah, but now we've got the internet."

Hennie snorted. "If it was up to me I'd shut it down today."

"Are you a communist, Hennie?"

"My dad was a socialist, much good it did him. I'm more in the way of a king, but to be a king you have understand how the game is rigged."

"Well you can't blame me for the wars or the internet. I'm not a farmer anymore."

Jason fell into what seemed to be a thoughtful trance.

Hennie was peeved that his historical analysis had not provoked greater admiration.

Jason said, "We shouldn't have left that girl."

"Forget about the girl."

"We should've at least called an ambulance."

Hennie felt a familiar rage simmer in his chest.

"Jason, do you know what 'tolerate' means?"

"Tolerate? It means we should try not to hate the blacks."

"That's a narrow definition," said Hennie, "but it's a start."

"Uncle Rudy says we shouldn't bother."

"More generally it means that when a situation—or a person—is a pain in our bollocks but either we can't do anything about it or the cost of doing so would be more than its worth, we grit our teeth and put up with it. For instance, we tolerate the sun, the dust, the mosquitoes. We tolerate the whims of women and the tantrums of children. And yes, we tolerate the blacks, and Rudy's wrong, you should bother, because you're not going to get rid of them any more than you're going to get rid of the sun."

"I see your point, Hennie."

"No you don't because I haven't made it yet. My point is, I tolerate you."

"I always thought you were a good bloke, too."

Hennie looked in the mirror to see if Jason was taking the piss. He wasn't.

"You might also say that I suffer you. For Dirk's sake. But if you don't shut your mouth, that can change."

"I don't want Dirk to suffer."

"Jesus. Are you still pissed?"

"She couldn't have seen Dirk. Pity he didn't see her."

Hennie glanced over his shoulder.

Jason was wringing his hands and staring down into the space between his knees.

"She saw me," he said. "Did she get a good look at you?"

Hennie braked slowly and opened the electric window.

"They say we all look the same to them," said Jason. "You could always shave the beard off."

Hennie stuck his arm out and waved at Simon to overtake them.

Jason said, "I wonder what Margot will say." He noticed Hennie's maneuver, the white Toyota swooping past. "What's wrong?"

Hennie pulled over and stopped. He left the engine running. He got out and opened the rear door on Jason. Jason cringed, like a dog who knows he's done something wrong but not exactly what. Hennie pitied him, but not enough to shirk what had to be done.

"Out."

"What do you mean? Why?"

"I'm tired. You drive."

Jason's lips quivered with gratitude. He stuck one foot on the tarmac and ducked his head and one shoulder out of the door. Hennie stepped behind him and slid his right forearm across Jason's throat. He grabbed his own right elbow with his left hand and levered his left forearm into the back of Jason's neck. He dragged him, choking, from the car and dumped him in the scrub at the side of the road. Jason rolled onto his back and stared up at him, panting with fear.

"Listen to me you stupid, drug-addled juice-monkey. Margot isn't going to say anything because Margot's never going to know. Neither are your mates, your uncle Rudy, and most of all Dirk. Only you and I know. And if I ever hear that anyone else does, I will recycle you into the shit of carnivorous beasts. It takes about two days and the smell is peculiar depending on whether or not you get eaten alive. Have I made myself clear?"

Jason nodded. He started to get up until Hennie stabbed a finger at him.

"Stay down."

Hennie took a gun from his jacket pocket. Jason's Vektor Z-88, a Beretta 92 produced on license for the cops. He ejected the magazine and the cartridge in the chamber and dropped the gun at his feet.

"The next man who takes that off you might not be so friendly."

Hennie took the chance to examine the back of the Range Rover in daylight. The bumper, the trunk, the window. He rechecked the surfaces from various angles. After a moment he was satisfied. Not a mark on it. There'd be traces of something, but he'd get one of the men to give it a scrub, wax, and polish. He tapped the gleaming metal twice.

"British engineering, mate."

Jason had not dared move. Hennie slammed the rear door without looking at him and got back behind the wheel. Dirk moaned and shifted but didn't waken.

"Jesus, Hennie, you're not going to leave me here—"

Hennie closed his door and drove away.

He watched Jason, reflected in the wing mirror, scramble to his feet. He stood there, frantically going through his pockets. It felt like abandoning a giant child. But these lads had to grow up.

Hennie found Rudy Britz's number on his mobile and dialed it. In the rearview, he saw Jason run after him, waving both hands above his head.

"Christ," said Rudy. "Seven on a Sunday morning? What do you want?"

"I want you to hear this from me," said Hennie. "You'll be getting a call from that nephew of yours. He's been a silly boy."

THREE

The girl looked as dead as any corpse Turner had seen.

She was a black African, mid-to-late teens, and lay prone with her left cheek resting on the sunbaked dirt of the lot. Flies crawled over her eyeballs and her desiccated lips. A bruise bulged from her right cheekbone. She didn't appear to be breathing. But greater diagnosticians than he had zipped the living into body bags, and he was the first responder. He had to be sure.

He squatted and felt for the carotid pulse between gloved fingers and thumb.

After a moment, he withdrew his hand.

He guessed she weighed well under forty kilos. Her short, thin cotton dress, pale green with yellow flowers, had been torn from waist to hem to reveal emaciated buttocks and thighs. Soiled underwear, more recently soiled with moist red clots and excrement. Her right hip was grossly deformed, the overlying skin pulverized and sheared aside in a ragged, shriveled flap. Raw, white-and-red shards spiked through the breach in her flesh, their edges and spicules rimed with an obscene coagulant of marrow and blood. More feasting flies.

Turner's guts rose inside him with something more than mere disgust, something that evoked outrage and confusion, and a memory he rarely dared revisit and never willingly: of another young woman lying broken and dead on another sunbaked street. The police had stood over her body, too. But not in search of evidence, least of all justice.

His mouth flooded with saliva, acrid yet sweet. He stood up and looked away and marked a spot at the edge of the lot where he might vomit without contaminating the scene. He swallowed. He took a deep breath and exhaled slowly. Balance the chi. Engage the mind like the moon. Cool, distant, objective, aware. The memory sank back into the darker regions of his psyche. He turned back to his work.

The girl's right leg was fractured below the knee, the skin tented above one broken tip of the fibula. He stepped around the corpse. Her left hip was swollen with a huge hematoma, but the skin was unbroken. Her whole pelvis seemed abnormally canted from the axis of her spine.

Her left arm was trapped beneath her body. No reason to disturb her until the techs showed up. Her right arm was out-stretched and its clenched fist swarmed with copper-colored fire ants. A narrow column scuttled away with their winnings. He bent for a closer look. The ants were harvesting an organic material extruding from between her fingers. He pried the fingers open and saw a mass of bread and ground meat, mixed with a pale-yellow goo. The ants swarmed in. He dusted the insects from his gloves before they could bite him.

He assumed the cause of death to be catastrophic internal trauma. A more expert assessment was up to the techs and the coroner. Where were the uniforms? Lost in the maze of unmapped and nameless alleys. Or doing battle with the living rather than standing over the dead. Statistically, by the square meter, Nyanga township, Cape Town, was a competitor for the title of highest crime neighborhood on the continent.

Turner stood up and took out his phone.

He circled the body, taking photos from a variety of angles.

He took photos of the blood trail that led five meters to the garbage dumpster.

He had noted the dumpster on his walk from the car. It stood at the rear of the vacant lot where she had died, distinguished from its neighbor on either side by a depression punched into the galvanized metal about a meter above the ground. He took a photo and examined the surface. Spray-painted black. At the rim of the depression the paint was marked by fresh abrasions and cracks where clean metal shone through. He assumed that paint fragments would be found on the girl's dress and skin. He snapped two close-ups. A blue Bic lighter lay on the ground. He shot it and bagged it. He took photos of the tire marks scored into the dirt in front of the dumpster.

Turner went back to the corpse and sat on his heels. Around her neck was the sling of a handbag. One tatty corner stuck out from beneath her chest. He tugged it free and lifted her head to free the sling. He looked inside the bag. Four coins. A dirty handkerchief. A child's finger puppet—a penguin. Nothing else but a grubby business card. He looked at the card.

WARRANT OFFICER
RADEBE TURNER

Underneath his name was his office phone number. He turned the card over and saw his mobile number, written in his own hand. He studied the girl's face.

He studied her for a long time. Her blighted youth. The

desperation that had marked her even before her death. The mask of her final agony in this barren trash-strewn garden. Not merely her own history written there, but that of a failing civilization. He looked again at the handwritten number on the card, as if it represented an indictment from some higher court of his own role in that failure. He was certain he did not recognize her. He did not know how or why she had come to be carrying his card. He handed them out often enough to witnesses. He added his own number less often, for people who might need his help. He hadn't been much help to her.

He stood up and turned as he heard a sound behind him.

A lean African, thirties, bearded, leaned against the doorway of the shebeen, rubbing the corner of one eye with the first knuckle of his thumb.

"Nothing worth stealing on her, man. Police be here soon."

Turner was dressed in light mountain boots, khaki hiking pants, and pale blue hiking shirt that hung out to cover the gun on his hip. The shirt was one size too big to give him the room to move when he needed to. He took no offence at being mistaken for the lowest kind of scum. He held out his identification card in his gloved hand.

The African straightened up and retreated behind a sudden barrier of fear.

Turner took a photo of the front of the bar. The timber was painted green, peeling here and there in the heat. A hand-painted sign named it THE DUBLIN CASTLE. A second sign promised LUXURY! Turner walked closer as something caught his eye. He studied the fresh white wood and splinters that surrounded a bullet hole. He took a photo. He looked at the African. The African hunched his shoulders and sucked his teeth.

"What's your name, sir?"

"Khwezi'll do."

"Did you call this in, Khwezi?"

"Yeah, about three hours ago. Lucky it wasn't something important."

"Busy night. Do you know who she is?"

"No, I never seen her before."

"What did you see?"

"I didn't see the accident."

"That wasn't my question."

"I saw her lying there when I closed up, when I took out the trash, around three o'clock."

Turner watched him for a moment. Khwezi shuffled in his flip-flops.

"At first, I thought she'd just crashed out, you know? It happens."

Turner watched him some more. For township boys like Khwezi, giving information to police carried a vague stain of dishonor, no matter what the end. It was a mistake to get impatient with them. Let them get impatient.

"That's it," said Khwezi. "She was dead so I called the police. Three hours ago. I just need you to get rid of her before I open up again."

"Must have been a big vehicle," said Turner. "Gangsters?"

"Shit, they weren't no gangsters."

"So why are you afraid of them?"

"Afraid of who?"

"The people who killed her."

"I never seen them before, either. And I wouldn't know them if I saw 'em again."

Turner nodded. "Do you sell cheeseburgers?"

Khwezi was taken aback. "Yeah, we sell cheeseburgers. Why?"

"The girl fished one out of the garbage."

Khwezi glanced at the dented dumpster, then at the dead girl. His head bobbed up and down, as if some lingering question in his mind had been answered.

"How did it get there?" said Turner. "The cheeseburger."

"Now you're asking me to speculate."

"So you're an educated man. Relatively speaking."

"I know the way things are, as in those fuckers are never going to pay for it."

"But you think they should."

"Damn right they should but they won't, so you're wasting both our time."

"Give me something to work with. I'll make them pay."

Khwezi laughed. "Excuse me, officer, but you the one needs educating. It doesn't matter what I saw or what I say I saw. I make a statement, my name comes up as a witness, then I've got some private investigator on my back who gets paid twice what you do, and he's digging into my shit, my family's shit, my bar's shit, shit I did ten years ago. He's standing on my throat while you've got your boot on my balls. So let's say I'm more stupid than you think I am and I wear the cheap shirt and tie you buy me and I stand up in court. A crowd of fat white lawyers take it in turns to piss in my face and I'm the one who looks like he should be doing time."

Turner said, "You're right."

Khwezi blinked twice. "Okay then."

"Your name won't come up. You don't make a statement. You're not a witness. You just tell me what happened. I'll work with that."

"Shove her in the ground and move on, man. Nobody gives a shit. Nobody ever did. I mean, just fucking look at her."

"I have looked at her."

Turner let that hang while Khwezi shuffled on the spot. He held the business card in front of Khwezi's face.

"Ask around," said Turner.

"Turner. Maybe I hear a bell. What will they tell me?"

"That my word is good. That you don't want my boot on your balls."

Turner bagged the card and put it in one of the pockets of his pants.

"See?" said Khwezi. "They'll get away with murder, I'll get fucked for selling my grandma's mampoer."

"Is that what the driver was high on?"

"If I didn't see the accident, like I told you I didn't, how could I see who was driving?"

"So tell me who might have been driving."

Turner saw Khwezi glance past him, a change of expression, a further retreat. Four boys in ragged shorts and bare feet had appeared. They were watching the work of the ants at a respectful distance. An audience wouldn't help his efforts to loosen Khwezi's tongue. Turner reached in his back pocket and called to the boys.

"Hey, come here."

The boys shrank away. Turner waved a fifty rand note. The boldest led them over.

"Any of you know that girl?" asked Turner. "Or see what happened to her?"

The boys exchanged glances and shook their heads.

"She got hit by a big car," said Turner. "You ask around for me, see if anyone did see it. If they did, you come back and tell Khwezi. Now go buy yourselves a cool drink."

The leader snatched the note and skipped away with his comrades in pursuit.

"So now I'm the neighborhood snitch," said Khwezi. "Thanks a lot."

Turner said, "Kinetic energy."

"What the fuck are you talking about?"

"The vehicle that killed her didn't move very far. To smash her up that badly in a short distance, it would have to be powerful and heavy. Say a high-end SUV. You said these people were white."

"I didn't say that."

"But they'd hire white lawyers."

Turner looked into his eyes and Khwezi held his gaze. Turner let his instinct make the calculation, then gave Khwezi the victory his pride required. He broke the stare and looked away at the shanties down the street. He sensed Khwezi recover himself.

"I grew up in Khayelitsha," said Turner. "The cop is our enemy. Our money in their pockets. Friends tortured. Relatives who disappeared. I know." He turned back to Khwezi. "But I am not that cop. And you are lucky, because you are not my enemy."

"Whatever you say, man. I'm not trying to make this personal."

"I am," said Turner. "I don't believe you're the kind of man who could see a girl torn apart and not give a shit."

Khwezi took a breath through his nostrils. "If anyone tossed the burger it was the black they had with them. Personal security motherfucker. A Zulu, so we thought. Dressed like James Bond, had a gun, we thought maybe a Steyr. Most of the time he was out here, watching the cars, but he came in to get some food. Guess he's too used to eating with the quality folk."

"Cars?"

"A white Toyota 4Runner and a Range Rover, I don't know, dark brown, or maybe red." He pointed to the dumpster. "The Range Rover was parked right there, pointing out, like for a getaway."

"License plates?"

"No. Just two cars, six men, and one dead girl."

"Tell me about the other five."

"Tourists on a trip to the zoo, you know, so they could brag about going down to jungleland."

"They speak English or Afrikaans?"

"Both, but mostly English. One was older, the babysitter.

Fifty-something but fit with it. A beard. He drank water. The others were rugger buggers, talked about yesterday's game. Not kids, midtwenties? They caned the peach brandy, four shots apiece at sixty percent. The mampoer made them loud. Was like having an elephant taking a long loud shit in the middle of the room and laughing at the smell. Drove half my people out. The richest fucking people in the country and they just can't stand it that we've got something they haven't, even if it's piss-fucking-poor. They have to drop in and steal our Saturday night, too. Oh yeah, they were from out of town. Country boys. They talked about going back to the hotel but not which one."

"Time?"

"They arrived around midnight and left an hour later, before they got eaten alive." Khwezi pointed at the bullet hole in the wall. "One of them pulled a gun and took a shot at my poster of Madiba."

"Any reason why?"

"Four shots of mampoer, you don't need a reason. The older guy took the gun off him and knocked him off his chair. He was fast, a slick mover, I'll say that. Then the Zulu comes in, waving his Steyr like we're the fucking gangsters. Then they ran like little bitches."

"The Zulu was sober?"

"Bottled water. So yeah, they've got two clean drivers, but there was a fight over the keys. 'Dirk, give me the keys. Dirk, give me the bloody keys, you're too bloody pissed to walk.' That's the big older guy. He sounded different from the others. Foreign, I'd say British or maybe Australian. Not American."

"So you think Dirk killed the girl."

"I'd had enough of their shit, I came back inside. I didn't see it happen so I can't say."

"Any other names?"

"Dirk for sure," said Khwezi. "Maybe there was a Simon? I

think that was the Zulu. That's all I know. But I meant what I said about not going to court."

"So did I," said Turner. "Anything I can do for you?"

Khwezi scratched his beard with a thumb, shook his head. "No, it's stupid."

"Try me."

"You got to promise me I won't get fucked."

"I have to know what you want before I promise that."

"Last time the city shut me down, the paperwork to get legal again took more than a fucking year to go through the system. Times are tough, the margins are thin, we're always on the edge. If I go down again I'll never get back up." Khwezi hesitated.

Turner said, "Go on."

"Well, it's like what you said about my cash. And cops putting it in their pockets."

Turner's lip curled. Khwezi took a step back from the cold anger.

"Okay, man, just forget it."

"Give me names," said Turner. "You will not be the one who gets fucked."

"You're serious?"

"A promise isn't worth making unless it's serious."

Khwezi weighed him up and grinned. Before he could speak they both heard a muffled riff of heavy metal music. The riff repeated. Behind Turner.

Turner strode over to the girl as the riff cycled a third time, louder now. He stooped and rolled the girl's body over. In her left hand she held a smartphone. Turner pried it loose. The caller ID read, RUDY. Turner swiped the answer button with his thumb.

A voice said, "Jason? It's Rudy." A white man. Afrikaans. Forties or older.

"May I ask who is calling, sir?" said Turner.

The caller paused. When he spoke again his tone expressed

a threat and a contempt with which Turner was familiar. "This is Sergeant Britz of the Longhill police. Am I making myself clear to you?"

"Yes, sir, quite clear."

"Good. Now where's my nephew?"

"That would be Jason?"

"Don't get clever, son. Where is he?"

Turner said, "Jason isn't here."

FOUR

For the first few kilometers Jason walked as fast as he could. If you walk fast enough you can't think about much except the walking. He didn't want to think … or remember. He stared into the distance without seeing anything and pushed himself on.

By five kilometers the alcohol and dehydration had slowed him down, and he thought and remembered, and a violent rage rose inside him, black and red. His muscles strained at his bones and joints as if trying to tear himself limb from limb, to collapse his chest into his lungs. His teeth ground into each other. Small sobs escaped from his throat. He screamed at the desert sky. A fantasy of pulling his own eyeballs out came and went. He stomped the ground with each step until his ankles hurt. He grabbed his shirt in meaty hands and tore it apart, tore it, ripped it, stripped it, balled it, strangled it, and threw it in the road. Nausea flooded up his gullet and he stopped and bent over and tried to vomit. Nothing came up except acid and a thin green bile. He could have spit it out but he swallowed it back down. Swallow it, cunt, swallow it; swallowing it is what you're good at.

He stood bent over, his hands on his vast thighs, and growled as he tried to hold back burning tears. Those fuckers. That bastard. His rage redoubled, fueled by self-disgust. Where was the rage when he needed it? He had grown up manhandling livestock, machinery, tools. He could eat pain. He was a fucking farmer. He could tear that clever, clever English cocksucker to pieces; he could crush his skull into cheese with his bare hands. The vain, strutting, gloating English turd.

But he hadn't. He hadn't raised a finger. He hadn't even raised his fucking voice. He'd lain on the ground and showed him his throat like a bullwhipped bitch. He'd let him take the piss because he was stupid and … okay, he was stupid, he knew that, he'd been told so often enough by his teachers, his mother, his uncle—by anyone who thought they had the right to a fucking opinion— but what was he supposed to do about that? It didn't mean he had to smile when they handed him a plate of shit and a knife and fork to go with it. But he did smile, didn't he? He let Hennie wank in his face. He let that old cunt take his gun and slap him down in front of his friends and a bar full of blacks. He let him take the piss out of his family, his dead land, his fucking English. He never even tried to speak English until he met Dirk.

"You haven't got the balls," he said to himself.

Another fantasy, not so fantastic. Take the gun from his belt and eat the fucking thing. Blow his brains out, here on the tarmac. Let them swallow that.

Another bitch move. His head felt swollen, his face. He straightened up, panting. The land rolled away from him in every direction. It was hard and it had no pity, he knew that better than any of them, stupid or not. It wouldn't keep you alive for a day unless you gave it your blood. He hated it, he loved it, it was the only land he knew. It was his. He'd given it all he had and he'd failed. The land had erased over twenty years of slog and left a hole in his chest where his pride should have been. It had given him nothing in return, not even hardness. He lived alone and had come to find comfort in his aloneness, a warmth, a defiance. Fuck 'em. He'd never felt so alone as he did now. Today it was no comfort at all.

His rage was spent.

His thirst was terrible. He couldn't feel his tongue.

The dying girl came back from the dark and choked him.

Alone? He didn't know the meaning of alone. She'd been alone. She'd looked at him with her insides bleeding and begged him to not leave her alone in all that dark. And he hadn't had the balls. He had more in common with that girl than he did with Hennie, more by far, but what had he chosen? If he'd opened that car door that Hennie had slammed in his face he could've broken the fucker's shinbones without even trying. He wondered if the girl would have helped him if the tables had been turned, and as soon as he wondered he knew the answer and he felt sick again.

He turned and looked northwest. He could head across the veld, away from all this shit, all this shame. From here you could reach the Kalahari without crossing another road. Of course, you'd never reach it. The state he was in he wouldn't reach sundown. But it wouldn't be a bitch move. Let the land take him back. Wipe the slate. Nasty way to go out, though. He'd have to throw away the gun he had in his belt or he'd end up using it.

He heard a car engine and looked up the road toward Langkopf. It was still too early for heat haze, but it seemed a long time before the vehicle came into view. He saw the shape of the light rack on the roof.

He realized that for a while there, raving and weeping and vomiting on his own soul, he'd actually been doing alright for himself. He'd been getting somewhere, crawling toward something worth finding. He knew that because he felt it all shrivel away leaving something much smaller, someone who wasn't going anywhere at all.

It was Rudy's patrol car.

Jason watched it roll by and slow into a U-turn. It pulled up beside him, and Rudy leaned over and opened the passenger door. He flicked a cigarette out onto the tarmac.

"Jump in."

The land had beaten Rudy, too, broken him and driven him into town long ago. But it had left him with a splinter of its hardness in his heart. Jason got in and shut the door.

"Where's your shirt?" said Rudy.

"I lost it," said Jason.

Rudy drove off.

"You lost your phone too."

Jason shrugged. The last he could remember of his phone it was lying on the table in the shebeen. He'd taken some selfies, and maybe been online, he wasn't sure. Everything after that was confusion. Hennie slapping him, the smell of the barroom floor, the escape to the cars. Everything but the girl and the look on her face. He'd never forget that. He stared through the windshield.

"For a second I thought you'd been kidnapped, or worse," said Rudy.

"Why would you think that?" said Jason.

"Because when I called you a black fella answered."

"I lost it in Cape Town. Because I'm stupid."

"Well you're in luck. He picked it up in the street when it rang. I told him I was a police, and he promised to drop it in the post."

"You think he will?"

"Oh I think so. Said he was on his way to church. A respectful type, the way it used to be." Rudy smiled. "They're not all criminals, you know."

The girl's face came into Jason's head again. He rubbed his eyes until she went away.

"So you had a spot of bother with Hennie."

"Hennie's a turd."

"Anybody who knows him can tell you that," said Rudy.

The gun in his belt was digging into Jason's ribs. He pulled it out and made sure the safety was on and laid it in his lap. He saw Rudy's glance.

"What did Hennie say?" said Jason.

Rudy nodded at the gun. "He said you'd fired that off in some dive and upset the local riffraff."

Jason nodded. He wanted to tell Rudy about the girl. But he couldn't. At that moment he would gladly have sent Hennie Hendricks to the floor of the pit. If the girl was dead, it was Hennie that had killed her. But he couldn't drop Dirk in there with him. He couldn't betray a friend. Dirk was the only true friend he'd ever had.

"I did worse at your age," said Rudy. "Forget about it."

"You're not going to come down on me?"

Rudy lit another cigarette. He inhaled and blew out the smoke with exasperation.

"Jason, when it comes to the rest of the world and every bastard in it, I'm with you. I'm always with you. Come hell or high water."

Jason felt his eyes sting with tears. He turned away and wound down the window and stuck his face in the warm wind to dry them off before Rudy could see them.

"That's what I promised your mother when Oscar died. That's what I promised her again in her own last hours. I may not have made a good fist of it, but I'm with you. Never forget that."

Jason took a deep breath and held it until he knew that his voice would be steady.

"Thanks, Uncle Rudy."

"And remember, I'm the only one."

"There's Dirk, too."

"Listen. I understand why you've held Dirk's hand—because have no doubt, he needed it more than you did—all these years.

You're a thousand times the man he is. You could crush him like a dung beetle. But he will drop you like a used rubber the minute it suits him. That's what the rich do with the likes of us."

Jason didn't want to believe that. But he probably did.

"I'm sick of feeling smaller than I am."

Rudy took another deep drag. He nodded.

"Welcome to the club."

FIVE

Margot's dream mansion was a gorgeous pile of wood—or as the architect had put it, "natural timber"—glass, and stone in what Hennie understood to be the African Zen style. More impressive, to Hennie's mind, were the four hectares of flourishing greenery in which it sat. More plants grew here—more sheer chlorophyll—than in the surrounding thousand square kilometers combined. Swimming pool, koi ponds, water features, gardens galore, with solar power, geo power, and all the eco-friendly bells and whistles that the owner of an environmentally disastrous mining operation could wish for.

Hennie was particularly proud of the security features, which he had supervised. The estate was enclosed by three-meter-high walls, clad in travertine stone and topped with an electric fence that was lethal to humans. The concrete was embedded with seismic sensors. Reinforced steel bars extended three meters underground to prevent tunneling. Four armed guards. Cameras covered every angle and were monitored twenty-four hours a day in the gatehouse security module. The American Embassy in Mogadishu wasn't better protected; if the Yanks hadn't been run out of town, Hennie couldn't remember. Some might think these measures overcautious but in this country they weren't unusual, and Margot had more reason than most.

Outside the compound were two clay tennis courts with a small pavilion for spectators, a stable for Margot's three horses, and a hangar for the Cessna 172 Skyhawk. Hennie, Dirk, and Simon were all licensed to fly it. The small plane wasn't a toy. No one apart from engineers wanted to come to Langkopf for meetings, so it was used often enough—and it put them in range of a decent rugby match or even a night at the theater in Kimberley. To Hennie it was priceless. It made him feel less trapped in the middle of Hell's creation.

As the gates opened and Hennie drove through he wondered what kind of mood he would find her in. Margot's moods could never be predicted and bore no necessary relationship to whatever was going on at the time, or at least to what appeared to Hennie to be going on. If there was an opportunity to get worked up she seized it with both hands and her teeth. If things were rosy, as they usually were, this did not rule out the chance that she would find something somewhere with which to torment herself and anyone else in range.

Hennie felt no shame in admitting to himself, even if to no one else, that he was a little scared of her. His machismo, if that was the right word, was so extreme, and so often validated by life-threatening experience, that he was able to concede that emotionally, intellectually—in all realms other than the sexual and physical—she was the dominant partner. After some early clashes had neared Armageddon, on which occasions he had backed down because it was clear that she never would, he had realized that this was why he was madly in love with her. And so he still was. The previous women in his life, his memories of whom were as lost to him as those of his toenail clippings, had never scared him for a second. Maybe it was one of those Freudian things. His mother had been a battle-ax in her day.

He had no doubts he'd done the right thing in abandoning the girl. But he wasn't sure it was right to keep Margot in the dark. He couldn't recall the last time he'd kept something significant from her. It was possible he never had. But this cock-up involved Dirk. If he told her about it she would worry and the worry would grow as she imagined the worst. It would go on for weeks, months. It would be like infecting her with a tapeworm. He was scared to tell her he had failed. But not too scared to do it if it was right. He knew how to hold his hand up. He had to protect her from that worm. He had to keep the worm inside his own gut.

He slowed down and poked a finger into Dirk's ribs. Dirk shifted but didn't surface. Hennie felt along the upper rim of Dirk's eye socket with his thumb and found the notch in the bone and compressed the supraorbital nerve. A trick for rousing the almost dead he'd learned from a medic in 1 Para. After a few seconds, Dirk opened his eyes and reached toward the pain drilling into his skull. Hennie withdrew his thumb.

"Oh, God."

"Wake up, Dirk, we're home."

"I feel like I've got a brain tumor."

"Tell me, what do you remember about last night?"

"Oh, Jesus. I've got tunnel vision."

"Last night, Dirk. Think. Think hard.

"I remember the first shot of sixty percent mampoer. If I remember the second I'll throw up. Shit, I need a piss, too. Pull over."

"You can wait, we're nearly there. Is that all you remember?"

"Why? What did I do?"

"You didn't do anything. Can you remember that?"

Dirk nodded dismissively and grabbed the water bottle and drained it.

As they approached the house, Margot emerged onto the decking. She was wearing her blue silk dressing gown and holding a coffee cup. Ash-blond hair disheveled. Head and shoulders held up and back as always. Magnificent as ever. She wasn't smiling.

Hennie parked and got out and walked round the car to open the door for Dirk. He mustered a grin for Margot.

Margot said, "What's wrong?"

"We're fine, love, nothing's wrong." The tapeworm felt like a large poisonous snake. "Nothing that a hot shower and a few hours' shuteye won't cure."

"Dirk?" Margot turned her pale-blue eyes on her son.

"Mum, please, I've got raised intracranial pressure."

"You weren't due back until tonight."

"We got rat-arsed in a shebeen," said Dirk. "Christ, I'm still rat-arsed."

"A shebeen where?" said Margot.

"I don't know, what does it matter? Some township."

Margot looked at Hennie. With that look he was on the rack.

"After the game and dinner and a strip club the lads were feeling bullish. Dirk wanted to take a walk on the wild side. You know how they are."

"No, I don't."

"Young lions. They want to see the world, get a whiff of danger. With me and Simon on board a whiff is all it was ever going to be."

"What was wrong with sleeping it off in the hotel?"

Hennie almost stumbled. Then the answer was on his tongue before it had passed through his brain. "Jason fired a gun at a poster of Nelson Mandela."

Dirk squinted as if affronted by this information. "When?"

"I told you not to take that cretin."

"Don't start on Jason, Mum."

"Pissed-up tomfoolery," said Hennie. "He didn't hit Nelson or anyone else. But with Dirk just passing the bar exam—"

"On his third attempt."

"—I didn't want to chance any bother with the cops, so I brought them straight home."

A fair point. Margot managed to swallow it. "What was Jason doing with a gun?"

"I carry a gun, you carry a gun," said Hennie. "I could hardly frisk them all every time we stepped outside."

"You know why I failed those bloody exams?" said Dirk.

"You're right," said Margot. "You're still rat-arsed."

"Because I don't want a career as a lying bastard."

"I've given you the best education money can buy."

Dirk said, "I hate the law."

"Then you should have chosen something else. You're a grown man."

"I did it to please you."

"It does please me. I'm proud of you. What you do with it now is up to you."

"I'd rather shovel shit with Jason."

Hennie saw it coming. The set of her mouth. Her nostrils. Cold rage at white heat. He felt sorry for her. She couldn't help herself.

"I didn't know Jason was that talented," she said.

"You never liked him," said Dirk, "even when we were kids. I don't know why."

"Jason's gay," said Margot. "A homo. Maybe you didn't know that."

Dirk looked at her as if she'd stabbed him. "That's ridiculous."

Margot shrugged. "Maybe he doesn't know it either. Maybe he doesn't dare see it that way; they say these things are possible. But he's in love with you."

Hennie wondered if she was right. She usually was. It hadn't occurred to him but he had no sense for such things. His prejudices in that respect, being strong and impervious to persuasion, blinded him to all but the obvious. It didn't matter. He had to stop this incipient catfight.

"Come on, love," he said.

"That's all perfectly fine with me," said Margot, to Dirk. "I don't care what he is. Is it fine with you?"

"Jason's my best friend."

Margot said, "Is he shoveling your shit or are you shoveling his?"

Dirk stared at Margot, trying not to blink. Margot didn't have to try. Dirk trembled and his fists clenched. One day he would go for her. Maybe he needed to. Maybe that's what she wanted him to do. But not today. Not while Hennie was around. He clapped a hand on Dirk's back.

"Let's go, sport."

Dirk dropped his eyes and nodded. Hennie gave his shoulder a squeeze. Dirk shrugged him off and walked past his mother without looking at her. Margot clenched her eyes shut. She still held the coffee cup. It was steady. Dirk disappeared into the house. Tears formed beads along Margot's eyelashes. She wiped them away on the edge of her wrist. Hennie walked over and put his arm around her waist.

"I'm sorry," she said.

"He'll get over it."

Hennie took the cup from her fingers and tossed it in a long arc. Coffee sprayed the grass. The cup splashed into the nearest koi pond, scattering the dozing Jap carp.

Margot said, "Why did you do that?"

Hennie stooped and swept her up in his arms like an old-time film star.

"For what I've got in mind, you'll need both hands."

SIX

Turner swung his Land Cruiser off the M18 and headed for Woodstock. The dashboard clock read 07:34. If they were as drunk as Khwezi said they were, there was a chance he could catch them in their hotel beds.

A search of the national database had validated his instinct not to tell Sergeant Rudy Britz that his nephew's phone had been found on a fresh corpse. Jason Britz had been arrested three times, twice for possession of marijuana and once for an affray that had left two men in the hospital requiring reconstructive surgery. Despite the severity of the latter offense, Jason had never been required to stand before a judge. All charges had been dropped. It wasn't likely that Sergeant Rudy would have helped to put his nephew in a Cape Town interrogation room. Turner had offered to deliver the phone to Jason's hotel. That had made Rudy cagey but he'd given him Jason's name and address and that was enough. Jason lived in Langkopf, a small town on the other side of nowhere in the Northern Cape. The smartphone would tell him more about Jason than his uncle Rudy knew.

The forensics crew had arrived with a squad car and two uniforms in tow and Turner had left them to it. While he'd waited for them he'd called Mohandas Anand and told him what he needed from him. Anand asked if it was an iPhone. On hearing it was a Motorola running Android, Anand laughed and said, "No problem."

In Woodstock Turner parked illegally on a street of semi-detached Victorian houses. Ten years ago you could buy heroin on this street; now it had an eco-café where, for the price of a Big Mac and fries, you could buy a ginger-and-pineapple smoothie. He rang a bell and a lanky Indian answered the door.

"Anand," said Turner. "I appreciate this."

"Always my pleasure to assist an agent of state oppression," said Anand, "as long as that agent is you."

Anand was an immigrant from Bangalore. At twenty-seven he ran a thriving cybersecurity business, including corporate espionage, most of which amounted to employers spying on their own employees. These days people didn't think twice about putting information in their phone that in the recent past they would have trusted only to their lawyer. It was rumored, though not proven, that Anand was a member of the African Anonymous hacktivist collective that had embarrassed the Gupta empire in 2016. He and Turner exchanged favors. The police department's computer forensics team could have handled the job, but it would have taken them two weeks.

Anand gave Turner a cup of coffee. Turner gave him a pair of latex gloves and Jason's phone. He followed Anand to his home office on the first floor. Two tables, one desktop computer, two laptops. The room was cool and uncluttered. Two Herman Miller chairs. Anand offered one to Turner.

"This phone is almost two years old," said Anand. "My Python script is way ahead of it."

Turner nodded. It was why older phones commanded a better price on the black market. Easier to crack and recycle. A stolen late model iPhone wasn't much more than sixteen gigabytes of scrap.

"PIN lock, not pattern. You know who this belongs to?" asked Anand.

"Jason Britz. A petty offender on holiday from the Northern Cape."

"Doesn't sound the type to use sixteen-digit alphanumeric encryption. Do you know his date of birth?"

"I thought about trying that but decided to leave it to the master."

"We put in five four-digit pins and the screen locks. Python script will extract the salt and give me root access. Brute force will do the rest."

"I like the sound."

"However, in proceeding to screen lock we don't risk anything by trying the obvious numbers."

Turner said, "Sixteen, ten, nineteen-ninety-three."

Anand tapped in one number, then a second, then grinned, and showed Turner the screen. The desktop wallpaper was a photo of two young men laughing.

"Voilà," said Anand. "One-nine-nine-three."

Turner opened the photo app. The title at top of the screen read: Today. Underneath the title were nine thumbnails. The first photo was gold. Turner tapped to open it.

Five white men stood in front of a white Toyota and a red Range Rover in an almost full-length group portrait, four with their arms across each other's shoulders, grinning into the lens, the fifth, older man standing behind them and trying not to scowl. Most numbers of both license plates were visible beyond their legs.

Turner double-tapped to zoom in. He scrolled across the faces. Four young men, out on a spree. He spread the image between his thumbs to zoom in further and scrolled over them again. Well-fed, strong-boned, captured in a moment where they had not a care in the world. They didn't know it, but they were about be tested.

Turner said, "As the Mennonite said, there is no such joy in the tavern as upon the road thereto."

"Beautiful," said Anand.

"That's life."

"Surely not." There was pity in Anand's surprise. "Surely not always."

"No, not always. If you're lucky."

Turner reexamined the photo and scrolled over the older, taller, bearded man at the back. His eyes were red in the flash, lending him a demonic aspect that was not out of keeping with his features. He scrolled again. The garbage dumpsters, if a little blurred, were caught behind the vehicles. He tapped the information button. The photo had been taken at 12:07 a.m.

"I can pull GPS data off those photos, too," said Anand.

"I know where they were taken."

Turner swiped through the other photos. A second, tighter group shot in the same location. Another portrait of the younger four outside the shebeen, their fingers pointing in mockery at the LUXURY! sign. A tall black man at the edge of the frame, his face turned away from the camera.

The other shots had been taken inside. One proved that by many standards the sign outside was no boast. Cozy lighting. A rough plank floor. Tea candles burned on half a dozen tables. On the benches around the perimeter men sat passing a galvanized pail of sorghum beer. The walls were decorated with posters and magazine covers. Some were of old movies—*The Harder They Come*; *Dirty Harry*. Some were political—*Malcolm X* "By Any Means Necessary"; a map of Ireland, pierced through the north by the barrel of an AK-47, promoting the Belfast Brigade. Shamrocks. A toucan with a glass of Guinness balanced on its beak. Khwezi had a passion for the Emerald Isle. At the rear was what appeared to be a small dance floor and two speakers. From behind a zinc-topped bar, Khwezi glared at the camera.

A portrait of the young invaders, lifting shot glasses of peach brandy.

Two selfies showed a man with a thick neck, huge shoulders, and the kind of tan that is painfully hammered out from years of raw sunburn. Short, fair hair; clean-shaven. Something childlike in the rough, rounded features. Something frightened in the eyes, something defeated, as if in looking into themselves they did not find what they hoped for. A strange sympathy stirred in Turner's chest. Jason Britz. He was glad that Jason seemed unlikely to be the driver.

The last two shots were studies of another young man. Handsome, sun lotion–tanned, expensive, dark hair. In the first he raised a shot glass, unawares. In the second he looked at the camera with mild irritation—perhaps disdain. Somehow Turner knew that this was Dirk. He felt no sympathy at all.

In none of the faces, except for the bearded one, did he see anything that would resist even polite questioning for more than a few minutes, if he could talk to them without a lawyer or their red-eyed minder in the room.

"If you find that any of the phone's apps are protected," said Anand, "he probably uses the same PIN."

Turner nodded, opened Jason's messages. The first lines of recent texts were tabled down the screen. Eight of them were either to or from "Dirk." The fifth began: "We'll be staying at the Elysium Hotel. Check their website! Phone is …" Turner opened it, noted the number, and rang the Elysium from his own phone. He exchanged greetings with the receptionist.

"Do you have Jason Britz staying with you?"

"Just a moment, sir."

Turner waited. He could be at the Elysium in fifteen minutes.

"Hello? Mr Britz checked out this morning, sir."

"Can you tell me at what time?"

"I'm not sure I should. Let me ask my supervisor."

"I'm Warrant Officer Turner, Cape Town Homicide. You'd be saving me considerable inconvenience."

"He left at one forty-seven a.m."

"And his companions? He was part of a group booking of six."

An anxious pause. "They all checked out at the same time, sir."

"Could you verify their names for me?"

"Only if you have them, sir."

Turner knew he'd already done well for a voice on a phone claiming to be a cop. Anyone could claim to be a cop. To get more information he'd have to show up in person with his badge.

"You've been very kind, miss," he said. "Thank you."

He hung up and thumbed his way back to the first group portrait on Jason's phone and zoomed in on the bearded minder. He didn't look like hired security. A professional, such as the Zulu, would have no good reason to join the gang, even if invited. What he did look like was the man in charge. The man who made the decisions.

"Bad news?" said Anand.

"The wicked flee when no one pursueth."

"You pursueth, don't you?"

"They didn't know that when they left their hotel at one forty-seven this morning instead of going to bed to sleep off the mampoer. It means at least one of them was aware of what they'd done and decided to run for home."

"What did they do, if I may ask?" asked Anand.

"Hit-and-run. They killed a girl."

"I'm sorry to hear that."

"To be more precise," said Turner, "they crushed her against a dustbin and left her to die in the dark."

"That sounds worse."

"It is."

"How did you get the phone?"

"Jason dropped it in the parking lot. The girl found it but didn't get the chance to use it." Turner handed the phone to Anand. "Can you clone this thing?"

"I could," said Anand, "but it would take some time and I don't know why you would want me to. This is GSM, they all are now. The network won't authenticate both the original and the clone, even if they appear identical. It would just lock out one or the other. Perhaps you mean, can I make a copy of all the information inside it?"

"That's what I mean," said Turner.

Anand looked at the photo on the phone in his hand and tapped the screen. "Do you want to know their names before or after I dump the copy?"

"That's a smug smile."

As Anand thumbed the screen, Turner caught up with him. "Jason posted the photo on Facebook, from the bar."

"At twenty past midnight," said Anand. "The faces are tagged. Mark Lewis. Dirk Le Roux …"

Turner rolled his chair over to look.

"Chris Gardner. Jason Britz. The big man at the back has no tag."

Turner said, "Which one is Dirk Le Roux?"

SEVEN

Eric Venter was sixty-one, trim in build, and gray in both hair and spirit. He wore an unfashionable mustache that stopped short of the edges of his thin-lipped mouth. He was down on one knee in his back garden when he heard an engine and the crunch of tires on the gravel of the driveway on the other side of the house. He was tending a bed of tall blue-and-white flowers, *Neomarica gracilis*, with a trowel. They had lasted longer than usual this year, he didn't know why, but now they were fading and drooping, and it was time to help them propagate for next year.

Venter wasn't willing to admit to himself that he enjoyed gardening. It was tedious and repetitive; the job was never over; results came slowly; and nature conspired day and night to undo one's efforts. Yet he liked the sense of order it imposed, and it mattered that he imposed it himself rather than via some hired hand. He was told it was good for osteoporosis, high blood pressure, and depression. He hadn't noticed any marked effect on the latter condition, but he could say the same for the latest round of pills his doctor had prescribed. "You're a young man!" the doctor, who was perhaps forty, had exclaimed. "You can expect another twenty years of tolerably good health." Venter had left his office feeling suicidal.

The truth was he had never had any great experience of happiness, even in his youth. "When were you at your happiest?" a therapist had once cheeped at him, no doubt recycling the latest mumbo jumbo imported from the States. Venter had trawled his memory for fifteen silent minutes without finding an honest answer. He suspected he was at his happiest when in dreamless sleep, though that too was hard to come by, and waking to the defeat of each new dawn was a particular purgatory.

"Captain," said Turner.

Turner stood over him, brimming with vitality and a strange physical magnetism that Venter had never been able to fathom, though he envied it. "You're the patron saint of the violently dead," Turner had once told him, intending this, as far as Venter could tell, as a sincere compliment. Venter oversaw the machine tasked with honoring those dead with something approximating to justice. To what exact point, Venter no longer knew. He was like a doctor whose experience was immense but whose compassion had long since burned out and who viewed each new consultation with a vague dread. Perhaps that was the kind of doctor he needed. Turner, an enigmatic figure to all and a thorn in many sides, seemed to hold Venter in high esteem, though Venter did not know why.

Venter indicated the flowers. "Walking irises, an unusual bulb. As you see, they're on their last legs, but if you bend the stem down and bury the dying flower near the mother bulb, it will take root and grow into a second plant." Venter stuck the trowel in the soil and stood up. "I'm sure there's a metaphor there, but I can't think of one that pleases me."

"They're us," said Turner. "Homicide. Our heads are buried in the dirt."

"Not bad," said Venter. "But where are the beautiful blooms?"

"That would be someone like me."

Venter said, "Now I'll have to dig them all out. Every time I look at them, they'll remind me of you."

Turner wasn't sure how to take that. He looked almost wounded. How strange. The man was a relentless predator. Colonel Nyathi, his tongue only partly in his cheek, called him the Lion of Nyanga. A meticulous observer of procedure without a single accusation of brutality on his record, his tenacity was indefatigable, if exhausting for everyone else. He was lethal when crossed. He had fired his gun in the line of duty on four occasions and had killed four men, including a colleague caught importing heroin who unwisely chose to make a stand. All four shootings had been judged good. Turner managed to be superb without being vain. He was everything Venter was not, and Venter hated him for it.

Venter smiled, "Just kidding. Let's have some tea."

Venter himself had never been a good street detective. The dirt didn't agree with him. But he had a genius of sorts for management, for handling the beasts, like Turner, who did thrive in the township jungles of Cape Town—both the most beautiful city on the planet and the crime capital of Africa. Its homicide statistics were 30 percent worse than those of Ciudad Juárez.

If Venter hadn't been white, he would have made major, and probably colonel, years before. His resentment of this injustice had not helped his prospects, which were and would remain zero. No one was going to promote him and bump his pension on the verge of retirement.

He and Turner sat under a hinged awning on the patio and Venter poured iced tea. The house was small and modern, under ten years old, part of a suburban gated community in white flight land. A little piece of paradise, according to the developer. But two failed marriages had cost Venter significantly grander dwellings. He dated the birth of a certain toxic bitterness in his soul to the loss of the second. As Orson Welles had put it, "What do I have after thirty years? A little turkey ranch."

"Thanks for seeing me, Captain," said Turner.

"I'm sorry for spoiling your weekend off, but we racked up a lot of bodies last night. I hope the overtime is welcome."

"This is an important case."

"If I understood your briefing we have a street girl killed by drunken driver. I don't see the headline."

"It's important to me."

"Why?"

"It's important because you need to ask me that question."

Turner's voice was low and easy but his gaze, without meaning to be so, was intimidating. Turner had black skin and green eyes, uncommon but, in this vast swill of DNA, not exactly rare. Venter had always found them disconcerting. What did he mean by his answer? Some implication that Venter wasn't sufficiently committed? Or that he didn't understand Turner's zeal, which was true enough.

"What do you want to do?" said Venter.

"Push it hard, close it fast," said Turner. "I need your permission to go to Langkopf to interview the suspects."

"Langkopf." Venter searched his memory.

"The Northern Cape," said Turner. "Population around four thousand."

"That's a long way. I don't just mean the mileage."

"I can be there by dark."

"You want to go today?"

"I'll have a confession by tomorrow."

"The evidence is that strong?"

"Strong enough," said Turner. "One of them killed her. It's just a question of who. Confessions will put it to bed. But if we let this drift, they might walk."

"Spare yourself the strain. Get the Langkopf police to conduct the interviews."

"They'd bury it deeper than shark shit."

"Is that based on something more than your usual opinion of our brethren?"

"One Sergeant Rudy Britz is the uncle of one of the suspects, Jason Britz. Jason has avoided prosecution for at least three serious crimes, including a double aggravated assault. It's a good bet the rot goes higher than Rudy."

"Why?"

"You'll see," said Turner. "First, I need something more from you, sir."

"Go on."

"A priority autopsy on my victim, this afternoon. You have the power to move her to the top of the list."

"The morgue must be like a bus station."

"Bread and butter cases. Shootings, stabbings, cerebral hematomas. Paperwork for the courts. Not one of those reports will assist an early arrest. Except mine."

"I'm not following you," said Venter.

"The autopsy on the girl will be grim reading."

"Aren't they all?"

"Let me put it this way, even I'll find it grim. Here, look at this."

Turner opened a folder and took out an enlarged A4 print of a group portrait: five white men posed in front of two gleaming SUVs. The photo had been taken at night. The flash gave it an ugly, paparazzi clarity. Turner pointed to each of four smiling youths in turn.

"Look at their faces. These are decent people. Privileged people. They have no experience of horror. They feel pity. They feel guilt."

Turner displayed a second photo, a close-up of a young man raising a shot glass.

"I believe he's the driver. With an autopsy sheet I can show him how much pain he dropped on the girl."

"Whereupon he'll confess," said Venter.

"It can only improve the odds."

Venter trusted Turner's instincts in such matters. He took a swallow of iced tea. "Who is he?"

"Dirk Le Roux. Last Monday he passed his bar exam, in Pretoria."

The case began to offer a little more interest than the usual tales of mindless human bestiality.

Venter said, "Culpable homicide isn't the brightest career move."

"Dirk invited his hometown pals for a weekend in the big city, to celebrate," continued Turner. "His farewell to the troops. He bought them tickets to the rugby match. It's all on Facebook. By one o'clock this morning he's too drunk to think straight, gets in his car, and shatters the girl's pelvis like a popadam. He might not even know he hit her."

Turner pointed to an older, bearded man at the back of the group.

"But *he* knew."

Venter studied the face. "I don't see a bleeding heart there."

"Lionel 'Hennie' Hendricks, Dirk's stepfather. British. A former mercenary. He decided to leave the scene while the girl was still alive."

"How do you know?"

"He's the boss man." Turner produced a printout of a magazine article and handed it over. "Dirk's mother, Margot. From *Business Times Africa*, last April."

The title read: "Le Roux Manganese Rejects Chinese Takeover Bid."

Above the text was a photo of an imposing woman who didn't feel the need to smile. Classical but flinty good looks, which appeared to be unimportant to her. Clearly not a bloodsucker. The kind of woman Venter should have married, though he doubted such a woman would have accepted him. The caption identified her as Margot Le Roux. Venter scanned the article. He felt the case dig its hooks into his guts.

"The bid she rejected was concealed," said Turner, "but industry sources estimate it couldn't have been less than seventy million US dollars."

"Manganese?" said Venter.

"It's an essential ingredient in the manufacture of steel and aluminum alloys. You can't make a car or a battery or a Coke can without it. Margot's sitting on half a billion tons of ore."

"Can I keep this?"

"I've got copies."

Venter put the article aside for later.

"Here's a headline for you," said Turner. "'Manganese Millionaire Kills Township Street Girl.'"

"You read the tabloids."

"It would make the *Guardian* and the *New York Times*, too."

Venter thumbed his mustache. "You believe you can make an advocate confess to culpable homicide."

"It's his only intelligent option. Perjury isn't as easy as it looks."

"We're pretty good at it," said Venter

"We get a lot of practice."

This was a little rich. Turner had undermined more than one case by refusing to back up his comrades' lies. Venter let it pass. "You could be in for some heartache. I've had more dealings with such people than you have. People with money and the connections that go with it."

"Afraid of the pressure?" said Turner.

"I never resist pressure from on high. It's futile. But I'd worry for you. Have you ever been to the Northern Cape?"

"No, sir."

"It's another world up there. Farming stone and sand breeds a certain stubbornness. Pride. The generations who fought the wilderness, the blood of the forefathers, so forth. Even a mild paranoia. One way or another, the world always seems to be against them. And all that space alters your mind—no visible boundaries, no perspectives—you could say all that freedom. They get used to doing what they want."

"You want me to let them get away with it?"

Again Venter had to look away from Turner's invasive stare. No wonder he didn't need to torture suspects. A fantasy flashed through Venter's mind, a voice, "a little turkey ranch," but it vanished before it was ever really there, rejected in terror by his conscience before it had a chance to germinate, as when one conceived some forbidden sexual image too repellent to be fully formed. Perhaps it was the antidepressants. He forgot the fleeting idea—there was nothing to remember—yet he was aware that the seed of it was lodged in his unconscious where he'd never dig it out.

He blinked and snapped his attention back to Turner's question. He was about to point out that none of these men would ever see the inside of a prison but found himself saying, "Of course not."

"They think they're entitled to get away with it. But I can be stubborn, too."

"Don't we know it."

"That distance you're talking about can work against them. They won't be expecting the knock on the door. That's why I want to go today."

"Shock tactics." Venter nodded. He was curious to get back to the piece on Margot Le Roux. He stood up. Turner stood up too. "You'll have the autopsy report by the time you get there."

They shook hands.

"Thank you, sir."

"Keep me up to speed," said Venter.

He watched Turner walk away. An unusual gait, as if he moved on rails. His feet made no sound, despite the stout boots he wore. As if he were some kind of phantom. Venter was glad Turner wasn't on his tail. He picked up the magazine article. Seventy million dollars US. And a rand was worth what? A nickel? Or was it a dime?

EIGHT

On his way home Turner dropped by the supermarket and picked up two bags of groceries for his downstairs neighbor, Mrs. Dandala. She was eighty-eight years old, and as scrawny and demanding as a new bird. She was laid up with a diabetic foot ulcer on her left heel. Turner had got her fitted up with a total-contact cast to take the pressure off while it healed. Mrs. Dandala complained about it bitterly. Without it she would probably lose the leg above the knee.

"I'd be better off without the leg," said Mrs. Dandala.

"You wouldn't survive," said Turner.

"I've known plenty of people with one leg. They were as happy as everyone else. Or I should say they were no more miserable."

"You wouldn't survive the surgery. Your doctor said so."

"My doctor is useless. He treats me like a child."

"Your pills are in the tray."

"I know how to take a pill. I've been rattling for twenty years."

"The nurse will visit tomorrow."

"Jesus save me," said Mrs. Dandala.

"I'll be back in three or four days."

"What's so important that you have to leave?"

"Work," he said.

"I don't understand why an intelligent man would choose such a stupid job. It never ends, nothing changes, and no one ever thanks you. It isn't even well paid."

Turner finished unpacking the groceries. He smiled and bowed in farewell.

"Call me anytime, as always."

"I've told you before, you should have been a criminal. You've got the eyes for it."

In his own apartment Turner packed a rucksack with spare light hiking pants, three cotton hiking shirts—just back from the laundry and still sheathed in plastic on wire hangers—T-shirts, spare socks and underwear, his MacBook Air and chargers, and a Kobo e-reader. He threw a toothbrush, old-style safety razor, and toiletries into a supermarket shopping bag and added it to the pack. A sweater. Running shoes. Spare pens and notebook.

He called police constables Gola and Qoboza and told them to meet him at the police vehicle pound in twenty minutes. When Qoboza objected to getting out of bed on a Sunday morning, Turner said, "You can get up now or wake up tomorrow in a cell."

At the station he checked Jason's phone and the cigarette lighter into evidence but not the business card. At the police vehicle pound he had the duty mechanic check his Toyota Land Cruiser for the long haul. It was eleven years old, had two hundred ninety thousand kilometers on the clock. It might have been time to trade up but he liked driving a tank with bad bodywork. It kept other drivers at bay. And it was marginally less likely to tempt thieves. While the mechanic changed the oil and filters he found the two constables in the parking lot.

Qoboza was the senior by three or four years; a big man with angry eyes, ready for a fight. Gola wasn't much more than a rookie. Both dressed in civvies. They had arrived in the same patrol car.

"What this about, Warrant?" asked Qoboza.

"How much money do you have in the bank?" said Turner.

"That's none of your business, sir."

"Tomorrow you'll take twelve thousand rand from your account—or wherever else you keep it—and you'll put it in an envelope—" he glanced at Gola, "—along with your twelve thousand, then you'll deliver the envelope to Khwezi at the Dublin Castle. You will thank him for the loan and apologize for the late repayment. You will give him your word that he will never hear from either of you again, unless he needs you."

"I hope this is a fucking joke," said Qoboza.

"I know you do," said Turner. "It isn't."

"I only got fifteen percent, sir," said Gola.

"Shut the fuck up," said Qoboza. "What if we don't?"

Turner said, "I will destroy your lives as well as your careers."

Qoboza thought about that. "That's way more than we took."

"I've added interest at standard credit card rates."

"We didn't keep all of it, we had to kick some up," said Qoboza.

"That's not Khwezi's problem. It's yours."

Qoboza clenched his fists and jutted his chin forward. "You'd better speak to our sergeant."

"I will, after I've filed charges against him on the basis of your testimony."

"You motherfucker."

Turner rapped him just behind the right hinge of the jaw with the knuckles of his right index and middle fingers. The blow struck the Triple Warmer 17 point, a yang polarity fire meridian connected to the pericardium. Qoboza staggered as the energy shock blazed from his heart to his brain. His thighs wobbled like tubes of wet clay. If Gola hadn't stepped up to support him he would have toppled to the oil-stained concrete. His eyes struggled to focus on Turner's face.

"If you've taken out any other loans elsewhere, pay them back before I find out. You won't feel like speaking for about thirty minutes, and I wouldn't advise you to try, so nod if you understand me."

Qoboza managed a slow, unsteady gesture, as if afraid his head would fall off.

"We carry the law," said Turner. "It is heavy. It is an honor. If you don't want to carry it, go and flip burgers."

Turner walked back into the workshop to collect his Land Cruiser.

By twelve fifteen he was on the N7 heading north. The girl's killers would probably be sleeping. He was less than twelve hours behind them.

The magnificent grasslands, citrus farms, and fertile valleys of the Western Cape gradually fell behind him and Turner crossed the mountains and dropped down into a country he had never seen before, and where all forms of life seemed unwelcome.

He drove through hundreds of kilometers of desolation, featureless and flat to the visible curvature of the earth, where neither hill nor tree nor habitation defiled its parched immensity. In every direction the view did not vary in the smallest particular. Pale brown dirt and broken stones, bare rock; leafless gray shrubs, ankle-high and so brittle and dry it was hard to believe they were alive, if alive they were.

He cruised at a hundred and twenty, but the naked vastness made it seem like a crawl. Nothing ever seemed to get closer, yet he felt the increasing size of the emptiness behind him. He was obscurely disturbed to think that this country was his. He felt like a trespasser.

At a small, scorched town whose reason for being there he could not imagine, he filled the tank with diesel. He bought and ate a sandwich that tasted as if it had been made some weeks before. In the short walk back to the Toyota the sun was sufficiently intense to make his scalp tingle. He went back into the service station and bought a milk-white all-terrain hat. As he left he turned to check his reflection in the window. He did not look cool in the hat, but his head felt cool. He drove on.

His phone displayed a "no service" message for almost two hours. By the time he got a bar of connection back, the landscape had become a little less forsaken. Thorn trees appeared, and broad patches of yellow grass invaded the scrub-and-rock desert. He saw a dozen or so black-faced sheep patiently cropping out a living. As the lower rim of the sun reached the western horizon, the GPS told him he was twenty kilometers from Langkopf.

He saw a figure by the side of the road up ahead and slowed down. It was a Bushman sitting cross-legged on the yellow grass, watching the sun go down. Turner braked and pulled over a few meters beyond him. He recognized the man as a San. The first people. The original human beings. They fought no wars. They craved no power. They lived in a wilderness no one else wanted and devoted their lives to play. Turner took off his shades and left them on the dash and got out.

The San was small and slender, perhaps thirty years old, it was hard to tell. He wore a cloak wrapped about his shoulders and held a spear propped up in the crook of his left arm. Turner nodded in greeting and the San nodded back and smiled. Turner asked with a gesture if he might join him. The San nodded and mimed smoking with two fingers.

Turner opened the back door of the Land Cruiser. He dug out a carton of Winstons and took a pack. He didn't smoke but they were useful currency. He levered a two-liter bottle of spring water from a six-pack and put it under his arm and closed the trunk.

He sat down by the San and gave him the cigarettes and opened the bottle. He offered the San a drink and the San accepted a sip. While Turner rifled water down his throat, the San took out a cigarette. Turner lit it for him, declined the proffered pack, and gave him the lighter. The San accepted with a smile and a dip of his head but did not speak. Turner saw no reason to do so either. They sat and watched the astral inferno decline beyond the far rim of the earth. The desert turned gold and copper, then garnet red, and for the first time Turner saw its beauty. At once it was dark.

A dull glow of light from the far side of a broad, low hill marked Turner's destination. He capped the water bottle and gave it to the San and the bottle disappeared into the man's cloak. They stood up together. Turner indicated the car, offering a ride. The San declined. They saluted each other and as Turner walked back to his car, the San walked away into the wilderness. Turner got in and started the engine and switched on his lights. When he looked again, the San was no longer to be seen.

The road curved around the hill to the north and east and he was in Langkopf. On the left a new industrial park: warehouses, agricultural stores, livestock pens, Lewis' garage. On the right a petrol station. Then a mix of residential and commercial buildings that conveyed the bleached, exhausted feeling of a small arid community. On the right an old, red-brick, three-star hotel, long but only two stories high, with faded yellow paint work. Two banks. The police station appeared on the left side of the main street. As Turner pulled into its parking lot his phone announced the delivery of the autopsy report.

At the front desk inside Turner found a bulky, sour-faced sergeant watching soccer on a portable TV. When the sergeant saw Turner loom toward him he stood up and some primitive reflex sent his right hand to the butt of his pistol. He was half a head taller than Turner, far from peak condition but powerfully built. Some gray in his hair with jet-black brows. Small nose and full mouth. He had the eyes of a man who was generally disgusted by the world. His name tag read: BRITZ.

"What do you want, boy?"

Turner presented his ID card. "Warrant Officer Turner, Cape Town Homicide."

A variety of expressions competed on Rudy Britz's face, most of them suggesting inner distress and none that Turner was welcome.

"Cape Town, eh?"

"I'd like to see Captain Mokoena."

"The captain's probably at the Office."

"I'd be grateful if you'd let him know I'm here."

"The Office is the Captain's private headquarters," said Rudy. "He's not in the building. He might even be at home. I can make you an appointment to see him tomorrow morning."

"If he's within range of my car, I'll see him tonight."

"He won't appreciate being disturbed."

"Why don't we find out?"

Turner indicated the desk phone. Rudy picked up the phone and squinted at Turner while he dialed.

"I know you, don't I?" said Rudy.

"We've never met."

"The religious type, a church-goer, if I remember correctly."

"I'm not a believing man," said Turner. "Though to not believe is equally absurd as neither position can be verified."

"I can verify this: there's no bigger trouble on earth than a clever black."

Rudy flinched at a muffled voice from the receiver.

"No, sir, not you. I've got Cape Town Homicide standing at the front desk. Warrant Turner would like to see you. Seems urgent." Rudy listened. "Yes, sir." He put down the phone. "I'm to give you directions. It's not far."

Turner pointed at a machine behind the desk. He took out his iPhone.

"Does that printer use Bluetooth?"

"Why?"

"I need to print a report."

"What kind of report?"

"Police business."

"I am the police."

Turner opened the flap in the desk and walked toward the printer.

"What the fuck do you think you're doing?" said Rudy.

Turner discovered the printer on his phone and tapped PRINT. The machine hummed.

"Is there is a hospital in this town?"

"If you can call it that. Six beds and a trainee with a stethoscope from Bloemfontein."

"Call me 'boy' again and you'll need to fly his boss in."

Rudy stared at him, his face reddening with a mixture of anger and, if Turner wasn't mistaken, shame.

"If I was you," said Rudy, "I'd—"

"I'm not," said Turner.

Turner collected the sheets from the printer. As he walked back to the gap in the desk he stopped and eyeballed Rudy from a distance close enough to smell his breath. He didn't wait for him to blink; he didn't give him the respect of a contest. He turned away and walked back out to the parking lot.

He sat in the Land Cruiser and switched on the dome light. He speed-read the autopsy. It was more ghastly than he had expected. He placed it in a folder with the photos and got out of the car and locked it. After nearly eight hours at the wheel he was glad to follow Rudy's directions on foot.

He walked down a street lined with small, shabby shops, glancing at door numbers. He was looking for twenty-nine. He carried the folder under his left arm. He reached a glass window emblazoned with the words:

LA DIVA
HAIR AND BEAUTY

Behind the glass he saw bad photos of various hairstyles and a row of empty roller chairs facing a long wall mirror. The salon was unlit. The door bore no number. He stepped back to check the shop next door. It was a bookmaker's—a licensed betting parlor—closed and shuttered; its number was thirty-one. The door of La Diva opened and a colored woman in her midtwenties looked at him. Her skin was a milky brown. Strong features and eyes that put him in mind of a panther were framed by a black cloud of unprocessed hair. The eyes checked him out, head to toe. He couldn't tell if she liked what she saw. He did.

The woman said, "Winston's inside."

Turner followed her past the chairs and mirror. A faint but rich smell of cooking made Turner's empty stomach ache. They passed through a door and a short corridor, the smell getting stronger, into a dimly lit room the same size as the salon where boxes of shampoo and hair products were stacked along the walls. A burgundy-red leather sofa sat in front of a wide-screen TV. A large wooden table dominated the remaining space.

Behind the table a big African rose like a king from a swivel chair, upholstered to match the sofa. He had two inches on Turner and his shoulders filled his shirt like cannonballs. He was in uniform, the collar undone. He gave a smile of such encompassing warmth that Turner felt he was meeting a long-lost uncle. Considering the captain's history, which Turner had looked into before he left, it was quite a talent.

"Warrant Turner. Winston Mokoena, late of robbery-homicide, Johannesburg, now happily out to pasture in the Thirstland. Or Dorsland, as the Afrikaners call it. Please, be welcome."

Mokoena was sixty-three and formidable in stature and energy.

His head and face were cleanly shaven, oiled and perfumed, accentuating the illusion of greater youth. His features were those of a man who had witnessed every extreme of human nature without surprise. His eyes not only took part in his smile but were its true, deep source; yet at the same time they had the quality of bullets. Mokoena offered his hand across the table and Turner shook it.

"Sit down, my friend. Your timing is impeccable."

Turner sat and set his folder down against the legs of his chair. Amongst a clutter of papers, receipt rolls, a laptop, three smartphones, and an ashtray holding a smoking cigar, the table was set for dinner with wooden bowls, plates, and spoons wrought with delicate and artful design. The woman reappeared with a matching serving dish that steamed with the extravagant aroma. She set it in the middle of the table and sat at the third place setting.

Mokoena took Turner's bowl and raised up a ladle brimful of stew.

"I hope you like your curry hot," said Mokoena. "Iminathi has no mercy."

Turner said, "What right man does not like his curry hot?"

NINE

Mokoena watched the way Turner looked at Imi as she cleared the table. He had watched them both throughout the meal. Neither had said much to the other beyond compliments given and accepted on the excellent goat curry, but beneath the lingering pungency of the chilies, Mokoena sensed the pheromones circulating. Why not? He loved Imi, in a strictly fatherly way. Imi had emerged from her last, and to his knowledge only, romantic affair with painful wounds that had not yet healed, though she would have denied this. Turner was a fine figure of a man and worthy of her, which could not be said of anyone else Mokoena could think of.

He wondered how this might be put to his advantage. He was sure he would need one. He offered Turner a cigar from a humidor of polished ebony. Turner declined.

Mokoena liked the younger man for the same reasons that made him afraid of the trouble he had undoubtedly brought with him. Turner was not incapable of fear—everyone was capable—yet it was not clear where in Turner it resided, and Mokoena had spent his life in the study of fear. With the skill of a seasoned interrogator Turner had avoided answering every personal question he had been asked. A big man, yet his body seemed strangely weightless. A sense of balance, of calm cultivated by discipline; his movements precise and flowing with a liquid energy. Not an African energy. Chinese, perhaps. He had asked Turner which martial art he practiced, and Turner had answered, "I try to take care of myself."

The energy contained and masked a deep anger, Mokoena was sure. Turner would not be swayed by mere authority. Mokoena would not even try. Here was a man committed to himself and his own purpose, but Mokoena could not tell what that might be. Turner would reveal his intentions soon enough, but would he reveal his purpose? Was he a good man or a bad man, or did he exist, as did Mokoena, beyond such distinctions? And what kind of man needed to cultivate such balance? One thing was clear: though he did not wear it, and few would have the eyes to see it, Turner was a killer of men.

Imi returned to the table and looked at Mokoena. He nodded for her to join them. He wanted to see how she conducted herself while two dangerous men discussed business.

He chose his cigar and lit the end amid a fragrant cloud of smoke and brief bursts of flame. He closed the lid of the humidor and showed Turner the back, into which was screwed a small brass plate. The plate was engraved with the name SIR PHILIP ABERCROMBIE.

"Philip Abercrombie was the magistrate who founded this town for the Great Empress, in 1866," said Mokoena. "For twenty years it was the most remote settlement in the Cape Colony. It sometimes amuses me to think of myself as his successor, though I'm not sure it amuses his ghost. There's a story behind his arrival on this God-cursed plain, somehow emblematic, I feel, of our condition. Though I am no philosopher."

"That I don't believe," said Turner.

Mokoena laughed.

"Tell me the story."

"Abercrombie was sent, with a contingent of native police, to put down an anti-colonial rebellion by the Griqua. Are you familiar with the Griqua?"

"I know it's the nickname of the Kimberley rugby team. I don't know much about the original tribe."

"They survive but are scattered amongst us, barely identifiable as a group. Abercrombie made his base camp on this spot and with time it evolved into a town. But it's the Griqua rather than his deeds that merit our attention."

Mokoena drew on his cigar and continued.

"When the Dutch East India Company founded their outpost on the Cape, they had no fantasy of creating a state, let alone our own happy republic. They sought only wealth. But as the settlers came and began to resent the Company's autocracy, the trekboers struck out into the interior. Most of them were single young men and naturally they made free with indigenous women—the Khoi, the San, the Tswana. In effect they often married them, though such unions were not Christian and therefore unlawful. Hence many children were born whose social and legal status for all concerned was, to say the least, uncertain."

"The Bastaards," said Turner.

"You are familiar. I'm impressed."

Turner shook his head. "Just a name in the back of my mind. Please, go on."

"When the boys in question came to manhood, the trekboers conceived the idea of using them to fulfill the military duties of their fathers, who were permanently fighting their new neighbors. They trained them to replace their own commandos and so there came about a new tribe—of mixed-race, Dutch-speaking sharpshooters, who lived on the backs of their horses and were expert in guerrilla warfare." Mokoena smiled.

Turner said, "What's not to love about that?"

Mokoena laughed. "What not indeed? As any right men would—I like that phrase—they soon abandoned their paternal communities and struck north beyond the confines of the colony, bearing allegiance to no one but themselves. Slaves ran away to join them. They became the scourge of the indigenous peoples along the length of the Orange River and challenged the colonials at their own game. A century later their descendants, calling themselves the Griqua, established their own rival state."

"Griqualand," said Turner, his memory finally stirred. "Which was where the British discovered diamonds."

"Such is life," said Mokoena. "Even the Griqua had to kneel before the power of commerce."

Turner took the point. He didn't smile. He picked up the folder from by his chair and laid it on the table.

"Can I offer you a glass of Irish whiskey?" asked Mokoena.

"You can."

Mokoena glanced at Iminathi. She rose and left the table and returned with a bottle and three glasses.

Mokoena uncorked the bottle and poured. "Writer's Tears. Because when the Irish poet cries, he sheds tears of whiskey."

"I was at an Irish bar, of sorts, this morning."

"Another admirable race."

"They're bastards, too, when the circumstance demands it."

"I will not hear a word said against them."

Turner said, "That wasn't meant as an insult."

"A toast, then. To bastards of all nations."

They clinked their glasses and emptied them. Mokoena poured refills. He gestured at the room with the bottle.

"You may have been surprised to find me here," he said, "but I learned in Johannesburg that a beauty salon makes an excellent base of operations within the population. You'd be amazed how much intelligence flows beneath the hair dryers. Most things worth knowing are known to the women. Isn't that so, Imi?"

Iminathi didn't answer. Mokoena saw that she was anxious for Turner. She couldn't read him as Mokoena did.

"I also own two bars but they generate more mayhem than information. Nothing that would call for your talents. Petty theft, whores, a few tik and weed dealers. As in prison, a drugged population is a docile population. My most profitable investment is the licensed bookmaker's next door. The miners like a wager."

He had made it clear where he stood in the matter of modest, harmless, and intelligent corruption. He gave Turner the chance to disapprove.

Turner said, "Small business is the lifeblood of the economy."

"I have three officers under my command and one of the lowest murder rates in the country. I'm proud of that." Mokoena gestured with his brows toward the folder. "If a local man committed a homicide, even as far away as Cape Town, I would expect to hear whispers."

"These locals have the wrong kind of hair to whisper in here."

Mokoena caught his first glimpse of potential crisis. "I see."

Turner glanced at Iminathi. She didn't move. He looked a question at Mokoena.

"Imi's my personal assistant, my right arm. I keep no secrets from her."

Turner opened the folder.

"Just after midnight this morning six men stopped at a shebeen in Nyanga township. They killed a bottle of sixty percent mampoer and fired a gun at a portrait of Madiba, no harm done."

Mokoena waited for the punch line. Turner took out a photo of the dead girl's face and laid it on the table.

"On their way home they killed a teenage girl. With a red Range Rover."

Mokoena felt cold. His face turned stony. He had sat in Margot's red Range Rover many times, admiring the custom interior. Cream leather, arctic air-con, cooling massage seats. There wasn't another in the Northern Cape.

"Who was she?" he asked.

"She's unidentified," said Turner. "Chances are she'll stay that way."

"A tragic accident, then. They probably don't even know they hit her."

"Her death wasn't instantaneous. From the pattern of the hemorrhage, which were numerous, the coroner estimates she lived for around thirty minutes after the collision. At least one suspect knew she'd been hurt when they fled the scene."

"How do you know that?"

"All six checked out of their hotel at one forty-seven a.m.," said Turner. "A surprising decision for intoxicated men enjoying a holiday weekend. They grabbed their bags and ran."

"Speculation," said Mokoena, without conviction.

Turner handed him several sheets of paper.

A full autopsy report. Written up in less than what? Twelve hours? Mokoena resisted an urge to wipe his brow. He scanned the pages. Details leapt out at him.

"Severe malnutrition … Microcytic anemia. Megaloblastic anemia … Hepatitis C … Multiple metastases?" He looked up at Turner. "This girl already had both feet in the grave."

"The cause of death was massive internal trauma, caused by two tons of metal and a drunk."

Turner's tone was even. Relentlessly so. No challenge or accusation. Just the sense that this man would move forward, no matter what stood in his way. Mokoena dragged on his cigar and blew a gray plume from the corner of his mouth.

"Read past the blood work," said Turner. "Fracture dislocation of the pelvis at the sacroiliac joint. Fractured neck of femur. A ruptured left kidney. Anorectal avulsion. Her cervix plucked from the neck of her vagina—"

Iminathi let out a groan and put a hand to her mouth.

"You've made you point," said Mokoena.

Turner laid out the photos of the suspects.

Mokoena didn't need to look at them. But he did.

"Jason Britz, Mark Lewis, Chris Gardner, Lionel "Hennie" Hendricks, Simon Dube, Dirk Le Roux. Do you know any of them?"

Mokoena said, "I know all of them."

"Good."

"Is it?"

"They'll accept an approach more easily coming from you," said Turner. "If you'll invite them down to the station tomorrow, I'll take their statements."

"And if it doesn't come from me?"

"I'll run them down myself."

Imi picked up a close-up of Dirk Le Roux raising a shot glass and stared at it.

"Imi, put it down," said Mokoena. She did so. Mokoena looked at Turner. "Where did you get these photos?"

"When I found the girl's body, she had Jason Britz's phone in her hand."

"It would have to be Jason's," said Mokoena.

"He must have dropped it in the lot as he got in the car. She crawled five meters to get it with a shattered pelvis but wasn't able to make a call."

"I presume Jason was the shooter, too."

Turner nodded. "He posted the photos on Facebook, from the shebeen."

Mokoena forced an involuntary grimace into a smile. "Any eyewitnesses? To the accident?"

"Not in Cape Town. All eyewitnesses to the accident are here."

"Who is your prime suspect? The driver?"

Turner said, "The barman believes, based on an exchange he witnessed, that Dube, Lewis, and Gardner left in the white Toyota, on the instructions of Hendricks. He also witnessed a fight over the car keys between Le Roux, who was staggering under the influence, and Hendricks, who was stone-cold sober. It's likely that Le Roux was the driver."

Mokoena had a vision of two trains steaming toward each other on the same track. Neither train could see the other yet, but he could see both because he was standing in between them, chained to the middle of that track. He drew on his cigar, but the taste had soured. Various courses of action ran through his mind. None were attractive. All were dependent on the decisions—more likely the irrational compulsions—of others and were beyond his control.

His best hope lay in Turner … and his obscure purpose. With luck it was greed. A force so potent, so unpredictable, that the bravest and noblest men that Mokoena had ever known had been buckled into its yoke like stunned oxen. Not that he blamed them. No city so strong that it cannot be conquered by gold. He gave Turner the opportunity to pump up the price.

"For the moment, that's conjecture."

"Someone killed her," said Turner. "Someone decided it was in their interest not to call an ambulance. Either they tell the truth or they conspire to pervert the course of justice. Whichever they choose, I'll be making arrests."

"Local warrants will be hard to come by."

"On a charge of culpable homicide, I don't need one."

"Do you know who Dirk Le Roux is?"

"You're talking about his mother."

"Fifteen years ago this town was on its knees in the dust, a glorified petrol station on the way to no place anyone wanted to go. Then Margot inherited her husband's farm. She gambled everything on a geological survey and discovered deposits of high-grade manganese ore. Nothing in her life prepared her for what she went on to do. She was born and bred here, pregnant at sixteen, a sheep farmer's wife. This is a woman who spent her honeymoon in Kruger shooting antelope and lions. She'd never had a passport. But she went out and found investors, partners, in Frankfurt and Shanghai. She built nine kilometers of road. She built a water pipeline from the Orange, a reservoir in the desert—"

"It doesn't matter to me if she put a man on Mars. Margot Le Roux isn't a suspect."

"You can't be that naive. Her mine has pulled billions of rand into the region. A smelter plant in Upington. New housing, a school. She's created hundreds of jobs and her politics are impeccable. These are good people—"

"I googled her," said Turner. "She's a remarkable woman, a blessing to the community, and throws cash at the ANC. But I missed the part that said her son was above the law."

"There's an old African saying," said Mokoena. "Where a woman rules, the streams flow uphill. Round here we have another: Margot gets what Margot wants."

"Captain, if you feel unable to cooperate—"

"To the contrary. Take my advice and let me handle this. Relax. Imi can show you natural wonders galore. In a day, two at the most, I guarantee you a docile prisoner with an airtight confession. Your paperwork will flow. The court will be delighted. The machinery of justice will grind on undisturbed. Your Captain Venter will pat you on the back for a swift and efficient clearance."

"A pat on the back from Margot, too?"

The perfect solution. But Mokoena saw the glimmer of contempt in Turner's eyes, heard it in his voice. He didn't like this game. The disrespect was a toad in this throat, but he swallowed it. While there was still a chance, he had to play.

"Why not?" he said. "A generous contract, let's say as a security consultant, would in no way be illegal."

Turner stood up.

This game, at least, was over. The next would call out the rusted guns of pride.

Turner bowed to Iminathi. "Thank you for dinner."

He nodded, once, to Mokoena. "Goodnight, Captain."

Mokoena stood up. He leaned across the table. His voice was dark.

"Be reasonable, Turner."

"There's nothing reasonable in asking me to do wrong."

"I'm sorry the girl died under Dirk's car last night, instead of next month in a ditch waiting for a doctor to show up. A hundred like her died while we were eating dinner. No one cares about them either, don't tell me you do. If you want to make the world a better place, leave this to me."

"We carry the law," said Turner.

"Have you any idea what the law required when I first took an oath? We were a gestapo. Homosexuality was against the law. Interracial marriage. A man like you or me couldn't walk down the street without breaking a law."

"The girl was killed," said Turner. "She's entitled to justice."

"There is no justice. There's just us. And a thin chance to get along without fucking each other."

"If the girl had rolled an SUV over Dirk and left him to die, Margot would mobilize an army to see her crucified, malnutrition or not."

He was right enough about that. Mokoena tapped the ash from his cigar.

"You know no one will go to prison for this," he said.

"I don't answer for the corruption of the courts," said Turner. "I answer for myself."

"I know things about Margot you won't find on Google. When it comes to Dirk she would rather break than bend. I hope I'm wrong, but if you push this too hard, there might be bloodshed."

"If there is, that won't be my fault."

"Fault, blame, guilt—these are irrelevant abstractions," said Mokoena. "My concern is with reality. In my town enforcing the law comes second to keeping the peace, and for that I make no apology. I like peace. I spent a lifetime wading in the alternatives and have come to appreciate its virtues."

"I respect your position," said Turner. "I respect you."

"Then I ask you again, from my heart, let me resolve this case."

"I can't do that."

"Paris is worth a mass. This country knows that better than any."

Turner's gaze held no more compromise than the bore of a shotgun.

"When I go back to Cape Town, the men who killed the girl will go with me. Or I'll not go back at all."

"You'd rather break than bend, too."

"Anyone who tries to break me will die where they stand," said Turner. "Go and tell Margot."

So there was his purpose. To test himself against the mighty. A law more ancient than any ever written down. Mokoena understood. He felt old. He felt sad. He was afraid. He looked at Imi. Her chin was upturned, a certain light—a fire—in her expression. She was for Turner. Mokoena knew why. There were lots of whys.

Turner held out his hand.

There was no more to be said.

Mokoena put his cigar in the ashtray. He shook Turner's hand.

Turner dipped his head to Imi once again and turned and walked out.

Mokoena knocked back his whiskey. Turner's refill was untouched. He drank that too.

Imi collected the autopsy report and the photos and put them back in the folder.

Imi said, "He forgot his file."

"He didn't forget anything." Mokoena put the folder under his arm. "Thank you for a splendid dinner. And for keeping the peace."

Imi said, "I don't understand."

"I know you don't," said Mokoena. "Lock up."

He grabbed his phone and his car keys and hurried through the kitchen to the rear exit.

Outside, he paused to look up at the stars. They were of a brilliance and infinitude that could only be seen from nowhere. He did not miss Johannesburg. He thought of Turner. He liked the man more than ever. He felt afraid, but not for his own life. If the time came when that would be put at hazard, he would already have been witness to a bloodbath. To take sides in that was a choice he prayed he would not have to make.

As he opened the door of his Grand Cherokee, Mokoena speed-dialed Margot Le Roux.

TEN

On Sunday evenings Margot and Hennie played chess on the terrace while jazz drifted out from the open glass doors of the kitchen—right now Bill Evans live at the Village Vanguard. Margot had visited New York for the first time three years before and had made a pilgrimage to the club.

She'd been appalled; her fantasies shattered. You couldn't talk at your table without being shushed by some floor manager, unless a glassy-eyed fan had got their own objection in first. You had to sit still and stare at the band as if you were on the front row of a papal mass. She had almost expected to be told to keep her elbows off the table. No one danced, no one circulated, no one dared move. No joie de vivre; not a whiff of the wild, devil-may-care good-time spirit she had imagined. She doubted anyone had kissed in there since 1973. If Evans rose from the dead and turned up there tomorrow, the staff would drag him off to detox halfway through his first set.

And of course you couldn't smoke, though this was no surprise. The whole city had left much the same impression on her as the jazz club. Whatever it had once been, it wasn't anymore. How could anything original emerge from a city where you couldn't smoke and

drink at the same time unless you stood outside in the rain? She'd
been wrong; you couldn't do that either. A passing cop had told her
it was illegal to drink in any public space, had checked if there were
any warrants out for her arrest, and handed her a civil summons for
twenty-five bucks, with the reminder that she was lucky because
before the recent change in policy, she would have been arrested.

Margot had been happy to return to the back of beyond.

She lit a Dunhill and took Hennie's h6 pawn with her dark-
square bishop, which left the bishop hanging. If Hennie took
it he would be saying goodbye to his queen in four moves, and
Hennie, from painful experience, suspected something of the sort
but couldn't see it. When they'd met he had considered himself
a strong player, having played thousands of games in tents, bars,
and barrack rooms around the world. Since then he had matured
into a decent player but had never learned to channel his innate
aggression to best effect. Margot always gave him rook odds. He
did manage to squeeze out the occasional win, about which he
would invariably brag for days afterward.

Margot's phone rang and she answered it while Hennie
worked up a sweat. She listened to Mokoena.

"We're on the terrace," she said. "I'll have Simon bring you up
when you arrive."

She hung up, tapped her phone screen, and listened again.

"Who was that?" asked Hennie, still trying to calculate her
next moves.

She didn't reply. Simon Dube answered her call at once.

"Sorry to disturb you, Simon. I need you to meet Captain
Mokoena at the gatehouse and bring him up to the terrace. Ten
minutes. Thank you."

As she spoke she watched Hennie. At the mention of
Mokoena, his interest in the game vanished. He looked up from
the board. He made no attempt to disguise his worry.

"Bollocks. What does that gloating bastard want?"

"He just said it was important and that Simon should sit in."

Hennie nodded. He scrubbed the flat of one hand over his crew cut hair. Anxiety, embarrassment, resignation, and anger flitted in quick succession across his reddened face.

"You told me you didn't want to risk any bother with the cops," said Margot. "What really happened down there last night?"

Hennie tossed both hands and let them fall to his thighs. "Dirk hit some girl with your Range Rover."

"Some girl?"

"A teenage skinny lurking behind the car, probably up to no good."

Margot felt a cold dread wash through her insides. She stared at Hennie and waited.

"That fucker, Jason," said Hennie. His fists clenched. "Two minutes of chaos, that's all it was. I had to take his gun, slap him down, pay the damages, and get the lads out before it got ugly, and it could've been very ugly indeed. Dirk still had the car keys from the drive up. He got behind the wheel before I could stop him, I mean physically stop him, and he was in a mood. Wrong gear, left the handbrake on, revved her up, and *BANG*. Reversed straight into a rubbish dumpster. Only drove two or three meters. But the girl got crushed in the middle."

Dread clenched at Margot's insides. She dragged on her cigarette. She needed to keep Hennie cool and to do that she needed to be cooler. She suppressed an impulse to lunge across the chess board at his throat. All problems could be handled. She'd had a lot of practice. It would be fine. Dirk would be fine.

"What state was the girl in?"

"The surgeons would have had their hands full, but she was alive."

"So, by now she might be dead."

"Sounds like we'll find out soon enough," said Hennie. "They die like flies down there. Jesus, they're dying like flies all over. Nobody'll give a shit."

"If Dirk killed her we'd better start giving one."

"I'm sorry, Margot. I let you down. No excuses."

Margot wasted no energy on recriminations. Hennie's guilt was painful enough, even to witness.

"I had two pissed-up rugger buggers on my hands in the worst ghetto in the city. Okay, going there was mistake number one, but they're not children; it was Dirk's weekend." Hennie picked up the black king from the board and squeezed it in his fist. "Point is, the cops just dream of getting their hands on the likes of us. Saturday night in the Nyanga tank? I'd have had to kill someone just to keep Dirk alive till morning."

"Hennie, you don't have to justify yourself."

The gratitude in his eyes was so intense she thought she saw a gleam of tears. Hennie had his faults but he was loyal as a war dog. She couldn't have accomplished all she had without him, couldn't have taken the first step. It was his savings that had drilled the first hole, when everyone else had thought her mad. He had never sought credit, never wavered in his iron faith, never tried to dissuade her from the awful risks she'd had to take. When she'd turned down a fortune from their Chinese partners he hadn't raised a single objection, even though she knew there were a thousand places he'd rather be than here, in the Thirstland. "I'd be happy to live in a tin-roofed shack as long as it was with you," he'd say, and he meant it. The battles she had fought for the business were exclusively with men. Knowing that this man stood behind her, with his fearless vitality, his cheerful cynicism, and knowing that he was hers, had made those other men seem to her as soft as wormy apples.

Hennie rolled his shoulders to collect himself. "Besides," he said, "five minutes under the hot lights and Jason would have spilled his guts like a gored cow."

"Jason saw everything?"

Hennie nodded.

"Anyone else?"

"No. I told him to keep his mouth shut, but maybe he blabbed to Rudy."

Margot stood up, walked over beside him, and put a hand on his shoulder. She felt his hand wrap over hers. She looked out into the darkness of the gardens. She heard a car engine in the distance. She heard it stop.

"It's not like Dirk to keep something like this to himself. What did you say to him?"

"Dirk doesn't know," said Hennie.

"What do you mean he doesn't know?"

"He doesn't know he hit the girl. Doesn't know he pranged the car. He was as full as a frog. He doesn't even remember the bloody gunshot."

ELEVEN

Iminathi opened the passenger door of Turner's car and looked at him as she climbed in. He didn't seem surprised. If he was she doubted he would show it. She closed the door. Her breathing was steady.

She said, "Winston doesn't know I'm here."

"Really," said Turner.

"I didn't run after you just to tell a lie."

"You're not out of breath."

"I run ten K three times a week."

"Cool," said Turner.

"You think he sent me to spy on you."

"No," said Turner. "And I don't think you lied, but I'd think twice before presuming to know what Winston does not know."

"Known unknowns and unknown unknowns," she said.

"It's the things we know but don't want to know that cause the problems."

"Can we go?" She glanced at the windows of the police station behind them. "Before Rudy spots us?"

Turner started the engine and switched on the lights.

"Which way?"

"Take a left. I want to show you something. It's out of town."

"They've already dug a hole for me?"

"You'll see why that's not funny when we get there."

They drove north on an empty road. The glow of the town vanished and absolute wilderness emerged from the dark, as if it had been lying in wait. Turner kept his eyes on the yellow wedge that streamed from the high beam headlights. Beyond the lights, the land reached as far the stars.

She stole glances at Turner's face. He was a portrait of ease, but how could he feel easy? He'd arrived as if from nowhere and thrown Winston into as close a state of panic as she'd ever seen him in—and which she wouldn't have thought possible. He had threatened to bring down a chaos he couldn't imagine. He had no idea what or who he was dealing with.

"You haven't asked me where we're going."

"I'm enjoying the suspense."

"Don't you want to question me?"

"What do you want to tell me?"

"I'm not sure."

He looked at her. "Tell me everything."

She realized that she wanted to, badly, and with that desire came a loneliness she wasn't aware was in her. She had no one in her life to whom she'd ever revealed very much, not even Winston. There was no point. In a world as small as the one she lived in, opening herself would only make it seem smaller.

"Winston's been good to me," she started, without knowing how to go on. She said, "Don't hurt him."

"Winston doesn't want to get in my way. If that's where he finds himself, he'll step aside."

"You think he's afraid of you?" asked Imi.

"Forty years ago Winston Mokoena ran a death squad for

Umkhonto we Sizwe. They assassinated policemen, blew up Wimpy bars, tortured informers. But we won't hold that against him. At exactly the same time, he was also building his career in the Johannesburg police force, the heart of the enemy empire. Cop by day, violent revolutionary by night. At any moment, for two decades, he could have found himself strapped to an interrogation chair. The ANC chiefs called him 'the sharp edge of the spear.'"

"How do you know all that?"

"I'm a detective."

She felt as if something had been stolen from her. Winston was the kindest man she knew.

"Winston's not afraid of me or anyone else," said Turner. "He's afraid for the status quo."

"But you don't care about that."

"I'm here to arrest a drunken driver."

"When Winston arrived, four years ago, the town was out of control," said Imi. "Hundreds of men had come in from as far as Joburg and Durban, looking for work. There were nowhere near enough new jobs. They had nowhere to live, they built shanties on the edge of the desert. You could smell it. There were riots over water, food. It was the one thing Margot hadn't prepared for, the sudden immigration, the scale of it. She lost control. And there was a dispute at her mine over digging the second shaft. Safety and pay. In theory Rudy Britz was the law, but all he knew was how to crack heads. Rudy never had any control to lose. Shotguns and tear gas. A week wouldn't pass without a killing. The company was spending more on security than on mining ore. So Margot had a captaincy created and brought Winston in."

"She picked him personally."

"I don't know how those things work, but that's what Dirk said."

Turner looked at her. She felt uncomfortable.

"So you know Dirk well."

He didn't phrase it like a question, so she didn't answer.

"Winston restored order. Like a magician. He bulldozed the shanties, gave every man without a job a fifty-rand note and bused them out of the province. He had them dumped by the road in townships all over the country, a hundred here a hundred there, not enough to cause an outcry. No one knew if it was legal or not, but who were they going to complain to? The police? Winston convinced them they were getting a good deal."

She wondered now if there wasn't more to it than that. She loved Winston. She didn't want to think of him strapping a man to a chair.

"You know, I've never seen him wear a gun. He says he doesn't need one to the keep the peace. Like Gaston Boykin."

"I don't know Gaston Boykin."

"He was an old-time lawman in Texas, so Winston says."

"How did you and Winston team up?"

"I was a hairdresser in the salon. He asked me if I could type and handle a computer. If you watch him trying to navigate online he looks like he's dismantling a bomb every time he clicks the mouse. And in case you're wondering, he's never suggested anything sexual."

"I could see that."

"He paid for me to do a bachelor's degree online. Politics and economics. I just started on my master's."

"Congratulations," said Turner.

"My thesis is on the history of the mine workers' unions. It's a bleak story, but it needs to be told."

"Would you say Dirk Le Roux is an honorable man?" asked Turner.

The question took her unawares. Before she could answer it, she saw the memorial flash by in the edge of the headlights.

"Stop the car, we're here."

Turner braked and slowed.

"It's behind us," she said, "set back from the road."

Turner made a U-turn, crunching through scrub before regaining the tarmac. A few meters from the edge of the road rose a cairn of stones, a cone about waist high. Turner angled the car to flood it with light and stopped. Iminathi got out and Turner followed her.

The cairn was mounted on a concrete base and was composed of rocks of various sizes bonded together with mortar. Threaded down the center of the cone by its wooden handle was a pickax. The work was crude but honest. There was no plaque to identify its meaning. Iminathi had sometimes wondered why the company didn't destroy it. But in leaving it untouched they announced that they didn't care what it represented, and why should they? No one else did. If the cairn was a heartfelt memorial, its continued existence was an expression of contempt, not respect.

Turner studied it without expression. He looked at her. "A grave?"

"No, a memorial," said Iminathi. "This is the place where my father died. This is where they found his body."

TWELVE

The council of war on the terrace: Margot, Winston Mokoena, Simon Dube, and himself.

Hennie had broken the seal on a bottle of Bruichladdich and was on his third dram. He could neck a quarter of a bottle without noticeable effect, so he was well within the zone of responsibility. Winston had made a performance of refusing the Scotch, opting instead for mint tea, but Hennie sensed he'd knocked a few back before coming out here.

In the meantime Hennie and Simon had between them laid out the whole sorry tale and Winston had filled them all in on this motherfucker from Cape Town and the fact that by tomorrow he'd be knocking on doors. All of it—*all of it*—thanks to that fucking stupid ox, Jason.

To Hennie it was a mountain out of a miserable, meaningless molehill. But that would suit Winston, wouldn't it? Winston to the rescue. Give him a new car, another house, another fucking hair salon. A suitcase of those Krugerrands he loves to run through his fingers at night. The bald gloating bastard loved to see Hennie on the spot, too, and boy did he like to keep him there. "Measured by the square meter, Nyanga is more dangerous than Mogadishu ... So you let Dirk have the car keys ... So Jason knows everything."

Hennie would love to have known what really passed between him and this Turner character. It looked to be the perfect opportunity to squeeze more blood from Margot's balls. It wouldn't have surprised Hennie if Winston had put Cape Town up to it.

"Good morning, Captain Mokoena, we've got a sack of human shit here that someone in your manor turned into a sack of human shit with a ruptured uterus, or whatever the fuck it was. We don't give two shits, but what do you want to do about it?"

"I'll tell you what to do about it, son. Get up here on the first bus and we'll put their lily-white feet to the fire."

Simon was solid, of course. Hennie had picked him himself, straight from the 1 Parachute Battalion after Simon had been wounded at the battle for Bangui, when two hundred paras had given three thousand well-trained rebels a bloody nose. Simon was as ruthless a bastard as a Zulu could be, and given their history, what more could you ask for in a head of security? One of the great warrior nations of the earth. Even the British at their best had needed Gatling guns to put them down. It wasn't 'ardly fair, as Kipling said, but that was nothing compared to what they'd had to swallow under apartheid. Oh well, the wheel turned. Decline and fall. Look at Britain now—if you could find it. In any event Simon would be in, whatever was necessary. And being Zulu, he despised Winston and his ANC bullshit too. This comedian from Cape Town had no idea what he was getting into.

Hennie knocked back a third dram and poured a fourth from the blue bottle.

There had been a pause while Margot lit a Dunhill and dwelled on the information. She leaned forward and looked at Winston, and Winston prepared himself to spout more pompous bilge.

Margot said, "Exactly how serious is this, Winston? Legally speaking."

Winston didn't disappoint them. "Nothing is more serious than death."

"That's a pile of moldy old cock," said Hennie. "There's fifty murders a day in this country—that's murders, not killings, suicides, dead babies, or buildings that fell down because your pals built them on the cheap. Death is the national sport."

"What are the possible charges?" said Margot.

Hennie made himself relax. Let Margot handle it.

Winston spread his palms as if displaying his wares. "Culpable homicide. Drunk driving. Leaving the scene of an accident. Failure to render assistance—"

Hennie couldn't let that pass. "It would take days for an ambulance to show up in that piss-hole."

Winston continued, "To which, it seems you have added destruction of evidence and conspiracy."

"What evidence?" said Hennie.

"You said you washed and waxed the car."

"They can't prove any of that," said Hennie. "They can't prove Dirk was drunk, they can't prove Dirk was driving, they can't prove we ever knew she was there."

"The caliber of criminal lawyers you can afford might well get the lesser charges dropped in a plea bargain. But whatever else happens the charge of culpable homicide will stand. *Res ipsa loquitur.*"

"This isn't the time to show off," said Margot.

"The facts speak for themselves," said Winston. "No one is entitled to kill someone with a car, even if it happens all the time. If you do so, negligence—and hence culpability—is automatically presumed. The driver is held to blame until proved otherwise, and in this case it appears that no such proof is possible. The girl did not, for instance, unexpectedly run in front of a moving car. The car reversed at speed and crashed into a dumpster. The dumpster proves this was an irrefutable act of reckless and negligent driving. Culpability is established. The girl was indisputably and unlawfully killed. Hence, culpable homicide."

Margot said, "Let's say this Turner has his way, and he arrests Dirk. Walk me through it."

"He'd be fingerprinted, charged in Cape Town, and held in custody until bailed. Then it would depend on whether or not he fights the charges or pleads guilty. I would advise the latter."

"Why not fight?" said Hennie. "We've got the money."

"The world is surprisingly forgiving of dangerous driving. Most of us are guilty of it from time to time. But drunken driving and leaving the scene propel us into much more odious moral territory. Plus a sentence of up to fourteen years in jail."

"Fourteen years?" said Hennie. He looked a Margot. For a moment he saw something in her eyes that he'd never seen before. Naked fear.

"And if he pleads guilty?" said Margot.

"The criminal justice system is overwhelmed, not least in Cape Town," said Winston. "A plea bargain limiting the charge to culpable homicide, by negligent driving—no alcohol, no leaving the scene—would be welcomed by the court. You can call in some favors, spread some cash. A defendant with a stainless reputation, the appropriate expressions of contrition, etcetera. The driver could expect community service and a fine."

Hennie thought it sounded reasonable, all things considered. A slap on the wrist. If that was all Dirk was looking at, Hennie's gamble in leaving the girl had been a good call. A hell of a lot better than if Dirk had been breathalyzed, fingerprinted, and locked up in Cape Town. They'd all be in jail right now, waiting for the lawyers to cut through a jungle of red tape. He relaxed a little. Winston glanced at him. The Captain sensed a win, too. Margot's expression, on the other hand, was unreadable. An unreadable Margot usually meant trouble.

Winston tried to push her. "You certainly want to avoid a jury trial," he said. "The charges would multiply. Blood would be in the media water. Crocodiles the world over would weep for the girl. Dirk would be on TV for weeks. So would you. The pressure for a harsh sentence would be intense. Your allies would distance themselves—"

"There won't be jury trial," said Margot.

"I'm glad you see it my way," said Winston. "A plea bargain is by far the most *harmonious* solution. There'd be some brief media exposure but no ongoing drama."

Hennie saw a change in Margot's eyes. "But Dirk would be convicted of homicide."

"Well, that's what justice requires," said Winston. "He killed her."

Margot said, "Am I right in believing that he'd never be allowed to practice law?"

Winston's confidence wavered. He stared at her.

Margot had that set look on her face, her no-retreat, no-surrender face. Hennie fancied he heard the toll of a distant bell.

"That's correct," said Winston. "A conviction that serious would see him disbarred for life."

"Years of effort wasted," said Margot. "His character stained forever. His career ruined before it's even started. Dirk's an idealist. He has a vision. He wants to do good, to work for the unfortunate. What about them?"

"It's true," said Hennie. "Dirk's not in it for the money. He wants to make a difference. He's told me that many times."

"All that thrown away," said Margot, "for a poor nameless girl who wasn't long for this world anyway."

"It's a double tragedy," agreed Winston, "but—"

"Where's the justice in that?" said Margot. "Tell me, what

earthly good will come from destroying Dirk? Who will it help? Where is the utility? Where is the logic?"

If she expected an answer, Winston didn't have one. He looked at Hennie, as if for help. He wasn't going to get it. If it was that important to Margot, the argument was over. If the Devil himself drew a line in the sand, Hennie would stand with Margot, whichever side she chose, right or wrong. He didn't have to make a decision, it was just the way it was.

"That's a nonstarter then," said Hennie. "So I'll cop to it. I'm as 'culpable' as Dirk is, maybe more so. No one will notice another stain on my character."

"I appreciate the offer," said Margot. "And I know you mean it. But that's unacceptable."

"Why?"

"It would be a stain on the company, on me. Mining's a dirty business—Brett Kebble, Marikana, the rest—but we've worked hard to create a pristine reputation. Investors like it, the market likes it. I don't want this to come anywhere near any of us. Winston, we've pulled bigger strokes than this together. You must have an alternative."

"A ringer," said Winston. He didn't seem enthusiastic.

"Jason," said Margot.

"It was that stupid fucker who lit the fuse," said Hennie.

"Jason does have a record," said Winston. "The charges were dropped, but it's there. The system never forgets. There's also the matter of the gunshot. It's a portrait of reckless disregard for the law. The judge might well feel obliged to impose a custodial sentence."

Margot said, "So Jason does three months and comes home to a real job with a big fat signing bonus."

"It might be rather more than that."

"Then we'll pay him more."

"What if he's unwilling?"

"Jason will do as he's told," said Hennie.

Margot said, "I'll deal with Jason."

"We're missing the point here," said Winston. "By a 'ringer' I mean I know any number of men who would confess to being the driver—your chauffeur, so to speak—for a plate of beans. He wouldn't have been seen in the shebeen, we keep Dirk out of it, we give the prosecution a nice neat clearance. Some legal acrobatics and some money and it would be done. But all this is to ignore our new friend Turner. I already explored that solution with him. He rejected it out of hand."

"He rejected letting some poor stooge take the fall," said Hennie. "You said he can't prove Dirk was driving."

"He can prove it with witnesses. That would be you and Jason. We can count on you to stand up to the pressure. Can we count on Jason?"

"Then let's tuck Jason up," said Hennie. "Jason was there, he fired the gun, he caused this girl's death. And Turner gets to put a white man inside."

"I don't think that would satisfy him."

"What would?" asked Margot.

"The truth," said Winston.

"He must have a price," said Margot. "Maybe not in hard cash, but there are other currencies that carry no risk and needn't prick his conscience. Advancement, a transfer, a new career."

"He's chasing corpses in Nyanga," said Hennie. "It's not much better than digging their graves. Who wouldn't want to move up? You just made the first offer, so of course he turned it down. He's trying to pump up his price."

"Some men have no price," said Winston. "They can't be bought, they can't be persuaded."

"Then we'll put his tail between his legs and send him home," said Hennie.

"They can't be scared off either."

"You think Turner's like that," said Margot.

"I think he's waiting for you to try."

"What's he trying to prove?"

Winston thought about it, as if he had an answer but couldn't put it into words. He said, "I don't know."

"He'll obey orders, won't he?" said Margot. "Who is his boss?"

"Captain Eric Venter. I don't know him but I'll look into it. Now, I am a great believer in greed—"

"And don't we know it?" said Hennie.

Winston blinked at him slowly like some giant lizard. "—but you can't just pick up the phone and buy a police captain."

"That's news to us," said Hennie. "It's true there must be a few fresh apples in the barrel, but it's worth a try. The president of Interpol was bent, the police commissioner of the whole country, drugs, assassinations—Jackie What's-his-name?"

"Jackie Selebi," said Winston. "But he went to jail, and that's my point. It would be a blind bet, and if you lost it would be a disaster. Such things take time. Discretion. Research. We don't know these people. We don't know which boss to buy. Turner is here. He plans to make arrests tomorrow."

"You don't have the authority to stop him?" asked Margot.

"Not if he doesn't wasn't to be stopped. I can't fire him, I can't suspend him or arrest him. He's doing nothing wrong."

Hennie looked at Margot. "A hundred cops a year die on the job. Why not a hundred and one?"

Winston stood up. "I can't listen to this."

"You do have a price and we pay it, so drop the performance," said Hennie. "Give Turner a choice between a hole in the desert and a wad of cash and he'll change his tune as fast as anyone else. The kind of man you describe doesn't exist, especially not in this country."

"I once knew one well," said Mokoena.

"We all know the edge of your spear isn't that sharp anymore, but Jesus, Winston, what did he do to you to get you running this scared?"

"I've nothing to be scared about, Hennie. I didn't leave a girl to die on a garbage heap."

Hennie lunged up from his chair and faced him, chin up, eyeball to eyeball.

"I won't take lip from a man who smells like a kicked dog."

"You can kick your dog all you want. It won't change what I saw in Turner. Walk softly, my friend, or you will see it too."

Winston held his eyes and Hennie saw the contempt buried in there. It enraged him.

"Now that they've done their pissing, can the dogs sit down?" said Margot.

Hennie had other things to say but he swallowed them. He backed off and sat down.

"Simon," said Margot, "this concerns you as well. What's your take?"

Simon Dube had followed the proceedings with his customary impassive cool.

"Take it out of Turner's hands, get ahead of him, cut him out. Let Jason carry it. Captain Mokoena can arrest him and wrap up the legal paperwork—write the confession for him, Jason signs it. Normal procedure. We present Cape Town Homicide with a fait accompli. If Jason doesn't like it, threaten to throw him to the wolves on the gun charge and leaving the scene. Let him sell some sheep and hire his own lawyer. He's going down whether he likes it or not. If Turner objects, that's a war he'll have to fight with his own boss, not with you, Captain."

Hennie was slightly peeved that he hadn't put it that way himself. He gave Simon an approving nod.

"Our security firm is licensed for prisoner transfers," Simon continued. "We could ship Jason straight to a Cape Town cell, tomorrow. He'll be wearing orange while Turner's still looking for someone who'll talk to him. As long as we keep Dirk and Hennie out of Turner's way, there's nothing else for him to do up here." Simon dipped his head to Margot. "But you give the orders, Mrs. Le Roux."

Margot looked at Winston. "Can you get Rudy behind this? Jason won't agree to it without him."

Winston nodded but didn't look any happier. "Margot, please reconsider. We are embarking on a serious criminal conspiracy. Not for the first time, to be sure, but it is the first time without extensive preparations. Simon's plan is strong but far from foolproof. There are too many imponderables. The potential consequences are catastrophic. If you get the lawyers in and Dirk makes a plea there will be minimum damage at virtually no risk. Turner can't stop a plea bargain, that's out of his hands. He already expects it."

"Minimum damage?" said Margot. "My son will not be convicted as a killer. I will not put that weight on his back. If you won't help us, we'll take alternative measures, as Hennie suggested."

That shut Winston up. He gave Margot a fatalistic nod.

"I'll talk to Jason in the morning," said Margot. "Better still, I'll see him in person. Winston, you set it up so he knows it's official. A lawyer will be waiting to bail him out. We'll keep him in Cape Town until he pleads. Make it clear he'll be well looked after. Protection inside, whatever else is necessary."

"Sorted," said Hennie.

Margot stood up. So did the others. It was over. Winston still had a doubt on his face.

"How will Dirk feel about Jason taking the blame? I understand they're close friends."

"Dirk won't know anything about it. He's going back to Pretoria on Wednesday to start his new job."

Winston blinked. Hennie himself was impressed by her cold-bloodedness. Winston half-turned away and paused, as if another thought had struck him. He turned back.

"Does Dirk even know that he killed this girl?"

"My son knows nothing about the whole affair," said Margot. "That's the way it's going to stay."

Winston hesitated. He looked like he was carrying a thousand pounds of brick on his back.

"Speak your mind," said Margot.

"I don't have the moral authority to say that Dirk is entitled to know—and would want to know—that he has taken a life—"

"No, you don't," said Margot.

"But I will say, as your admirer and I hope your friend, that a secret—a deception—as dark as this one, is a dangerous bargain to make with someone you love."

"We are friends," said Margot. "I appreciate that you offer this advice in that spirit. But don't imagine I am unaware of the nature of the bargain I am making, or of its dangers. And never again presume to tread on the relationship between me and my son."

They exchanged a long look. Winston nodded.

"Goodnight, Margot."

"Goodnight, Winston."

"Let me know when you want me to make the arrest."

Winston walked across the terrace and down the steps and disappeared into the dark.

Hennie judged it best to keep his mouth shut. He reached for the blue bottle.

"Mrs. Le Roux?" said Simon.

"Simon." She was all business again, the cold rage gone like that.

"Turner will try to make direct contact with Dirk. If he's got Jason's phone, he's got Dirk's number. We should take Dirk off the radar."

"Can you do that without his consent?" said Margot.

"His phone is on a company contract. I can kill his service with a call, right now. In the morning I can spin him a story and give him a spare until the problem is fixed. With your permission."

"Do it," she said.

"Then there's email, Facebook, Twitter, or a dozen other online routes, and Dirk can access those from any computer, yours for instance. The only solution to that is to shut down the Wi-Fi to the whole compound, for a day or two."

"How much of a problem is that?"

"It isn't a security problem. What would be a problem, if I understand the situation, is if Dirk were to get a message from the police asking him to present himself for questioning. They don't have to say why. That's all it would take to let the cat out of the bag."

"Where is Dirk tonight?" said Margot

"He's playing Texas Hold'em," said Simon. "At Lewis' garage. He went in his Audi. I sent a man with him to drive him home."

"Have him brought home now. Shut down the Wi-Fi."

She nodded to dismiss him. Simon rose to leave.

"And Simon?" she said. "Thank you."

Simon was too cool show he was pleased. He was already tapping on his phone as he left. Hennie basked in the reflected glory. Why not? Simon was his man. Cybersecurity? Christ. What had happened to the days when it was all about the barrel of a gun? Chairman Mao, now there was hardcore. Where was the Chairman Mao de nos jours? Hennie missed the old days. Who didn't? Including the youngsters who didn't even know what they'd missed? Turner was an underpaid nobody. It was a shame Hennie wouldn't get the chance to put that bastard in his place. A man with no price, okay, he did know the type. He'd been that type himself, once upon a time, just like Winston. But that kind of—whatever it was, integrity? Honor? Principle?—was a

weakness to be conquered, it was immature, it was out of touch
with reality. It did more harm than good. Look at the fucking
Americans. He blamed the movies, all the lies they peddled, all
that good and evil bollocks.

He looked up from his single malt reverie and found Margot
watching him. He saw that she loved him. He wasn't always convinced of that, but that's how she kept him on his toes. Sharp as
a scalpel. That's why he loved her. But now there was something
more. She needed him. His heart expanded to the limits of his
massive chest. That was a feeling worth dying for. She held out
her arms. What a woman. He put his glass down and stood up,
perfectly steady of course, and grabbed her hands and pulled her
against him. She seemed at the same time so small and yet twice
his size. He stroked her short blond hair.

"Should I call Herzfeldt?" she said.

"He wouldn't tell you any different than Winston," said
Hennie. "He'd just charge a lot more. Unlike Winston, he'll only
bend the law as far as it won't hurt him, and we're bending it
well beyond that. Let's keep it tight and play it by ear. We haven't
reached any point of no return."

She turned her face up toward him.

"I don't know if I'm doing the right thing," she said. "By Dirk."

Hennie laughed, from his belly. Not a shadow of a doubt
clouded his judgment.

"You always do the right thing, love."

THIRTEEN

Turner drove back toward town on the empty road. His eyes were gritty. His back ached. He'd been on the move for over sixteen hours. He needed to find a hotel, a shower, a bed. First, he had to find out what Imi was after, and if she had anything for him.

Imi was a puzzle. After her studious silence in Mokoena's den she had proved herself quite a talker. She was relaxed around men, dangerous men. She was beautiful, in that way only a mixed-race woman could be, or a man, come to that. Something you couldn't classify or describe, a face you couldn't compare to any other, as if it were the first face you'd ever seen. She didn't seem to know it, or didn't know how to use it, or she'd decided that that just wasn't the way she wanted to be or how she wanted to make her way, which increased her allure to no end. Her mother had died when she was a child and her father had been a miner, taking her with him from pit to pit, one tumbleweed town to the next; a hard road to travel, so maybe no one had ever had time to tell her she was something special.

She was driving through the night with a strange cop from the big city and was as cool as if she'd been going to the movies with an old friend. He had some idea of what it might be like to sit beside someone like him. A job got into you, any job. A cabbie, a doctor, a soap star, the owner of a mine. You carried it whether you liked it or not. Homicide was a lot to carry. His colleagues were heavy; it had nothing to do with their size. What they knew was heavy. Their vision was dark. They weren't easy company. They had fewer reasons than most to admire the human race. Meanwhile, Imi just watched from the passenger seat, waiting to hear what he had to say about her father's death.

Her father had collapsed from dehydration and had roasted to death in the sun ten meters from the road. His body, or rather the vultures taking it apart, had been spotted by a passing truck driver.

"What was the coroner's verdict?" said Turner.

"Accidental death," said Iminathi. "Misadventure."

"That satisfied Winston."

"Papa died about a month before Winston came here. Rudy Britz said he died from stupidity and bad luck, in that order."

"Rudy has a way with words."

"He didn't even ask why Papa was thirty kilometers off road in his 1993 Suzuki. It made no sense. Papa hated the desert. He had the desert in his lungs, under his fingernails, in his teeth."

"He was working for Le Roux Manganese," said Turner.

"On the first shaft they dug."

"Any sign he was coerced?"

"You could find cuts and bruises on him any day of the week. There'd been violence at the diggings, strike meetings. Papa was an organizer for the AMCU."

"Translate that for me," said Turner.

"Association of Mineworkers and Construction Union."

"Rivals to the NUM."

"The NUM is rotten to the core."

"Marikana," said Turner.

"Right," said Iminathi. "Marikana."

The Marikana massacre had taken place five, six years ago as he remembered it. A platinum mine near Rustenburg in the North West. An elite police unit armed with assault rifles, in support of company security forces, had killed over thirty striking miners, some already in handcuffs, and shot down dozens more. The strikers were AMCU. The National Union of Mineworkers and the Communists defended the police. The company share price rose. No one was punished. The media sucked the bones dry and everyone moved on.

"An unfortunate incident," said Turner.

"Are you quoting Zuma?" A flash of anger. "Or is that your take?"

"I'm not a political man."

"We're all political," she said. "Whether you like it or not."

"Was your father at Marikana?" he asked.

"No. Platinum is about the only thing he never dug for."

"Were they striking at Le Roux when he died?"

"They were talking about it."

"A union man snaps a timing belt in the desert and dies of thirst. No bad headlines there."

"It didn't even make the local paper," said Imi. "The strike never happened."

"And then Winston arrived. Maybe they were clearing the decks for the new management. At that stage they couldn't be certain he'd stand still for that."

"So you agree my father was murdered."

"If it's not filed as murder it wasn't murder. They did a good job."

A bullet would have been kinder, but he didn't say so. He glanced at the pain in her eyes.

"There's nothing I can do about it," he said. "There's nothing anyone can do. Even in cases of unequivocal murder, the conviction rate is under twenty-five percent. For the perpetrator, the odds are that good."

"That's what Winston said."

"So why tell me?"

"I wanted you to know you're dealing with more than a drunk driver."

"I appreciate the warning. Why should you care?"

"They're all on your list."

"The men you believe murdered your father?"

Imi nodded. "Hennie, Simon, and Mark. Rudy Britz."

"Are these known knowns or just your theory?"

"I've seen the way Hennie looks at me. He's seen the way I look at him."

Turner believed it. Murder was routine.

"Back then I was a hairdresser. I didn't know anything about them. Bit by bit I picked up enough to see it. Hennie's a bully, a thug. He was a sergeant in the British paratroopers. He likes to boast about his mercenary days, but it was mainly shouting at recruits in training camps. He likes getting his hands dirty. I think it makes him feel young again. The decision to kill my father wouldn't have been taken any lower than him."

"Margot?"

"I don't know. She wouldn't have to give an order. If she complains about the heat, Hennie turns up the air-con. She's a control freak. After the strike danger went away, she boosted the wages anyway and raised safety standards sky-high. There hasn't been a fatality at the mine in three years. She's proud of that. Things have to be done her way."

"Maybe she felt guilty."

"I don't think Margot does guilt," said Imi.

"You seem to know her well."

"I admire her." It galled her to say it. "How couldn't I?

She's a woman, she hires women, she's built this business, she's generous to charities, and she started out as a widow with a ten-year-old son and two hundred sheep. And she isn't a racist."

Turner doubted that. Everyone was a racist when the moment demanded it, himself included, but it wasn't a subject that much interested him anymore. They were stuck with it, like the desert waiting for rain.

"But she had the air-con turned up on your father."

Imi paused but didn't bite. "Simon Dube is ex-army; no line he won't cross if he's told to. Mark Lewis' family has the contract to service all the company's motor vehicles, including plant at the mine. Mark was the mechanic who wrote the report on my father's truck."

"And the others?"

"Jason's too unreliable. He has 'roid rages and smokes tik. And he's not too bright. His uncle must have been involved, but not Jason."

Imi shifted in her seat. She seemed uncomfortable.

"So tell me about Dirk," said Turner.

"Dirk's a rich mama's boy. She's always kept him clear of the business. She made him study law in Pretoria."

"She made him?"

"Margot's always had a plan for him, Dirk's always followed it. But he won't do that forever. He wants to go into politics."

Her tone sounded more complex now. A familiarity, threads of regret, frustration. He remembered the way she had studied Dirk's photo.

"Will he own up to it?" asked Turner. "The death of the girl?"

"You're sure it was him?" she said.

"That's what I'm here to find out."

Imi thought about it. Some inner conflict tightened her lips.

"Dirk wouldn't leave a girl to die. He's not that much of a coward."

"I've heard better character references," said Turner.

"That wasn't fair, I mean I wasn't being fair. He's a good guy. A genuine white left liberal. A twenty-first-century post-apartheid man. He can afford to be, but it doesn't mean it's not real. I know him; it is. We need his kind. We're drowning in our own lies. We need him. So he got drunk. If he knew he'd killed her, I believe he'd do the right thing. So I don't think he does know. Is that possible?"

"That's why they call it blind drunk."

Imi controlled her distress but it was real. "Let him go," she said.

Turner wondered why people imagined he had a choice in the matter.

"I know what that might mean to you," she said. "I know what I'm asking."

"I don't think you do."

"Dirk's not a killer," she said.

"I never thought he was. But he appears to be a person who has killed."

"I appreciate the distinction. But the real killers walk free. The Hennies, the Simon Dubes."

"Hendricks has a case to answer," said Turner. "He'll answer."

Imi said, "Because you're a killer, too."

"We're not talking about me."

"You're right, we're not. Why is that?"

"You got in my car, you asked me to drive, I'm driving."

"Give Dirk a pass. He's not a bad person."

"What do you have going with Dirk?"

He face closed up and she looked away. "I don't have anything going with Dirk."

So Dirk was her ex. That had to explain something. Turner wasn't sure what, beyond the confusion he was feeling. He was probably picking that up from her.

"Who broke it off?" he said. "You or him?"

The lights of town rose out of the darkness ahead.

"Will you drive me home?" she said.

"Sure."

He waited while she fought whatever battle she needed to fight with herself. She must have fought it before, but such battles existed to be refought. Her ex-boyfriend was the scion of the family she believed had murdered her father. A hero father who had not had much chance to be there for her and was probably not so inclined. She hadn't let his death stop her forming a relationship with Dirk—or working for Mokoena who worked for Margot. She'd educated herself. She was more than just surviving, much more.

He would have been confused as well. He often was. Keep it clean and simple; carry it hard and true. He drove down the main street and she indicated a turn and he took it.

"You can pull over here, please," she said.

Turner stopped outside a short terrace of three new single-story brick houses. Small, functional, security bars over the windows. Classy by local standards but utterly without character. A few potted plants struggled for life along the pavement outside.

"I broke it off," said Imi. "Because Margot persuaded me to." She looked at him. He didn't speculate on what she was feeling. "Dirk asked me to marry him."

She seemed to expect a response. Turner didn't have one.

"Does that surprise you?" she asked.

"Surprise cuts down on reaction time. I stopped doing it," said Turner.

"I'm not being honest," said Imi. "Margot paid me. With this house. She said the marriage was never going to happen but she preferred not to go to work on him. 'I want to keep our relationship at least at par,' she said."

"Why not throw a fight you can't win?" said Turner. "Especially for a payoff."

"That's funny, coming from you. Why don't you throw your fight? Don't you know how high your payoff could be?"

"You mean, 'be reasonable.'"

"The whole world's at it, read a newspaper. It is reasonable."

"If I throw this one, why not the next? And the one after that? For money, for a friend, for a promotion. Then one day I'm arresting some teenager who's just stabbed his neighbor for a fistful of tik straws and what will I have become? Just another jackboot."

"Isn't that what you already are?"

Turner didn't look at her because he didn't want to frighten her with what her insult made him feel. He had more reason than most to share that view of his profession. He understood now why she'd taken him to see her father's memorial. She wasn't looking for justice or even sympathy. She'd sold what she knew was best in herself, perhaps more than once. It was a lonely place to be. She wanted company. She wanted him to join her, to ease her aloneness, to banish her shame.

"You made your choices," he said. "They seem like good ones. I don't see anyone judging you."

She uttered a short, bitter laugh. "You just arrived in town so how would you know? And you can't see your face."

He smiled. "You're just looking at a face that's been on the road since daybreak."

"We've all walked past that girl in the street. We walk past her every day. Why does she matter so much now that she's dead?"

"Because mattering now that she's dead is the only right she has left."

Imi stared at him.

"Maybe it was the only right she ever had," said Turner. "But it's fallen to me to defend it."

Her emotional confusion vanished. She looked cool and beautiful again.

"You must excuse me," he said. "I need some sleep."

"Stay with me," she said.

He saw no ambiguity in her eyes. Turner thought about it, but not for long. Long enough to feel regret that the circumstances were not otherwise. She was a grown woman holding her own in a snake pit of killers, thieves, and millionaires, and making a good fist of it. But that wasn't the issue.

He couldn't abandon the discipline without abandoning himself. The dead girl demanded it, the case demanded it, any and all cases demanded it. He was a beast on a chain. Without the chain he was a mad dog unleashed in a field of sheep. The chain was the rule to which he had committed himself. He yearned to snap the chain. He would have died for the joy of it. But he had chosen against joy. He had chosen the chain. It was a long time since he had questioned it, since he'd had cause to question it. The woman looking into his eyes gave him cause.

For a moment his soul felt at hazard.

If he walked through her door, his case was poisoned. Another man could have fucked her without such compromise, but he was not that man. Fucking a woman was a serious matter for a serious man. He brought into his mind the parchment features of the nameless girl's death mask. He could not contain within himself both the girl and the fucking without breaking the chain.

He held out his hand to Imi. "Promises to keep," he said.

She understood. His regret became deeper.

She took his hand and squeezed it. She was strong.

"I'll swap numbers," he said.

"Sure."

She gave him her number, and he stored it and rang it so that she had his.

Turner dropped a question he had been saving. "Did you ever tell Dirk about your father?"

"Does it make you feel good to humiliate me?"

"That's not my intention. I want to know what kind of man I'm after. His reaction to that story would interest me."

"No, I never told him. How could it have changed anything for the better, to tell him I thought his family were murderers? I was in love. I didn't want to spoil what we had."

"No reason to blame yourself for that."

"Good luck," said Imi. "You'll need it."

She opened the car door and climbed out and closed the door and walked to her house. She opened the door and went inside without looking back.

Turner drove to the hotel on the main drag and parked his car. He shouldered his backpack from the trunk and walked inside. Rudy Britz sat in an armchair in the lobby.

Turner went to the desk and booked a double bed with a mosquito net. He got his key. He wasn't in the mood to be harassed. He felt the chain stretching thin. He walked over to Rudy and looked down at him.

"If you've come with an apology, I accept it. If not, get out of my sight before I break you."

Rudy stood up. "I do apologize." His eyes were as sincere as a pig making a promise to lose weight. "I've got something else to offer, too."

"Goodnight, Sergeant. I'll drop by the station in the morning."

"By then it'll be too late. They're circling the wagons."

Turner studied his face. He had no idea what was going on behind the black brows. No one was more skilled at lying than a seasoned cop.

"You're so far out of your depth you can't see land, Cape Town." Rudy snorted. "Do you really think you can go toe-to-toe with the power? With your little badge? The best you can hope for is to go home looking like a fool. The worst ..." Rudy smiled. "Well, believe me, it's a lot worse."

"You're the third person tonight to tell me that. What do you want?"

"The same thing as you."

"Oh yes?"

"Let justice be done though the heavens fall."

FOURTEEN

The hotel bar was small and empty and opened onto a patio laid around a giant thorn tree. They sat at a table outside. Rudy Britz smoked. The night air was cool. Turner enjoyed it.

"Mokoena called me," said Rudy. "You've got him sweating like a birdbath."

Turner couldn't quite see the image, but Rudy seemed to find it pleasing.

"You'll need more than luck to arrest Dirk Le Roux. I doubt you'll ever set eyes on him. You should see their compound."

"I have. Google Earth."

"You'd need an air strike and a Black Hawk to get in there. Or a warrant, but you won't get a warrant from any judge in this province, not with the evidence you've got. So you'll talk to your people, and they'll talk to our people, and our people will talk to other people. Then you'll be taken off the case and sent to direct traffic in Khayelitsha. I'm a noncom too. I know where we stand. I know how little we're valued."

Rudy's bitterness seemed real enough. Turner remembered

that Mokoena had been parachuted in above him. "Must be tough scraping by on a sergeant's wage."

"Oh I get my turkey at Christmas. I'm talking about respect. Rudy do this, Rudy do that. You can always count on Rudy."

"I can?"

"I'd like to see the look on Margot's face when you slap the cuffs on her darling son."

The spite in Rudy's eyes went all the way down to what passed for his soul.

"Show me the noose," said Turner. "I'll see if I want to put my neck in it."

"You know what would get you that warrant, don't you?" said Rudy.

"A sworn statement from your nephew putting Dirk behind the wheel of the car."

"The truth and nothing but the truth. Jason remembers all of it."

"Isn't Jason in with the in crowd?"

"Jason's the only family I've got and vice versa. His father, my brother Oscar, died when he was a lad. Melanoma. Sucked him down to skin and bone in six months. Horrible. I've done my best for him. Took him hunting, helped out on the farm, a shoulder to cry on. That kind of thing gets under your skin. And this is where that arrogant bitch has gone too far. I went to school with her, you know. Poor as dirt. I used to drink with her husband. Look at her now. I don't know the inside of that compound any better than you do. I've never been invited. I remind her of what she was."

Turner took a drink of Black Label. Rudy was taking pains to establish his motive for going against Margot, as a police would. No doubt the bone had been in Rudy's throat for a long time, but he was hardly choking on it. Turner set the beer bottle down.

"So the rich girl's in her castle and the poor boy's at her gate. Why is it in your interest, or Jason's, to make my case?"

"They want Jason to go down in Dirk's place, to claim he was the driver. Then Dirk swans off to be an advocate in Pretoria while Jason's in a cage with a crowd of animals."

Jason's phone, and the photos, placed him at the scene. With the right lawyers on hand to strike a plea, a false confession would be hard to crack. The public prosecutor would be unlikely even to try. A clearance was a clearance.

"They'll pay him off, of course," said Rudy. "They'll 'look after him.' But if Jason goes inside he might not come out again. When that switch gets thrown in his head, he's a terror. If he kills someone or tries to—because once he goes berserk that's what it looks like—then 'a couple of months,' as Winston puts it, becomes fourteen years minimum."

"What makes Margot think he'll go for it?"

"Arrogance. Disrespect. Because Rudy will rubber-stamp it for them, won't he? They're so fucking haughty it makes them stupid."

"Jason will do whatever you tell him to do."

"No," said Rudy. "He'll do what I think is best for him because he knows I'm the only one who gives two shits."

"They won't be happy with you."

"What can they do? Chop my monthly bonus? They can have it if they dare take it, but they won't. We're all chained together in the same boat—Margot, Hennie, Winston, me. If one goes overboard, the rest go with him. I know where the bodies are buried, as they say. Literally. That's the funny part—Dirk's not chained to anybody. He's pure as driven snow. Or he was until last night. Let's face it, he's not going to prison no matter what happens."

Turner didn't see any more in Rudy's face than what he was giving out. It was simple. It was believable. In his gut, Turner didn't believe it.

Turner said, "So what are you offering?"

"I'll prep Jason tonight, you and me go out there first thing tomorrow and get his statement. You take him straight back to Cape Town and keep him safe until you get your warrant. You'll be gone before they know they've been outfoxed. When you come back you bring a partner and you'll be bulletproof."

Rudy raised his glass, inviting him to drink to it. Turner clinked his bottle. They drank. Rudy stood up.

"I'll meet you outside in the parking lot at seven."

"Make it eight," said Turner.

"Eight, then," said Rudy. "Sleep tight."

Turner went to his room and took a long shower.

His gut didn't feel any easier. His gut knew how easily he could die out here. He considered calling Venter and taking advice but couldn't face another hour on the subject of the Le Roux. Nothing he had seen or heard had surprised him. It wouldn't surprise Venter. In any case the captain would back him.

He put a chair against the handle of the door, something he hadn't done in a long time. He checked his Glock and put it under his pillow; ditto. He plugged his phone charger into the power outlet by the bed.

Before he went to sleep he set the alarm on his phone to 6:00 a.m.

PART TWO: MONDAY

ALL MANNER
OF MADNESS

FIFTEEN

Turner checked out of the hotel at 6:30 a.m.

He drove the Land Cruiser to the service station and filled the tank, checked the water, and corrected the tire pressures. He programed the coordinates he'd copied from Google Earth into the GPS and headed for Jason Britz's farm. Thirteen kilometers. He found just one road through Langkopf, two lanes running north and south. Half a dozen single-lane roads branched off within a few kilometers of town but all were culs-de-sac that fed only local farms and the Le Roux mine complex. Jason's farm was to the southwest.

The scheme Rudy had laid out had merit but he didn't want Rudy along. If it proved legitimate, there was no good reason Jason shouldn't jump in the car and head back to Cape Town with him. If it was a setup, he'd rather not find himself standing in the tumbleweed with one Britz in front of him and a second behind his back.

Twelve kilometers in, while the tarmac continued across yellow grass and scrub, a metal gate in the barbed wire fence marked a dirt track that angled off to the right. The GPS told him to turn. The gate was open and he drove through it. In the distance he could see a small cluster of buildings and the tall skeleton of a windmill pump. He passed a dozen black-faced sheep grubbing for a living on land that even by local standards looked barren. In the rearview mirror dust spiraled up from his wheels. If Jason was up, he'd see him coming. He could see no phone or power lines to the house; presumably a generator. Turner checked his phone: two bars.

His rearview mirror included a 1080HD camera that captured a near one-eighty-degree image through the windshield. The camera was synced to supplementary high-sensitivity microphones at either end of the dashboard. The data was stored on a microSD card and, when in Cape Town, could be networked live to headquarters. He washed the thin film of dust from the windshield and switched the camera on.

He saw a wind pump that fed an open circular tank on the ground and a row of rusting water troughs. Seven silage bales in black polywrap, stacked three on four, had melted and rotted into a misshapen redoubt by the side of the track. A faded blue tractor had grass growing up around its wheels. An old stone shearing shed. A flatbed Suzuki truck stood in the yard by a single-story farmhouse, probably four rooms.

The house looked old, a century or more, built of rough pale stone with a low-pitched roof of red tiles. A black iron chimney rose from its center and a satellite dish, for TV or broadband was bolted to one corner. A broad stone stoop was painted a faded, peeling red and, like much else about, hadn't seen attention in years. Turner stopped in the yard about eight meters from the front door.

Jason stood on the stoop doing mixed-grip sumo dead lifts with what looked like 120 kilos on an Olympic bar. He wore tight black leggings that emphasized the girth of his thighs and a bottle-green bodybuilder's vest that displayed the enormous musculature of his torso. His face maintained a fixed grimace that masked whatever he thought about Turner's early arrival. Eight reps didn't seem to challenge him too much, though by the end he was short of breath while trying not to show it. He set the bar down on the stones and straightened up. His shirt was printed with a slogan in white letters: GET BIG OR DIE. Epic orchestral music thundered from two speakers set to either side of the front door.

Turner displayed his badge and ID through the windshield. Jason beckoned him; come on, no problem. Turner got out and left the door open. He didn't move closer, in part to limit the impact of the music. It was on a repeat loop and made Turner grit his teeth. Propulsive drums, blaring brass, and stirring strings battled to outdo each other in heroic drama, as if exhorting the listener to invade a foreign country. It wasn't that he didn't like it; it didn't give you any choice: if you didn't like it it would kill you.

"Amazing sounds," said Turner.

"Basil Poledouris, *Conan the Barbarian*, 1982," said Jason. "It helps me push through the barrier." He slid another twenty-kilo plate onto either end of the bar. Turner noticed beads of dried blood on his left triceps. "This is the best time to train, before the heat gets up. You train?"

"A little tai chi, when I get the time."

"I thought that was for health, migraines and shit."

"I haven't had a cold in ten years."

"You're missing out, man. One more set to get the pump and we'll talk."

Jason knocked out five reps, music soaring, veins bulging from his forearms, temples, and delts. To hoist up the sixth he bellowed with rage.

Turner had to grant him a certain magnificence. He wondered about spending seven hours with the man in the car. He considered encouraging a couple more sets, to wear him out if that was possible, but he didn't want to hear any more bellowing. Jason dropped the bar to bounce on the stoop. A two liter plastic jug from a blender sat on a small table nearby. It was two-thirds full of creamy yellow liquid. Jason picked it up and poured a long slug down his throat. He gasped with pleasure and wiped the back of his hand across his mouth.

"Two scoops of whey protein, three eggs, two oranges, peanut butter, and a banana. Top it up with coconut milk. Build while you burn, see? You want some?"

Turner said, "No. Thanks."

Jason clicked an MP3 device on the table and the music stopped. He picked up a towel and swabbed the sweat from his face, neck, and pecs. He looked at Turner as if giving him his full attention for the first time.

"Turner, right?"

"Right."

"Where's Rudy?"

"I thought we'd best handle this without him."

"Okay."

"Rudy said you'd make a witness statement."

Jason waved the jug. "I didn't hurt a fucking fly in Cape Town."

"I didn't think you did."

"Now Rudy tells me they want me in a cell, shitting in the same bucket as five blacks."

"Tell me what happened early Sunday morning, outside the shebeen."

"You know what happened."

"I wasn't there," said Turner. "I need to hear it from you."

"Dirk was dead drunk. He even drank my last shot, I was close to puking after three. When we left the bar Dirk had the keys, he blipped the locks and I got in the back. I expected Hennie to drive but Dirk got behind the wheel and started her up."

Jason took another chug on his smoothie and put the jug down. He wiped his mouth on the towel.

"I warned him, so did Hennie, but Dirk was too pissed to know what he was doing. He shoved her in gear, it's an automatic, and trod on the gas but the hand brake was on. I warned him again. He dropped the hand brake without moving his foot, so we shot backward into a trash dumpster. Bang. That got through to him. Dirk turned off the engine and Hennie gave him a mouthful and made him move over. No big deal. That's when I saw the girl on the ground, all mangled up, blood and bone."

Jason paused. He coiled the towel in his hands into thick rope.

"I knew it was bad. I couldn't find my phone so I told Hennie to lend me his—that's when he saw her lying there too. She couldn't speak—shock I suppose—but you could see it in her face. Begging us for help. It was—" He paused to choose the word. The memory moved him. "It was a shame. A rotten shame. I started to get out, see what I could do. I wasn't really thinking, just doing it. But Hennie slammed the door on me. Then he climbed in the car and drove us away."

"Did Hennie say anything?"

"Yeah. Hennie said, 'Time to hit the road to dreamland.'" Jason flipped the roped towel over his head and sawed it against the nape of his massive neck. "Hennie knows everything. Dirk knows nothing. I did nothing." Jason shrugged. "Will that do it for you?"

"You'll swear to all that."

"I swear it before almighty God."

"Rudy said you'd be willing to come with me to Cape Town today."

"For once in my life I'm going to follow Rudy's advice. Let me get changed."

Turner nodded. Jason dropped the towel on the table and went inside.

Any other witness, in any other place, and nothing might have disturbed Turner's instincts. Most witnesses gave their honest version of the truth, even if they were often inaccurate or wrong. But something didn't sit right, he didn't know why. His habitual level of suspicion was high; Iminathi had cranked it higher. Maybe that was all. He lifted the tail of his shirt up and tucked it into his pants to clear the butt of the Glock 17 on his hip. He could have drawn it but it might spook Jason, and the only way to get him back to Cape Town was if he wanted to go.

When Jason reappeared he hadn't changed his clothes. He had to turn slightly sideways to get through the doorway, his left shoulder in the lead. As he cleared the door Turner saw he carried a Franchi SPAS-12 combat shotgun in his right hand, its extendable metal stock locked out and his bulging forearm crammed into the stabilizer hook for one-armed shooting. Semiautomatic; no pump necessary. He held it by his leg, the barrel pointed at an angle to the stoop. His grip on the weapon was familiar, confident. His eyes had a strange, euphoric glaze. His breathing was shallow and quick.

Turner could have killed him right then, but Jason was the only witness he was going to get. Turner let his weight sink into his left foot without changing his stance and raised his left hand and extended his palm out. He kept his lateral vision on the muscles of Jason's right arm. The muscles would move before the shotgun did. The SPAS-12 weighed about five kilos. With Jason's strength he could raise it as fast as most men could raise a pistol.

"I ask you to put the gun down, Jason. If I draw mine, I will kill you."

"If I wanted to put it down I wouldn't have picked it up."

"You must have doubts or you'd have come out shooting."

"No doubts. But I'm not a coward. We go man-to-man."

"That doesn't sound like Rudy's advice," said Turner.

"He says I can shoot an armed black on my own land without being charged with a bloody thing."

"In this town I expect he's right. Is Mokoena backing this?"

Jason shook his head. "Rudy's idea."

"I can see why he wanted to be here. You're not a killer."

"I first killed a sheep when I was eight years old. My dad made me. Can't be any harder than that was."

"You're tougher than me," said Turner. "You must be, you live here. You're stronger than me, probably faster. But I've done this before. You haven't."

"Doesn't matter to me. I'm tired of feeling smaller than I am."

"You think this will give you some size with Margot and Hennie. It won't."

"Those fuckers think they're better than me."

"They're wrong. You tried to save the girl."

"That's the point," said Jason. "I didn't. I didn't have the balls."

"If you want to show some balls, help me take down Dirk Le Roux."

"Dirk's my friend. He's the best friend I ever had."

"People like Dirk don't have friends. They have servants. He even expected you to serve his time."

"No. Dirk's not in on any of this. It's all their idea."

"How can you be sure?"

"I know him."

"So you know that if Margot told him to cut his own ears off, he'd ask her to pass him a knife."

"You black bastard."

Turner cast a glance at the interior of his car. Jason didn't miss the glance, but he didn't read it as a feint. Turner made sure he didn't by backing down.

"Okay, forget about the witness statement. Put the shotgun down and I'm out of here."

If Jason would have let him, Turner would have gone. The dashcam video would be enough to push a warrant through. He felt no pity for the hulking young farmer, but he had no desire to kill him.

Jason said, "Your only way out of here is in a plastic bag."

"We can both walk away from this. Dirk Le Roux isn't worth dying for."

"Depends who's dying, doesn't it?"

Jason's shoulders and neck tensed with anger. All three heads of deltoid were visible. The rage had simmered inside him for a long time. Others had provoked it and fed it, not Turner. But Turner was standing in front of him.

"For once those rich cunts'll be in my pocket."

"There are no pockets in a shroud."

They looked at each other across a narrow but bottomless abyss. Turner had stood here before, facing other sad young men. To have reached this abyss was his failure, because here he had no more choices. The choice was Jason's. He could step across or he could fall. He was pumped up on iron and steroids and the need to prove himself to himself, yet for a moment Turner thought that he'd see reason. Then Jason blinked and glanced away with a frown, as if a sudden thought had annoyed him.

"Shit," he said. "I should've put the music back on."

Jason's right deltoid and biceps flexed.

Turner shot him. *Bam-bam-bam.*

He dipped his left shoulder toward the open car, the payoff of the feint. His weightless right foot stepped the opposite way and his body followed. At the same time he drew the Glock, raised the front sight to Jason's chest, and fired three times. The SPAS-12 boomed and blew out the window of the open car door. Jason's tremendous thighs gave out like pillars of blancmange. He keeled backward across the Olympic bar as two ropes of blood spiraled from his sternum, entwining around each other as he twisted and fell. Then his blood pressure collapsed and the blood merely flowed to pool across the red stones of the stoop.

Turner reckoned him dead before he'd fired the shotgun. A man of lesser strength couldn't have squeezed the trigger. Turner put two fingers to his own carotid pulse. His usual resting heart rate was fifty. It was fifty now. He walked over and crouched to study the corpse.

The slogan on Jason's shirt was stained red. The holes between his pecs were in a vertical line, three centimeters apart. Blood drained from a single exit wound in his back. The third shot had gone through the side of his throat and blown out through the bony angle of his lower left jaw. Turner checked Jason's pulse. There was none. He noted the color of Jason's eyes for the first time. Its luster faded as he watched, as if the color were being erased from the palette of creation. As indeed it was. A kind of baby blue, but Jason's alone.

Turner holstered his gun and walked away.

He returned to his car and ejected the SD card from the dashboard camera and stored it in the safe pocket inside the waist of his pants. He took a spare SD card from the glove box and reloaded the camera.

There was no one he could trust within five hundred kilometers of where he stood. Not even Iminathi. The Britzes could have devised this setup by themselves or they could have been acting on orders, from Winston Mokoena, Margot Le Roux, Hennie Hendricks, or any combination thereof. At the very least Rudy would be out for blood. Turner called Mokoena.

"Warrant Turner, good morning."

"Not for Jason Britz. I just shot and killed him."

A short silence followed while Mokoena weighed the pros and cons of this news. As to whether or not he'd been aware of the Britzes' intention to murder Turner, his voice when it came gave no clue.

"I'm sure you had your reasons," he said.

"He threw down on me with a SPAS-12 at his farmhouse."

"Why would he do that?"

"Rudy's idea. To gain favor with Margot."

"Working toward the führer," said Mokoena.

"I'm not with you."

"It is said that one reason the Nazis became so insane is that everyone tried to come up with ideas that they thought would please Hitler." Mokoena sighed with disgust. "I'll be right out there."

"No. Go to the hotel parking lot and wait for Rudy. Go now. I'm supposed to meet him there in seventeen minutes. Tell him Jason is in my custody and no longer at the farm."

"Two perfect half-truths," said Mokoena.

"Just keep him away from me. I don't want to kill two Britzes in one day."

"Stay at the scene until I get back to you."

"Play it straight, Winston, or you'll rue the day you left Jo'burg."

SIXTEEN

Turner snapped half a dozen photos of Jason's corpse, the shotgun hooked to his arm, the fatal wounds. He felt a sudden nausea, a weakness in his limbs as his inner self reacted to the taking of a man's life. He couldn't think his way out of the moment, couldn't rationalize the killing. Or rather, there was no point in trying. The feelings—the guilt, the horror, the anger—just had to be endured and absorbed. The burden had to be carried. He breathed and looked at the empty blue sky until the moment passed.

He hadn't taken the time for breakfast or even coffee. He walked back to the stoop where the first flies had arrived. The pooled blood was trickling over the edge of the stones and soaking into the dust. He stepped around it and took the blender jug from the table and tasted Jason's smoothie. It was good, the orange zest bitter and bracing. He drained the jug and set it back down.

He had used deadly force. He knew the procedure, if Mokoena wanted to follow it. That would take most of the day. He could leave by evening, drive through the night. Tighten up the case with the video of Jason's statement before returning for Dirk. He saw nothing more to be achieved by staying in Langkopf, unless

Dirk Le Roux decided to surrender. Jason had said Dirk knew nothing. Turner set his phone to record the conversation and dialed Dirk's number, the one he'd taken from Jason's mobile.

An automated message told him the number was no longer in use.

Dirk had gone dark. Turner could have called him yesterday but it wasn't usually a good idea to give a prime suspect forewarning. He considered calling Hendricks but couldn't imagine what good that would do. He called Eric Venter. By the sound, Venter was in his car, hands-free.

"Go ahead, Turner."

"I just killed one of our suspects, Jason Britz."

"Before or after breakfast?"

"He didn't leave me a choice. It's all on the dashcam."

"Give me the essentials."

Turner gave him an account of the relevant events and personalities. Venter listened without interrupting.

When Turner finished, Venter said, "What are your intentions?"

"Follow procedure with Mokoena and come back home. Work on the warrant for Dirk Le Roux."

"The dashcam footage includes Jason's testimony putting Le Roux behind the wheel?"

"Yes, sir."

"He wasn't coerced or entrapped?" asked Venter.

"Purely voluntary. He said nothing to retract it. Didn't spot the camera. He just tried to shoot me."

"The statement could be gold. Can you send me the data file?"

Turner glanced at the satellite dish on the roof. "I think so."

"Do it as soon as you can. I'll deal with the warrant application. Stay in Langkopf until I update you."

"If you say so, sir."

"Are you in danger?"

"It's the Wild West."

"You were warned," said Venter. "But if they kill you they'll find our tanks camped on their lawn."

"See that my grave is kept clean."

"Send that file."

Venter hung up.

Turner collected his laptop from his backpack and went into the house. The front door opened into the living room. Clearly the digs of a young, single man. A large flat-screen TV was dominant; an Xbox and joystick. A shelf of DVDs. A balding blue velveteen sofa and two matching armchairs. Clothes draped here, boots piled there. A rugby ball. Bodybuilding mags. Unwashed glasses and plates. No photos, no art, no knickknacks. An atmosphere of loneliness, or sadness; but then his corpse was still bleeding outside. On a scarred wooden table by the window was a laptop, a mobile phone several generations old, and a modem, its lights blinking.

Turner entered the modem's password into his MacBook Air. He was online.

He went back to his car, where he could keep an eye on the road. The Wi-Fi signal held strong. He slotted the microSD card into an adapter and inserted it into the Mac. He copied the video file of Jason's statement and death onto his desktop. It was 1.3 gigs. He compressed the file. He sent it to Dropbox to upload to the cloud and emailed the link to Venter. He emailed the same link to Anand; he told him not to open it unless he heard he was dead. It was 8:25 a.m. He put the laptop on the passenger seat and left the file to upload. The timer fluctuated but it looked like the upload would take well over an hour. He was likely to be stuck here longer than that. He replaced the spent shells in his Glock.

He walked back to the house and into Jason's kitchen. It was surprisingly neat and clean. He found a hand brush in a cupboard under the sink. Back at the car, he brushed shattered glass from the driver's seat and footwell. He cleared the crazed glass still clinging to the window frame. He saw a whorl of dust in the distance where the dirt track left the tarmac, the dust more obvious than the vehicle.

He was expecting Mokoena, but it might be an enraged Rudy Britz. The timing would work for either man. Turner got in the Cruiser and turned it around to face the yard and the dirt road. He reactivated the camera system. The file was still uploading from his Mac. He left the engine running, got out of the car and left the door open.

He opened the black metal lockbox in the base of the cargo trunk and slid out the wide lower drawer. It contained a variety of gear including a vest, a night-vision surveillance monocular, ammunition, medical kit, a box of oatmeal energy bars probably past their sell-by date, and a standard-issue R5 assault rifle in a brown canvas case. He took out a pair of 8×42 Athlon Optics binoculars and focused on the approaching vehicle.

The oblique rays of the sun flashed from its waxed paintwork. It was neither Mokoena nor Rudy Britz. It was the red Range Rover that had killed the girl.

SEVENTEEN

Simon drove. Margot stared out of the passenger window at the landscape she had been staring at all her life. Nothing green. Pale yellow at best. A land so arid they were reduced to celebrating the camelthorn tree—though most of those had been cut down and burned for firewood.

When she was fifteen Margot had promised herself that she would leave Langkopf forever as soon as she could. This decision was provoked by stumbling upon a tatty paperback copy of Albert Camus's *The Stranger* in English, at a church rummage sale. The portrait, by Villon, on the cover of a man with no eyes had terrified and excited her; an almost pornographic excitement for she knew that this was a book that her parents wouldn't want in the house. That portrait haunted her still. She had identified intensely with the hero, Meursault. She was awed by his indifference to feeling, to the crushing banality of the society around him, to other people, to his own fate. The stifling heat, the ingrained colonial corruption. Meursault's world was her world. She believed that his fate could also become hers but knew she lacked his heroism, and this frightened her.

She would go to university and study French. She would go to
Paris and play chess in boulevard cafés with existentialists; even in
the mideighties there had to be a few left. She wondered now why
she had never dreamed of falling in love. Perhaps that was why
she never had. Her elder brother, Pieter, had escaped to England,
despite the bitter opposition of her father, so she knew it could be
done. She had been too young, though, to understand the hand-
icaps and hazards of being a girl in a remote, conservative sheep
town in the Northern Cape.

Thirty years later she was still here.

She sometimes asked herself, had she been able to turn back
the clock, if she would exchange everything she had—the power,
the millions, the luxury, and prestige—for the chance to have
climbed on a bus, any bus, going anywhere, when she was fifteen.
The answer always came within a single wrenched beat of her
heart and tears would spring to her eyes. Then she would think of
Dirk and, reluctantly, the answer would change.

Her parents had owned and run a grocery store, which had
evolved into a small supermarket. She had never been a particularly
happy child, though like any child she knew the meaning of pure
joy. By that age the joy was almost exclusively confined to working
through chess books in her bedroom (no one she knew was worth
playing) and to being on the back of a horse. The latter pleasure
was uncommon: once, sometimes twice a month. Horses were
almost unknown in those parts. Expensive to feed and keep, not
particularly useful, needless extra work. The farmers preferred Jap-
anese four-wheel drives. But the Le Roux family had a mare called
Lottie who belonged to their son, Willem. Willem's sister, Annette,
was in Margot's class and he taught them both how to ride. He was
eight years older than Margot. When she was sixteen, he raped her.

She was certain he didn't see it that way, but she did. When
she became pregnant, Willem married her before Dirk was born.

Depressed, saturated with hormones, and chivvied by her parents, she submitted like Meursault to her fate, the crowds within her mind howling in execration. Instead of going to Paris she became a sheep farmer's wife. But she had Dirk.

As Simon slowed and turned into Jason's gate, Margot's phone rang. Winston Mokoena.

"Winston."

"Margot, forgive me if I'm brief. Don't go to Jason's. Your meeting isn't going to happen."

"Why not?"

"Things are in motion. I'll explain later. Just go home."

"Explain now—"

Mokoena had hung up. Margot looked at the clock on the dash. Eight thirty-nine. The meeting had been set for nine. Simon glanced a question at her. She didn't tell him to stop. As they got closer to the wind pump and the farmhouse she saw a big black Land Cruiser parked in the yard.

"Do you recognize the car?" she asked.

"No, ma'am," said Simon. "It's either the United Nations or Warrant Officer Turner."

Margot watched a tall, lean black man step out from behind the SUV and walk toward them. He had an unusual way of moving, she couldn't say why. A lightness, as if he were gliding, yet at the same time rooted, solid. She assumed he had Jason in custody, perhaps on the gun charge. How much intelligence did it require to keep one's mouth shut? Very little, though in Jason's case that was no comfort. They should have come earlier, but at least she could reassure and advise him.

"What did Mokoena say?" asked Simon

"He said go home."

Simon headed on toward the farm. They passed the wind pump. Turner stopped and held his hand out, palm upraised. His face was impassive behind his sunglasses. Simon unbuckled his seat belt. She could feel a sudden rise in his vigilance. She became aware of the gun on his hip. The gun on Turner's hip. Simon stopped the Range Rover five meters short of Turner.

"Will you stay in the car, ma'am?"

"No."

"Until I check things out."

"What is there to worry about?"

Turner held up his ID and badge.

"Jason's dead," said Simon.

Margot wound the window down and leaned her head out. In the gap between the battered SUV and Turner she saw what Simon had seen. Jason was splayed backward across a giant barbell on the stoop. She couldn't see his face. An enormous pool of blood was dripping from the edge of the stones.

Margot discovered that she felt nothing for Jason. If anything she felt a sense of relief. A corpse made a better ringer than a frightened man in a cell. The only eyewitness left was Hennie. The only thing that Hennie was frightened of was her.

"He's killed his only witness," said Margot.

"So far, so good," said Simon. He pushed his sunglasses on top of his head and peered forward. "But there's a camera on us."

"Where?"

"In his rearview mirror. Look at the shape. Without doubt it was on Jason, too. Don't say anything, ma'am. Please wait here."

Turner circled behind the Range Rover. She twisted around to watch him. He was examining the Camargue-red paint. Simon left the engine running and got out.

"Warrant Officer Turner," said Turner. "Stay in the car."

"Simon Dube. Director of Operations, Le Roux Security." He nodded at the back of the Range Rover. "If you want to get any closer you'll need a warrant."

Simon turned and walked toward Turner's Land Cruiser.

"Sir," said Turner. A classic cop's tone; politeness as threat. "Keep away from the vehicle."

Turner followed him for two paces but stopped by Margot's window. Another contest between men. She was fascinated by these unspoken duels, the way they jabbed at each other's pride. Turner didn't want the indignity of running after Simon. His authority, his voice, should have been enough to stop him. But Simon defied him. He didn't stop until he reached the Cruiser's open driver's door. He ducked his head to look at the rearview mirror, she presumed to study the controls for the camera. Something else caught Simon's eye. He straightened up and faced Turner.

"Are we going to fight in front of the lady?"

"Whatever the lady wants," said Turner. He took off his shades and put them in his pocket.

"You're pretty sure of yourself."

"As sure as I need to be."

The two men were entirely capable of killing each other. Simon was bigger—Turner didn't carry much weight in the shoulders—yet he seemed untroubled by either the corpse a few meters behind him or the prospect of more violence. She suppressed her inclination to get out of the car and take charge. She had to trust Simon. Simon walked toward the stoop.

"I want to see what you did to Jason."

"Stay away from the crime scene," said Turner.

"If you want to shoot me in the back, go ahead."

Turner couldn't shoot him, not legally; no one's life was threatened. To physically restrain him would be no easy feat. She was fascinated to see how much of a policeman's power was no more than thin air, if you had the nerve to defy it. But why was Simon pushing him? Hennie would do it for no more than the pleasure it would give him. Simon was as cold a calculator as she'd

ever seen. Turner seemed of similar mettle. He wasn't a man to
indulge in wasted gestures or idle threats. He had to be perplexed
but didn't show it. He didn't show anything. Simon halted at the
bloody stoop and looked at Jason's body.

"Two in the chest and one in the throat," he said, with the
respect of a fellow craftsman. "I'd say the first shot burst a ven-
tricle and he dropped down into the third."

"That's as far as you go," said Turner. "No more warnings."

Simon beckoned to Margot. "Mrs. Le Roux?"

Margot opened the door and got out. She'd been invited
to play a part in Simon's mysterious stratagem. Diversionary,
perhaps. Turner came to the same conclusion. He ran, without
seeming to run, at Simon. Simon jumped up the step and darted
inside the house. Turner stopped and waited.

Simon reemerged holding a gray plastic modem box in both
hands. He smashed the box to pieces with two blows against the
doorjamb. He let the pieces drop. *Why?* thought Margot. Simon
looked at Turner with a certain fuck-you triumph. As he stepped
from the stoop Turner hit him in the belly.

What followed took place in a second, almost too fast for her
to follow. Turner's first blow was so fast, so short, so casual that it
hardly looked like an attack. He flicked his hand, as one might flick
at a fly, and struck Simon with his knuckles in the solar plexus. It
wasn't a punch, it had no power that she could see. Simon, almost
as fast, parried the arm with his left hand just after the impact and
threw his right fist at Turner's head. Turner moved without seeming
to move, the fist missing by a hair, and, bing-bang, hit Simon on
his biceps with these odd, light, snapping strikes. Simon's face was
already twisting with pain, his arms falling, as Turner hit him again
in the right side of the throat, below the jaw, with the back of the
first two fingers of his right hand.

Turner stepped back as Simon doubled over and fell from the

stoop to his knees, his tongue sticking out as he gasped for air. He tried to raise his arms but couldn't. Turner stuck two fingers into the left side of Simon's throat and crouched, gracefully, as he forced—guided—Simon to lie on the ground. He reached out and stood up holding Simon's gun. Simon, choking as if for his life, tried to lash out with a kick. Turner stepped away, without apparent hurry, and the kick missed. He walked toward Margot.

His stride was not purposeful or aggressive; it was loose, almost a shamble, but much faster than it appeared to be. She saw that he had green eyes. The anger in them was hidden deep. She felt chilled. He ejected the magazine from Simon's gun into one hand and jacked a shell from the chamber. He circled past her, with a strange courtesy, and tossed the gun and the magazine through the Range Rover's open window. He had moved from courtesy and patience to crushing violence and back with scarcely a change in the expression on his face. She was not frightened of him—because, she realized, he did not want her to be—but she was equally aware that he was a force that threatened the core of the only good reason she had for existing. Of that she was frightened indeed. She felt confident that she wouldn't show it.

Turner glanced over his shoulder at Simon. Margot looked back. Simon was struggling to his hands and knees, still trying to breathe. She didn't feel for his pain; she did feel for his humiliation.

"What did you do to him?" said Margot.

"He'll be fine." He looked at her. "If I didn't want him to be fine, he'd be dead."

Margot lived and worked and survived amongst men. She had no woman in her life she considered important to her, no female friends with whom to exchange small talk, let alone to pour out her heart. The social obligations of business and politics demanded enough of the former, and she could wear that mask well enough. As to the latter, no woman had listened to her when she was sixteen, including her mother, and she had never asked a woman to listen to her since. She lived and worked and had succeeded amongst men, without ever exploiting sexual wiles of which she was ignorant, and she had grown to expect them to fear her, and at the worst to respect her.

Turner was giving her respect. Yet she sensed that he would have given her that no matter who she might have been. She thought of the dead and nameless girl who had brought him here. A sudden window opened for her, into his implacability. He wasn't an idealist. No one was, in the accepted sense. The notion was a myth. He had created for himself an ideal, a code, a principle, to which he clung for dear life. She understood that. So had she. In the larger scheme it didn't matter what the principle was, only that it be the rope that kept you from drowning.

She said, "I'm Margot Le Roux."

"I know who you are," said Turner.

"I'm glad we have the chance to meet."

"Why?"

"I want to talk with you."

"I want to talk with your son," said Turner. "If you make that happen, I'll be grateful. Beyond that, you and I have nothing to talk about."

"I understand you're investigating an accident, a tragic accident."

He looked at her, as if to say, *Go on.*

"Perhaps you don't realize but you've already closed your case. He didn't deserve to die for it, but it was Jason who killed that poor girl."

"He died because he tried to shoot me," said Turner. "Before he died, he denied harming the girl."

"Well of course he denied it, why wouldn't he? You're a policeman. Denials, confessions, statements, retractions.

Reasonable doubts. Bargains. Appeals. Figments in an elaborate game, aren't they?"

"You're absolutely right," said Turner. "Those are the rules and they're designed to be broken. But for some it isn't a game. They might be stuck inside it, because they have no other place to be, but they're not playing."

"Do you play chess?"

Turner shrugged. "Once upon a time, in the army. Never seriously."

"Chess is one of the few things in life that isn't a game. It's an experience of how life should be. In chess it is impossible to tell a lie. Everything is there to be seen and known. At any given position everything can be seen and known, even if you can't see and you don't know. Nothing is concealed. It's all there right in front of you: the board, the pieces, a handful of rules that a five-year-old child can learn. At the close you either win, or you die where you stand, or you are not yet dead but you resign—you embrace death, rightly or wrongly, and sometimes even on the brink of a certain victory that is right before your eyes but which you do not see. There is no possibility of hypocrisy, of corruption, of deception. Self-deception—and every kind of blindness—yes, certainly, but that's not the fault of the pieces. There is only the position and your opponent and you, and your courage, and the next move."

"Beautiful," said Turner.

"You should take it up," she said. "It would suit you."

"Maybe I will."

He looked past her and she turned and watched Simon approach. He dusted dirt and dried blood from his black suit. He was furious. As he passed the SUV he ducked into the open door, reached up and fiddled with the rearview mirror. Turner was too far away to stop him. He showed no reaction. Simon stood up and showed them a tiny square of plastic between finger and thumb.

A microSD card. He put it on his tongue and swallowed. Turner appeared unmoved. Simon stared at him as one wild dog might regard another, ready to go again. Margot moved him back to safety.

"Simon? Turner tells me that Jason denied killing the girl."

Simon pointed into Turner's car. "He's got a Mac in there, uploading a file transfer. It's got to be a video from the dashcam."

She understood why he had destroyed the modem and swallowed the card. She fired a brief, humorless smile at Turner. "But you killed Jason, so he's lost his chance to tell the truth."

"You were supposed to find my body when you got here," said Turner. "Jason and his uncle wanted to impress you."

"I haven't spoken to Jason in months or Rudy in years," she said. "If I wanted you dead, I wouldn't send two buffoons to do the job."

Turner inclined his head. He accepted that.

"Whatever Jason said to protect himself," said Margot, "living witnesses—without a demonstrable history of drug abuse, mental instability and violence—will swear otherwise. Isn't that right, Simon?"

"I was there," said Simon.

"Any decent trial lawyer could discredit anything Jason said in ten minutes."

"Then let's go to trial," said Turner. He glanced at Simon. "You can perjure yourself however you like." He looked at Margot. "So can Dirk, if he wants to. If he's got any intelligence, he won't. If you've got any, you won't let him."

A coil of anxiety tightened in Margot's stomach and she felt anger rise in her chest. Her natural reaction to threat was to counterattack. She restrained herself. She couldn't see any good options. What did he know about Dirk? Who'd been talking to him? The idiot, Rudy. Perhaps Iminathi, the amateur scheming bitch.

"When Dirk was nine years old his father, my husband, was

murdered," she said. "His grandparents and his aunt, my sister-in-law, too."

"I'm sorry to hear that," said Turner.

Images of the bloodbath flashed through her mind. She had never loved Willem. She had hated her life with him, cloistered in mindless tedium with his family, surrounded by parched nothingness, the bleating of sheep, the endless, repetitive chores. The horror of discovering the massacre had been real, but the event had marked her liberation. She wondered if Turner could read her mind.

"It was only by chance that Dirk and I weren't there," she said. "A farm attack. As you know they've killed thousands of us. The police never caught the killers, didn't even try. But certain others knew who they were. Three local men. They sold the guns they'd stolen from the house. These certain others captured them. And I remembered a story, perhaps a legend, about Shaka Zulu. To punish a murderer, Shaka had him locked in a shack with a pack of hyenas."

"It's no legend," said Simon. "Shaka was a general to King Dingiswayo. A rival king, called Zwide, captured Dingiswayo and beheaded him. In revenge, Shaka locked Zwide's mother, Queen Ntombazi, in the house. After the hyenas had eaten her, he burned the house down."

"Then it's as well I'd heard the wrong version," said Margot. "The point I'm trying to make is that it left me very sensitive to threats against my family."

"We all have sad tales to tell," said Turner.

"Jason would no doubt agree," she replied. "Why not give this one a happy ending? Surely two deaths are enough to square the account. Though if that's not so, there are other ways. Other kinds of account."

"I don't keep accounts. I do my job."

"I respect your integrity. I wish it were more common. So let's talk about doing something of value, real value. Let some good come out of this. You must know the ancient tradition of the blood debt. You atoned for a killing by paying money or goods—cattle, land—to the family of the dead. This girl, it seems, has no family. But I could build a medical clinic in your township. A clinic for women like her. God knows they must need it."

"Don't let me stop you," said Turner.

The anger thickened in her throat. His intransigence made no sense.

"Thousands of murders go unsolved, uninvestigated, even unrecorded, every year."

"I regret that more than you do," said Turner.

"This was just a terrible accident."

"The girl was unlawfully killed."

"Then let me make amends," she said.

"That's not my judgment to make."

"There was no malice, no intent—"

"What if the girl had been drunk," said Turner, "and she had killed your son? What would you be saying to me now?"

A low blow and it hit her hard. She struggled to keep a snarl from her lips. "I don't mean to offend you, Warrant Turner, but you seem to be out of touch with reality."

Turner glanced at Jason's corpse. "I don't think so."

"The girl was a piece of human waste." She saw something dark pass through Turner's eyes, but she couldn't help herself. She pressed on. "Even you know that, so don't pretend that you care. Nobody cares, or she wouldn't have been crawling in the filth."

"I don't disagree."

"Then for God's sake, man, how does your rejecting my charity help anyone?"

"Charity doesn't come with a price," said Turner.

"You can't be that naive. How does persecuting my son—who is innocent—make the world a better place?"

"If the law won't stand for a piece of human waste, we have no law. If we have no law, we have no country."

"This country eats because people like me—and my son—put food on the table."

"Your generosity is appreciated," said Turner.

"You want a rich, white scalp to hang on your belt."

"Self-pity doesn't become you."

"Self-pity?" The insult struck to her gut. She couldn't even understand it. She didn't know why it should hurt her as it did.

"It's not a racial matter with me," said Turner. "Nor a matter of economics. I've sent a thousand people to jail. Most of them were poor and black. They all had better excuses than you. Or Dirk or Hennie. Or Jason."

He said it almost gently. As if the truth didn't require anything more. His tone goaded her. She felt her fury swell toward the breaking point. The conversation was going nowhere good. She couldn't win it on his ground. She had to stop. Reevaluate. Retreat to other ground. She had to talk to Hennie.

"You've killed the guilty party," she said. "Be satisfied. Fill in the paperwork and go home. Before it's too late."

"I'll leave when what I came here to do is done."

"Stay away from my son."

"Your son is in a hole. Stop digging."

"I'll pay for your coffin."

She found herself leaning up into his face, chin extended, her teeth clenched. Her head throbbed with blood. For the first time she wanted to kill him. He was wrong. He was irrational. Psychopathic. He had to be stopped.

"Mrs. Le Roux?" said Simon.

She felt the blood drain from her face. For a moment she thought she might faint. She stepped back. She hadn't broken her stare into Turner's eyes, nor he his into hers. She felt a deep, scalding hatred. She made herself turn away. She caught a glimpse of the concern—the muted shock—on Simon's face. She put one hand on the hood of the Range Rover and took a deep breath. She looked into the far parched distance. The only land she knew. The barren soil in which she had grown and, against all odds, flourished. If the land had a lesson it was patience. Wait and the rain will come. Wait and the sea will turn into sand.

All the accumulated rage and hatred of her life had somehow flooded up inside her. She felt a kind of panic, transmuted into aggression. It wasn't a question of whether Turner deserved it or not; she didn't care. He was no one to her—had Jason shot him she would have felt nothing—a stranger; a cop; one of the lowest forms of life. And he was violating her and all she'd built; threatening to bring down her fragile tower of, if not happiness, at least tolerable contentment and pride. But panic, rage, and hatred would not help her win.

She nodded to Simon and opened the car door and got in and closed it. She did not look again at Turner. She did not dare. She stared out through the windshield. At Jason's corpse, the great muscles of his arm and shoulder and chest shiny with blood. In death he had achieved a strange grace, a sculpted beauty, that had wholly evaded him in life. Sadness constricted her throat. A thin ribbon of shame. She had never respected him. She had rarely resisted the urge to mock him. A poor provincial redneck. Yet what had she been? Did her money make that much difference? Jason had truly been Dirk's friend; perhaps—the thought disgusted her—her competitor. Whatever his uncle's crude plan had been, she knew that Jason, in his heart, had died to protect Dirk.

Simon got behind the wheel and closed the door. He reversed out of the yard. As he swung into a semicircle she saw Turner standing, loose and shabby, watching them. Simon turned onto the track and drove toward the road.

"Maybe it's time to bring the lawyers in," said Simon.

Margot stared at him. "The lawyers?"

"As you say," Simon shrugged, now embarrassed, "Turner's killed his only witness."

"Didn't you hear how that low-rent ghetto cop spoke to me?"

For an instant Simon's face froze with a kind of dread. She could see his mind racing, as if envisioning where this path might take them. He was clearly dubious as to its wisdom. She didn't care. She paid him to do what she wanted. His face became impassive again. He had been humiliated by Turner. He was in.

Simon said, "Yes, ma'am."

"Can we kill him?"

"Turner can be dead by lunchtime. The problem is the busload of Cape Town murder police who'll show up for breakfast."

Simon reached the gate and swung onto the tarmac. Their speed increased, the road noise diminished. Margot's phone rang. She looked at the screen. Number withheld. She answered.

"Hello?"

"Mrs. Le Roux?"

She didn't recognize the voice. A white South African man, well-spoken. Middle-aged. She tapped on "speaker." She wanted Simon to hear him.

"Who is this?" she said.

"A potential friend and ally, or so I hope," said the man.

"Say what you want or get off my phone."

"I've just seen a piece of video that puts your son Dirk in an awkward position."

Margot tapped the mute button and looked at Simon.

"Captain Eric Venter," said Margot.

Simon nodded. "Let him play James Bond."

"Has he seen the video?" asked Margot.

"Ten minutes minimum of HD, say a minimum one gig. At local residential upload speeds, I don't believe it. He knows what's on it, but he hasn't got it."

"Hello?" said Venter.

Margot tapped the mute button off. "Horseshit," she said.

Venter laughed. The laugh was meant to convey confidence, but it was nervous, weak. "Well, all that can wait. I just wanted to ask you to make a rough calculation, to see if it tallies with my own."

"Go on."

"How much money is it going to cost you in legal and, let's say, ancillary services just to keep Dirk out of jail?"

"I can afford it."

"Bear in mind that even if we—as your lawyers certainly will—define that as success, your son will be a convicted killer, with all the associated ... disadvantages. A very substantial sum for a less than ideal outcome, I think you will agree. Unless you want to go through the circus of a jury trial, in which case the cost would be very much more."

"What ancillary services are you offering?"

"You have one fundamental problem that you can't buy your way out of," said Venter. "Unless I overestimate you, you must know who I'm talking about."

Margot suppressed an impulse to step on him, as she might step on a maggot. "So you would call him off."

"That's not within my power," said Venter. "I can order him home but I can't call him off. No one can."

"More horseshit," said Margot. "Why not?"

"His case is too strong now," said Venter. "You may not be aware, but he has already killed for this case. Literally. I doubt you can understand what that means. Let's just say it makes it personal, deeply personal, for any cop. And this isn't any cop. This is the cop of your nightmares."

That much wasn't horseshit. She was disturbed to hear it from Turner's commander.

"You're saying you can't control him."

"You don't know this man. I do. He hates the police. He despises them. That's why he became one."

"What do you mean?"

"His history doesn't matter," said Venter. "What matters to you is that he's not going to let anyone bury this case. Not you. Not Mokoena. Not me. Not now."

"He's a psychopath."

"A psychopath has no conscience. Turner is the opposite. His conscience drives him. That's the problem."

"So what makes you think you can filch my money?"

"Because if your problems were to be reduced to matters of procedure, that is to satisfying the demands of the judicial bureaucracy, you would find no barrier to the smooth functioning of the market."

"You haven't done this before, have you?" said Margot.

Silence drifted from the phone. Margot adopted the Hennie approach.

"If you had," she said, "you would know that all this clever-clever devious roundabout I'm-not-going-to-say-anything-to-incriminate-myself bollocks isn't worth a pint of your piss. You claim to know Turner—I doubt it—but you don't know me. If this doesn't work, you will go down. Because I will take you down. I could take you down right now. I will pay your fee but understand that that makes you my dog. Never pick up the phone and threaten me or my son again. Never imagine that you can hold anything over me. Because I am not afraid to go down, into hell and beyond. But you are. Do you understand me, Captain Eric Venter?"

Another silence. Margot let this one ride. In the silence she could hear his fear. If she had scared him away, she was no worse off. If not, the hierarchy of power would be established.

"I'm simply asking you to think about it," said Venter.

"You think about it."

"I'll get back to you in an hour," said Venter. "And please don't neglect that calculation. I think doubling the result, and perhaps rounding it up, would be more than fair. Remember, Pistorius spent seventeen million rand. And went to jail."

Venter hung up. Margot turned to Simon. He raised one brow in disgust.

"Tell me what you're thinking," she said.

"It's not polite."

"I can take it."

"What a cocksucker," said Simon.

"Agreed," said Margot. "But did you hear what I heard?"

"He's saying we can bury Turner along with the case, without that busload of cops showing up."

"You believe the video is still trapped in Turner's laptop."

"I'm sure it is. It may be on his phone too. Either way, it hasn't reached the cloud."

"I want that video," said Margot. "Venter mustn't get it. Then we'll bury Turner."

She sensed a heaviness fall upon him. She understood. A man not dissimilar to himself, a fighting man, a man who risked his life for his code of honor, was going to die. A cocksucker was going to get rich. It was disgusting. She was disgusted. But on the scale of disgust that she had endured and survived, these fighting men were boys.

"Yes, Mrs. Le Roux," said Simon. "You give the orders."

EIGHTEEN

Turner sat in the Land Cruiser and plugged his phone into his laptop. The upload was stalled, about 20 percent completed. He copied the video file into his phone. He then mail-dropped the file from the phone to the cloud and forwarded it to Venter, Anand, and himself. He had two bars of 3G coverage. At phone upload speeds of at best one meg per second, he was looking at more than two hours before it was sent.

He had studied a map of phone and broadband provision at Anand's. Langkopf had appeared as a small blotch surrounded in every direction by thousands of square kilometers without coverage. If he was lucky he'd find a five meg per second upload in town that would finish the job by laptop in thirty minutes. He took the original SD card from its adapter in the Mac and put it in his safe pocket.

He considered his position and found it wanting.

Rudy had been stupid enough to try to murder him. He was still at large with his badge, still as stupid, and the desire for revenge was unlikely to improve his cognitive abilities.

Margot was highly intelligent but that made her more, not less dangerous, if she wanted to be. She had to know that murdering a police risked bringing a storm down on her head. She and her son might well survive it. Far more scandalous crimes had gone unpunished; many more had gone undetected. Turner was no one special. Cops were buried at the rate of two a week. He wasn't the girlfriend of a world-famous athlete. There might not be a storm at all. Venter had said that resisting pressure from above was futile. And Margot was a gambler—her success was proof of that.

But what did she stand to win or lose? She won if Dirk walked away untarnished, with Jason's corpse taking the blame. But if Turner sent the video out that option disappeared. She would lose. If she killed him then, she added an obviously motivated murder, of a cop no less, to the problems she already had with Dirk. Lose-lose. He didn't believe she would take that risk out of spite.

If, on the other hand, she knew that the video of Jason's testimony had been destroyed, the attractions of killing him would be real. A fake car-hijack, for instance. Hijacks happened every day. Mokoena would be in charge of solving any local murder. No doubt he could supply plausible forensics along with the corpses of the perpetrators. A neat clearance to present to anyone Venter sent north—along with a neat clearance of the girl's homicide, too. To overturn either would require a major investigation, with piles of filthy police laundry being washed in public and no guarantee of a conviction. Venter might go for it, but his superiors would not. If she destroyed the video before it flew, killing him, for her, was a win-win.

She was ruthless enough. She had money, connections, and as many armed men as a city police captain. She had no moral boundaries. She had Simon Dube, who was unlikely to be caught by surprise a second time. She had Mokoena to tie it all up in pink ribbons.

Turner had a car, inadequate technology, and no one he could count on within range of four hours' travel, even if they chartered a Cessna in the next ten minutes. If he didn't get the video out into the world, and prove it to Margot, he was probably dead.

He searched inside the farmhouse and found two boxes of twelve-gauge shotgun shells in a cupboard beneath a gun case. He returned to the stoop, where the flies were now out in force. He took the SPAS-12 from Jason's body and folded the metal stock above the barrel and recharged the magazine. He stored the shotgun where he could reach it in the rear footwell of the Land Cruiser. His laid his binoculars on the passenger seat.

Time to leave. It was 9:57.

Turner drove down the dirt track toward the road.

He stopped at the gate. The tarmac ran dead straight for the horizon through the flat featureless land. At a distance of, he guessed, three to four kilometers, he saw a low mass of some kind squatting in the road. He took the binoculars, steadied the heels of his hands on the top rim of the wheel and glassed the road. He focused the left lens and then the right. Two vehicles were parked one beside the other, blocking the road. The first looked like an old dark-blue Freelander; the second a silver-gray flatbed truck. He couldn't see inside the cabs. He could think of no good reason why they might be sitting motionless in the sun. He could think of a bad reason.

Two vehicles; at least four men. They hadn't come up to the farm while they'd had the chance. Maybe to deny him the cover provided by the buildings. Had Margot passed them? For the moment that was irrelevant. Assume: Rudy and some hired hands. In Cape Town you could hire a professional hit for the price of a new iPhone. If all you wanted was a desperado willing to point and fire a gun, the price of a pair of Levi's would do it.

The equivalent of the latter must have existed in Langkopf. Rudy could afford them and would know who they were.

He set his phone to record calls and rang Mokoena on the car's Bluetooth rig.

"Where's Rudy?" asked Turner.

"I don't know. He wouldn't listen to me—"

"So he knows Jason is dead."

"The half-truths didn't fly. I told him to go home—"

"I'm looking down the road from the farm at two stationary vehicles. A dark-blue Freelander and a silver truck, maybe a Hyundai, both seen better days. You know them?"

"I do. They will, without doubt, be reported as stolen within a couple of hours."

"Whoever they are, they're waiting for someone."

"It shames me to say this," said Mokoena, "but I can no longer guarantee your safety."

"It was nice while it lasted. Twelve whole hours before someone tried to kill me."

"This situation is not of my making. I wash my hands of it."

"Call him off or you'll be washing them with blood."

"There's nothing I can say to him I haven't already said. He's enraged and half-crazed with guilt."

"Who does he have with him?"

"I can think of a dozen candidates who would kill you for a can of hair grease."

"Get in your car and bring me in."

"Turner, I lost my taste for gunplay a long time ago. For what it's worth, you have my blessing. I will sanction any action you deem necessary."

Turner had to laugh at that. Mokoena laughed too.

"There's little I'm willing to do to help you," said Mokoena, "but I won't raise my hand against you. I tried to persuade you and I tried to persuade them. My advice was ignored. As always, I will pick up the pieces."

"There could be more pieces than you think."

"But I won't be one of them. I can't say my conscience is clear but I haven't been able to make that claim since 1976."

"You're feeding all this to Margot."

"As a matter of fact I'm not taking her calls. I'm going to switch off my phone and watch the test match. There's been heavy betting on Pakistan and I want to know why."

"I'll see you later," said Turner.

"You may not believe this," said Mokoena, "but I sincerely hope so."

Turner hung up. He glassed the vehicles again. They hadn't moved.

He wondered what Rudy's plan was and suspected he didn't have one. Rudy had been moving fast, on raw emotion—killers, cars, weapons, roadblock. He would be a marksman; perhaps a scoped hunting rifle. What now? Was he hoping Turner would drive at them head on?

Turner called him. He listened to the ring tone. He imagined Rudy seeing the unfamiliar number and making the appropriate deduction. The voice that answered trembled with hatred.

"Save your dirty black breath," said Rudy. "You are a dead black motherfucker."

"We're veteran police. Let's act the part."

"Oh, I intend to, mate. I've got a tire and a can of petrol in the back of the truck. I'm going to necklace you, dead or alive."

"I thought that was an ANC trick."

"You'd be surprised," said Rudy.

"I'm sorry I had to kill Jason."

"He didn't have a chance."

"He threw away all his chances when he fired that twelve

gauge," said Turner. "We both let him down so let's do what's right. Let justice be done."

"Fuck off. And drop this 'we' business. I've no more in common with you than with a pile of street shit."

"Get out of the car, lay down your arms, and send whoever's with you home. I'll take you to Mokoena and you can take care of Jason's body."

"Are you out of your fucking mind?"

"I don't want to spill any more blood."

"Then you lay down your arms," said Rudy, "and leave the rest to me."

Turner had tried. His best chance was to goad Rudy into coming at him.

"How many paid guns have you brought with you?" he asked.

"More than enough," said Rudy.

"Jason went to it like a man."

"Jason was a fool."

"He adored you."

"Shut up."

"If it's any consolation it was quick. Two in the chest and one in the throat."

"I said shut your fucking black mouth."

"It was you, Rudy. It was you."

"You bastard." Hoarse with guilt and rage.

"You killed him. Now you're hiding like a bitch."

"It's on," said Rudy.

"I'm here," said Turner.

The line went dead.

Turner got out of the Cruiser with the SPAS-12 and propped it against the front wing. He walked to the trunk and opened his lockbox. He briefly glassed the road again and saw the two vehicles start into motion. He had maybe three minutes. He set the binoculars down and strapped on an Armour Express Razor level II ballistic vest. He unsheathed the regulation R5 assault rifle from its case, loaded it, and shoved two spare 35-round magazines into the thigh pocket of his pants. The R5 was a licensed copy of the Israeli Galil. The 5.56mm cartridge was lethal at a thousand meters.

He watched the two cars start along the road toward him and accelerate. The Freelander in front. Say twenty meters per second. No easy target for light weapons, until they slowed. He was not afraid of gunfire from a moving vehicle. They weren't Special Forces. Turner slipped the two-point tactical rifle sling across his chest and set the R5 to fire single rounds. He went down on one knee behind the engine block and watched through the binoculars.

The Freelander had three men on board. Rudy was driving. The rear window was down and a rifle barrel angled outward. It looked like an AK. The truck was a Hyundai, two black men in the cab; another assault rifle. At about a thousand meters the Hyundai swerved off the road and crashed through the jackal-proof fencing onto the yellow grassland, the long wheel base seesawing as the wheels hit uneven ground. A crude pincer movement. Their coordination was poor. The Freelander slowed to give the truck time to draw level.

Turner felt calm. Everything was clear, visible. No civilians to consider. Focus on technique. It would be over in three minutes that would feel like three seconds. In terms of stress, it hardly compared to a night search of a crack house in Nyanga. At four hundred meters automatic gunfire rattled from both vehicles. The bullets came nowhere near the Cruiser that he was aware of. He saw Rudy open his mouth, red-faced, shouting, probably at the waste of ammo. Turner laid down the binoculars and shouldered the rifle and tightened the sling. At two hundred meters he started firing at the Freelander.

Due to the angle of the car's approach and the need to lead it, his point of aim was into the thin air above the horizon. Educated guesswork. On the fourth shot he saw a white blur burst in the windshield. With the seventh shot another. Then another. The Freelander swerved back and forth in a violent zigzag. Turner heard more gunfire from the truck approaching to his left. He ignored it. The Freelander at a hundred meters: he tracked the left edge of the windshield with the front sight, firing a steady two shots per second.

The windshield was two sheets of curved glass with a layer of plastic laminated between them. A bullet hitting the surface tumbled as it went through, deflected downward. He'd put a dozen slugs through the moving car's interior. Noise and destruction. The ripping of furniture and flesh. Ricochets from metal and plastic. To be inside such a car is an experience of terror and helplessness magnified by speed. The car is now as deadly as the gunfire. The panic contagious. The driver plunged into indecision. Faster or slower? Left or right? A mist of pulverized glass. Blood.

Rudy gave up the zigzag and accelerated straight ahead to escape the fire. Turner swiveled, pumping rounds through the doors as it swept past. A rear side window blew. Turner continued the swivel three hundred degrees until he sighted the Hyundai bearing down fifty meters beyond the Cruiser.

A gunman leaned head and shoulder from the passenger window, trying to draw a bead with an AK. The rough ground gave him no chance. Turner fired as fast as he could aim and squeeze. Six shots. The windshield turned opaque. Flame and smoke from the barrel of the AK. Ten shots. The bolt snapped empty. The shooter fell back into the cab. The truck braked and swung in a desperate arc, lumbering back toward the road and flight.

Turner slid the rifle behind his back and cinched the sling tight with the speed tab. He grabbed and shouldered the SPAS-12.

Twenty meters. He could see the driver through the side window, his blood-flecked face grimacing as he heaved the truck into the swerve. Turner shot him twice through the door and saw him slump against the wheel. As the truck lost speed and rolled toward the fence Turner swiveled again to check the Freelander.

Rudy had plowed through the fence on the far side of the road and was skidding through the grass in a wide turn, back toward town. A hundred meters. Turner sprayed the Freelander with two rounds of buckshot and watched it pick up speed and pull away. The Hyundai had nosed into the fence and come to a stop without breaching it.

Turner loped over behind the truck from where he could cover both doors and moved in. He glanced into the flatbed and saw the tire and the jerry can. He heard groans of pain. The passenger door swung open.

A pair of legs and the barrel of a rifle swung clear of the seat. An AK barrel. Turner aimed and fired. The lower thighs exploded into gore and raw meat as the close-grouped buckshot half-severed one leg and plowed on into the other. The AK fired a burst, a reflex, the bullets clanging through the truck's door. The shooter slithered out, gibbering, his legs folding beneath him like blood-soaked laundry, his left arm extended back inside the cab as if trying to pull himself back in. Turner shot him through the armpit. The body slid down into a bleeding heap.

Turner didn't look at his face. He swapped the shotgun to a left-handed grip and moved in, aiming, listening. He heard the drone of the engine but nothing human. He looked inside. The driver's face was cradled in a gap in the steering wheel. His torso was drenched in blood. He was dead.

As Turner walked back to the Land Cruiser he put two fingers to his neck and checked his pulse. It was fifty-four. He reloaded his guns and stowed them inside and collected his binoculars.

The Freelander was back on the tarmac, making speed toward Langkopf. Rudy was a lucky man. Turner climbed behind the wheel and started after him.

Just short of the intersection with the main road Turner saw two bodies sprawled by the fence. He got out and examined them. One had been shot twice, through the face and the upper left chest below the collarbone, by his own 5.56 rounds. The second body had a rifle wound in his left shoulder and a close-range gunshot—a starburst wound and scorched hair—in the side of his head; probably a nine mill. He couldn't have been over twenty years old. Rudy hadn't needed the aggravation. The Freelander was long gone.

Turner got a bottle of water from the trunk and drank. He stood in the blinding sun and thought about what he had done. He thought about the life, and the world, that had required him to do it. He thought about the fact that he was thus capable. He would live with it. He capped the bottle and put it back.

As he got behind the wheel, Venter rang.

"Turner? I'm still waiting for that video file."

Turner collected himself.

"Turner?"

"If I can find a connection without getting shot you should have it within an hour. Rudy Britz tried to hit me with a team of low-rent locals."

Venter was silent for longer than Turner might have expected.

"How many?" Venter seemed too shocked to be amused.

"Four dead. Rudy got away."

"Jesus Christ. Are you hurt?"

"No. Amateur hour."

"You think Le Roux was behind this? I mean Margot?" Venter sounded nervous.

"No, but now that Rudy's jumped the gun she might try. He says he can take their ship down with him."

"Can you get clear?"

"I intend to."

"Can you find a safe place to hide until I get you some backup?"

"I'd feel like a mouse in a bathtub. Better to get out and run. But if they've decided to take me down they've got faster wheels than me and three hundred kilometers of desert road to do it in. If I can get that file to you, at least I'll know it won't be for nothing."

"Where's your local support?"

"There isn't any. Winston Mokoena is watching the cricket."

"Cricket?"

"He's sitting on the fence."

"What can I do for you?" said Venter.

"Nothing until I finish this upload. Once that goes through, I can talk my way out of town."

"When you find that connection, call me. Don't take any chances you don't have to." Venter hung up.

Turner glanced at the laptop in the footwell. There would be no Wi-Fi hot spots in Langkopf. An internet shop, probably; much of the population wouldn't own computers. The hotel. The police station. Various local businesses. A lawyer's office? He could get access with a badge. But each of these possibilities would occur to Simon Dube as well. Turner tapped a number on his phone.

Iminathi answered. "Turner?"

"Where are you?"

"I'm at La Diva, why?"

"Is Winston around?"

"No, I've been trying to find him, too. In the mornings he's usually at the station but he's not there either. He's not answering his phone."

"He's probably dancing around a cauldron with Margot."

"You should hear this as well," said Imi. "A girl came to the salon. She asked me if Winston would talk to her boyfriend. A friend of his knocked him up out of bed and she heard them talking about stealing cars, getting guns. She doesn't know what they're planning but she doesn't want him to go to jail again."

Turner thought of the youngster Rudy had executed; the three men he had killed.

"She's probably better off without him."

"What do you mean?"

There was no point trusting her more than he had to.

"When you make contact with Winston, tell him to call me."

Turner hung up and headed on toward town.

NINETEEN

Turner spotted the lookout at the petrol station on the edge of town. It was the car that first caught his eye, a small, white three-door hatchback, looked like an Aygo, very clean, maybe two years old. In a small, rural mining town it struck him at once as a company car, the kind security firms include in their fleet as a cost-efficient patrol vehicle. It was parked by the air pump and a black man, thirties, stood beside it holding the hose and pressure gauge. No uniform, but his white shirt was crisp, his khakis pressed, his black boots polished. As Turner saw him, and he saw Turner's big black Toyota, he crouched down in a pretense of checking his front tire but kept an eye on the road.

The private security industry in South Africa was huge. In manpower it outnumbered the national police force and the army combined by more than two to one. At the top of the pyramid would be someone like Simon Dube, expert in a wide range of surveillance, protection, tactical, and combat skills. At the base were hundreds of thousands of low-paid, low-skill guards, expert only in the endurance of boredom. Standing at gates, checking ID, checking padlocks, doors, fences, industrial machinery.

Turner made a sudden right-angled swerve into the forecourt, blipped the accelerator for a burst of speed, and braked to a halt a meter short of the startled guard, who dropped the air hose and staggered two steps back. Turner slid out and the guard saw POLICE emblazoned in white on his vest. Turner pointed at the car's hood.

"Hands on the car, sir."

The man obeyed with the sullen grace of one caught out. He didn't ask any questions, confirming the diagnosis. He wasn't carrying a gun. Turner patted his shirt and pants and took his mobile phone.

"Stay where you are."

Turner opened the driver's door. A hip-holstered Z-88 pistol lay on the seat. Turner took it. No in-car radio. Just the mobile. He took the keys from the ignition. He shut the door and looked at the man.

"How many more of you?"

The guard shrugged and made a sound with his tongue and teeth. Turner jabbed him with a spear hand in the liver 13 meridian point, just below the tip of his right floating ribs. The guard collapsed flat across the hood and slid down to his knees. He vomited onto the radiator grill. Turner tossed the gun and the keys into the back of the Land Cruiser. He crouched down by the guard, who gasped as the wave of agony ebbed from his gut to a tolerable level. It would linger there, lapping at the edges of diarrhea and nausea, for a good half an hour.

"You don't get paid enough for this," said Turner. "How many more?"

"Two."

"Where?"

"I don't know. In town."

"How many more?" Turner repeated.

"Four others, down the road. On the other side of the hill."

Turner hauled him up by one arm and guided him, hobbling, to the driver's seat. As he shoved him inside, Turner jabbed him in the liver again. The guard doubled over the wheel so fast he bashed his face on the rim.

"Better sit this out," said Turner.

The guard began to heave again. Turner shut the door.

He got back in the Land Cruiser and reversed to face the road. Two more spotters. Where would they put them? One in the hotel parking lot: from there he could cover the police station and a fair length of the main street to the north. The second further down the main street, probably on foot, mingling with the pedestrians. They weren't here to intercept him, just to warn Dube.

Turner nosed up the road. The nearest oncoming traffic was half a kilometer distant. He swung into the right-hand lane, against the traffic, and accelerated hard. He made three hundred meters in the viewing shadow of the hotel before the far corner of the parking lot appeared. He slowed and went up onto the pavement and gained another fifty meters. The entrance to the hotel was from the parking lot, not the street. He stopped as close to the hotel wall as he could and still get the door open. He grabbed a canister of pepper spray from the center console and put his white sun hat on.

He walked to within two paces of the corner of the building before he saw the nose of a 4×4 on the edge of the parking lot. White. Clean. Thirty meters. A four-second sprint. Doors almost certainly unlocked. The spotter would need to think and move fast to hit central locking. If he did, it would be a bullet to shatter the window. He wouldn't have time to make a call.

Turner sprinted.

The spotter—who else would be spending Monday morning watching the street from a white 4×4?—didn't see him until he was halfway there. He saw POLICE running at him. The guy was still thinking about what to think when Turner opened the passenger door, stuck his arm inside, and hosed his face and head with five seconds' worth of bear-repellent-strength capsaicin. He kept his own head outside, above the roof of the car, listening to the bellow of shock transmute into racking and uncontrollable coughs. He stepped back and glanced inside. The driver was coughing so hard his chest was slamming into the steering wheel, one hand clasped to his blinded vision as his eyelids bubbled and boiled and searing pain swamped his face, scalp, and throat.

Turner circled the front of the 4×4, pocketing the canister. He opened the driver's door. A mobile phone fell from the spotter's right hand and onto the tarmac. Turner took his hat off with his left hand and used it to yank the keys from the ignition. He picked up the phone the same way and wrapped phone and keys in the hat. He shut the door and left the spotter to recover; a minimum fifteen minutes before he could stagger to the hotel; more to make himself understood; much more to come up with the phone number he had probably never memorized; and most likely straight to the bathroom, where the water he would splash on his face would bring him no relief.

Turner drove back into the left lane. Most of the town sprawled in a grid on the flat land to the west, opposite the hill. He drove as fast as he dared down the main street. Not many pedestrians in the heat. He saw no obvious reactions in the rearview mirror. The road ran straight beyond town, where he had driven Iminathi the night before. When he reached the last turn to the left he braked and took it. It was unlikely to fool the last spotter into thinking that he'd headed north, but it put him in as much of a maze as Langkopf offered. He took the second left and headed back, parallel to the main road.

The town had expanded onto cheap land so it was laid out with plenty of space. Streets where buildings faced each other alternated with alleys lined with parched gardens and the back lots of shops and businesses. He passed a new building with a sign reading LE ROUX MEDICAL CENTER. He drove on and took an educated guess and chose an alley and slowed down to study the backs of the properties. About where he expected it to be he saw an empty parking space and two wheeled garbage bins. Above the bins a plastic sign screwed to the wall read: LA DIVA—DELIVERIES.

He pulled in parallel to the bins and jumped out. Between here and the main street a hundred meters away, there were enough obstacles, cars and low walls, to conceal his Land Cruiser.

At the last moment he hesitated. Could he trust her? He had detected nothing in her words or behavior that suggested she'd conspire to murder him. Even Mokoena didn't want any part of that, and Turner believed him, because it was the captain's only intelligent choice. And Turner wanted more from her than the Wi-Fi.

He hammered on the door. He went back to the Land Cruiser and retrieved his laptop and returned to the door and hammered again. As he took out his phone to call her, Iminathi opened the door.

"I need a favor," said Turner.

"But you didn't trust me enough to ask on the phone," said Imi.

"It's a big favor," said Turner. "I want to you save my life."

TWENTY

Turner hooked his Mac up to the Wi-Fi network in Winston's office and resumed the upload. Forty-one minutes estimated. A long time to dangle in the wind. He closed the laptop on Winston's table to free some bandwidth.

"Anything else running on the Wi-Fi here? Music, radio?"

"There's another laptop in the salon," said Imi.

"Can you take it off-line for forty minutes?"

"Why? What's this about? How is this saving your life?"

"I'm not going to explain," said Turner. "The less you know, the better it is for you." He walked toward the back door. "Off the other laptop for me. I'll be back in five."

He left before she could ask more. He got in the Land Cruiser, reversed back up the alley, turned in the street, and drove back to the Medical Center. A second sign with an arrow pointed to a parking lot. He drove into it and stopped. He took the R5, the SPAS-12, the car keys, the gun he'd taken from the guard, and the second phone in his hat and dumped them in the trunk. He locked the car. There was nothing in sight worth stealing and the gaping driver's window, still rimmed with broken glass, made it look like it had already been robbed. If the third spotter found it, a medical center was a place where a police might ask to piggyback some Wi-Fi. The decoy would give him more time—he hoped enough to make a difference.

He jogged back to the rear door of La Diva. He saw few people and no one who took any notice of him. He'd left the door open. He went back into the office through the kitchen. Imi stood by the table. She was anxious and a little angry, the one feeding off the other. She waved her mobile phone at him.

"I'm going to call Winston, but I didn't want to do it behind your back."

"Winston doesn't want to be called."

Turner glanced at the upload. Thirty-four minutes still to go. He took the original SD card from his pocket.

"If the Wi-Fi reaches the salon it must reach the bookmaker's next door," said Turner. "I'm going to take the Mac and finish the file transfer there. If trouble comes, I don't want it to land here. If anyone asks, tell them I used the Wi-Fi last night, with Winston's permission. They've no reason to question that. You'll be out of the picture."

"What picture?"

"An ugly one. I want you take this."

He handed her the SD card. She hesitated, then took it.

"That's not for my benefit," said Turner. "It's for Dirk's."

"What's on it?"

"A dashcam video of Jason putting Dirk behind the wheel of the Range Rover when the girl was crushed."

"Jason turned against Dirk?"

"Not as he saw it. It's complicated. The video is ugly, too. By the end of it Jason is dead. I killed him."

Imi swallowed as she looked into his eyes. She was appalled. She must have known Jason at least reasonably well. Something in her retreated from Turner. She didn't speak.

"If Dirk watches that and he's half the man you say he is, he will turn himself in and there will be no more violence. No more conspiracies, no more crimes. It will be over."

"Why should this fall on me?" said Imi.

"Because no one else has the courage to reach to out to him."

"You mean go against Margot."

"That's why Dirk needs to see it. As Winston said, he won't go to jail. It's the best thing anyone can do for him. His mother is keeping him in the dark."

"She'll never let go of him."

"He needs to let go of her. If he doesn't, he's going down. All the way down."

Turner picked up the Mac. Thirty-one minutes.

"Think about it," he said. "And thanks for your help. I owe you."

He carried the open Mac to the door into the corridor. He looked back at her.

"You want some advice?"

"Not really."

"If I were you I'd sell up and get out of this town. Whatever it's got to offer, you don't need it."

Turner walked through into the salon. Two stylists were blow-drying hair. Four pairs of eyes watched him from the long mirror. He smiled.

"Good morning," he said.

He walked past the chairs as the greeting was returned and opened the glass front door. He stuck his head out and scanned the street, up and down. Hot and bright. No one was moving fast enough to be a spotter trying to find the Land Cruiser. Turner walked out onto the street and pushed open the door of the bookmaker's.

Five punters inside. They all stared, motionless, at the word POLICE on his vest. A narrow, smoky room, bare except for two counters sheathed in red plastic running down either wall, where punters could write their bets. The floor was littered with used betting slips and cigarette ends. A TV suspended from an armature bolted to the ceiling displayed a cricket match. At the far end a plexiglass window, heavily grilled, with a narrow slot at the bottom above the counter and a small mesh screen through which to speak to the bookie. At the right side a door clad in metal. The bookie, a wiry man, midforties, was smoking a cigarette. He watched Turner with the kind of blank stare essential to his trade.

Turner checked the Wi-Fi signal. It hadn't diminished. Twenty-nine minutes to go. He put the laptop on the left-hand counter. He brandished his badge.

"Everybody leave, right now. No questions, no problems."

The five punters bumped into each other as they straggled for the door.

Turner walked toward the bookie's window. The bookie didn't move.

"Put your hands on the counter."

The bookie put his hands on the counter behind the glass. His expression didn't change. Winston wasn't paying him enough to do anything rash. Turner pocketed his badge and dug out a hundred rand note. He pushed it under the glass.

"For the inconvenience. Stay cool. You're not being robbed. Twenty minutes and I'm gone. Give me your phone."

The bookie took the hundred and slid his mobile under the slot. Turner put the mobile on a side counter.

"Lie on the floor, belly or back, whichever's most comfortable. If I hear you try to leave, I'll shoot you. If the landline rings, ignore it. If you try to make a call from the landline, I'll shoot you."

The bookie lay flat on his back behind the counter and continued smoking. Turner walked to the front door and tripped the lock. A standard cylindrical pin tumbler. No bolts. He checked the upload screen. Twenty-seven minutes.

His phone vibrated. It was Captain Venter.

TWENTY-ONE

Eric Venter sat on the toilet in the senior officers' bathroom and tried to overcome the panic that had already overwhelmed his gut and threatened to do the same to his mind. He'd been prone to irritable bowel since the protracted legal proceedings for his second divorce. In his youth he had acquired a taste for prostitutes, which had then lain happily dormant for twenty years. In his late forties, provoked in part by internet pornography, the taste had returned as a compulsion, and not for the sex itself but for the thrilling self-disgust it had evoked. That pleasure too had waned, the last hurrah of his sexual life, leaving only catastrophic cost in its wake.

He was uncomfortably aware that the disgust he felt now, at the prospect of feeding, or rather selling, Turner to the wolves, was perversely similar.

His self-image was that of a man of principle in an unprincipled world. That was the reputation he had cultivated; but he knew it flattered him. More accurately, he was simply a man who followed the rules. He had always been nagged by a mild sense of shame about that. He had been of the generation that had lived through the glory days of the anti-apartheid struggle, and had never taken part. He did not consider himself a racist. It was self-evident that God had distributed all human abilities and failings with perfect equality across the human race. Hatred, it was equally self-evident, did not need racial difference to flourish. If the entire human species had been the same color, it would still have had all the other innumerable and microscopic differences in religion, politics, language, class, and kinship to justify mutual loathing. The evil and stupidity of apartheid had been apparent to even the meanest intelligence, yet throughout his early career he had played his part in enforcing its laws with only mild reservations. When the rules changed he had changed with them. The rules were the rules.

Transgressing those rules now excited him. Calling Margot Le Roux that morning had excited him. But excitement and terror were merely markers on the same road. The distance between them could close with astounding speed. There was the money, too, of course. He had found the suitcase in the desert, almost literally, and it was full of cash. He knew how that story was supposed to end, but that was just the Sunday-school morality of fiction; history and reality refuted it at every turn. Of course it was possible to get away with betrayal, murder, and corruption. He had to be clear in his mind. He was not battling with a moral dilemma. A moral man would have no dilemma. He'd crossed that boundary when he'd called Margot, without thinking it through, as if accepting a dare from some inner self previously concealed from him. He had to think it through now, here, with his thighs going numb on the rim of the toilet seat.

The choice towered before him in his noxious cubicle. He hadn't yet crossed the Rubicon. A single unrecorded conversation, in which he had merely made allusions, all deniable. All he had to do was, well, do nothing and he was safe. The attempt on Turner's life had shocked him into reality. Turner could actually be killed. They weren't fantasizing up there; they were acting; they were firing guns. Like Turner, he didn't think Margot would shoot unless Venter agreed to help with the cover-up. In effect it was up to him to pull the trigger. The cover-up itself would be easy enough, if, as seemed the case, he could count on Mokoena's help. And the rogue actions of Sergeant Rudy Britz had strengthened Venter's hand. Margot now needed him more than ever. Why, then, was he hesitating?

Fear, pure fear. He had never been seriously tempted to corrupt himself before, but he had never before had so much as a glimpse of the suitcase. There had never been such a prize to tempt him. Most criminals were poor—even poorer than everyone else. A regular trickle of cash from some miserable tin-pot kingpin was insane: the constant danger, 24-7, of discovery and disgrace simply wasn't worth it. But this was a one-off opportunity with no ongoing commitment. It would be over in a week. Margot would have nothing on him that he didn't have on her, and she had the most to lose. And if he got Turner's video, he would have even more security. He wouldn't have to cower in the suburbs, eking out his pension, paying the mortgage on a house he hated.

It was time to shit or get off the pot.

Venter stood up, his legs tingling with pins and needles, and flushed the toilet a second time. He pulled up his pants and washed his hands. He left the bathroom and took the elevator down to the parking lot and sat in his car. A welcome, if relative, quietude had settled on his bowels. Decision was always more painful than action, a strange truth. He took out his regular phone and called Turner.

"Captain," said Turner.

Venter could hear the dull murmur of what sounded like a TV or a radio in the background.

"Where are you?"

"I'm at the bookie's."

"The what?"

"The bookmaker's here in town. I'm uploading the file. You'll have it in twenty-seven minutes."

"Your safety is my top priority. If the risk is too great, forget the bloody file and get out of there right now."

"I'll call you from the road."

Turner hung up. Venter felt a stab of guilt. No. He mustn't hesitate. He'd made his decision. He took out the anonymous phone he had bought that morning. He looked at Margot Le Roux's number. It was the only number in the phone. To get it had required a chain of six calls to three different cities and a good deal of delicate dishonesty. He pressed dial. A male voice answered.

"Venter?"

"Who is this?" said Venter.

"I'm going to give you another number. Memorize it and call us back."

A white Englishman. London. Margot's husband, Hennie Hendricks. Other voices in the background. Venter's anxiety spiked. The voices receded. Hendricks gave him the number. Venter didn't like the idea.

"This wasn't the arrangement. Where's Margot?"

"Listen you little worm, there is no Margot. There is no arrangement either. There never was. Call the number or don't call the number, I couldn't give two shits. But if you don't, you'll wake up some dark night and find me smiling at you."

Venter's irritable bowel flared.

"Could you repeat that number, please?"

TWENTY-TWO

Margot leaned both hands on the granite top of the kitchen island and stared between her arms at the oak floorboards. She had to order her thoughts, and without emotion.

Rudy Britz had driven up to the gate in a bullet-riddled car and announced that Turner had killed four more men. Twenty-four hours before she had been in bed with Hennie enjoying an indulgent Sunday morning. Now the flotsam of a small war had washed up at her door. This was worse than the water riots, the clearance of the shanties, the strike crisis. No one who had died then had had any status or authority. Some didn't even have names, or none that anyone cared to know. Their deaths had caused no more ripples than their lives had. Turner, living or dead, was a tsunami.

She was bewildered. What she had wanted had not seemed—still did not seem—very much. She wanted Dirk to avoid a lifelong stigma, a stigma which would affect no one but him and which would benefit absolutely no one else. For that she was prepared to pay handsomely. She despised those who took bribes; of course she did. She felt no pride or pleasure in giving her money to devious scum. Everything she had she had earned through guts, commitment, and labor. She was hard-pressed to name a single national leader world-wide who was not, either actually or morally, a criminal. Criminality and injustice were woven through the fabric of civilization. Everyone swallowed this, unperturbed, every time they watched the news. For Dirk to avoid the penalty for his actions, a penalty that, within the law, would be no more than symbolic, was, yes, a crime, but a miserably small one. To atone, instead, by building a clinic in a hellhole was more than reasonable, it was enlightened. She was willing to pay the blood debt, the ancient, the intelligent, way of making things right, but not with Dirk's reputation.

The thought of Turner rejecting the clinic made her angry again. Don't me let stop you, he'd said. The bastard. As if she hadn't built many such projects already—irrigation, roads, medical centers, schools—with more to come. Now Turner had killed five men, and he was right and she was wrong? She shook her head to clear her mind. She didn't know how to proceed. She looked up at Hennie, who sat watching her from a high stool, a glass of orange juice in his hand. He was at risk, too.

"I need some help here," she said. "What are my options?"

"Seems pretty clear-cut to me," said Hennie. "Either we own up and face the music for the dead girl, which wouldn't kill us, or we kill Turner. If we can get Venter in the bag, that's a done deal. Turner had his chance, he threw it in your face. He's shut out all the options."

"Hennie, I've got a bad feeling."

"So do I, but not about stepping on him. He's a maniac, a mass killer."

"I thought we'd left this kind of thing behind us."

"You have. This is on me. It's been on me since the start. Margot, you've done nothing wrong. You're clean. You'll stay clean." Hennie's pirate grin gleamed through his beard. It was his grin she had fallen in love with. "Remember, I like getting my hands dirty."

"What about Rudy's fiasco, these men he hired?"

"Men?" he laughed. "Four unemployed tik freaks? No one will know they're gone, much less care. Anyway, it was nothing to do with us. It does put the grocer's thumb on the scales for killing Turner. If we let him get away, he'll be after Rudy, too. That could be awkward. Then Rudy might have to be found in that stolen car, that's to say, a sixth body to Turner's credit. Then we'd be back to square one—plus this damned video of Jason you say he's got."

Jason, another maniac. Why had he betrayed Dirk? What was in it for him? Was he simply that stupid? The bullets in his muscle-bound corpse proved that, she supposed. She felt entangled in the whims of morons and lunatics.

"I want that video," she said.

Hennie gestured his chin beyond her shoulder. "Simon's on it."

There was a knock on the glass door. She turned. It was Simon. She waved him in.

"Rudy's in the gatehouse drinking hot sweet tea," said Simon. "He's in shock but suffered nothing worse than glass cuts. Looking at the car, it's a miracle."

"Turner couldn't even do us that favor," said Hennie.

"Where is Turner?" said Margot.

"I've got three men in town to spot him, ma'am," said Simon. "Strictly surveillance only. They'll let me know if he tries to hook up that laptop. Four more set up on the road a kilometer south with H&Ks. They'll stop his car on my order." He looked around. "Why isn't Winston here?"

"He's sitting this out," said Hennie. "Squeamish about offing a fellow officer. Hear no evil, see no evil, as if he was kidding anyone."

"Has he turned on us?" said Simon.

"Then he'd be kidding himself," said Margot. "He'll do what's necessary after the fact."

Margot's phone rang. Number withheld. She passed it to Hennie.

"Venter?" said Hennie.

Dirk walked into the room. He wore tennis gear and carried a racket bag. Hennie walked quickly to the open door and out onto the terrace. Dirk smiled at Margot and her heart melted. So tall, so handsome, so brilliant.

"Sorry to interrupt," said Dirk, "but you promised me three sets."

"Darling, I completely forgot," said Margot. "I'm sorry."

"If it's a bad time—"

"No, no," said Margot. "I wouldn't miss it for the world. I just need fifteen minutes to finish up here and get changed."

"Anything I can help you with?" asked Dirk.

"No, you practice your serve. I'll be right there."

Dirk exchanged a smile and a nod with Simon and left by the glass door. Hennie clapped him on the shoulder as he passed. Hennie came back inside and gave Margot her phone. He went back to his stool where two phones lay on the granite top. One of them rang and vibrated.

"This is secure, right?" said Hennie.

"It's all set," said Simon.

Hennie reached for the phone. On impulse Margot snatched it up first. "No," said Hennie. "We agreed, I'll do it, you stay clean."

"It's my son, my fight," said Margot. She answered the phone.

"This will be short and sweet," she said. "Especially sweet for you if you play your cards right. If you play them wrong you'll never sleep soundly again, because the purpose of my life will be to fuck you."

"I—"

"Shut up. You will listen to my one-time offer. You will accept it or reject it. There will be no haggling. If you accept, I buy your absolute obedience. Is that clear?"

Hennie jabbed a finger at his ear. Margot tapped the speaker on.

"Absolute obedience is a bit much," said Venter. "We need to set some parameters."

"The unfortunate death of Warrant Officer Turner, should it occur—and that depends on you—will require investigation," said Margot. "That investigation will be conducted by the local authorities. You will come to Langkopf and take part in that investigation, to ensure that the Cape Town authorities will be satisfied with the result. Is that within your power?"

"It is," said Venter.

"You will also close the investigation into the homicide of the unknown girl, committed by Jason Britz, again to the satisfaction of the Cape Town authorities."

"No problem," said Venter.

"You will share all relevant intelligence as and when we need it."

"Relevant, as and when. I can do that."

"Those are your parameters. When it's over, we can each take our own path to hell."

"That's your end," said Venter. "What's mine? I asked you to make a calculation."

Margot glanced at Hennie. He raised his right thumb above his fisted hand and shook it.

"Three hundred Krugerrands," said Margot.

A silence. Good. Her instincts had been correct. No Swiss accounts. No footprints. Just solid gold. Its power over the human soul had not waned in millennia. She knew. She had a safe in the panic room half-full of it.

Venter coughed, nervously. "I'm not sure what that's worth."

"At current rates," said Margot, "it's worth four hundred thousand US dollars."

"Help me out again," asked Venter. "What's that in rand?"

"In rand?" Margot laughed. Hennie's grin caught her again.

She channeled his coarse energy. "You poor fucking peon," she said. "I thought you were a big city boy. Who gives a fuck about the fucking rand?"

"I need to put it in a context I can grasp," said Venter.

"Something over five million," said Margot.

Another silence. This one longer. Venter was stunned.

"That's eight kilos of twenty-two karat gold," said Margot. "If you've got what it takes to pick it up. Do you?"

"I'm sure I could get it to my car," said Venter.

"Yes or no. In or out."

"Yes," said Venter. "I'm in."

"Where's Turner?" said Margot.

"I'll try to find out. I suggest you send some men, good men, to cover the Cape Town road and—"

"The deal's off," said Margot. "You're going to jail, Captain Venter. This conversation has been recorded."

Margot hung up and put the phone down. Seconds later it rang again. She answered.

"Where's Turner?" she said.

"I don't—"

"Shut up. Turner is uploading his video to the cloud, which is why you won't tell me where he is. You think it will give you some leverage but you are an idiot. Turner is not an idiot. When he mails the file to you he will mail it to one or more others as backup, as would any half-intelligent person in fear for his life. Yes?"

"It's a reasonable supposition," allowed Venter.

"Once that video is out, I've failed—so I won't need you anymore. I'll pay my lawyers and Dirk won't go to jail. The other thing I won't need anymore is to kill Turner, because killing him won't change the case against Dirk. Instead I will send Turner my own mail, with the recording of you and I plotting his murder. Then I'll pay my lawyers again. And I won't go to jail either. But you will die there. If Turner doesn't get to you first."

"He said he's in the bookie's." Venter almost shouted. "The bookmaker's in town. You've got—twenty minutes. Then he'll run."

Hennie grabbed his phone and walked toward Simon. He stopped as he passed Margot and leaned toward her. She muted the phone. Hennie kissed her on the lips.

"You're beautiful," he said.

The double compliment touched her. He looked her in the eye to be sure she was sure.

"Last chance," said Hennie.

Margot said, "Get rid of him."

Hennie grinned. He turned to go, but she stopped him.

"Take Rudy with you." She saw the question in his face. "He's a wild card with a badge and a gun; he's out of control. I don't want him hanging round here and I don't want him causing chaos elsewhere."

She watched Hennie and Simon stride out of the door.

"Hello?" said Venter. "Hello?"

Margot unmuted the phone. "We agreed: all relevant intelligence, as and when."

"I was wrong, I apologize, but—"

"You broke our deal," said Margot.

"Nothing's changed—"

"Oh yes it has. Your purchase price just dropped by a third. To two hundred Krugerrands."

"What?"

"How does it feel to lose a couple of million rand in less than a minute?"

She listened to Venter's silence. She enjoyed his pain. She could feel its dimensions. The basic visceral horror. The bitter self-torment that would rankle till the end of his days. The battle with his own cowardice.

"I assume you consider that fair," she said. "I consider it more than generous."

Venter uttered strange, grunting gasps, like a man fighting to control his bowels.

"Bear in mind that if you betray me again, I will use a small portion of the money you just squandered to have you killed."

"It's fair," whispered Venter.

"Text your number to this phone, now," she said. "Be ready to travel on my word. I'll tell you when to be here in Langkopf."

She hung up. She picked up Hennie's orange juice and drank it. She didn't feel bewildered anymore. The world would turn wherever it would turn, for her or against her, as it had turned before. She remembered Meursault and the four shots he need not have fired. The corpse of his mother that he chose not to see. The memory gave her an odd comfort. She put the empty glass down on the granite counter. This wasn't just about Dirk. Perhaps it wasn't about Dirk at all.

Margot went to change into her tennis outfit.

TWENTY-THREE

The road from Margot's compound to the highway north of town was seven kilometers long and private all the way. One of the things Hennie didn't like about this part of the world was that all the bloody roads were straight as bloody arrows. You could go to sleep at the wheel in one town and wake up an hour later in the next. So when they had planned the road to the new house and compound he had insisted on incorporating a variety of chicanes to give him some driving pleasure. The builders hadn't liked it, but when experienced from the controls of a 5L supercharged Jaguar engine the results were spectacular. Today he could have done without the bends but he couldn't help laughing from his belly as he screeched through the curves, straining the onboard computer and daring the two-ton Camargue-red behemoth to roll over. It was a shame he hadn't thought to time the run.

Simon Dube sat next to him, as cool as a glass of lager in Alexandria. He had a Benelli M4 tactical shotgun propped between his knees, muzzle down. Rudy sat in the back, grunting at each roll of the car. In normal circumstances he would have grit his teeth and kept quiet, but his nerves were shot from his encounter with Turner. The left arm and leg of his uniform was blotched with dried blood, none of it his. Hennie had told him not to get it on the leather or the seat belts.

Simon opened a box of surgical-quality latex gloves and took out three packets. He passed one to Hennie who shoved it into his shirt pocket. He tossed one to Rudy and opened the third for himself.

"Rudy, put the gloves on," said Simon.

"I don't take orders from you."

"Oh dear," said Hennie. "It's Rudy's time of the month. I hope he's not going to fuck things up for us. You're the man to go to for fuckups, aren't you Rudy?"

"Jason's lying dead on the stoop of the old family farm—" said Rudy.

"So Jason knows what I'm talking about."

"I'm not in the mood for your famous fucking British humor."

Hennie glanced in the mirror. Rudy's face was a portrait, in various shades of red, of grief, rage, and car sickness. They entered another chicane.

"Well that's put me in my place," said Hennie. "I feel quite chastened."

"Where are we going?"

"We're going to finish what you started so you'll do exactly what Simon or I say. You might be a joke but Turner isn't."

"Let me take him," said Rudy.

"You couldn't take Turner if he was nailed to a tree with a bag over his head. You couldn't take Coco the Clown. You're here strictly as an observer."

"Jason said you were a turd. I said anybody who knew you could tell me that."

"One more word and I'll leave you by the side of the road."

Hennie watched him try to summon up a comeback line. The side of the road would be the best place for him but they couldn't afford the time. If Rudy decided to sit there like a big stubborn ox, they'd have to shoot him to get him out.

"Listen, Rudy," said Hennie, in his friendliest voice, "we have to take Turner alive and well and without a mark on him. Get it?"

Hennie watched him work it out.

"Okay," said Rudy. "A bullet would be too good for him anyway."

Hennie came out of the last chicane. The last kilometer was straight. He put his foot down.

"The bookie's," said Simon. Down to business.

"Never been in there," said Hennie. "Tactics?"

"Turner's using their Wi-Fi. If he gave them a few rand, he might just be sitting there with the customers. That would suit us, we could just walk in. Civilian cover, he won't want to shoot it out. But he's got a badge and gun. If I was him, I'd clear the shop and lock up."

"Let's assume he has."

"The windows are painted and grilled," said Simon. "We can't see inside. The back door will be locked. Assume he's locked the street door too. There's a door at the betting counter, locked from the inside. No high security, Winston's too cheap."

"You're very familiar. You like to play the odds, do you?"

"Winston asked my advice. That's how I know how cheap he is."

Hennie braked sharply and turned onto the highway. They'd be there in under five minutes.

"I can make a silent entry through the back," said Simon. "You'll have to take the front door down." He patted the stock of the Benelli. "This has two breaching rounds ready to go. When you blow the lock, I'll throw down on him from behind. You don't have to come through the door. Turner will be in the far left hand corner of the room."

"Timing?"

"Keep your phone on vibrate. When I'm ready to go through

the counter door I'll text you: twice for go—on your own time, I'll be ready. Once for abort. Wait for the second buzz. If it's not going to happen I'll be back outside and I'll ring you with an update—that's a different vibration, longer, right?"

"He is a shooter," said Hennie.

"We don't know his mind-set. If the video's flown—and the timing of that is unpredictable—then as Margot said we don't want him dead. He may have worked that out, but he doesn't know if we have."

Hennie had not quite got his head around all that but deferred to better brains than his. "In short, if has to go, he has to go."

"It's his choice."

"How good is he?"

"As good as you or me, maybe better. We've been out of practice, he hasn't. But there are two of us."

"What's this video about?" said Rudy.

Hennie decided it was easier to tell him. "Dashcam. Turner filmed Jason talking about what happened in Cape Town. We don't know what he said but we've got to stop Turner posting it to his people."

"I want to see it."

"We'll deal with that later." Hennie turned to Simon. "Where's the bookie in this? Is it just him, or a girl on the till, or what?"

"Just the bookie. I'll improvise."

"What do you want me to do?" asked Rudy.

"You stay in the car," said Hennie. "We've had enough of your improvisations for one day." He rubbed the back of his hand on his beard. "Not ideal, this. Lots of holes."

"Simon looked at his watch. "Whatever Venter meant by twenty minutes, we've got less than ten left."

Hennie had an idea. "I'll make sure the bastard doesn't shoot."

He drove up to the rear of La Diva. He got out with the shotgun, turned back to wag a finger at Rudy, and shut the door. He put his phone in the pocket of his shirt. He pulled his latex gloves on.

Simon was already working on the lock of La Diva. He inserted a small tension wrench into the keyhole and held it taut, then slid in the thin steel rod of a snap gun. He clicked it five times and the tension wrench swung up and the door opened. Simon moved on to the rear door of the bookie's. Hennie walked into La Diva.

Any of the women inside would do, Hennie thought, but Iminathi knew him so she'd be the easiest to handle, if she was there. If Winston was there, he'd better not argue or Hennie would lay him out. Hennie passed through the kitchen. It stank of curry. He pointed the shotgun at the floor, no need to terrify her, and entered the office. Iminathi sat at the table, her back half toward him, texting on her phone.

"Hello, Imi."

She jumped to her feet with a short cry and dropped the phone on the table.

Hennie smiled, he hoped reassuringly. "I need you for five minutes."

She looked at the shotgun. She was scared. Fair enough.

"I haven't done anything," she said.

"I never said you did. I just need you to come with me for five minutes."

She shook her head, too scared to speak.

"I prefer you to be conscious," said Hennie, "but unconscious will work too. Now be good and you'll come to no harm. Come on—"

He gestured toward the salon. She walked in front of him, her body stiff with tension.

"Right out to the street," said Hennie. "Say to the ladies: 'There's no problem, girls, this is a friend of mine.'"

They passed through the corridor and into the salon. Four faces looked at him in the mirror.

"No problem, girls, this is a friend of mine," said Imi.

Hennie smiled into the mirror. Iminathi opened the door to the street. He seemed to remember she was a keen runner. She certainly looked fit. He grabbed her firmly but gently by her wrist and they stepped outside. Not too busy. Maybe a dozen pedestrians up and down the street. Langkopf was never busy. He rarely set foot in the town. Whenever he did he remembered why. It was a crap-hole. He stopped her just short of the bookmaker's window.

"What do you want from me?" said Imi.

"Keep very quiet. All I want you to do is to stand in front of that door."

"Why?"

"I'm going to shoot it open." Her eyes widened with horror. "The shells fire a kind of powdered steel mixed with wax. No ricochet, no danger, perfectly safe."

"So why do you need me?"

"What's important now is that you stay cool. No sudden movements or no one will be safe."

"You motherfucker."

"I deserve that so I'll let it pass, but let that be enough."

Hennie's phone vibrated in his pocket. Short. A text. He pulled Iminathi past the window and stationed her in front of the bookmaker's door. The lock was level with her collar bones. He raised the Benelli high by the pistol grip and canted the barrel down at forty-five degrees to the horizontal and forty-five to the plane of the door. The muzzle touched the wood just above the lock. He was peripherally aware of pedestrians turning around or crossing to the other side of the street. He reached around her, took hold of the fore stock with his left hand. Iminathi was now completely encircled by his arms and the shotgun. She covered her face with her hands, hyperventilating. The second text arrived.

"Put your thumbs in your ears," he said. "When you hear the shots, scream."

"Shit."

Hennie fired. *Boom-boom.*

The lock was blasted from the wood and the door swung half-open and Iminathi screamed and Hennie shouldered the Benelli and kicked the door the rest of the way. He stepped to the left, leaving Iminathi stranded in the doorway while he took cover behind the doorjamb.

He saw Turner right where Simon said he'd be, in the far left corner by the main counter, where he could watch the street door and the approach to the center door through the plexiglass. He had his Glock aimed high above the door, as if he'd reacted to cover the shotgun blasts, then again to protect Iminathi. He wore a vest. Hennie aimed below the vest, an easy shot. The center door opened and Simon's left arm leveled his Steyr at Turner's head.

It was done.

"Gun on the floor, kick it to me," said Simon.

Turner laid the gun down and kicked it over.

"Take the vest off."

Turner ripped open the Velcro side straps. He was staring at Iminathi. She was shaking, her hands still covering her face but no longer her eyes. Hennie pushed past her. He spotted the laptop on the left-hand plastic side-counter.

Simon stuck Turner's Glock in his belt. Turner lifted the vest over his head and dropped it. "Face toward the glass, on your knees, both hands on the counter."

"I've got him," said Hennie. He had the muzzle of the Benelli aimed at Turner's spine from a meter away. "Deal with the laptop."

Simon circled quickly around Hennie to avoid his line

of fire. He tapped at the laptop's keyboard. "I've stopped the upload. Now I need his phone." Simon circled again and reached straight for Turner's right pants pocket. "He might have hooked that into the Wi-Fi, too. It wouldn't make sense, competing with his own bandwidth, but we've got to be sure."

Simon pulled Turner's phone out and tapped and scrolled the screen.

"No password?" said Hennie. He realized that some futile caveman urge was competing with Simon's mastery of modern technology, a contest he was certain to lose. Simon had flattered him with that "as good as us" comment. He'd meant "as good as me." That was okay. Stark bollock naked and holding a sharp stone he'd still fancy his chances with either of them.

"He's a cop," said Simon, tapping and scrolling. "If he has to make a certain kind of call, the five seconds it takes to plug in a pin can be the same five seconds it takes someone to die." Simon stopped tapping and seemed satisfied. "The vid is on the phone but he was uploading through the carrier, not Wi-Fi. Another hour to go. The vid stays here in Langkopf." Simon circled a third time, back to the laptop. "Look."

Hennie side-stepped over, keeping the shotgun on Turner. He waited until Simon had covered Turner with his pistol, then looked at the screen where Simon was pointing.

"What about that, Turner?" said Hennie. "Estimated time to completion: two minutes. Looks like it isn't your day after all."

Turner stared at the red plastic fascia of the counter, perfectly still, perfectly relaxed.

"I'm deleting the video," said Simon. He clicked and tapped. "Secure delete. Disk utility. Erase free space."

"Can't they recover deleted files?" said Hennie.

"A deleted file usually sits there until you need the space, then the computer writes over it, but that might not be for months, or even never, so it's recoverable." Simon tapped the touch pad again. "Not this one. I've overwritten and erased it three times. It's gone. The CIA couldn't get it back."

Simon closed the laptop. The original file on the microdisk was in Simon's small intestine. No one would be recovering that either.

"Tape him up," said Hennie. "We don't want any of those Shaolin-temple tricks, do we, Turner?"

Hennie took a roll of duct tape from his thigh pocket and handed it to Simon. There was a tearing sound as Simon unspooled a length of tape. Hennie glanced at the doorway. Iminathi was still standing there, crying.

"You can go," said Hennie. "Thanks for the help."

Iminathi sobbed, "I didn't do anything."

Hennie wasn't sure if she was talking to him or to the back of Turner's head. He wasn't interested either way. "Go and straighten some hair. If you've got any complaints, call the police."

Iminathi stared at him with hatred. She turned and fled. What could she do? She was a bright enough girl, which was good, because she'd know that she could do nothing, and that no one would help her to do it.

Simon wrapped the tape four times around Turner's left forearm, over his shirt sleeve. He cranked that arm behind Turner's back, pulled his right arm to join it, and wrapped the right forearm the same way without breaking the tape. Then he bound both forearms together from elbows to shirt cuffs, round and round until the whole double sleeve of tape was several millimeters thick. He tore the tape free of the roll. Hennie covered Turner all the way.

"Stand up," said Hennie.

Turner rose from his knees in one smooth motion. He looked at Hennie. His face was blank. He had the coldest eyes Hennie had ever seen, and he had seen more than his share. They revealed nothing. Not anger, nor fear nor threat, not frustration, defeat nor defiance.

They were calm, still, disturbingly green. If they revealed anything, it was that he was at peace with himself. Since he must have known that he was going to die, that was as cold as a man could get.

"Quite the Zen motherfucker, aren't we?" said Hennie.

Turner continued to look at him in silence. Hennie realized, with a strange sense of confusion in his gut, that this man demanded absolute respect, and he, Hennie, had no choice but to feel it.

"Where's your car?" said Hennie.

Turner didn't answer.

"Can't be far away," said Hennie. "We'll find it. Depends on how much longer you want to stand in here listening to me."

Turner thought about it. "The Medical Center parking lot," he said.

Simon pulled a ring of keys from Turner's pocket. He also took the pepper spray and a Swiss Army knife.

"I'll bring the car round the back. Listen for the horn," said Simon.

"Call Mark Lewis at the garage," said Hennie. "Tell him no excuses."

Simon pointed at Hennie's shotgun. "Give yourself a bit more distance."

Hennie nodded. He was forgetting the basics. He took three backward steps away from Turner. Simon took the laptop and the Kevlar vest and went out through the street door and pulled it closed behind him. Hennie heard a faint rasp and a click and turned. He saw a plume of gray-blue smoke rise up above the main counter behind the plexiglass window.

"What the fuck?"

"The bookie," said Turner. "I'd give him a thousand and tell him to get that door fixed before Winston sees it."

"Oi, bookie," said Hennie. A man rose behind the glass like some prehistoric lizard. "Come here."

The bookie came out through the door, a cigarette smoking between his lips. Hennie dug his wallet out and gave it to the bookie. "You heard him. Help yourself to a grand and fuck off."

The bookie opened the wallet, took out the bills, showed them to Hennie, and returned the wallet. Hennie put it in his pocket. The bookie walked out of the street door and closed it behind him.

"You do know," said Hennie, "that he's never going to pay for that door."

"Why should he?"

Hennie laughed. "I'm the only one who gets it, you know."

"Gets what?"

"Gets why you're here. Gets you."

Turner didn't answer. Hennie felt a strong impulse to make some connection with him. He didn't know why he would want to do that with a man he was about to kill, but there it was. And because he was about to kill him, why not?

"I mean, okay, nobody ever gets anybody else, anywhere, ever," said Hennie. "Nobody gets their wife, their children, their parents. Nobody gets John Coltrane, nobody gets Shakespeare. How the fuck could they? They might think they do, but they don't, not really, not completely. Only in flashes, moments."

"You think you've had a moment," said Turner.

"They're all asking, what the fuck is wrong with this guy? Why doesn't he take the job, the money, the clinic, the keys to the kingdom? What's his problem with this fucking dead girl? I said you were a maniac myself. But now I see you're not."

"What do you see?" said Turner.

"You don't care what I see."

"No I don't."

Hennie laughed again. "You're a man who sees the way things are. Which is that it's all bullshit. It's meaningless. It's fucking chaos. But somewhere in that gigantic, bottomless ocean of pure bullshit, the man who sees the way things are has to choose the worthiest bullshit he can find and make a stand for it. It might be that woman who makes you feel a thousand feet tall. It might be the flag of a country that will shovel you into the ground with no more thought than a cat burying its own turds. It might be a girl with no name lying dead in the street. But it's that knowing that if you walk away from it, if you take the money and run, you'll be ghost to yourself. You'll be nothing. It's that feeling in the blood, when you know you have to ride it till it crashes."

"Does Margot see the way things are?"

"Like a fucking eagle."

"You should let me go," said Turner. "Cape Town murder police will hunt you down."

Hennie smiled. "I'm sorry it's going to end without giving you a chance." He wasn't sure he meant that, but he felt like saying it.

"I have a chance," said Turner. "You don't."

"We'll see," said Hennie."

There was a distant double blast on a horn from the rear of the building. Hennie motioned with the shotgun toward the door past the counter.

"Time to hit the road to dreamland."

TWENTY-FOUR

Turner knew where he was headed from the moment Simon started to tape his arms up. Handcuffs or flexicuffs would potentially leave marks on his wrists; certainly if he chose to make them. Simon had been careful: the tape was inescapably secure but not too tight. The glue was only on his shirt, not his skin.

They were going to drive him out into the desert in the Land Cruiser and leave him to die—like Iminathi's father.

As he talked with Hennie, Turner ran escape options through his head. They hadn't taped his legs. They were aware that his death would have to stand up to a professional investigation. They didn't want glue on his pants. His shirt was easily replaced. He'd be helpless enough without his arms. Hennie didn't want to blow him apart in the middle of town. They wouldn't be able to conceal the forensics. They wanted an accidental death. A clean corpse that would pass examination by a coroner. No marks, no blood—no mess.

Turner considered attack strategies. The bookmaker's building was the same length as La Diva. Probably the same basic layout. Corridor with bathroom, large middle room, kitchen. The middle room doorway: spin and sidestep to get some cover from the wall;

Hennie constricted in the corridor. Kick the shotgun barrel aside; a stomp kick—wherever he could land it. Take it from there. Turner couldn't see what he had to lose.

What then? A chase through the streets with his arms taped behind his back. Who would cut him lose? A hair stylist? The hotel clerk? A doctor or a nurse? A bound man was bound for a reason, usually a good one. He had his badge in his pocket but whoever helped him would need some courage.

Iminathi?

On the list of suspects of who had told Hennie where to find him, she was number one. At the door she had appeared horrified, but after standing six inches from a double shotgun blast, blind fear was more likely. Number two was the slim chance that the third spotter had seen him slip into the bookie's. He didn't have a number three. Logic would insist on adding Captain Venter to the list, but it would also insist on a vast difference in probability. He'd known Imi for less than five hours; Venter for over five years.

Best case: he'd be at large, unarmed, a hunted man with nowhere to run. Chances of getting that far: very poor. Worst case: dead in the kind of faked random-murder scenario Rudy had had in mind. Chances of that: very high. The alternative: survive the desert. Chances of that: remote. But not zero.

"Time to hit the road to dreamland," said Hennie.

"A Johnny Mercer fan," said Turner.

"Just full of surprises, aren't you?"

Hennie motioned toward the inner door. Turner walked through. Hennie kept a good distance, two meters. The attack idea dissolved into the realm of fantasy, where it had always belonged. He'd just be boxed up in the next room; Simon would come. The best he could do would be to make them beat him bloody or shoot him. Any possible victory would be postmortem. Stay healthy while you can. He passed through the corridor. The kitchen door and back door were open. He could see the rear half of his Land Cruiser outside, doors open, waiting for him.

Rudy appeared in the back door frame.

Turner charged at him.

"You fucker," shouted Hennie.

Rudy cocked his fists like a boxer. Turner jumped and pounced from the run. As he landed he kicked Rudy with full force and momentum through the Conception Vessel 4 meridian point, between the pubic bone and the navel, focusing into the Dantian. Rudy hurtled backward and his legs gave out. The back of his skull put a new dent in the wing of the Land Cruiser as he fell.

Turner burst outside. Simon came at him from the right. Turner tried to weave around him but Simon was well on his toes this time and didn't give him an exit. He was smiling. His teeth shone. Turner spun and ran. Hennie dropped the shotgun as he came through the door and tackled Turner from the side. His left arm slammed across Turner's chest and dragged him into a crushing embrace. His right arm looped over his head and clamped his throat in the crook of the elbow, cranking his chin up. Turner relaxed, went with it. Protect the cervical joints. Breathe. Let the adrenaline settle, save energy. He could have crushed the bones of Hennie's feet, but there was no point in risking a broken neck.

"Bastard." Hennie's voice rasped into Turner's left ear. Turner let him wrestle him to the Land Cruiser. Hennie changed grip, one hand on his bound arm, the other round the nape of his neck. He had big hands. He walked him around the car, half bent over, and pushed him into the right rear seat. He pinned him with an arm across the throat while he stretched and inserted the seat belt across Turner's chest. He stood back and panted.

Hennie grinned, to hide the fact that, for a moment, he'd been alarmed. "You are a fucking handful. I'll give you that."

He closed Turner's door and went to help Simon drag Rudy

to his feet. Rudy moaned and struggled. He was concussed but the deep agony pervading his pelvis and bowels was bringing him around. He had lost his shades. They manhandled him into the front passenger seat, where he writhed, semiconscious. Simon sat beside Turner, no seat belt. Hennie collected his Benelli, stowed it in the trunk, and climbed behind the wheel. He took a short breath and blew it out, as if to credit himself for a tough job well done. He engaged drive and moved off.

At the main street he turned north. Parked by the curb at the edge of town was a dusty, well-used Land Rover Discovery. Hennie flashed it twice with the headlights. As they passed the Discovery Turner recognized Mark Lewis, the car mechanic and one of the group who had been in Cape Town. Lewis pulled out and followed behind them.

Turner had no doubts now. He was going to be stranded far from anywhere with a disabled Land Cruiser. He shifted his position to glimpse the temperature gauge. Outside it was forty-one degrees centigrade.

They picked up speed. No one spoke.

Turner had no good ideas. These men were committed. They'd done this before. They'd got away with it before. Yet he picked up a somber feeling from Hennie and Simon. Premeditated murder was a heavy matter. They were both ex-soldiers, proud of that and what it made them, both in front of each other and each in front of himself. They knew this wasn't war. War carried at least the illusion of honor. This was cowardly and squalid. No use in pointing it out: they knew it.

He thought about his impending death. From thirst. It would be slow and unpleasant. Then slow and painful. Then he would lose his mind. He had seen a couple of reality shows on the subject, by TV survivalists. Cacti and lizards. From what he'd seen from the road a cactus wouldn't survive any longer out here than an old lady—or a young man. The San Bushmen survived, but Turner didn't know how. Turner had had a glass of water in his hotel bathroom. He'd drunk some of Jason's milkshake. He was already thirsty. They would have to leave him his guns if they wanted it to look accidental. He wondered if he would get to the point where that would seem the intelligent way out.

The music of *Conan the Barbarian* struck up. Simon was watching the video on Turner's phone.

"What the fuck is that?" said Hennie.

"Jason's training music," said Simon. "Dead lifts. I have to admit, he was built."

"Fucking juice monkey, it's not real muscle. Get to the payoff, before Rudy wakes up."

Simon skipped forward, once, twice. Turner watched Jason waving his jug.

"I didn't hurt a fucking fly in Cape Town."

They listened to the exchange. Turner didn't need to see any more. He could see it anytime he wanted, in his head. He watched Hennie's jaw muscles bunching as Jason gave his account of the death of the unknown girl in Cape Town.

"He dropped me and Dirk right in it," said Hennie. "Bang to rights. What a cunt."

"Jason went inside the house," said Simon. "He's come back out with the SPAS-12."

They listened to the final exchange. Until it ended with a burst of gunfire.

"Beautiful," said Simon. "Hardcore. Turner gave him the first move. Do you want to see it, Hennie?"

"Jason?" said Rudy. His head came up from his chest. He was ignored.

"No. Scrub it," said Hennie. He seemed offended that Simon was impressed. "That's the last copy isn't it?"

"The original's traveling through my gut," said Simon, tapping and scrolling at the screen. "If you want that one you'll have to find it yourself."

"Jason!" raved Rudy.

Turner saw the pickax memorial pass by. Hennie slowed and swung off the road onto the scrublands. The ground was even, but it wasn't tarmac and the Land Cruiser bounced gently. Rudy groaned like a cow giving birth.

"Jesus Christ, Rudy," said Hennie. "You almost gave me a coronary."

"Get me to hospital."

"We'll see you're taken care of, don't you worry. Just sit still and take deep breaths."

Rudy tried a deep breath. He stopped halfway with another terrible groan. His body stiffened. His shoulders trembled.

"Fuck me. What did you do to him, Turner?"

"I wanted to ask, too," said Simon. "What style is that? Some kind of Chinese internal system, right? Something like Hsing-I?"

Turner wasn't inclined to indulge them. He didn't answer. Rudy moaned again and grabbed onto the dashboard with both hands to brace himself. His fingertips clawed the plastic. His whole body shuddered with pain.

"Where are your gloves?" said Hennie. "You're leaving prints all over the car. Keep your fucking hands to yourself."

A vision sprang to life, fully formed, in Turner's mind's eye.

Rudy's prints.

The vision was atrocious. The mythical reasonable man inside him recoiled, but only for a moment. In extreme circumstances, even he could justify extreme measures.

"Tai chi," said Turner.

"I thought that was old people and hippies, yoga teachers, vegans," said Hennie.

"I'll tell you, Hennie," said Simon, "I've been punched and kicked by the best of them. KO'd, choked out, broken nose, ribs. I took two rounds in the chest at Bangui. But I never felt pain like that before. I was paralyzed. It was like someone had injected snake poison into my spinal cord."

"I'm not doubting you," said Hennie. "I've worked in the Far East. Manila. Bangkok. Hong Kong before we gave the bloody thing away. Different laws of physics out there. Sort of related to acupuncture and all that, isn't it?"

"Sort of," said Turner.

"So where did you learn this Chinese malarkey?"

"From a Chinaman."

"Come on, man," said Simon. "I'm interested."

Rudy entered another groaning cycle. He broke wind at great volume.

"Fucking hell," said Hennie. "Can't you do some acupuncture on Rudy?"

"What he needs is a good surgeon and Intensive Care," said Turner.

"Now, now, don't upset him any more than he already is," said Hennie.

"You bastards," gasped Rudy.

"Go on," said Simon. "I want to know."

"I hit him in the Dantian, point number four on the Conception Vessel meridian. If it had been number seven, he'd be dead, but he had that covered with his arms."

"But how does it work?" asked Simon.

"That's like asking how to play a violin concerto," said Turner. "It doesn't matter that all the notes are written down, or that you can read them, or even that you're a good violinist. You have to reach a place where you're not thinking about what you're doing anymore, you're just doing it. Even the Chinese can't explain it in words, it's all metaphor, symbols. You can't learn what you call the internal style directly, that takes you down the vegan route, good for your health but no threat to anyone else's. You have to start with an external style—Hsing-I, you were right. Then you slowly strip away the bits you don't need as you move into combat Tai Chi. You replace strength with energy. Something like that. All that matters is that it's real."

"Handy for a police," said Simon. "No bruises."

"Depends," said Turner. "Rudy's probably bleeding from the kidneys and small intestine. Maybe the spleen. His blood pressure is double what it should be. His heart is skipping beats, his intracranial arteries—"

"Shut him up," said Rudy, his teeth gritted.

"This ride isn't doing him any good, either," added Turner.

Hennie was driving at a steady eighty kmh. Mark Lewis in the Land Rover Discovery was running parallel, clear of their dust. The Land Cruiser was eating the scrubland but the bumps and bounces were constant. The air con was doing its best but due to the missing window the car was stifling. On every side there was nothing to see but pale brown flatness baking in the midday sun.

"Maybe you don't want him to get back alive," said Turner.

"What are you saying?" said Rudy.

"Whatever kind of chain they're making here," said Turner, "you're the weak link."

Hennie looked at him in the rearview mirror. He changed the angle of his head to look at Simon. Neither spoke. Rudy turned his head to glare at Turner with deep hatred.

"They know that better than I do," said Turner. "As you said last night, you know where the bodies are buried."

"You black bastard." Rudy turned to Hennie. "I only said that to set him up for me and Jason."

"Take no notice of him," said Hennie. "He's trying to divide and conquer. We'll have you at the hospital in an hour."

"This is far enough," said Rudy. "He'll never walk out here."

"Another twenty clicks."

"Jessis."

For several minutes the ground got rougher. Rudy moaned and maneuvered in his seat, hoisting his right hip up so he could lay his head against the window.

Turner worked on the rest of his plan. The atrocity. Polishing the details in his mind's eye. It was sound. He had nothing to lose. The Cruiser steadied and the wheels were suddenly running on smooth, perfectly level ground. Hennie picked up speed.

"Salt pan," he said. "The bed of a dry lake. Now we'll rack up some miles."

The pan was a pale reddish brown. A fine spray of particles was sucked in through the open window and drifted back over Turner. In the distance he saw shimmering patches that were snow white. He didn't know if they were pure salt crystals or some mirage effect. They drove on.

Every kilometer was another nail in his coffin. He was waiting for Rudy to make his move. He'd given him enough reason to. Rudy had cleared the way to reach his gun on his right hip. Whatever else he lacked he didn't lack guts. He might try to shoot Turner but the muzzle would have to travel a long way at an awkward angle, and the pain would slow him down. Either Simon or Hennie would stop him well before it got there. Best give him another push. Turner's arms were cramped and aching behind his back. He leaned forward as far as the seat belt would allow. It put his head closer to Rudy, making any angle of attack even more difficult.

"How's an hour from the hospital looking to you now?" he said.

Rudy snatched out his Z-88 with a gasp. Hennie reacted fast. He reached out to grab Rudy's arm but Rudy was ahead of him.

He passed the gun to his left hand and aimed it across his body at Hennie. Simon shoved his gun against the back of Rudy's head. Rudy ignored him.

"I've fired a thousand rounds through this, and the trigger's squeezed as tight as it will go," said Rudy. "So make your mind up, Hennie. Either we stop here or you get a bullet. Or your boy shoots me in the head, and we both get one."

"All right, Rudy. Gently does it." Hennie took his foot off the accelerator. The car slowed. "Simon, put it away." Simon holstered his pistol. "Rudy, ease off that trigger, then I can brake. I told you, he's playing us off against each other. That's how he killed Jason. Don't give him another win."

Rudy relaxed his finger but didn't withdraw it from the trigger guard. Hennie braked softly. He threw Turner a venomous look in the mirror. Mark Lewis drew alongside them in the Discovery. Hennie hit the horn twice. Both vehicles slowed to a halt. Hennie looked at Rudy.

"You stay here. Ten minutes and we'll help you over to Mark's car. Okay?"

Rudy nodded. Hennie reached under the dashboard and triggered the hood catch. Simon unlocked Turner's seat belt. Hennie got out and opened the rear door and dragged him out. Turner stepped onto the pan. The air con had seemed ineffective but the heat now hit him with a force that almost made him stagger. In seconds he felt it rise through the soles of his boots.

"Nice try," said Hennie. "But this is where the road ends."

TWENTY-FIVE

Hennie slammed the door of the Cruiser and walked to the cargo trunk. Turner followed. Simon was already rummaging through Turner's rucksack. The Benelli shotgun was propped against the rear wing.

"Keep your distance," said Hennie. He pointed. "Over there."

Turner retreated three steps and stopped and watched. Simon pulled out one of Turner's spare shirts and removed it from the plastic and the wire hanger. He laid the shirt aside and shoved the bag and the hanger back into the rucksack. He slid Turner's laptop into the rucksack and closed the buckles. Methodical as a bone surgeon. No emotion. No need to show off. Nothing a performance, just tasks to be accomplished as well as they could be done. Not a Hennie. A samurai mentality. Worth twice whatever Margot was paying him.

Mark Lewis walked over from the Discovery. He was young and sullen and afraid. The Discovery was a work vehicle rigged for the environment. Off-road tires. A shovel strapped to the hood. Big plastic jerry cans, red and blue, spare diesel and water, in steel baskets welded to the rear wings. Lewis raised the hood of the Land Cruiser and propped it up. He stepped back from the engine heat, wafting his hand. He was wearing thin canvas work gloves. He did not look happy to be there and avoided looking at Turner, as if the less he knew the better.

Hennie hauled the pack of five two-liter bottles of water from the trunk, still wrapped in plastic. He set them on the ground.

"Hennie," said Mark Lewis. "I can use one of those."

Hennie pulled a bottle free and tossed it to Lewis. Lewis caught it, opened it, and emptied it over the engine bay. Steam billowed from under the hood. Hennie took a second bottle. He unscrewed the cap and smiled at Turner.

"We're forty kilometers from the road, give or take," he said. "To walk that far in these conditions a trained soldier needs to drink eight liters of water to stay on his feet—and that's if something on wheels or four legs carries it for him. That's the science. The military logistics of the Gulf War. You walk, you sweat, you breathe, you dehydrate. Your blood turns to a salty sludge, your brain shrinks to the size of a pickled walnut. Then you die."

Hennie poured a long draft of water down his throat, his Adam's apple bobbing. He gasped with satisfaction.

"Hot enough to brew tea, but it still tastes good."

He emptied the rest of the bottle over his head and shirt and shook the last drops out onto the sand. He threw the empty bottle at Turner's feet.

"That's why urban types like you come to grief in places like this. You don't think to carry enough water for an emergency."

"Hennie?" Simon was shoving Turner's plunder into his pockets. "He's got the keys to two of our cars, two of our phones, and one of our guns in a holster. From the lookouts we sent."

"What did you do to them?" asked Hennie.

"They had to take a sick day," said Turner.

"There's a trumpet in here," said Simon.

Hennie's brows rose and fell. "A man of many talents, eh? I'll pick it up tomorrow. It'll make a nice souvenir."

Simon went to the driver's cab. He came back with the keys and opened the lockbox and slid out the drawer. "I'll lock up the long guns or he'll shoot us while we're driving away."

"Okay, but we leave everything else exactly as it would be if he'd never met us," said Hennie. "We just take the water. We don't want some clever bugger asking, "why is this or that missing from his kit?" It's a simple story. He went for a drive in the desert—tourists do it all the time. It was just his bad luck the most reliable motor ever made broke down on him."

Simon packed the SPAS-12, the R5, the pepper spray and the Kevlar vest and locked the drawer.

"You expect someone, somewhere, to believe I became a tourist in the middle of an investigation?" said Turner. "Before I logged a report?"

Hennie shuffled on the spot. "It'll do."

"It may have worked before to get rid of some local difficulty. It won't work for a Cape Town detective on a case."

"What do you mean, 'before'?"

Turner didn't want to involve Iminathi any more than she already was, but he didn't have to. "It's obvious. Special Forces couldn't invent this plan from scratch in the time you had. Four men and not one of you ask any questions on the way?" Turner nodded at Lewis. "The mechanic cripples a car in the desert like it's all in a day's work? It's a routine. The problem with your simple story is you'd have to be fucking simple to believe it."

Hennie seethed in silence.

"I can tell you a better one," said Turner.

Hennie stared at him through his shades. He struggled with the impulse to tell him to shut his mouth. But he knew he wouldn't, and although Hennie's vanity was excessive, he badly wanted to know what Turner had to say.

"All right, let's hear it."

Turner retreated several more paces, out of earshot of the broken window. Hennie and Simon followed but still kept their distance.

"You've still got your weak link," said Turner. "He's only going to get weaker. Grief, guilt, bitterness. Resentment, envy. Whoever applies the pressure, Rudy's ready to break like a dead twig. Even if he doesn't, he's going to want more status, more money. He's a millstone hanging from your balls."

"I'm not hearing a story I don't know," said Hennie.

"Then you should know this, too, but maybe you haven't had time to think about it. Rudy tried to kill me this morning. You've still got four bodies to prove it—bodies you'll have to make disappear, if your plan's going to work. Somebody hired those corpses. Four local losers didn't wake up today with the bright idea of killing an unknown cop—who'd only been in town twelve hours—all by themselves. That finger points at you, before it points at Rudy. Plus you have to keep their loved ones quiet, if they have any. That's a tall pile of dirt, even for Mokoena. The only place to sweep it is under Margot's carpet. Because Margot's got the only carpet in half a day's drive."

Hennie flinched microscopically. "So what's the improved version?"

"Rudy went after me. Revenge for Jason's death. I wiped out Rudy's murder squad, just the way it happened, but they're not dirt anymore—because Rudy took me prisoner. Five against one, why not? Rudy didn't shoot me on the spot because he had a plan, based on your old routine. Drive me out into the desert. No, make me drive, with a gun to my head. Out to the salt pans where the ground is soft not stony. Rudy needs my car to get back home so he can't fake an accidental death, but he can get some payback if he wants to. Make me dig my own grave. Bury me alive, under the dry lake bed where no one will find me. All he needs is a shovel. Motive, opportunity, means, concealment. And Rudy's prints are in the car. To a murder police, it's the perfect case."

Hennie stood thinking. He looked at Simon. Simon shrugged one brow: not bad.

"What happens next?" said Hennie.

"That's the twist. Rudy doesn't get his payback. I put up a fight, kick him in the gut, maybe hit him with the shovel. We struggle for the gun and I shoot Rudy dead. But it's not my day either. The most reliable motor ever made breaks down on me."

Again, Hennie wordlessly consulted Simon.

"He's right about sweeping up the dirt," said Simon. "And the carpet. And clearing the case. All the dirt becomes evidence—against Rudy. It doesn't need sweeping anywhere. For us it's two birds. Six if you count the losers. Seven if you count Jason. It is better. It's much better. It's clean, it's logical. He's a cop, he knows how cops think. The dead Land Cruiser's a stretch but it always was. That's why I told Mark to come up with something clever."

Hennie took his shades off and squinted at Turner. "Why do us this favor?"

"If it wasn't for Rudy, I wouldn't be here. First, he set me up. Then he cost me twenty minutes."

"Revenge. Didn't Confucius say dig two graves?"

"Mine's already dug."

"You know," said Hennie, "it's a pity you didn't accept Winston's offer to go on the payroll." He glanced at Simon, then back to Turner. "You might have put us both out of work."

"Is the job still open?" said Turner.

Hennie laughed. He held out his hand to Simon and Simon gave him Turner's Glock. Hennie checked the chamber and shoved it in the back of his belt. "Give me his phone, too." Hennie put Turner's phone in his pocket.

Mark Lewis stepped around the engine bay. "Car keys?"

Simon tossed him the keys. Lewis slotted the key into the ignition. The starter motor turned over but the engine wouldn't catch. He tried again with the same result. He left the keys in the car and looked at Hennie, again avoiding Turner.

"That's it," said Lewis. "I've shorted the EFI relay—"

"We don't need to know," said Hennie. He pointed at the three remaining water bottles. "Put them in the Land Rover. And bring me that shovel."

As Lewis picked up the bottles he finally risked a glance at Turner. Behind his shades Lewis was sickened and scared. He carried the bottles to his truck, put them in the trunk and unclipped the shovel from the hood.

"What if you and Rudy shot each other?" said Hennie.

"Hard to believe," said Turner. "Hard to stage. More forensics. More questions. More ways to make the mistakes that will hang you. But if the choice is between a bullet and a pickled walnut, I'll leave it up to you."

Hennie walked over and took the shovel and stuck it in the ground. The blade crunched in to half its length. Lewis got back in behind the wheel. Hennie waved at Simon and they walked to front passenger door of the Land Cruiser. Hennie opened it and looked down at Rudy.

"Let's get you to the hospital. We'll take your weight on each arm. And put that bloody gun away."

Rudy swung his legs out one at a time, grunting with agony. Simon and Hennie took his arms by the elbows and hoisted him upright. Rudy groaned. He was absorbed in his own pain. Hennie took Rudy's phone from his pants and slid it into the left breast pocket of Rudy's shirt.

"What's that for?" said Rudy.

"You'll be more comfortable," said Hennie. "You could do without that gun on your hip, too."

"Don't touch it," growled Rudy.

"Have it your way."

They led Rudy around the front of the Cruiser, Rudy shuffling. Hennie let go of his arm and walked ahead and grabbed the shovel. Simon took a step backward.

For a moment Rudy wobbled, unsupported, bent slightly forward from the waist. Confusion flitted across his features.

Hennie swung the shovel as he turned. He hit Rudy square across the cheekbone. A good clip but not full force. Rudy's head flapped against his shoulder and he fell to his knees and sat back on his heels, his hands groping his thighs for balance. Hennie tossed the shovel to Simon.

"Wipe that down."

Hennie drew Turner's Glock. He bent over and put the muzzle against the phone in Rudy's shirt pocket. Then he shot him in the chest.

Rudy swayed on his knees. His shirt was scorched and smoking over the shattered phone. No blood came from the bullet hole but below the pocket the cotton was rapidly saturated. His mouth drooped open as if he was surprised but at the same time knew that he shouldn't be. He tried to muster a final sneer but fell over sideways, his bloody cheek crunching into the salt. Hennie ejected the magazine, jacked the round from the chamber, and dropped the Glock on the ground. He saw Mark Lewis staring at him through the Discovery's open window.

"Jesus, Hennie, I didn't sign up for this."

"You mean you only signed up for one murder not two?"

Lewis' mouth moved but no words came out.

"You'd better tighten your bollocks, son, before someone cuts them off."

Hennie went to the Land Cruiser and collected the Benelli. He beckoned Turner. As Turner walked over, Simon took Turner's knife from his pocket and opened the blade. Hennie pointed with the gun barrel.

"Kneel."

Turner knelt. The heat of the salt pan seared through the cloth of his pants. Hennie covered him from the side with the shotgun. Simon cut through the tape binding his arms. Turner flexed his joints and fingers. Simon closed the knife and tossed it on the ground.

"Take your shirt off," said Hennie.

Turner unbuttoned his shirt, arms still encased in tubes of duct tape. With difficulty, he stripped the sleeves off. Simon held out his hand and Turner took his shades from the pocket and gave him the shirt. Simon nodded at the tire tracks leading away across the salt pan.

"Are the Discovery's tracks a problem?"

"No," said Hennie. "We're the ones who're going to find him. There'll be tracks and footprints galore. Have we forgotten anything else?"

"The dashcam," said Simon. "I'll install a blank SD card when we come back. That's all."

Simon got in the rear of the Discovery. Hennie backed away, still aiming the shotgun.

"One question," said Turner. "How did you know I was in the bookie's?"

"Work it out for yourself."

Turner stood up and put his shades on. The sun on his skin was fierce. Hennie got in beside Lewis, who started the engine and swung the Discovery in a U-turn. Hennie wound the window down and called out.

"The official advice in these situations is to stay with your car until help arrives."

Hennie laughed. The Discovery plowed away through its own tracks.

Turner watched the vehicle warp into a quavering black phantom, levitating motionless in the haze above the salt pan. It disappeared, then it reappeared, then it disappeared for good. Turner went to the trunk of the Land Cruiser and put the clean shirt on. It would help to retard sweat loss. He found his hat. He picked up the shovel.

They'd left him to die of thirst but they'd left Rudy Britz with him.

Rudy was 60 percent water.

TWENTY-SIX

Margot was in no mood for smiling but she had managed to smile most of her way through lunch with Dirk.

The fake smile was something she'd been forced to master as the company had grown into a powerhouse and she into a part-time politician with it. She had neither sought nor welcomed that role; she had played it solely to become rich and free. She had become only rich. She hadn't expected the chains that came with it.

Looking back, she had been pitifully ignorant, and worse than ignorant, naive. Hennie had been almost as ill-informed as she, but she thanked God for his cynical view of the world as one big no-holds-barred cage fight. It had saved her many times on the learning curve she had climbed. To become rich by ripping minerals out of the earth was to enter politics at its most squalid. Without politics you couldn't pick up a shovel. She had been manipulated, cheated, humiliated, and betrayed on the curve; but that was the curve, and she had learned. She could smile with disarming warmth at people she despised. Somewhere inside she was ashamed to find herself using the same smile on her son, but it was for his own good. It was all for Dirk's good. Including the anxiety now gnawing at her stomach.

She smiled at Lisebo, the housekeeper, as she brought two espressos out to the terrace and set them on the table. "Thank you, Lisebo. Please tell the cook that the lunch was excellent."

The anxiety had risen to the pitch of a panic attack while she'd been in the shower after her tennis with Dirk. She hadn't had an attack in years. The last had been when the town had seemed about to explode with the influx of immigrants and Rudy Britz was firing birdshot at semistarving shanty dwellers more or less every day. The last she remembered previous to that had been the night before her wedding to Willem Le Roux. Three in twenty-odd years seemed reasonable; she was hardly a neurotic.

The attack in the shower had started with a tingling around her lips and the realization that she was breathing too fast. Then her vision had shrunk to a circle surrounded by blackness and pure fear had overwhelmed her. Her legs had given way and she slipped down against the wall, hugging herself under the spray of hot water. The fear was blind, empty of content or object. She felt as if she were going to die but knew she wouldn't. An image of Janet Leigh in *Psycho* popped into her mind and she laughed, and in that instant the panic fled as quickly and mysteriously as it had arrived. She stood up unsteadily and hosed herself with cold water for three minutes. She felt fine, or as fine as she could feel while her husband was out kidnapping and murdering a policeman.

She thought Dirk had enjoyed the tennis and the lunch. She wanted his last days here to be good ones. She dreaded him leaving. He had left before, to go to university in Pretoria, and even though she'd known he would be back soon enough, it had broken her heart. This time he was leaving to start a whole new life.

"What's wrong, Mother?" said Dirk. He was flushed with exercise and youth. So handsome. So gentle. So unlike either his father or herself.

"Nothing's wrong."

"You were off your game today."

"You're sixteen years younger than me, three times as strong, and you're a man. I haven't beaten you in ten years."

"But you usually fight for every point as if your life depended on it. Today you were just letting them go."

"I don't know, maybe it's because I'm sad that you're leaving. This time it feels like you're leaving for good. I know it's wonderful, a new stage in your life, but I'm your mother. I can't help it."

"When I woke up my phone was dead. No coverage. No Wi-Fi."

She felt hurt that he was ignoring her need for a more intimate conversation, but he was a man, a young man, so she wasn't surprised he was more interested in banalities. "There's no Wi-Fi to the whole compound today. All I know is that they're working on it. Ask Simon about your phone."

"I did. He gave me a spare and said it's a problem with the carrier network. He'll get onto it."

"There you are then," she said.

"Don't you think it's a bit weird? My phone and the Wi-Fi?"

"We can survive without Wi-Fi for a few hours. Last year, while you were in the city, thieves stole two kilometers of telephone cable from the poles out on the road, for the copper wire. In the middle of the night. The whole town was cut off for a week. That's why we installed wireless broadband. But it's machinery. All machinery malfunctions. Try raising a ton of manganese from three hundred meters beneath the desert and you'd know that." From Dirk's point of view it had to be weird—and he was right, she'd taken him off the radar—but his whining got on her nerves.

She couldn't help adding, "You can't change a light bulb, so have some patience. Being cut off from your Twitter feed isn't going to kill you."

The ease with which he let these barbs bounce off him gave her pause. Maybe she had thrown too many for too long.

"So what was going on this morning? When I interrupted you?" he said.

"Business."

"You looked like you were planning a bank robbery."

"Dirk, I'm not in court. Stop cross-examining me."

Dirk sipped his espresso. "I'm sorry I was so rude to you yesterday, when we got back."

"It's forgotten. You weren't at your best."

"That's no excuse. I regret it because I meant what I tried to say, I just put it badly, very badly. I don't like the law, I don't like the people, I don't like what it does to the people. They play this giant game with thousands of rules whose ultimate value is supposed to be the truth, but almost everything they do is an attempt to either hide the truth or subvert it if they do find it, which they try their best to avoid. No trick is too dishonest or absurd, as long as it fits the rules, and the rules are designed to encourage that. Of course they are, lawyers designed them."

"The world is the way it is, dear, not the way we want it to be. It's called growing up."

"That's an admission of defeat. That's my point. The partners in Pretoria, my bosses, have won first prize in the lottery of life, at least in theory, but inside they're defeated. Beneath their tans they're gray and shriveled and empty by the time they're forty. They're enslaved to a contest where the one who wins is the one who's best at cheating. Their lives are devoted to lying. Their triumphs are victories for evasion and deceit. You've seen them. All those smiles and handshakes, that's when the guilty go free. The game is so cynical you can't play it without ending up that way, and that's not the way I want to be."

Margot felt uncomfortable. And annoyed. "So what are you saying? That you should have been a doctor?" She realized that a homicide conviction would stop him from pursuing that too. "A sheep farmer?"

"I'd like to give it a couple of years to see if I can find a niche. If not, I want you to take me into the business."

"You think you can do what I've done without lying and cheating?"

"So why don't you sell up?" said Dirk.

"And then what? Drink martinis in the Bahamas or whatever the idle rich are supposed to do? Windsurf? Go shopping? I built this, it's mine. It may be just a stack of money to you. To me it's, I don't know, a dream. My dream."

"You don't trust me to share it."

"Of course you share it, everything I have is yours."

"Then why did you tell Simon to switch my phone off? What don't you want me to know?"

Margot's phone rang. She grabbed it with gratitude. Hennie. Calling to talk about murder. The gulf between her and Dirk and his naive scruples suddenly seemed infinitely wide. And that made it more important than ever that he know nothing of the mendacity and criminality that circled around him even now as he bleated about lawyers and their timid little games.

"Excuse me." She stood up and walked down to the garden and answered. "What news?"

"All manner of madness," said Hennie. "The video's safe, wiped, eradicated. It never left town."

"Our friend from the south?"

"We've got end-to-end encryption on these phones, no need for code—"

"Dirk's nearby."

"Okay. Turner's stranded on the salt pans with nothing to swallow but his own tongue. Rudy Britz is dead."

Margot almost shouted at him but kept the volume down a hiss. "Two dead police? Jesus, have you gone blood simple?"

"Don't lose your grip," said Hennie. "Don't go all Lady Macbeth on me—out, out damned candle and whatnot. It doesn't suit you. If it all goes tits-up you're shielded, but it won't. This is perfect, its foolproof."

His attempts to reassure her seemed only to confirm that she'd lost control of events. "Come home."

"First I need to get Mokoena on the job—he's got bodies to shift. And we need our other new friend from the south to come up here tonight. It'll all be wrapped up by tomorrow."

"How can you be sure?"

"Well, I'll take the Skyhawk up and spot Turner. Official search, so to speak. Maximum effort by the community."

"What if you don't find him?" said Margot.

"Where's he's going to go? He's like a beetle on a tablecloth. No human being could walk out of there without water, not even a Bushman. You walk, you sweat, even at night. It's biology, it's mathematics. If he sits tight he might last two days. If he walks, at best he'll be babbling on his knees by breakfast. A little hand-to-mouth suffocation and it's over. All our ducks will be lined up for Venter and Mokoena. A few rubber stamps and it's done."

"You need to get back here now. I want more details."

"I was going to find Mokoena," said Hennie. "He'll be hiding at home."

"No, I want to be in on that. I'll call Venter."

"I'm on my way. Half an hour."

Margot hung up and returned to Dirk at the table.

"What's Hennie up to?" said Dirk.

"Nothing that concerns you."

Dirk stood up. "I'm going for a drive. Get the smell of horse-shit out of my nostrils."

Margot stood to face him. "Don't you talk to me like that."

"Then don't lie and avoid my questions."

"I don't need to tell you my business. You don't tell me yours."

"I don't have to, you already know it. This place is like a five-star prison. Guards, walls, cameras, electric fences."

"How dare you. Only someone who has never lived in fear would say that."

He knew what she meant. He'd only been a boy and he hadn't seen the corpses of his relatives, but he remembered.

"I'm sorry. I just need to get out for a while. I'm going to see Jason."

"Jason's dead. His place doesn't have a wall."

The color drained from Dirk's face.

"Jason's dead?"

Margot immediately regretted the outburst. "I apologize. I didn't mean to tell you like that."

"Did you mean to tell me at all?"

"Dirk, I know you were close. I was trying to protect your feelings."

"How did it happen? When?"

"This morning. We don't have all the details yet."

"What details do you have?"

"He was shot." Margot floundered under his look. She remembered the four cowboys Rudy had hired. "It's possible it was another farm attack. But we just don't know. In any event, there's nothing you can do. The police are investigating. I want you stay on the property until we know it's safe."

"Until Winston decides what story best suits him." Dirk didn't hide his contempt.

"You're too fond of that high horse, Dirk. When you fall off, it's going to hurt."

She had a sudden urge to tell him everything. That half a dozen people were dead because he was vain and pampered and too weak to hold his liquor like a man. That he was blind to the price that she and others had paid to secure him in his ivory tower. She resisted.

"Winston Mokoena was one of the best detectives in this country—your country—which he has served with courage and honor through its darkest days. He has nothing to prove to me. And nothing to prove to a privileged white boy like you."

Dirk's lips tightened. For a moment he looked far too much like his father.

"I don't want to talk about this anymore," she said. "Just stay here, in 'the prison.' At least it is five-star. God forbid that the great Dirk Le Roux should put up with anything less."

She saw him flinch and crumble. She had beaten him down, as she had so many times before. She was still angry enough not to regret it, yet. He was a disappointment to her. She couldn't hide it from herself, though she spent great energy in denying it. But that was why she couldn't have him follow her into the business like a little duckling, why she had pushed him into the law. He had wanted to study the history of art, for God's sake—what, so he would know which paintings to spend her money on? She needed him to be someone she could be proud of. Someone to worship. As a boy she had worshipped him but as man her emotions just would not blind her that much. She missed having someone to worship. She wanted that back.

"I'm going for a walk," said Dirk. "In the garden."

"Will we see you for dinner?"

Dirk waved vaguely without turning around.

Margot had other things to do. Like keeping him out of court.

If he saw what the law game was like from the wrong side of the witness box, he'd change his tune soon enough. She went into the kitchen and found the secure phone. She called Venter.

"Hello?"

She was amazed by how much stress could be conveyed in a single word. She hoped Captain Venter would hold up. At the moment hopes were the only wings she was flying on.

"You need to be here in Langkopf by breakfast," she said. "Tomorrow's going to be a long day."

"How do I get there?"

"Our regional airport is an hour north. Charter a Cessna, hire a car. And make the trip official, all in the open, no cloak and dagger. One of your officers is missing and you're going to coordinate the search."

"I'll need notification of that from Mokoena."

"You'll have it within the hour."

"Where will I stay?" said Venter.

She understood what he was asking for: an invitation to stay at the compound.

"There's a tolerable three-star hotel in town."

A crestfallen pause. Then, "Dinner?"

"Let me know when you arrive," she said. "I'll send a driver."

"And the fee we discussed?"

"Ready and waiting," said Margot. "As am I."

TWENTY-SEVEN

Iminathi watched the video that Turner had left with her twice.

The second time she stopped it before Jason was killed. She ejected the USB adapter and the SD card and put them both in the watch pocket of her jeans. She sat at the table in Winston's office and stared at the screen saver and thought about Dirk and Turner and her life and what she should do.

She was afraid—of everything. She was afraid for herself. Hennie hadn't realized she had helped Turner, but he had been in a hurry and it might occur to him later. She had witnessed Turner's capture; then, so had others. They really believed the town was theirs to do with as they pleased. They were right. Winston wouldn't let them harm her, she was sure of that, but only if she kept to her place. What if she stepped beyond it? She couldn't take them on alone, could she?

She knew, instinctively, that they had taken Turner to the desert, just as they had taken her father. Tears sprang to her eyes and she cried bitterly, for Turner, for her father, for herself. They would get away with it again. Another good man would die in agony. Their corrupt kingdom would flourish. Could she drive out there and find him? Not in her own car. It was a ten-year-old Polo. She had no friends with a 4×4. Except Winston, who wouldn't let her get involved, and Dirk, and she didn't know if Dirk were friend or foe.

She hadn't done anything wrong, so why did she feel so guilty? Because she had done nothing to avenge her father? Because she had become a tiny cog in the machine that had killed him? Because she remembered the look on Turner's face in the bookmaker's: he believed she had betrayed him. He had advised her to leave, and that had frightened her too. She had come to feel safe here, which made no sense anymore, if it ever had. She was a coward.

Was Dirk a coward, too, or had he simply not found his moment? Could she help him find it? She had loved him. And though she had denied it this past year and a half, she still did. He was funny and gentle and beautiful; the sex had been intense, deep, at times transcendent. Her body had wanted his children, instead she had broken his heart. She still had his bewildered emails and texts. She didn't believe, she had never really believed, the explanations she had invented for herself, that he had been captivated by some liberal fantasy of a beautiful interracial marriage, that the spell wouldn't last, that a man like him would never stand by a woman like her. It was all a justification after the fact. She had never had those fears while they were together.

She had ended their engagement because she was afraid of Margot, afraid of what she would do, not just to her but to Dirk. To make Dirk end it Margot would have had to break his pride, and there was the problem: neither Margot nor Imi had any doubt that she could do it. Why? Why didn't they believe in him? Why did everyone believe only in Margot? It was a power far beyond her money. The money had grown from that power. Turner had defied her power and money both. Now he was roasting alive in the Thirstland.

She called Turner's number. Voice mail replied. She hung up.

She shut down her laptop and put it under her arm. She locked the office and left by the back door and walked home, to the drab and soulless little house that had been the price of her self-respect. She had a shower but didn't feel any cleaner. She stood naked in her living room and looked around at her possessions. They were paltry. The only thing that reflected any pride was her bookshelf. She went to her bedroom and curled up on the pillow and hugged herself. She closed her eyes but didn't sleep. She didn't know how long she lay there.

She sat up. Winston paid her a good wage, and in Langkopf there was nothing to spend it on. She had some money in the bank, enough to tide her over for a few months. She stood up and dressed in the clothes she had taken off. She pulled her wheeled suitcase from on top of the wardrobe, laid it open on the bed, and started to pack. Her degree certificate and papers. The deeds to the house. She paused.

She had a girlfriend in Kimberley, Sizani, who would put her up for a few nights at least. They had done the same degree course, had met at workshops, spent the occasional weekend together. Things would be clearer there. She called Sizani. It was no problem. She could stay as long as she wanted.

An hour later Imi put her suitcase in the trunk of the Polo and took the road north. She'd turn east on the motorway and be there in time for dinner. As soon as the town fell behind her she felt lighter. It wasn't her battle. It was only as the tension started to ease from her stomach, her shoulders, that she realized how frightened she had been. A man with a shotgun had dragged her into the street. She had never been that close to gunfire, she'd never seen a gun fired at all, only heard them at a distance. She was entitled to be shaken up.

Her father's memorial appeared in the distance. She tried to swallow the sudden lump in her throat. She couldn't. She dug her phone out and called Dirk and listened. An automated voice told her the number was no longer in service. She understood at once. They'd cut Dirk off from the outside world. They would never let her through the gates. But she'd tried. What else could she do? As she approached the memorial she slowed down. She might never see it again. She had nothing to come back here for. She could sell the house by internet or phone. She stopped and turned off the engine.

She called Turner's number again. No answer.

She got out of the car. She crouched by the cairn and put her hand on the stones. She had adored her father without ever really knowing him. The man she had known had been too gentle to survive the mines. He had raised her and cared for her, made sure she was as well-schooled as she could be, taught her to love books. He had helped her to go far beyond him. She had a degree. He would have been proud of that. She cried again.

She said, "What would you do, Papa?"

She knew the answer even as she asked it. He had died for such answers. She stood up. She wiped her eyes. A few meters away she saw some loose scrub, recently uprooted. Other of the gray, brittle plants had been crushed to the ground and were trying to spring back up. She walked over and saw the tire tracks. At least two vehicles, clearly. Here and there one set of tracks were blurred or doubled. She followed them back to the road and saw smudges of dust and sand on the edge of the tarmac, where the tires had emerged from the desert and turned onto the road, heading toward Langkopf.

It was already done. Turner was already dying. Slowly.

Imi walked back to her Polo and started the engine. She made a U in the road and drove back the way she had come. She'd make one last try.

The Sharp Edge of the Spear.

TWENTY-EIGHT

Turner dug the first hole in the pan near Rudy's body and left the excavated soil in a single pile to one side. The ground had a thin, brittle crust. Below that it was firm and bone-dry. It crumbled easily, so he wasn't able to square the sides. He made the hole about twenty-five centimeters square and twenty-five deep. He scraped out as much of the base as he could without collapsing the sides. It would do.

He dug a second hole a meter distant.

He collected the two empty water bottles and their caps. He found his Swiss Army knife on the ground where Simon had dropped it and put it in his pocket. He rummaged around in the trunk of the Cruiser among the stuff that had accumulated there and found an empty soda can. He took the three sheaths of clear plastic in which the laundry had packed his shirts. The plastic was thin, but he didn't see why it wouldn't do the job.

He took the plastic sheaths, the can, and one bottle over to the holes. He dug a third hole. With his knife he cut the top off the can and cut the plastic bottle in two through the middle. He wiped sweat from his eyes. He rolled his sleeves up. He looked at Rudy and saw a knife buttoned in a leather holster on his belt. Turner took it and locked it open with his thumb. It was a Gerber with a semiserrated blade in a black, nonreflective finish. The nylon handle had a slight curve, a finger-stop, and seat-belt cutter. A good work tool for a cop or a hunter. Or a butcher.

There was nothing else to delay him. He found it strange that he should hesitate. He had examined hundreds of corpses in every state of mutilation and decomposition. He had witnessed dozens of autopsies. He had shot five men that day. And the water was going to be sucked out of Rudy regardless; Turner was just adding another stage to the cycle of nature, by catching it and pouring it through his own body. So get on with it. Find the iron in your soul. If the iron isn't there, there's nothing left at all. He held the knife between his teeth. Rudy was slumped over on his side. Turner grabbed him by the back of his belt and the collar of his uniform and dragged him headfirst toward the nearest hole.

Rudy uttered a low, rattling groan.

At first Turner thought the movement had compressed the air from his dead lungs. But then Rudy raised his face from the ground and twisted his head and opened his eyes. He took a breath, confused, then saw the hole just in front of him. The sheet of plastic. The halved bottle. He recoiled with the shock of perception.

"Jessis Christ on the cross."

Turner let go of him and straightened up and took the knife from his teeth. Rudy rolled onto his left side and looked up at the knife. He squinted at Turner. Rudy was a man of the desert. His family had struggled against it for generations. He understood what the holes meant. His crimson-flecked lips parted in a smile, as if he were enjoying some final, macabre triumph. As if he could see into Turner's heart. His voice was hoarse; a bubbling sound rose from his pierced lung.

"A fresh kill is even better. The blood will flow more easily."

Turner neither moved nor spoke. He hadn't contemplated cold-blooded murder. The law, whatever form it took, was unequivocal. Rudy was alive, even if his death was certain. The unknown girl had been dying, too, but Dirk had killed her. The health of the victim did not mitigate the crime. You couldn't walk into a cancer ward and shoot someone, even if they begged you to. And this crime would be worse to a wholly other degree. Not a blind accident of timing and folly, but premeditated and in violation of the most basic human values. He was looking at killing a wounded man and drinking his blood.

"What are you waiting for?"

"I'm waiting for you to die."

Rudy uttered a short laugh. "Better sit down, then. Let's see who goes first."

"I told your nephew he was tougher than me. It must run in the family."

"Prove yourself wrong, man, get on with it. You'd be doing me a mercy."

"I'm not a murderer." It felt like a lie the moment he said it.

"Are you trying to kill me with laughter? This wasn't Hennie's idea, or his nigger's. You put this bullet in my chest." Whatever he saw in Turner's face seemed to confirm it for him. "Hats off, my friend. The only law in this land is the law of survival. That's the way God made it. That's why I love it."

Rudy raised his right hand to shade his eyes. He glimpsed the sun.

"You're wasting time, man." He heaved for breath. He coughed blood. "Jessis." He spat out a clot of crimson phlegm. "If you haven't got the stomach, I'll do it myself."

He heaved a few more rattling breaths, steadied himself, sought the last dregs of his strength. He threw his hand at the gun holstered on his hip. His finger clawed for the butt, closed round it. He tried to drag the gun free but his last strength failed him. His arm flopped slack across his chest.

"Help me."

Pity churned with self-disgust in Turner's belly. With admiration, with horror, with fear; with confusion of every kind. And with the diamond-hard clarity of his mind. He was either a hypocrite or a murderer. If he helped Rudy to shoot himself, he was both. There was only one other choice. The only legal choice. No, he would not split hairs with his own conscience. Only one moral choice: hold the man's hand while he died and then sit down and die with him.

He would never get out of this desert without water. He had known that; they had known that. Yes, he had put the bullet in Rudy's chest, and had been pleased with his own ingenuity. It had seemed like pure self-defense. The primal right of any living creature. And so it was, wasn't it? He had made no threat to the lives of any one of them while they had abducted him at gunpoint in order to kill him. If he had somehow managed to shoot all four of them down, he would have been entitled to a righteous pride. And no philosopher of ethics could, or would, have contradicted him. So what was the difference?

His clarity collapsed back into confusion.

No place for philosophers here. His mind was no use to him. Nor was his conscience. If a better man—a weaker man? A stronger man?—would elect to die, then he was not that man. His being demanded life. His being demanded justice. His being demanded truth. His being would not play the role of the fool in someone else's story. He would rather play the monster in his own.

His being said: follow the law of the land.

Turner threw the knife to stick upright in the dirt. He stooped and took the Z-88 from Rudy's holster. He checked the bullet in the chamber and stood over him, casting his shadow across his face. Rudy looked up at him. Turner took his shades off so he could meet his eyes.

"When you take those bastards down, tell them you couldn't have done it without Rudy Britz."

"I will."

Rudy grinned. "Don't waste my brain. It was never much use to me."

Turner said, "I'm going to take everything you've got."

Rudy tried to haul himself the last few inches toward the hole. Turner stooped and grabbed his belt and dragged him. Rudy stared into the pit. For the first time he conveyed a sense of fear, though not of death nor of Turner.

"Into thy hands, dear God, I commend my soul."

Rudy turned his head sideways and nodded.

Turner placed the muzzle and shot him above the ear.

Blood exploded from the skull and he fired again and again, five, six shots through the same expanding hole, varying the angle. He put the gun down and knelt on one knee and lifted Rudy's head by the hair with his left hand. A large segment of skull cracked away, hinged and held in place by the scalp. He stuck his right hand down into the hole and felt for the far side of Rudy's head. A moist sludge was draining from the shattered skull, obstructed by shards of bone attached to rags of skin.

He took deep breaths to fend off rising nausea. He grabbed a handful of the saturated skeins and sharp fragments and ripped them free. His hand came up clutching a fistful of bloody skin and bone and hair. He dropped it into the hole. He reached in and around again and pushed his fingers through the gaping hole in the skull and scraped out tissue and membranes. Thin, tough ropes of artery and vein refused to snap. He felt blood pouring over his hand. He pulled his hand out, bright red to the wrist. He gasped for air. He put two fingers to his neck, felt a trickle of blood. His pulse was over eighty.

He enforced a total coldness on his mind. Do the job, just the job, do it well. No other thoughts. No other feelings. Feel it all later. Plead guilty later. But do it.

He took the knife and repositioned Rudy's head and reached the edge of the blade under to the left angle of Rudy's jaw. He cut deeply, sawing through the muscles, the jugular, the carotid, the windpipe and gullet, the vessels and muscles of the right side, all the way until he felt the edge grind into a vertebra. There was no pressure left in the vascular system but blood still flowed from the gaping stump. Rudy's skull was attached only by the spine. Even now some deep revulsion, some taboo, some last, useless, shred of decency, held Tuner back from cutting his head off. Some voice howled inside him that survival—no, the chance of survival—was not worth the price of his soul. Better to die himself. He heard inchoate grunts issue from his throat, as if it were not he that made them. A cold voice told him that his soul was already pawned, and that he'd never retrieve it. It was too late. The only path was to go on.

With the serrated half of the knife edge he cut through the cartilage between two vertebrae and slashed through the last shreds of muscle and skin and Rudy's head came off in his hand. The neck stump lolled over the hole and continued to exsanguinate. Turner staggered to his feet and carried the head to the second hole and laid it inside to drain. He leaned his hands on his thighs and panted. His shirt and pants were splashed with gore. His shadow lay before him on the compacted salt of millennia, foreshortened, hunched, grotesque. He felt as alone as any man had ever been. A murderer stranded with his prey in the blistering sun, abandoned by even his own humanity. He felt tendrils of madness slither through his mind.

He had planned this for the best part of an hour, ever since Rudy had left his prints on the dashboard of the car and the vision had come to him. The perfect logic. The moral reasoning. Survival. Self-defense against four men bent on murdering him by the same cruel method with which they had murdered at least one other. It was just. It was forgivable. Innocents by the thousand were bombed and slaughtered every week and the killers forgiven; celebrated; decorated. Yet his vision had been the palest fantasy of this reality. And the job was very far from done.

His body rebelled and his stomach contracted. He lurched toward the hole containing Rudy's head and bent over and vomited. Don't waste the vomit. But his stomach was empty. A few threads of bile trickled onto the dead face staring up at him from the hole. He straightened. His mind cleared. The tendrils retreated. He had to get the most out of the body.

He returned to the first hole. The leakage from the stump had waned. The blood was halfway up the depth, soaking in, but that was okay, it wouldn't be wasted. He put down the knife and rolled the body onto its back, the neck still over the hole. He took Rudy's right foot and cranked the leg upright, the boot against his hip, and kneaded the dead muscles of the calf and the thigh. The sensation in his fingers as he massaged the dead flesh disgusted him. He squeezed out perhaps another cup of blood. The veins had one-way valves; the blood wouldn't roll backward. He did the same with the left leg. He straddled the body and knelt on Rudy's belly, another repellent sensation. He raised the dead arms, one by one, and wrung out what drops he could. A constant battle with revulsion, with nausea, with his own degradation. He put his palms on Rudy's chest and with a perverted form of CPR he pumped out some more.

Enough. The blood would be evaporating. He dragged the body to the second hole and positioned the open neck. He returned to the first. It was more than half-full of bright red liquid mixed with bits of tissue, a skin already forming over the surface. He unzipped his pants and pissed into the blood. The urine was already amber. He had already wasted too much sweat. He took the bottom half of the plastic bottle and pushed it into the muck. It bobbed back up. Archimedes' principle. He removed the dripping bottle. Think. Think. It didn't matter what else was in the hole. The heat would evaporate the water regardless.

He set the bottle down and took the knife. He slashed the laces of Rudy's left boot and pulled the boot off. He pulled the sock off, too. He sank the boot into the hole. It sat at an angle. He crammed the bottle into the neck of the boot and propped it upright with the sock and the leather tongue. The blood covered the boot. The open top of the half-bottle was six centimeters below the rim of the hole.

He ejected the magazine from the Z-88. He laid a sheet of plastic across the top of the hole and weighted the four corners to the ground with the gun, the magazine, the knife, and his knee. With great care, he scooped dirt from the pile and heaped it along the four edges of the plastic to create an airtight seal, removing the weights as he came to them. By the time the whole sheet was pinned to the ground by the dirt seal, droplets of water were already forming on the underside of the plastic.

The solar still, or moisture trap, used the same principles of physics as the creation of rain. The sun's energy, shining through the plastic, evaporated any water in the organic material beneath. The vapor rose and condensed back into water on the under surface of the plastic. The water—pure and distilled—would drip down into the container. Turner had seen one built on Mrs. Dandala's TV. She loved reality shows.

The last stage was to create a drip point on the plastic above the open half-bottle. He needed a weight to tent the surface downward. He took one of the bullets and stopped. The nickel and brass was already warm after a few minutes in the sun. He feared that as it got hotter, it would melt through the plastic and destroy the still. Small stones would be best, but he couldn't see any on the pan. It was as smooth as a billiard table. He glanced at Rudy's remaining boot. The sole was black rubber. He could cut chunks off. He took the knife but as soon as he touched the rubber he felt the heat of that, too. He needed something that would heat more slowly.

Over the rim of the second hole he saw the hair on Rudy's head. He pulled the head back out and felt inside. Fragments of bone the size of the top of his thumb were still attached to the scalp. He peeled off two chunks and wiped them clean on the tail of his shirt and returned to the first hole. He placed the white chunk on the plastic right above the mouth of the bottle. It was just heavy enough to depress the thin plastic but he wanted a steeper slope so he added the second chunk on top of the first and pushed gently. The plastic sheet shifted but the seal didn't break. The slope improved. The condensing water rolled down the underside of the plastic to the drip point created by the bone and started to fall, drop by drop, into the bottle.

The first solar still was complete and working.

The concentration had helped clear his mind. His soul had lost and his conscience was silent. Just as well. He took the knife and went to the second hole. He pulled the severed head out and put it in the third hole. He knelt over Rudy's body and ripped his shirt open. The skin of his torso was many shades paler than his face. Turner felt calmer now. Coroners did this every day. One had told him that the word "autopsy" means "see for yourself."

"Let's see," said Turner.

He made the classical *Y*-shaped incision he had seen so many times, from the tip of each shoulder joint to just below the sternum, and from there straight down to the pubic bone. He wrenched the flaps of skin apart and cut them off and threw them in the hole. He sawed through the cartilage connecting the left ribs to the sternum and put the knife down and used both hands to rip the entire rib cage wide open. The joints snapped where the ribs joined the spine. The heart and lungs lay exposed, glistening in the sun, the surface moisture drying away even as he looked at them. He had to hurry. He cut out Rudy's heart and the big vessels going in and out of it. He tossed it into the hole. The lungs were mottled pink and varying shades of gray. He cut each one away from the air tubes connecting them to the trachea and peeled them away from the chest wall and tossed them in the hole. He put the knife down and slid both hands over the surface of the liver and tugged it down. Various vessels and ducts connected it from a central point. He cut them and wrenched the liver free and tossed it in the hole. He checked the hole. It was full of organs up to about a third of the way from the brim. He slashed and stabbed the liver and lungs to liberate as much moisture as possible.

He wiped his hands on his pants, he didn't know why. He had a choice. Aluminum can or half-bottle? The bottle held about three times as much. Was there more water in the organs or the bowels? He didn't know, but the bowels seemed the better bet. He lodged the can amongst the organs, shifting them around until the can was solidly wedged upright in the center. He took the second sheet of plastic and repeated the construction process to make the second still. Plastic, dirt seal, skull bone for a drip point. Again the condensation dappled the lower surface.

By now he was just working. Not thinking. Not feeling.

He removed the head and set it on the ground. He dragged the mutilated corpse over to the third hole. When he had made the vertical arm of the Y incision he had cut too deep and opened the sac containing the entrails. He had expected the smell to be worse than it was but he hadn't yet cut the bowels themselves. The intestines bulged yellow and violet and gray. He rolled the torso on its side by the hole and propped it by bending the legs into a kind of recovery position. He reached into the abdominal cavity with one hand and scrabbled and pulled and a mass of intestines slithered out into the hole. They settled in the bottom, almost filling it. He stabbed and slashed at the morass to ventilate the tubes. He severed the top end of the gut and pulled as much as he could of the rest of it free of the cavity, cutting arteries and ligaments with the knife as necessary. He explored the deep interior with both hands and harvested the kidneys. Then he severed the lower end of the colon. Now the smell hit him hard. But the worst was over.

He dragged the eviscerated corpse to one side and rolled it prone. He considered cutting pieces of muscle. There was water in them. But he'd had all the butchery he could take.

He took the second half of the plastic bottle, the one that narrowed down to the neck and the cap. He seated it steady in the center of the coils, which were already congealing in their leaking fluids into a kind of obscene pudding. He took the last plastic sheet and laid it down; he weighted it; he built the seal with dirt. He broke more bone with the haft of the knife and placed the pieces. He watched the droplets form and roll and drip.

It was done.

He stood back. Three stills. A severed head. A gutted corpse. Patches of blood-slaked sand already baked dry. He'd done what he'd done. He was what he was. Whatever and whoever that was, he did not know. He was drained. He was thirsty. He felt exhausted. He hoped he hadn't spent more sweat than it was worth. The blood holes were crammed with kilograms of flesh. Fifteen at least, maybe more. That had to be worth two liters.

He checked his pulse again. It was fifty.

He was splattered with blood, his arms caked to the elbows in a hardening dark red paste. It clung to his skin with a tightening grip. It revolted him. He dug up two shovels of the salty dirt and used it like water, scouring his hands and forearms.

He repeated the process until he was coated with only a crusty, dry dust, then he took his shirt off and rubbed his arms and hands clean. He dabbed a fingertip on an untouched section of the pan and tasted it. It tasted like sea salt. He recalled that such pans were mined for their salt. Would he need it? Would it poison him? A dead inland sea. Not just salt but the minerals of dead fish, seaweed, other organisms. He didn't know the science. He'd think about it. He collected his Glock and its magazine and the ejected shell. The sun scorched his shoulders and back. He needed shelter from the sun while he waited.

The Land Cruiser cast a narrow shadow to the east, the same side as the blood holes. He had perhaps five hours until sundown. He took a mylar space blanket from the trunk and opened both doors on the driver's side of the car. He draped the blanket between them. Enough shade to squat in. He put another clean shirt on. Pale olive cotton. The clean feeling was good. He opened the lockbox and took out the Kevlar vest. He put the vest on the ground beneath his shelter and sat on it cross-legged. He put his shades on.

He thought about what had brought him here. A girl who meant nothing to anyone but him. Something stubborn in his soul insisted: she deserved justice. She deserved it exactly because thousands like her never got it. That's what she represented, and he represented her.

Turner contemplated the horror he had wrought and asked himself what else he represented.

TWENTY-NINE

Mokoena heard the faint sound of an approaching vehicle and switched off the cricket match with the remote. Pakistan was ahead by a hundred and ten runs in the first innings with three batsmen to spare.

He was glad to be mildly depressed by the match. It distracted him from darker concerns. He had been waiting for Margot or one of her minions to arrive since last he spoke to Turner. Six hours ago. He had not attempted to compute the possible scenarios. They were too numerous and none of them good. He would know the situation when he knew it and would act according to his interests. He retained sufficient memory of his former ideals, like the blurred remnants left upon a palimpsest, to feel mildly depressed at who he had become and what he had made of himself. But that feeling was familiar, and common to any man his age, no matter what their dreams had been.

In the relative silence the note of the engine was that of a small car. Not something the high command would be caught dead in. He rose and walked to the front door and opened it. Iminathi's Volkswagen pulled into the driveway. He walked out to greet her.

The one tender spot that remained in his heart. He hoped she was here on some trivial errand. He hoped that she was not involved in whatever sordid events were currently in motion.

Mokoena's house was a large bungalow in the southern shadow of the long hill. His nearest neighbors were two hundred meters away in any direction and he owned most of the intervening land. He could have aspired to something grander, or more stylish, but had seen no point. It boasted all modern conveniences: it was clean, air-conditioned, and comfortable. He had grown up in a shack made of tin cans. He was more than content with a simple material paradise.

He had lived alone since his wife had died a decade ago, and he had come to like it. He found it a relief not to have to calibrate his emotions to those of another. To eat what and when he wanted. To be undisturbed. He had at last found the time for music and the solitude it required to be known with real intimacy. Pleasures shared were well and good but he had learned that other psyches stood in the way. Over the last two years he had set himself the challenge of forming a relationship with Beethoven's piano sonatas. A lifetime's work, he had soon realized, but better late than never. How could he be free to sob like an abandoned child at the sheer and incomprehensible beauty of the "Waldstein" with another person in the room? At such moments his existence at last seemed justified. His heart was torn apart and at the same time healed by some other rogue heart, beating yet across the centuries and the distance and the worlds that divided them. To feel this was to know that he had not entirely failed, that despite all he was not entirely lost.

He reached Iminathi's window and signaled her to wind it down.

"Put your car in the garage at the back," he said. "I'm expecting other visitors who might not be happy to see you."

Iminathi nodded and restarted the engine. Mokoena went

back inside to the kitchen and switched on the electric kettle. When it was boiled he warmed a teapot and dropped in three tea bags. He preferred PG Tips. He brought the water back to the boil and filled the pot. As Iminathi came in, he put the pot on the table and laid out two cups and saucers. He preferred them to mugs; he liked the thin lip. Iminathi pulled out a chair and sat down.

"Biscuits? Cake?" asked Mokoena. She shook her head. He sat down facing her. "Tell me everything."

He poured the tea. Like him, she took it with milk and two sugars. He listened. She told him everything. She moved him. It wasn't her intention, but she shamed him. When she'd finished, she put Turner's SD card, containing the video of Jason's statement and death, on the table.

"You take it," she said.

"If I take it, I will destroy it."

"Why?"

"Because it can only bring me grief. I've no reason to use it against Margot, though some would. If I show it to Dirk, my relationship with her is over. I like this town. I'm too old to move on and start again. And my loyalty to her is not merely venal. She has been, and I hope she will remain, an overwhelming force for good, in this district and beyond. If she were not hard she would have been crushed. She has risen above more than one tragedy of her own with extraordinary courage. That she hasn't been able to rise above this one is a matter for bitter regret but I won't damn her for it."

"What should I do, Winston?"

"Listen to Turner. At your age you should move on and start again. I'll miss you. But you can count on my most earnest endeavors to help you along any path you choose."

Her eyes filled. He saw her torment but he couldn't offer false comfort.

"What about Turner?" she said.

"What is he to you?"

"He's a good man."

"He's not the first good man to cause chaos."

"That dead girl deserves justice."

"You're a student of realpolitik. A lesser evil is often necessary to serve a greater good."

"There is no greater good in leaving him to die in the desert."

"Turner is not your father," said Mokoena.

"How does that refute my point?" She stared at him with a fire in her eyes. He conceded with a nod. "We could drive out there now and save him," she said. "All we have to do is follow the tracks."

"I told you, I won't betray Margot."

"But you'll betray Turner."

"Very few people are asked to risk something of value for what they believe to be right. Most of those who are asked refuse. Why shouldn't I? Why shouldn't you?"

"If you don't want to come along just let me use your car, I'll go and find him myself."

"When they come here and my car is missing Margot will get the picture like *that*," he snapped his fingers. "If they find you on the desert they will kill you both. That's one murder I wouldn't bury, but even if they know that, I won't put it to the test. I doubt I can bury Turner's murder without Cape Town burying us. This is a war which neither side can win. That's why you and I are going to stay out of it, at least until it's over."

"There's one person who can stop the war right now. And he would, I know he would." Iminathi held the data card in front of Mokoena's face. "Take it to Dirk."

This time there was no mistaking the engine that approached the house. Five supercharged liters. With Hennie at the wheel. Mokoena stood up and took the SD card from Iminathi's fingers. He opened a pedal bin with his foot and threw it in the garbage.

He took his cup and saucer to the sink and rinsed them and put them away. He took hold of Iminathi's arm and she stood up.

"Wait in my study. Keep the door closed. Stay there until I come to get you."

She didn't argue. He was relieved. He knew Iminathi had it in her to go up against Margot. He knew their history. The last time, Iminathi had compromised. Or surrendered. She'd never forgiven either herself or Margot. She'd grown up a lot since then. And now there was more at stake than a marriage. He led her to the study. He saw the look on her face as he reached to close the door.

"Imi, you are right. And the rest of us are wrong. But don't you see? We all know that. It's not about right and wrong. It never was. That's not what matters."

"It matters to Turner."

The front doorbell rang. Mokoena saw the hope die in her eyes. He nodded.

"That's why Turner is a dead man walking."

THIRTY

Turner woke from an uncomfortable doze. He shook off the aftermath of bad dreams and stretched his legs. The shade thrown by the blanket had grown but the heat was intense. He stood up. The atmosphere shimmered at a distance he couldn't guess, like some translucent but impenetrable barrier. The silence was eerie, absolute; the silence that would one day prevail over all things.

His throat felt raw, his tongue heavy. He was more thirsty than he could remember being, even during the forced training marches of his army days. It was a strange feeling, this thirst, this true thirst. He would never use it as a metaphor again. He would not thirst for justice, or vengeance, or love. He had never wanted anything the way he now wanted a glass of water. This desire wasn't confined to his throat, his tongue. His entire body murmured with yearning, a rising cellular desperation, as if his nerves and membranes and tissues, his spinal cord, knew that what was to come would transcend mere pain. Pain could be located; no matter how severe, that at least established some kind of distance. The torment of thirst would saturate his being; he felt its threat. He realized his body was afraid, and with that Turner was afraid, in a way that he had never been afraid before.

He walked over to check on his stills. Three holes in the salt pan, each covered with a clear plastic sheet, each sheet sealed to the ground by a miniature embankment of dirt running along all four edges. He crouched over the middle still, the one with the aluminum can. The plastic sheet was opaque with condensation. He couldn't see through it clearly. He removed the bone fragments weighting the drip point. They were hot but hadn't melted through. The inverted cone held its shape, permanently stretched. Through the gray blur he saw a ripple as a droplet fell onto a liquid surface.

He scraped back the dirt from two adjoining sides of the seal and lifted one triangular half of the plastic sheet. He jerked his face away from the smell. A foul stew of simmering human offal. The solar still was, in effect, a kind of oven. Out here where he stood the temperature was in the low forties. He could have cooked a steak on the roof of the car. Down in the hole, conditions were not dissimilar to those in a microwave. For all he knew that's exactly what it was. He swallowed on the urge to vomit and turned to look.

The organs—liver, lungs, heart—were a mixture of pale browns and grays, shriveled and sweating. The can was not only filled to the brim, it appeared from the water trapped in the creases around its base to have been overflowing for some time. He draped the lifted triangle of plastic across its counterpart and let it lie. He crabbed his fingers and thumb around the can from above and pulled, carefully. It resisted. He broke the grip of the clinging offal with the tips of his fingers and pulled again and the can came free with a sucking sound. A little water spilled over the rim. He lifted it slowly and rose to his feet and carried it away into a patch of clean desert air.

He put his lips to the rim and sipped. It was hot but it was wet. It was water. It didn't taste good but his tongue craved more. He tilted the can and drank in careful swallows until it was empty. He wanted more. He looked at the printing on the can: 330

milliliters. If he remembered correctly, it wasn't the stomach's job to absorb water. Give it a chance.

He looked at the sun in the west. Another couple of hours at least, he thought, though he had never had cause to make such a calculation before. The half-bottles in the other holes were three times as big. They wouldn't be full yet. He went to look. Through the clouded plastic of the first still he could make out the rim of the bottle, and a falling droplet, but no ripples.

He knelt by the second hole and mastered his nausea at the stench. He couldn't afford to vomit now. He slotted the can back into the cylindrical space it had left. He unfolded the triangle of plastic. In patches it was stuck to its opposite, tethered half. A mistake. He should have held it proud and drunk the water right here and replaced the can quickly. He slid his hand between the two halves and feathered the plastic sheets apart, millimeter by millimeter. He felt his own sweat beading on his brow. He flicked his head so that the drops fell into the hole. At last the whole sheet was unfolded. It was stretched and sagging in patches, but the surface was not breached.

He placed the corner of the sheet back against the ground and weighted it with the Z-88. He pulled the edges as taut as he dared, trying to even out the sags as he rebuilt the seal of dirt. The sags persisted. The end result was a poor imitation of its original, flat form. The noxious vapor resumed its condensation, but the sags, though shallow, formed new drip points, away from the mouth of the can, and their drops were wasted. He replaced the shards of bone in their shriveled cone without knowing if they were any longer useful. He wondered if the sweat he had lost to reconstruct the still would be worth its future yield.

He retreated to his patch of shade. His thirst had waned a little. The water from Rudy's liver, heart, and lungs had started to make its way through. The fear lingered. He thought about it. So he would suffer for hours, maybe a day, then he would die. The kind of fate he had glanced at in the paper a thousand times without troubling to read the details. An event of no importance. He could look that in the eye.

He remembered the San Bushman.

Turner would cross the desert, if cross it he could, in the cool of the night. He would walk in darkness. Whether he died in this desert or not, he knew he would walk in darkness for the rest of his life.

THIRTY-ONE

Iminathi was familiar with Winston's house. She had a key. As his assistant she was often sent there on errands official and domestic. To collect files. To deliver his laundry to or from the cleaners. To stock his fridge, to cook his dinner, to let the cleaning lady in on Thursdays. If he wasn't in his office at La Diva he often took paperwork home. He avoided the drab utilitarian confines of the police station as much as possible. So she felt no discomfort in sneaking from his study to eavesdrop on his meeting with Margot and Hennie.

It took place in the living room. No one sat down. The living room had two doors, one from the entrance hallway, and the one at which she listened that opened on the inner corridor to the study, bathroom, and spare bedrooms. Winston had left this door ajar. She was only three steps from the study. The first voice she heard was Winston's.

"The car breakdown is a little convenient. It might raise eyebrows in Cape Town."

She'd been right, about both Turner and her father. A faked breakdown in the desert.

"We've got our own eyebrows in Cape Town," said Hennie. "They'll go up and down on our command."

"That was quick," said Winston.

"You said we couldn't just pick up the phone and buy a captain," said Margot. "But there was nothing to stop the captain calling us."

"Venter?" asked Winston.

"He's on his way," said Margot. "What else do we need?"

"We have corpses to collect at Britz Farm before the vultures make the job more obnoxious," said Winston. "A truck and some trustworthy manpower would help."

"No problem," said Hennie.

"Legally speaking the death of the girl is discrete from today's events," said Winston. "Who killed the girl? Jason killed the girl. The end. I suggest I take witness statements from you and Simon today. We can close that case by tonight and have Venter sprinkle holy water on it when he arrives. Tomorrow your detectives will find Turner and piece together the regrettable case of—let's call it 'Rudy's Revenge'—from the abundant evidence you tell me we will find. I still think it will raise eyebrows other than Venter's, but no one will want to pursue it too far. Rogue cops killing each other leaves a nasty smell. Everyone will be happy to waft it away. The only remaining wild card is Dirk."

"Don't worry about Dirk," said Margot.

"Some media management will be required," said Winston.

"We can control that narrative," said Margot.

"I'd better get to work," said Winston.

Iminathi heard movement toward the far door. The voices retreated.

"I want you to come to dinner tonight," said Margot. "Give me a read on Venter."

"What time?"

"It depends on when he gets here. I'll let you know."

"Will Dirk have to join us?" The question conveyed Winston's doubts as to the wisdom of the idea.

"Perhaps you're right," said Margot. "I'll see what I can do."

"And do us all a favor, Winston. Have a shower and a shave."

Imi heard the front door open and close. She returned to the study, closed the door and sat down. A few moments later Winston appeared and waved his car keys.

"Duty calls," he said. "What are you going to do?"

Imi stood up. They walked to the living room. "I'm going to Kimberley, like I planned."

"Good. Take a few days. Let the dust settle. It always does, no matter how calamitous the storm."

"Thanks for listening to me."

"My pleasure. You are dear to me, Imi. At this point in my life you are the only person to whom I can say that." He smiled his big heart-melting smile. "So I hope you decide to come back—I don't know how I'll function without you—but as I said, if you don't, you can always count on me."

Imi kissed him on the cheek. He laughed and she felt guilty.

"I'll get my car," she said.

She drove out of the garage and found Winston waiting on the driveway in his big black Cherokee, the tinted windows down.

"Call me," he said. He smiled.

Imi waved goodbye and drove off down the road. He followed behind her until they reached the main road at the north edge of town. She turned right and watched in the rearview mirror until she saw the Cherokee turn left and disappear. She drove on for a while. Her heart no longer battled with her head; they were in agreement. It was just that she felt sick with fear. But what was the worst that could happen? Some embarrassment? She performed her second U-turn of the day and headed back to Winston's house.

THIRTY-TWO

Turner practiced his long notes in the twilight until a narrow ribbon of gold separated the sun from the horizon. Playing against the sky, blowing into all that space, gave him a volume he hadn't reached before, even on the mountaintop. He imagined the notes soaring around the desert until the end of time, unheard but freed from the urge to be heard. If he could have frozen the moment and stayed there forever, he would. But the Earth was still moving and he had to rejoin it.

Turner locked his trumpet in its case and put it in the trunk. He emptied his backpack. Every gram of weight would count. He opened the lockbox and stored his laptop inside. He took out the night-vision 2G+ monocular surveillance pack. Simon must have seen it but they weren't worried about him walking out at night; they'd expect to find him dehydrated and collapsed long before he got there. The full pack included a hands-free head mask, a long-range laser illuminator, and additional high-magnification lenses. Tonight all he needed was to see the tire tracks ahead of him, so he took only the basic unit. It weighed three hundred and fifty grams and was the length of his hand. He installed a fresh battery and put the monocular in the rucksack.

Simon had also left the box of oatmeal energy bars. Eating sucked water out of the blood for digestion. They were useless.

Turner stowed his Glock in its hip holster in the mesh pocket on the outside of the rucksack. He added a spare magazine. He took his boots off. Among his clothing was an unworn pair of hiking socks, merino wool and synthetics. He took off the socks he was wearing, checked his toenails, and put on the new ones. He laced his boots snugly. It got cold at night, no humidity, but how cold could it get? He'd be walking. He packed a lightweight hard-shell jacket and the space blanket.

He took a plastic evidence bag and used Rudy's Gerber knife to scrape a small pile of crusted salt into it. It was pale beige. More than he'd need, if he needed it. How would he know? He'd think about it. He emptied his pockets: he'd keep his badge, his wallet, and his house key. He took the medical kit. He packed it all in the side pockets with the Gerber.

There wasn't much in the rucksack. Was it worth carrying? He'd need it for the water. When the water was gone, he could abandon it. In the glove box he found the old car manual and tore off the laminated cardboard cover. He rolled it into a funnel and jammed it into the neck of the second, undamaged, two-liter bottle. He put the bottle cap in his pocket and went to check the output of his stills.

He stripped the plastic sheet from the first hole. Rudy's boot was mortared to the floor of the pit by a cracked, black mass of dried blood. The half-bottle stuck inside the boot was full almost to the brim. He removed the sock and eased back the boot tongue and carefully worked the bottle free. He lifted it out. He drank four swallows. Hot enough to shave with, but pure and good. He poured the rest down the funnel into the spare bottle and went to the third hole.

He took deep breath and held it and stripped off the sheet. A ghastly stench penetrated his nostrils. The entrails had shriveled and contracted into a gray, wrinkled pudding. The half-bottle had tilted as the mass had settled. It was full to the brim and water had spilled out over the lower edge. He worked it loose, rotating it back and forth. He lost a little more water before it came free. He poured it down the funnel and checked the level. He had, he reckoned, about 1.7 liters. It looked like plenty, but the proof of that would come in forty kilometers, if he got that far. He would have about nine hours of darkness. Five kilometers an hour seemed a reasonable pace. The difference between the first five and the last wasn't something he could worry about right now. He screwed the cap back on the bottle.

He opened the last still. The cola can had overflowed again. Turner worked it free. He recalled that it was best to drink before you became too thirsty. He poured the can down his throat and tossed it back amongst the cooked organs. Strangely, in the circumstance, he felt a stab of guilt for littering the wilderness. He recovered the can and threw it in the back of the Cruiser.

He put his bottle of water in the rucksack.

The heat had waned but remained fierce. He looked at the salt pan which had lain pristine and undisturbed for millennia and was now an arena of atrociousness. The decapitated hulk of Rudy's corpse with its one naked foot. The blackened and gaping void between his splayed ribs, the shattered, severed head, the face blistered, wrinkled, and sucked dry by the sun. The reeking holes, the blood-encrusted boot. The diverse stains baked into the surface of the ancient lake bed, as if even time would fail to erase them.

Twilight in Heaven. Sundown in Hell.

Turner took a moment to be there. To know that he was there. This was where his life had brought him. This was where he had somehow brought himself. Despite that he had been driven to this place at gunpoint, it was his own choices—many choices—that had made it happen. It was his place now, his alone. He took its truth into his spirit. It was harsh, it was bitter, but if he did not make that harshness his own, he would not survive.

Turner hoisted the rucksack onto his shoulders and tightened the straps and fastened the hip belt. He walked away from it all and started out across the salt pan without looking back.

THIRTY-THREE

Iminathi sat in the dark in the back seat of Winston's Cherokee and watched the front door of the bungalow, waiting for him to come out. Since turning back she'd waited for hours but it had given her time to get used to what she was doing and convince herself she wasn't insane.

She had left her Polo two kilometers away where she could be sure Winston wouldn't drive past it. After that she jogged back to the house, let herself in, and switched off the alarm. She recovered the data card from the garbage, wiped it clean of the remains of an omelet, and secured it in her watch pocket. She took a long shower and rinsed her hair only with water to be sure she didn't smell of perfume or any other beauty products. She wiped and dried the shower with a used towel from the laundry basket. She dressed in jeans, black sneakers, and a clean black blouse she had brought from her suitcase. She buried her T-shirt in the bottom of the basket. She called Sizani and canceled her trip but promised to see her soon. She set her phone to silent mode. She found Winston's spare car keys in the drawer of his desk.

By the time Winston returned from Britz Farm it was almost

8:00 p.m., and it had just gone dark. When Iminathi heard the Cherokee and saw his headlights coming down the road she reset the alarm and left by the back door. She watched him drive up and park and get out of the car. He wasn't carrying anything. He looked weary. He didn't lock the car so she didn't need the keys. Lights went on. She crept back around the house and stood by the bathroom window until she heard the shower, then she returned to the driveway and opened the rear door of the car.

The dome light came on. The back seat was empty. She sat inside and closed the door and waited for the light to die. The interior smelled of cigars. He was going to dinner. She couldn't think of anything he would need to take with him, no reason to open the rear door or look in the footwell. The front seats were wide and high. The windows were black. She watched the front of the house.

Thirty minutes later Winston reappeared in a dark suit, white shirt, and tie. She tucked herself down into the footwell on her back, her head behind the driver's seat. The door opened, the dome light flared, she felt his weight thump into the seat against her head. The engine started and a Beethoven piano sonata drifted gently from half a dozen speakers. She was on her way. Back to the compound for the first time in eighteen months.

Margot had never approved of her relationship with Dirk. It wasn't just Iminathi's color and lowly origin—she doubted Margot would approve of the Duchess of Cambridge—but her status had marked her as ultimately unacceptable from the start. As long as Margot had been able to frame the affair as no more than Dirk's wild oats, she had put up with it. At moments, at certain dinner parties, she had even been pleased to display her son's girlfriend as proof of the family's liberal values. Imi's appearance had done no harm. She did not consider herself vain—there wasn't much point in a dump like Langkopf and she had always wanted to make her way with her mind—but she knew she was the best-looking woman within a radius of two hundred kilometers. That didn't give her much competition, though Dirk had plenty of more appropriate choices in Pretoria. When Dirk had proposed to her, and told Margot, Imi had changed from a tolerable temporary consort to Margot's worst enemy.

Winston slowed as they approached the main road. Instead of turning right as she expected, toward the compound, he turned left toward town. Why? He was either picking up something from the office or the station, or another passenger. Or passengers. Her stomach cramped with anxiety. She reminded herself: the worst he'll do is send you home. A few moments later the car swung left and stopped. Neither the office nor the station. The hotel? Winston got out and left the engine running and the music playing. She flattened her body against the front seats as best she could.

Winston got back in the car. The front passenger door opened and someone else got in. She couldn't see who but assumed it must be Turner's captain, Eric Venter, whose name had come up over curry and who Margot had been expecting. The door closed and they drove off again.

"Nice car," said Venter. "You should see mine."

He sounded like a man under great stress trying to appear relaxed. Winston's performance was more accomplished.

He laughed softly. "The cost of living is cheap here, even if the cost of dying has risen in the last couple of days."

"I'm surprised a town this size can afford any ranks above sergeant."

"The town can't. The details of that arrangement need not concern you, and it would be impolite of me to pry into the details of yours. That said, I would like to make the nature of our association, and the task we face together, quite clear."

"By all means, do."

"Our primary role in this affair, Captain Venter, is to resolve two major crimes to the satisfaction of our respective public prosecutors. The culpable homicide of a young woman, and the murder of a police officer."

"Then Warrant Turner has been murdered?"

"He is being murdered as we speak. His body will be found in the desert tomorrow morning. Cause of death: dehydration."

"He's dying of thirst?" said Venter.

"Does that disturb you?"

There was a momentary silence, filled by a passage of Beethoven.

"No," said Venter. "I just expected him to die by gunshot."

"You will discover that this scheme is rather more subtle. Ingenious even."

"I'm intrigued."

"Hennie claims the credit. That's the only element I find hard to believe. Not only does the theory fit together like a watch, but all the potentially troublesome parties have removed each other. The tale the dead men will tell is the one we want to hear. All that's required of us is to follow normal investigative procedure and draw the obvious conclusions. We will not find it necessary to fabricate, erase, conceal, or lie, other than by one or two discreet omissions. No one will be able to fault us in either reasoning or technique."

"I'm delighted to hear that."

Iminathi found her body being pushed this way and that by the momentum caused by the curves as the car leaned into them. They were on the private road to the compound.

"Witness statements, time lines, phone records, photos, and much other evidence will prove, emphatically, that, in the first case, Jason Britz killed the girl in Cape Town while drunk in charge of a vehicle. And, in the second case, that Rudy Britz abducted Warrant Turner, with the intent to murder him and bury him in the desert. Turner killed him in self-defense but perished of thirst. All we have do is perform our jobs diligently and make sure that others, particularly in Cape Town, do not perform theirs with excessive zeal."

"Diligence is why I'm here," said Venter.

"Our own statements will be vital to the Turner case. He called me immediately after the death of the suspect Jason Britz and told me that in the course of questioning him, Jason tried to shoot him with a shotgun. Turner was forced to kill Jason in self-defense, confirmed by gun residue on Jason's right hand."

"Yes, Turner called me with the same information." Venter now sounded noticeably more at ease.

"Then our accounts will tally. Jason had injected steroids just before their interview. I logged a supply of the drugs and blood-stained syringe at his farmhouse and identified and photographed a fresh needle puncture in his arm."

"'Roid rage," said Venter. "A perfect explanation for his homicidal impulse when confronted with his guilt for killing the girl."

Winston laughed again. "Nicely put, Captain. I see we have nothing to worry about."

"We'll need statements to back up the Cape Town death, the girl," said Venter.

"I have two, Hendricks and Dube, already typed, printed, witnessed, and signed. You will check them in case you feel they need revisions or addenda before you take them home. I'm curious, and with all due respect to her soul, but this street girl—why didn't you refer it to me in the first place? Why send a warrant officer a thousand kilometers to pursue a drunken driver?"

"I told Turner to pass it on to you," said Venter, "but he knew that Dirk was guilty. And he knew that he was the son of Margot Le Roux."

"Any fool could guess that someone like Margot might hold sway over a tiny rural police force. My question is, why did you let him come here?"

This time Venter laughed. There was no warmth in it, but a certain cynical satisfaction. "It would have been hard to stop him and I had no reason to try. It's taken you and Margot a good deal of trouble to stop him. And you tell me he's not stopped yet."

"I take your point," said Winston. "I found much to admire in the man."

"Turner is the best detective I ever commanded," said Venter. "The colonel would tease him, he'd call him 'the Lion of Nyanga.' Once he sights his prey they're meat. He won't bend the rules of evidence, won't twist the truth in court. His casework is meticulous. Yet Turner is a paradox. He despises the police—our brutality and corruption, our history—yet he is a police. He has a passion for justice. I don't suppose he could satisfy it any other way."

"A revolutionary," said Winston. "A kind of entrist, as Trotsky had it."

"The only thing I know about Trotsky is that he was murdered with an ice pick."

"But you're a detective and Turner's case fascinates you. You must have a theory."

"I did do some research," said Venter. "It was remarkably difficult. Turner reveals nothing of himself and the official records are incomplete. You wouldn't believe how many people just disappeared."

"Oh, yes I would," said Winston.

"As far as I can tell, Turner's older sister was beaten to death with sjamboks by two policemen. Black policemen. During some demonstration. You remember what it was like."

"I remember."

"Turner would have been about nine years old," said Venter. "I've often wondered if he saw it."

"So that's why you've betrayed him. Because he is everything that you are not."

"You know," said Venter, "that's exactly the way I've explained it to myself. Why have you betrayed him?"

"Because I'm old, I fear for my comfort, and I lack the courage to be a better man. Once again Margot has managed to assemble the perfect team to serve her will."

Neither man spoke again for some time. Iminathi blinked tears from her eyes.

The car slowed down. Winston said, "Here we are."

"I'm impressed."

"You're meant to be. Unless they bring it up there is no need to discuss our duties over dinner. Indeed, it would discourteous. We have nothing to tell them that they don't already know. They haven't invited us out of kindness but to seal the Devil's bargain with an illusion of charm and a benign display of power."

"I understand."

They stopped briefly at the gatehouse and drove on toward the house.

"If Dirk Le Roux should join us," said Winston, "it's imperative that he learn nothing from us about either case."

"I understand that, too."

"He is completely ignorant of the accident and the girl's death. He has no idea it occurred. It must remain that way. He is aware that Jason is dead, but not why. Margot told him it was a farm attack, but I can handle that subject, should it arise. You, obviously, have no reason to know anything about it."

"And if Dirk asks why I'm here?" said Venter.

"We're old friends, aren't we? Between us we share seventy years of law enforcement, through historic and turbulent times. This little reunion of ours was planned two weeks ago, when you knew you would be passing through Langkopf. You can spin that, can't you?"

"It will be a pleasure."

"Dirk will be gone in a couple of days, then we can all get on with our lives."

"You give a good briefing," said Venter. "I appreciate it. I flew up here without knowing what to expect."

"Our work will be a walk in the park. The biggest challenge will be enjoying this dinner. Avoid politics, praise the food, admire the decor, and invite Hennie to pontificate about sports. He is a marvelous pontificator."

Winston stopped and switched the engine off. He and Venter got out and closed their doors. Iminathi waited for the dome light to go out and scrambled up and sat on the seat. She knew there were cameras around the house. She didn't know how closely they were monitored. She had decided against trying to evade them; if she was seen sneaking around, they'd flag her. Through the tinted glass she saw Hennie greet the guests at the front door. All three went inside. Iminathi opened the car door and stepped out.

A red Range Rover was parked parallel with the Cherokee. She walked across the gravel toward it and stooped in front of the wing mirror and did a pantomime of checking her makeup and hair. An intruder wouldn't do such a thing. If a guard was watching her, she hoped he would assume she was one of the invited party, that he'd be reluctant to disturb the house with a false alarm. She certainly didn't look dangerous. She straightened and continued to the front door, then turned and walked over to the decking that led to the terrace and the kitchen at the side.

If she could just find Dirk, she could shout out enough of what she knew before anyone could stop her. Dirk and Winston wouldn't let any harm come to her. If Dirk wanted to join their plan to leave Turner to die, then at least she'd done the right thing. She'd tried. She could leave all this behind with a clear conscience.

On the terrace a candlelit table was set for five diners. Iminathi walked through the open glass door into the kitchen just as Lisebo entered from the corridor with a vase of flowers. The cook was bent over the oven. Lisebo looked at Imi, her surprise almost imperceptible. Like all veteran domestic servants, Lisebo was expert at concealing her emotions while on the job. Iminathi gave her a bright, warm smile.

"Good evening, Lisebo. How are you?"

"Miss Imi, I'm well, thank you."

"Where's Dirk?"

"I'm not sure. Probably in his room."

"Is he coming down for dinner?"

"No, I'll take a plate upstairs to him. Should I bring two?"

"No, thanks, Lisebo. We don't want Mrs. Le Roux to know I'm here. Is that okay with you?"

Iminathi was counting on her to want to avoid embroilment in family politics.

Lisebo considered her. "Mr. Dirk's business is his own. If you'd passed through two minutes since, I wouldn't have seen you."

"Then that's when I passed through."

Iminathi smiled her gratitude. She slipped out of the kitchen into the short corridor that led to the back stairs. She ran up the teak steps lightly, silently. She walked along the landing. She heard Hennie's laugh float up the main staircase at the far end. She reached Dirk's door and opened it and walked right in.

The room was as she remembered it. Full height glass doors formed the corner angle of the house and opened onto a broad double balcony. The walls were lined with white silk, the ceiling with gilded paper. Oak floors, some rugs, a huge teak bed with Frette linens and a Schnabel framed above it, his twenty-first birthday present. A vintage sofa in green leather. Dirk was sitting at a table on the balcony with a bottle of whiskey. He hadn't heard her come in. Imi waded forward through a flood of mixed emotions and stopped short of the door.

"Dirk?"

He turned and stared at her. For an instant she saw the sadness that has preoccupied him. Then his eyes shone and he stood up and smiled with an amazed joy.

"Imi. My God."

She opened her arms and he embraced her and with her head against his chest she felt she was back in the safest place she had ever known. She turned her face up to his and they kissed. The raw lust that had never waned between them overwhelmed her and she stood back and pulled her blouse over her head.

Within seconds they were naked on the bed. The universe seemed to shrink until it contained only their flesh, their desperation to connect. The dead were forgotten, the dying too, and the murderers plotting down below. The world beyond the room seemed a sick and toxic dream to be abandoned forever. Inside the room was the only world that existed, the world of skin, muscle, lips, tongue, and sensation so deep it was painful. Where the love that had never died could be reaffirmed. She had read that love and lust were somehow separate, that one could be trusted and one not. She didn't believe it. The core of her feeling for Dirk was physical, innate, even savage, and if this wasn't love and it wasn't to be trusted then what could she trust in herself?

Food was left outside their door and Dirk brought it in and turned the key. The ate as they had made love, like young animals. They laughed. They spoke little and when they did it was not of life outside these walls, or of the past or the future, but of the now that had no end. They swarmed on each other, their eyes locked together, and they fucked again. When Margot knocked at the door, Imi felt no fear and she saw no fear in Dirk either. He simply said, "Go away." And Margot went. They turned out the lights and made love in the dark, stretching out the pleasure until their bodies were spent. They lay beneath the sheets and they were happy.

Midnight came and Dirk slept. Iminathi spooned against him, her arm around his waist. She heard a car drive away and a door close. Silence fell. She and Dirk had achieved something of beauty, yet for all her contentment she didn't sleep. Slowly, that other world crept back toward her from the night. Somewhere in all that night, a good man was alone and fighting for his life. She had to wake Dirk and tell him. She had to help Turner. She would. That was why she was here. Just a few more minutes of skin. Just a little more love.

THIRTY-FOUR

Turner sprinkled a pinch of salt on his tongue. He reasoned that if it was harmful, it wouldn't be enough to bring him down. If he was going to go down, that was already written. But if it did him some good, it might just keep him alive. He swallowed. The taste was sharp and tangy and his mouth filled with saliva. He swallowed again. Some animal knowledge in his nerves, his body, seemed to approve.

He raised his plastic bottle to the light of the half-moon. There were four fingers of water left in the bottle. He unscrewed the cap and put the neck to his mouth. The water was cool now. He drained it all. A brief, exquisite pleasure, then it was gone. He studied the bottle. To fill it he had stripped himself of every last vestige of his humanity. Now it was empty.

He was sitting cross-legged on the sand by a patch of scrub. He looked at his watch. It was 11:58. He had been walking for almost six hours. He had rested for five minutes in every hour. He was tired and hungry, and still thirsty. His feet were fine, no blisters. His ankles and knees ached. He didn't know how far he had come. He had reckoned on five kilometers an hour but doubted he had made that. He hadn't pushed himself too hard. He had tried to harmonize his movements with the qi energy of the desert. Earth and fire.

The salt pan had resisted long, fast strides. His heels sank too deep beneath the crust and dragged as he lifted them out. It was a tiny drain, imperceptible over a few paces but after a thousand it took its toll. He learned to take shorter, lighter steps, his feet parallel as if on rails, the way his Chinese sifu walked. His pace had slowed but he felt the energy saved was worth the time. Time, distance, speed, energy, hydration. Too fast would cost him in sweat and fatigue; too slow would cost him in distance and time. There had to be an optimal balance but there were too many variables to calculate. He had to go with instinct.

For the last three hours he'd been on rock, sand, and scrub desert. The ground was much firmer but brought different problems. Even small stones constantly turned his feet this way and that, microstumbles, each tiny correction wasting energy, straining ligaments, wearing him down. He came to feel the power of the desert lay in its slowness. It was a terrain that in its essence consumed vast quantities of time. It had been forged out of countless millennia and it still contained them. Nothing marked the passage of time, nothing came and went. No trees grew taller and no trees fell, nor flower nor blade of grass; no glaciers moved, no streams flowed, no species flourished and died. Everything that could go had long ago gone and nothing would be coming back. Motion had been exiled to the outer fringes of measurement. A scrawny gray shrub that struggled its way to ankle height and then died was speed's greatest triumph here. If he battled against the slowness it would crush him.

He decided to abandon the rucksack. He took his gun and clipped the holster on his hip. He clipped the Gerber knife to his belt. He put his badge in his pocket, with some paper money and a credit card. He kept his hat on. He put the monocular to his eye. The tire tracks were still there. Navigation at least was no real problem. On the rocky ground any one track was inconstant, disappearing for tens of meters at a stretch, but there were four of them. The black-and-green image always revealed some unnatural imperfection in the dust or the scrub. He would pick a mark fifty meters away and lower the monocular and walk blind toward it, then he would spot the next.

Turner dropped the rucksack and walked on.

His destination at any given moment shrank to the next mark. He didn't think about the road. He didn't think about kilometers. Keep the target small and slow, grind it down, turn the mountain into dust, the sea into sand. He felt more vulnerable without the rucksack, more naked, but that was just his mind. His body felt more free. Walk, spot, walk, spot. Do it again. The tedium was immense but he set it as his purpose. If he let the tedium chafe him it would burn him out. Resentment, boredom, impatience, desire, hope, all these would sap him, one molecule at a time. He surrendered his spirit to bleak and mindless repetition. He embraced the nature of slow.

He didn't think. Thinking used energy, psychological and real. Beyond the next step, the next mark, there was nothing to usefully think about. The only subjects he might consider were grim: the blood and death that lay behind him, the blood and death that lay ahead. He did not conjure memories or fantasies. Whether they evoked pleasure or regret, anger or sadness, they too would weaken him, because they were not of this slow dry world, this world that had destroyed everything upon it except dust and rock and the barest of skeletal plants, a world that had defined itself by killing anything that moved. He found no beauty here. He did not look for it. Beauty too could only weaken him.

It was Tuesday. Five hours until daylight, when conditions could only get worse. Don't think about it. Don't think at all. He stopped and raised the monocular and scanned the ugly green blur for the tracks and his next mark. There it was.

Turner lowered the monocular and walked on.

PART THREE: TUESDAY

RIDE IT TILL IT CRASHES

THIRTY-FIVE

They awoke just after six and before their dreams had faded they made love again with the same primal appetite that had consumed them the night before. Afterward, Iminathi sat up and hugged her knees, hid her face between her arms. She was afraid. For a few hours she felt she had had everything she wanted or needed. Now, in the daylight, she was going to lose it all.

"I'm going to Pretoria tomorrow," said Dirk. "Will you come with me?"

"I'd love to." She didn't raise her head.

"Imi, what's wrong?"

She got up and went to the bathroom and locked the door. She showered quickly and wrapped herself in a towel. She looked at herself in the mirror. Dirk had changed since she'd last seen him. Not in any radical sense, yet he seemed stronger, more comfortable with himself. Maybe because he was now an advocate. If she kept the secret she held—if she joined with Margot in protecting Dirk from the truth—there was a chance they could be together again, out of Margot's reach. She would not let Margot intimidate and manipulate her again. She would call her bluff. But then the secret and all it represented—cowardice, greed, and murder for greed and more—would sooner or later poison the love she felt. She felt that poison already. But if she told Dirk that he was a killer, that his mother was a killer, she took the risk of losing Dirk forever right there and then.

She went back into the bedroom.

"Let me take a leak," said Dirk.

While he was in the bathroom Imi dug the microSD card and adapter from her jeans. Dirk's laptop sat on the sofa, its screen dark. She hit the space key and it asked for a password. Dirk reappeared with a towel wrapped around his waist.

"What's your password?"

"I haven't changed it," said Dirk.

She typed it in. It pleased him that she remembered. She inserted the data card. She stood up to face him.

"I didn't come here last night to fall in love again."

"I never stopped being in love with you."

"Neither did I."

He blinked, puzzled, and started to form a question. "Then why—"

"That story can wait. I've something else to tell you. Something I have to show you. It's difficult and painful and shocking. It may change the way you feel about me. But you have the right to know. I believe you would want to know. Others have kept it from you. People have died to keep it from you. But I can't, because I love you."

"What are you talking about?"

She crouched before the computer and opened the file and clicked play. Dirk watched over her shoulder. The first few seconds of an unsteady shot of Jason's farmyard and house appeared. She paused the film. She didn't have the courage to look at Dirk. She didn't know what she would see.

"That's Jason's farm," he said. He noted the time and date frozen on the image. "Yesterday morning?" There was a sudden authority in his voice. His lawyer's voice. "This is a dashcam video. How did you get it?"

"It's brutal. It's sad. It's horrifying, even for me. I can't watch it with you. You need to watch it alone."

Dirk's face filled with questions and forebodings.

Imi knew that he knew that Jason was dead. Violently, unnaturally, unexpectedly, and needlessly dead. She knew—she had known, she had felt; she had embraced, in the hope of healing with love the wound—that Dirk's grief had been an element in the intensity of the sexual passion into which he and she had plunged. She had shared, to heal herself too, in that element. When death is shoved into your face—with killings and terror and shotgun blasts—the only intelligent response, primitive though it may be, is the fundamental affirmation of life.

She saw Dirk's confusion, his dread. What he was about to discover was worse than anything he could imagine. The remorseless logic of reality could not be refuted. His best friend was dead and the nameless girl was dead, because Dirk had drunk too much peach brandy, in the wrong place by meters and at the wrong time by seconds.

Her heart clenched. She was inflicting this torment on him; no one else. She suddenly understood why Margot would go so far to spare him. She was afraid of the guilt and rage to which he was entitled. She was even more afraid that he would see, and take, the way out that Margot had created. How could he not see it?

Dirk was the key, the center. He always had been, even if he hadn't known it. Dirk and the nameless girl. They had all realized that long before Imi had. Jason, Hennie, Winston, Margot, Simon, Rudy, Venter. And most of all Turner, who had chosen the risk of death over profit. Now six men had died. The Britzes, who had worked this land for a hundred and thirty years, had been eradicated. Turner himself was dying.

Now it was out of their hands, all of them. Hers too. It was in Dirk's hands, where it has always belonged. She had put it there. Nothing more she could do or say.

"I'll wait for you on the balcony."

Imi slid the glass door open and stepped outside and closed the door again. She sat with her back to the room. She looked out over the grounds and tried not to think. The grounds were beautiful, a miracle in a land without water. With that she thought of Turner.

She believed he was still alive. There was still time if Dirk would help her. Even so, she was ashamed she had lacked the courage to show the film to him last night as she'd planned. She was still stunned inside by the intensity of what had occurred between them. *That* she hadn't planned or expected. It had rolled over her in a tide of pure compulsion that emanated from all she was, body and soul. She had felt the same from Dirk. But civilization was the history of successfully quelling such moments.

She had quelled them herself, betrayed herself for the cheap little company house with which Margot had bought her off. She had never given Dirk the chance to stand up to Margot. She'd ended the relationship as Margot wanted without telling Dirk why. She'd had more faith in the mother than she'd had in the son. The man she loved.

Perhaps, if she had believed in him, in his love, in her own right to be so loved, in her own worth, then the unknown girl would still be alive, and Turner would never have come here. She had gone down on her knees before the power and locked the collar around her neck with her own hands. She could have left this town any time. That had been obvious to Turner. She had heard his advice as something like a fantasy. She had been as wrong as anyone else. If Dirk wouldn't now join her to save Turner's life, her heart would break. But she would have no right to judge him.

She tried to wipe her mind clear. In a few minutes she would need to be clear. She focused on the landscape, as perfectly demarcated from the world around it as the Garden of Eden. The flower beds and lawns, the arboretum and pools, represented an extravagant feat of engineering, and more than that, a not entirely balanced mind.

The thing that had always fascinated her about Margot's glorious compound was that no one would ever want to buy it for more than a fraction of what it had cost. No one with that kind of money would dream of relocating to a shabby little sheep and mining town, two hours by plane from the nearest decent restaurant and where even thorn trees struggled to grow. That must have been obvious from the moment this folly was conceived, even to Margot. Above all to Margot. But she hadn't built it to sell it. She had built it to live in, here, on her land. The land where she had struggled to grow and had flourished beyond anyone's wildest imaginings except, perhaps, her own. Better to reign in Hell than go to cocktail parties in Heaven.

Many times before, Iminathi had felt these contradictory feelings for this strange, tormented, and extraordinary woman who had built this absurd, heroic garden, along with so much else, in the middle of a wasteland. Imi feared her and hated her; she pitied her; she admired her. She was inspired by her. What would Imi have built with the tools Margot had started with? In a culture as brutalizing to a sheep farmer's wife as it was to almost everyone else?

Imi shivered as she realized, for the first time, that she loved Margot. Why couldn't Margot love her? Why couldn't they—why shouldn't they—build a beautiful and remarkable and inspiring family together? Here, in the heart of the Thirstland. Who else could? The Duchess of Cambridge? Some pretty young thing from Pretoria? Imi knew how to live and love and be in this land. She ran in the desert. She had educated her mind. She had observed the workings of its people from Winston's inmost cave. Her father, as he had told her, had dug a shaft inside it so deep it would bury the tallest building in Africa. She and Dirk and Margot could build that family, and all the others would follow them.

Imi held her breath, captivated by her vision. Then she saw Margot's face in her mind, her tragic and human limitations, the crippling emotional blocks that life had installed within her as deeply as she and Imi's father had dug their great shaft into the Thirstland. The vision vanished like a half-remembered dream.

Dirk slid the glass door open.

His face was drawn and pale. Grief and horror and guilt competed with his need to think. He had just learned that he had killed a young woman, on the word of his best friend. Imi had never warmed to Jason—he was pathetic and racist; stranded and alone—but she had respected Dirk's easy—natural, inevitable—affection and loyalty toward him. Jason was dirt. The same dirt Margot was risen from, which was why Margot had despised him. Dirk could easily have abandoned him, but he never did. He had followed his heart. And he had just watched that friend die, his enormous, muscle-armored body reduced to meat by the man she wanted Dirk to save.

"How long have you known that I killed the girl?"

"Since Sunday night, when Turner explained it to Winston."

"Why didn't you call me?"

"It was police business—"

"It was my business, Imi." His muscles were tight with contained anger. His eyes were cold. "I had a right to know."

"I tried to call you yesterday when I realized what was going on. Your phone wasn't working."

"I'm sorry, I'm not blaming you. I'm not angry with you." He turned away. "Everyone knew about this but me."

It seemed like a question. "Yes."

"They kept me cooped up like a chicken and fed me a pack of lies. The Wi-Fi, my phone, the farm attack. All the people I trusted most." He turned back. "That's how much they respect me."

"I don't think that's the way your mother sees it."

"Oh, please. There is no other way to see it. I can't blame them, either. If that is the way they see me, whose fault can it be but mine?" His mouth twisted. "'If Margot told him to cut his own ears off, he'd ask her to pass him a knife.' Jesus. A stranger comes to town and within hours he's learned that that's my reputation." He swallowed the sour taste in his mouth. "Well that's going to change."

He walked back into the bedroom toward the enormous walk-in wardrobe. Iminathi followed him.

"I want to see Warrant Officer Turner right now. Then I'll deal with the others."

"Turner's stranded in the desert."

Dirk stopped. "What?"

"Hennie and Simon captured him yesterday, I saw it. They drove him into the desert in his own car and faked a breakdown. He's going to die there, unless someone gets him out."

"They must be out of their minds."

"No, the opposite," said Imi. "This has escalated far beyond you and the girl. Rudy Britz is dead—"

"How?"

"Winston said Turner killed him, but it sounded like it wasn't true. They plan to finish Turner off today and blame it all on Rudy. They've already got a captain here from Cape

Town, Eric Venter, to oversee the cover-up. Winston said it fits together like a watch."

"And I was supposed to leave tomorrow without knowing a thing."

"You could still leave tomorrow."

"Imi, I can't stand by while a man is murdered in my name. I've already got two deaths on my conscience, and one was my friend. If I let them get away with it they'll have their fingers around my throat for the rest of my life. I'll be one of them. The gates of this prison will never open again. How long has Turner been out there?"

"Since early yesterday afternoon."

"Then he should be alive, unless he's walked himself to death. If he survives, Hennie and Simon are looking at life sentences, so they're not going to let us drive out of the gate, not until they've done what they need to do."

"Can they stop you?"

"Of course they can stop me. All they have to do is take the car keys. The reckoning with my mother will come but I don't want that now. By the time it was over Simon would be shoving Turner's face into the sand. And once Turner's dead, there's only your word against theirs. With two police captains on board, they're not going to be too worried about that."

"Winston wouldn't let them harm me."

"They wouldn't have to. If Mokoena says the plan's built like a watch then all the evidence will be in their favor. No one will corroborate your testimony and many will contradict it. There'll just be you, sitting in the witness box, face-to-face with the best lawyers Margot's money can buy, while you try to impugn two veteran officers. It's a fantasy. No prosecutor is going to waste millions on a case she can't win based entirely on your word, and without the support of her own police. Your evidence is worthless."

"Okay, I get it."

"But if Turner survives, they're doomed."

"So how can we help him?" She watched him thinking.

Dirk went into the wardrobe and came out with a sports bag and two rackets.

"We're going to play tennis."

THIRTY-SIX

Turner's right heel landed on a stone no bigger than a matchbox and before he knew it his face had raised a small cloud of sun-bleached dust as he hit the ground.

He had negotiated thousands of such stones. He had corrected a hundred such stumbles. Each had taken something out him that could not be replaced; not here. Again his ankle tipped over and his body lurched and he tried to lower and center his weight to correct his balance. This time his muscles failed him, along with his nerves, his joints, his eyesight, his strength. He didn't even manage to throw out a hand or roll to land on his shoulder. He just went down. He lay there and searched for the will to seek the energy that would get him back up.

Some detached pocket of his mind, his last reserve of Zen, observed with fascination. His will had vanished, all of it: conscious, unconscious, instinctive, reflexive. If he had fallen over a day ago, he would have been back on his feet before he'd decided to do it. No input from his mind would have been necessary; his body would have taken care of it. Now he couldn't feel a single cell that was willing to make the effort to stay alive. They were all of them, in their billions, content to ebb away into the void. And his mind was content to join them. An immense sense of relief filled his awareness. A sense of pure freedom. The crippling burden of existence was about to be lifted from his back.

He didn't know what time it was. He had thrown his watch away, along with the monocular, to save the weight. If he could have looked at it, whatever it would have told him would have had no meaning. Desert time had absorbed him. Slowness had absorbed his vain and grandiose odyssey as easily as the sand a drop of rain. He had been walking in sunlight for an eternity that might have translated, in the illusion of his former world, into two or three hours. He was long past the sensation of thirst; his system had burnt out the means to register it. While it had lasted, while it had risen and spread and intensified, thirst had gnawed its way from the familiar—tongue gritty, lips dry; a cold beer would be nice; it's getting difficult to swallow on nothing—to the inmost core of his sanity.

Mad with thirst. An ancient expression. No thousand words could better it. For nothing could begin to capture the raving, silent, relentless invasion not simply of his brain or his mind but of every particle of being by absolute want. A craving that rendered all previous concepts of desire null and void. Nothing so simple and clear as pain. The ache in his kidneys, the throb of his shrinking eyeballs, the constant oscillation of shards of broken glass in his gullet and throat, these came to seem as welcome distractions, then they no longer distracted. During one long trek, slogging from one mark in the dust to the next, he had dwelt upon the millions of creatures who had trodden this path before him; who were treading it now. Crying babies at the shriveled breast. Animals panting their last in the dry creek bed. Migrants who never reached a place to call home. Then with time, with the accumulation of the tiny distances he stole with each step, he stumbled beyond thirst, beyond the capacity to know it, into a slow descent that left his awareness of self behind. He lost his perception of "I." He became a walking no one.

He lay now on the desert floor and knew he was no more than a part of it. He accepted the rightness of this communion with rock and sand, with millennia, with slowness, with time. His muscles twitched and cramped, tensing randomly against another. His joints were loose, rickety; his teeth; he could feel the gaps between the lumps of cartilage in his sternum move as he breathed. His skin felt baggy, like a suit several sizes too big. He would have thought that his body would have stiffened, tightened, as it dried out, but the reverse was the case. All its pieces were shriveling into themselves, separating, leaving gaps. He felt like a sack of unrelated parts. For this he had killed and eviscerated a fellow man.

But that didn't matter now. Nothing did. He had the privilege of meeting death as a vessel of pure being, emptied of all feelings, all fears, all needs. He no longer even felt thirsty, even that vast and all-consuming desire absorbed into zero. Floating in this zero, he had a dream. Or memory that seemed like a dream. Or maybe a hallucination, played out in fragments behind his scorching eyelids.

A ghetto street and a gang of boys in rags and tags, thirty or so, banging sticks on cans, summoning the spirits of the warriors of old. Kicking a football between them. Their march had started on the wasteland they used as a soccer pitch; he didn't know why then, he didn't know now. A boys' game. An adventure. Make some noise, let the world know they existed. Chanting slogans of freedom they hardly understood. The only place they were going was back to the pitch for another game. They weren't angry, they were exuberant. It felt good to say fuck you, even if no one was listening.

But they were listening.

Two Casspirs arrived as if from nowhere, blocking either end of the street. Enormous riot-control vehicles, armored, grilled, and notorious. The cops poured out and the boys fled through the dust and the sjamboks hummed and cracked on flesh. The game had just become thrilling. As he lay now, prostrated on the burning rock, his spent nerves tingled still to recall the excitement. For a moment they were no more a carefree rabble, they were heroes. What stories they would tell.

Thandi should have stayed in the cash store where she worked. He didn't need her, not to get away from the kwela-kwela, even if he needed her for almost everything else. He had never known his parents; she had. Same mother, different fathers. Thandi was ten years older than him, and for as far as he remembered she had raised him. When she ran out into the street shouting his name, the adventure ended and he was no more a warrior. Two cops slashed her legs from under her and as she went down he saw the plastic whip lash her full force across the throat.

He didn't stop running.

After the street was cleared, he crept back. Thandi still lay in the dirt, cops standing over her in attitudes of mild annoyance. A young white officer crouched to feel the pulse in her swollen neck. He shook his head and stood up and gave an order, and they picked her up and threw her in the back of the truck.

Turner never saw or heard of her again.

Now he groaned on the burning cap rock. The memory was not new to him. But this detail was: the young white policeman in the street turned and looked straight at him.

It was Eric Venter. Officious and efficient as always.

Just doing his job.

Turner opened his eyes and raw sunlight fried the image from his brain. He tried but couldn't recall it again. Yet it was still in there somewhere, he knew, hidden where it had been hidden all these years. All these years of serving under him. Admiring him. Trusting him. He closed his eyes.

He saw Thandi's face.

He had to escape the past or he'd surrender and die there.

He conjured the girl's face.

The unknown and nameless girl, who had called him to this moment and this place. She hadn't surrendered. She had met death in agony and terror, but still fighting, crawling, dragging her bleeding innards toward the phone. Perhaps scrabbling for the card in her purse with his name printed on it, his number written in his own hand. Out of the zero within him, Turner imagined he heard her final desperate cry. As if she had made that call after all, as if, at last, she made it now.

He worked his hand into the pocket of his pants and found the polythene evidence bag containing the grubby card. He held it in front of his eyes.

There it was: the seed of will he needed.

He had not been able to save her. He had only been able to try to give her some shred of dignity, to honor her spirit by defending the only human right she had left, her right to justice. But perhaps *she* could save *him*.

If he no longer much cared whether or not he lived or died, he cared that he had failed her. He let that seed grow. He watered it with madness. To imagine he could get to his feet was madness. But madness was the one resource he had.

He had rested on the barren ground. He had reembraced the slowness and it had restored some of his strength. He could feel the heat of the sun on his face; he wasn't dead yet. He raised his head from the dirt and it didn't fall back.

He braced his elbows and raised his chest. He looked for the tracks. There they were. A gray shrub crushed and uprooted, a shallow rift in the dirt. He had wandered several paces away before his stumble. He pulled his knees up beneath him and took his weight onto the palms of his hands. His body desperately wanted more rest. Sleep. The sweet invitation of death. But his reserves were not totally exhausted after all. He pulled the pieces together, he reconnected the broken lines of energy into some semblance of unity. In one movement he straightened his back and rose to one knee and braced his hand on his thigh and stood up.

He put the card back in his pocket.

He looked down the broken trail of the tire tracks. They seemed to go nowhere. He had no idea how far he had walked. The road was just a strip of tar, almost flush with the desert floor. He wouldn't see it until he was on top of it. The first thing he would see would be vehicles. There wasn't much traffic into or out of Langkopf, but early morning was the best time to travel. The last things he carried were his badge and his gun. Enough to flag down a car. The gun had chafed the skin from his hips, his thighs. He had moved the holster dozens of times. He had carried the gun in either hand, in both hands. He had cradled it in his shirt. It had come to feel like it weighed more than he did. But he had not abandoned it.

Turner started walking again.

Slow and steady; watch for the rocks. Feet on rails. One careful step would earn him another; one careless could put him back on the ground and he might not get up again. One pace per second. Swing the leg, root the foot, swing the leg. Call it thirty meters a minute. Call it two kilometers an hour. He had an hour left in him. Maybe when he got there he would have more. Don't think about that. The next step is enough.

He squinted against the reflected glare and realized he had lost his shades. He didn't know where. He didn't turn back to look. To go back and find them might cost him the distance that would save him. To go back and not find them would break him.

He walked on. He walked on.

The sun got hotter. His mind blurred again. He held onto his picture of the girl. She drifted away. He lost her. He found her. He brought her back. Watch for the stones. Find her again. His ears had become accustomed to the absolute and measureless silence. It had taken into itself the sound of his own parched breaths, the crunch of his boots.

When it came, the sound of the plane was unmistakable.

THIRTY-SEVEN

Over the rim of her coffee cup Margot saw Mark Lewis drive up in his Discovery. She couldn't help feeling a certain tension. She had learned that she could stare down a Swiss banker, a government minister, a delegation of discontented miners, even a delegation of Chinese investors. None of them could compete with the eyes of Willem when he had raped her—nor with the sight of his tortured corpse when she had discovered it and, just in time, shielded Dirk. Her gaze had not faltered on any of those occasions either. Like Meursault, she was not afraid to look her own life in the face. But Hennie's wet work made her nervous for that very reason: she wasn't seeing it; she wasn't in control. She looked at him across the table on the terrace and he read the question in her face.

"I'll spot Turner from the air. He might have stayed on the salt pan but he's the type to try to hike out of there. If he did he'll have followed the trail of the tire marks, in which case he might have wandered off in the night and got lost. Mark's wheels will confuse the tracks. Simon takes some crime-scene photos—he'll do a better job than Winston would—and films Mark finding the blown fuse in the engine. Mark fixes it, they bring back Turner's car and the bodies. Then Venter and Winston write it all up. Signed, sealed, and delivered by teatime."

Simon met Mark as he got out of the Discovery and started to give him instructions.

"Do you think he's still alive?" asked Margot.

"Doesn't matter," said Hennie. "We took Turner ten clicks farther than Iminathi's dad. We learnt that lesson. And he'd been sweating in the mines for thirty years. He was tougher than a Special Forces veteran. But let's say an Olympic marathon runner walked from that salt pan. Without water he'd have collapsed about six hours ago, that's if he had the sense to wait until sundown. Scorpions can't survive out there. Flies. I'd give Turner a forty-sixty chance of being alive. If he is, he's unconscious. I'll put him away in sixty seconds without leaving a trace. If he stayed with the car he'll be conscious, but if he's still looking tasty, we just back off and pick him off later. Don't worry, love. We're golden."

After dinner last night Margot had given Venter a Console Vault security case containing his wages. She didn't see the point of all that half now, half later nonsense. Just buy him, do it, seal it. Chain him with gold. Was he going to run away in the night? He'd be more afraid of losing what he had than of losing what he hadn't yet got. Basic human nature. She remembered the look in his eyes as the weight had surprised his arm. Her own arm had given him no warning. The eyes of a man who had surrendered all the soul he had. His gratitude for the privilege of doing so had revolted her. It had confirmed her worst opinions of the species. She had recalled Meursault and soothed herself with indifference. She had let Winston witness the transaction. He would get his bonus. But let him stew in envy and doubt until the game was over.

"You think Venter checked his gold?" she said.

"He ran every coin through his fingers before he went to bed." Hennie laughed. "He slept with both arms around the briefcase."

"Cheap at the price."

"Aren't they always?"

She saw Simon glance toward the table, his raised brow a request to join them. She nodded and beckoned him. Mark Lewis tagged along as Simon walked over. She was about to offer them coffee when they all heard the sound of the Skyhawk's engine catch and fire up.

Hennie instantly looked at Simon. "Go."

Simon sprinted off down the path to the east gate.

Hennie grabbed Mark Lewis by the shoulder and shoved him toward the red Range Rover. "Get in my car. Now."

"What do you need me for?" asked Mark.

"We're going to find a corpse. I want a witness." Hennie turned to Margot. "I'll call you. Got to run."

"Why?" She was confused by the sudden action and anxiety.

Hennie backed toward the Range Rover, pointing in the direction of the airstrip beyond the walls. "That must be Dirk. Whatever he's up to, it isn't on our agenda."

Margot ran after Simon.

Dirk? She was running too hard to think. Just a sense of rising panic without a focus. Through the arboretum. Another two hundred meters to the airstrip. She heard the revs pick up, ready to taxi. If Simon got there in time he could stand in front of the nose. She could see the gateway in the wall, the reinforced door wide open. Beyond, the plane was moving. She dashed through the gate, saw Simon and the guard standing stranded on the tarmac as the Cessna swooped along the runway and left the ground. She stopped and watched as it gained height into the clear blue sky. Simon jogged toward her. Frustrated. Worried.

"Dirk?" she said.

"He told the guard they were going to play tennis."

"They?"

Simon hesitated. "Dirk and Iminathi."

"She was here?" Margot felt sick. "In the compound?"

"She must have been here all night."

All night? She remembered Dirk's curt, "Go away." She had thought he was grieving for Jason. That that was why he needed to be alone. Her heart had ached for him as she'd tried to get to sleep. But he'd been grieving with his cock. Fucking that scheming bitch. All night. In her house.

"Tell me how that's possible."

Simon was as cool as always but she read his eyes. She turned away to conceal whatever was written on her face. She knew it must be ugly. She tried to control her breathing. It was difficult, and not because of the run.

"The only way she could have got past the gatehouse is in Mokoena's car. He had no reason to bring her—that makes no sense, even if he wanted to jump ship. She must have hidden in the back seat."

"How much do you think she knows?"

"Depending on what Venter and Mokoena talked about on their way over here, she could know just about everything."

Margot walked back through the gate and half-ran, half-stumbled toward the house.

She had felt angry with Dirk often enough. Exasperated. Disappointed. All the rest. She was his mother, it was natural. Everything she had done, from sinking impossible shafts and borrowing impossible sums to this whole blood-drenched fiasco, had been for him. Now he had cold-bloodedly betrayed her, for a cunt and a pair of tits. For the first time since he'd been born, Margot felt something for him that she couldn't distinguish from hatred.

She reached the terrace and grabbed her phone. She called Hennie.

THIRTY-EIGHT

Less than five minutes after their wheels left the ground Iminathi saw her father's memorial. Beyond it a wide swath of tire tracks ran into the desert like the spoor of some fabled creature.

"Can we land down there?" she asked.

"Too dangerous," said Dirk. "The stones. Even if the tires survived a landing, they wouldn't survive taking off again."

"If we can't pick him up, what are we going to do for him? Drop bottles of water?"

"He'll welcome that for sure but the basic idea is to watch over him until the cavalry arrive, in the unlikely form of Winston Mokoena."

"I tried to persuade Winston to bring him in yesterday," said Imi. "He refused."

"I'm not going to persuade him. I'm going to threaten him."

"With what?"

"Prison food for the rest of his life. Venter too."

"How?"

"Our bent captains haven't done any wet work. Their fingerprints aren't on anything. All they've done is talk, which in court boils down to one bunch of liars accusing another. And they have all the best lies because they're cops. At this point they can still cover their tracks and back out before they're guilty of murdering a fellow policeman. If we give them reason to, they will. If they have to choose between saving their own necks or taking the long drop with their partners in crime, then Hennie and Simon will swing alone."

"Won't Hennie and Simon testify against them?"

"Not unless their lawyers have brain damage. The police and the public prosecutor will not want to see two captains dragged through the mud, because there's never any telling who else might get splashed and the government doesn't need any more bad head-lines. In a nice quiet plea bargain Hennie could save himself ten years and do soft time, instead of diving headfirst into Hell on Earth. If he even tried to take two veteran captains down with him, the judge would make sure that he died in prison. And to a certainty he would fail. The word of two cop killers, one of them a foreigner, against Winston Mokoena, hero of the struggle for national liberation? Hennie's lawyers would cut his tongue out before they'd let him testify. He'd be shooting his own hairy British bollocks off."

"Okay. I still don't hear the threat against Winston."

"Two witnesses. You and me. We find Turner, take photos, then I tell Winston to come and pick him up. If he refuses, and Turner dies, then that's a case that not even Winston can beat. I'll make sure of that."

"What if Hennie gets there first?"

"We've got a hundred and thirty kilometers an hour over the best Hennie can do."

"I mean before Winston?"

"We can stay up here for hours if we need to. Circle, keep Turner in sight. Hennie is not an impulsive type. He's not like my mother. He's a bastard but he thinks before he acts, he never panics. If we're up here, he'll know why. He's not going to swap attempted murder for the real thing."

They were now well into the desert, the tracks still clear with no end in sight.

"We should concentrate on watching," said Dirk. "He couldn't have got this far without water. He must be out here somewhere."

Imi had to ask the question she so far hadn't dared. "Do you remember the accident?"

Dirk didn't take his eyes off the landscape below.

"I wish I did," said Dirk. "The defining event of my life and I was too fucking pissed to even know it had happened. It's humiliating. And it's no defense. I'm guilty. I won't fight it. I believe Jason. If he'd taken those keys, Hennie would've broken his arm." He took his eyes off the trail to look at her. "And I would never have left that girl if I'd known she'd been injured. Never, drunk or not."

"I know that."

The desert swept by beneath them. She could see the far curvature of the earth. Between the horizon and her eyes, there was nothing.

"Do you see any footprints?" said Dirk.

"No."

"Probably too faint to see from up here. The cars weigh two tons. I can't believe we've missed him. Wait—there. Out on the salt pan."

The surface beneath them changed. It became flat and smooth, denuded of even primitive scrub and without the plates of rock, the numberless stones. Ocher sand blotched with enormous streaks of pure white. The wheel tracks were deeper and unbroken. Now she thought she could see what might be footprints, but she wasn't sure. Out on the pristine pan flashes of sunlight bounced from a shiny black mass.

"Turner's Land Cruiser," she said.

"I would chance a landing here, if he's down there."

They closed in. The car came into sharp focus. Another shape, irregular, a dark blot, shifted against the ground nearby. Closer. Lower. The shape broke apart and in a sudden explosion of sinister grace half a dozen Cape vultures soared flapping into the air on enormous beige and gray wings. Their departure revealed three black holes in the salt pan and the gutted hulk of man in ragged blue pants.

"That's a police uniform," said Dirk.

"Rudy?" said Imi.

"Jesus Christ. He cut his head off."

What the vultures left behind them seemed like the aftermath of some monstrous pagan ritual. Imi was sickened with horror and guilt. She had a terrible premonition that she had acted too late, that the violence unleashed here would not be contained, that the ritual was not over and would not be completed without more bloodshed.

THIRTY-NINE

As soon as Turner heard the plane he stumbled away from the track, bending over as far as he could without falling. Six, seven meters. He reached a patch of scrub, half a dozen stunted bushes sparsely scattered. He squatted to put his left hand on the ground and thrust his legs back to lie on his belly. The movement usually took him a fraction of a second. Today it took five, and his arm almost gave way. He rolled onto his back, his face screened by dead, gray branches. He bent his arms and legs flat against the ground to make his shape as irregular as possible. His face was caked in dust and salt. So were his olive shirt and his khaki pants.

Who was the only local outfit who might own a light aircraft? Le Roux. Who wanted him dead? Le Roux. They were looking to finish what they had started. But whatever calculations they had made regarding his actions, they would expect him to be much deeper in the desert. The two-and-a-half liters of water he shouldn't have been able to drink must have won him at least fifteen kilometers, maybe far more. They wouldn't be looking for him here. One man in the plane would be enough. Simon or Hennie. The sound of the engine closed in. He tried to think.

Forty kilometers to the salt pan. The pilot would be cruising slowly, one sixty or less. Fifteen minutes to the pan. He'd see the solar stills, then head back faster. Ten minutes. Turner had a twenty-five minute window. To do what? Reach the road, flag a car? Bury himself in dust? The plane would be out of range of a phone signal for most of that time. He couldn't land here. So call in the muscle in the 4×4s. Or maybe they were already on their way. That was the most logical: spot from the air; close in by land.

He was going to have to shoot it out. Good. What opponent was more dangerous than a man already dead? Today that was him.

The plane whined overhead. Fixed high wings. A Cessna. White with red trimmings. It passed right over him. He watched it soar onward. It didn't circle. The pilot had missed him. Turner clambered back to his feet. He drew and checked his Glock; holstered it. The bastards would still be reluctant to shoot him. They still wanted a parched dead tourist not a cop full of bullet holes. They'd be expecting to find a shambling human wreck with a walnut brain. About that they'd be right. They'd be expecting the easiest kill they'd ever made. About that, they'd be wrong.

At worst, they wouldn't get their tourist.

Wait or walk? Play dead? What if he was wrong? What if they weren't coming yet? That would leave him here frying in the sun. Better to move on, make for the road, flag that car.

Turner walked. Keep it slow. Steady. He detected a faint stirring of adrenaline. He hadn't thought he had any left. It felt good. Relatively speaking. His head ached badly, a pang each time his foot hit the ground. Apply some qigong. He rubbed his skull all over, briskly, with his fingertips. He pushed his fingertips into the Dantian, above his navel, and held them there for thirty seconds. He pressed his thumbs into the hollows on either side of the base of his skull, Gall Bladder 20. Thirty seconds. He pushed his right thumb into the central hollow at the base of his skull, Governing

Vessel 16, and with his left thumb and index finger he pressed the upper ridge of his eye sockets, just below the inner tips of his eyebrows, Bladder 2. Thirty seconds. He used the index and middle fingers of both hands to press up gently beneath his cheekbones, directly below the pupils of his eyes, Stomach 3.

His head still ached but his mind felt refreshed, clearer. He slid his clip holster to the small of his back and drew the Glock and carried it down alongside his thigh. He flexed his fingers around the butt, the trigger. He rolled his shoulders. His neck. Just as he thought that he was as ready as he was going to be, with amazing suddenness the big red Range Rover appeared in the distance.

Amazing, in part, because Turner realized he was no more than five hundred meters from the road. He now recognized the cairn that marked the spot where Iminathi's father had died. The car slowed and swung off the road and rolled toward him, the same car that had killed the girl.

Turner marked a low, dusty shrub and stopped beside it. He raised his left arm and waved at the car, as if in blind desperation. As he did so he sank to his knees, as if overwhelmed by exhaustion. Neither gesture required any great performance. He hoped these distractions would mask his right hand as he laid the Glock on the ground by his ankle, concealed by the bush. He waved with both arms.

The Range Rover hurtled toward him, bouncing on the uneven ground. For a moment he thought it might run over him. Then Hennie braked hard and the car smoked to a halt five or six meters short. A black man in a pale-gray uniform, same as the spotters had worn yesterday, jumped from the rear door and leveled a slung H&K UMP9 at Turner's chest. Turner slumped back to sit on his heels, his arms falling to hang by his sides in a gesture of defeat. The tips of his right-hand fingers touched the butt of his gun.

Hennie got out from behind the wheel. He carried the

Benelli shotgun by its pistol grip, the bore pointed at the ground. A third man sat in the passenger seat without moving. The glare on the tinted screen hid his identity. Hennie smiled and shook his head in admiration.

"You're fucking beautiful, Turner. I have never regretted killing a man in my life, but I will regret killing you. How did you do it?"

Turner gave him a blank, stunned stare. He opened his cracked lips and let his jaw droop. He swayed a little at the hips, as if close to collapse, and raised his left hand in a drinking gesture.

Hennie shook his head. "Sorry, mate."

The guard circled round, still aiming the submachine gun.

"Khosi," said Hennie. "Sling the gun and put the cuffs on him, from behind. And be careful, he's a kung fu expert. Aren't you, Turner?"

Khosi hauled on the sling and slid the H&K behind his back.

Turner scooped up the Glock and lined up the sights.

Hennie jerked up the shotgun.

Bam, bam, bam. Turner put three through Hennie's gut.

Blood gouts erupted from his back as Hennie groaned horribly and staggered. He fired the Benelli into the ground and dust fountained at his feet.

As Khosi struggled with the sling Turner shot him twice in the center of the chest. Crimson ropes of blood flew.

The shotgun barrel tangled in Hennie's legs. He toppled over. Both men hit the cap rock at the same time.

Khosi was stone dead.

Hennie's sunglasses fell from his face and he lay panting and bleeding, his breath catching in his throat as pride tried to stifle the sounds of his pain.

Turner covered the windshield of the Range Rover with the Glock but saw no movement from the man inside.

He stood up, slowly. He walked over to Hennie and stooped

and picked up the shotgun. He saw no sidearm. Hennie watched him through slitted eyes.

Turner checked Khosi. He lay in an enormous pool of blood, already soaking into the dust, it's surface skinning over in the rays of the sun.

Turner holstered his Glock and walked to the Range Rover and leveled the shotgun flat through the side window at Mark Lewis' face.

Lewis stared at him through his shades, his features rigid with fear. Turner repeated the drinking gesture. Lewis scrabbled around and came up with a half-liter bottle. He lowered the electric window and handed it out. Turner felt a waft of cooled air. He pointed at the bottle cap and circled his finger. Lewis eagerly flipped up the cap and pulled the valve open and presented the bottle again. Turner reached past it and took Lewis' shades from his nose with finger and thumb. Lewis blinked and cowered. Turner stepped back and beckoned him from the car.

The young mechanic seemed momentarily disappointed, as if he thought the bottle ought to buy him a ride home. Turner stared at him and Lewis' terror intensified. He opened the door and scrambled out and extended his arm with the bottle. Turner donned the sunglasses. The relief was immediate. Again he ignored the bottle. He jabbed the shotgun at the glove box and pointed two fingers at Lewis' eyes. Lewis got it. He popped the glove box and looked inside.

"There's a pistol in there," said Lewis.

Turner aimed the shotgun bore at Lewis' gut and held out the palm of his hand. Lewis took the pistol by the barrel as if it were a block of uranium and placed the butt in Turner's hand. It was a Steyr L9-A1, the same gun Simon Dube carried. Turner put it in his pocket. He took the bottle of water. He backed off again and directed Lewis toward Hennie.

They both walked over to Hennie and stopped and Turner looked at the bottle. Icelandic Glacial. Only the best. He knew he shouldn't drink too much too quickly. He couldn't remember why. His brain would swell; or was it shrink? He reckoned if he made this bottle last an hour, he'd be okay. He took a sip and held it in his mouth without swallowing. In seconds it was absorbed by his tongue and disappeared. A strange stinging sensation. He took another sip and another, without swallowing. He swallowed the fourth. It burned his raw throat. He didn't feel any surge of delight. One more swallow. His stomach cramped at the shock, then relaxed but felt jumpy. Enough for now.

"Get Hennie in the car," said Turner. His voice grated and crackled. He hadn't counted on it working at all.

"Fuck off," said Hennie. He was flat on his back, his shirt and pants drenched with gore. "I'm not going anywhere."

Turner pointed the Benelli at his crotch. "Margot can bury you with your cock and balls, or without them. Your choice."

Hennie grimaced with rage and pain. He nodded at Lewis. Lewis stooped and manhandled him into a sitting position, then he squatted behind him and threaded his arms around Hennie's chest and hauled him to his feet. Hennie uttered a series of guttural moans but somehow took his own weight. He leaned across Lewis' shoulder and shuffled to the passenger door. With another stifled groan he ducked into the seat and sat down. Lewis tucked his legs in. He shut the door on Hennie and opened the adjoining rear door for himself.

"What are you doing?" said Turner.

Lewis' mouth opened and closed. His lips writhed. His shoulders shook. Turner pointed at the H&K slung around Khosi's blood-soaked torso. A grin of panic-stricken relief broke out on Lewis' face. Like a dog eager to please his master, he hurried to the corpse and worked the sling over its head and arm. His hands were covered with blood. He gathered the spare magazine. He carefully held the gun upright by its barrel. Turner indicated the back seat and Lewis stowed them inside.

"Close the door," said Turner.

"You motherfucker," said Hennie.

Lewis put his hand on the door but couldn't bring himself to push it.

"This was nothing to do with me," said Lewis. "I don't even know what it's all about."

"It's about torturing a man to death."

"No, no, they just asked me for a favor with the car." In his terror, Lewis grinned like some deranged ventriloquist's dummy. "Anyway, you're alive, aren't you?"

"Imi's father," said Turner.

He watched Lewis' grin warp into a grimace, saw his mind struggle to deny the fact that his life was about to end, crushed by the visceral knowledge that here in the desert justice could settle for no less a penalty.

"Who?" tried Lewis.

"The miner."

Lewis' throat convulsed, as if trying to suppress vomit.

"Get it over with," called Hennie. "Shoot the spineless bastard."

"See what they're like? I had no choice," said Lewis. "What could I do?"

Turner said, "Close the door."

Lewis closed the door.

"Do you have children?"

"No." Lewis realized he had given the wrong answer. "I mean I plan to, I love kids."

Turner raised the bottle to his mouth. As he drank he leveled the Benelli and shot Lewis through the solar plexus. Nine buckshot with zero spread, each equivalent to a .38, cored a narrow cylinder through his stomach, aorta, and spine. The blood loss was catastrophic and instantaneous. Lewis folded to the dirt.

"Jesus," said Hennie.

Turner collapsed the stock of the Benelli. Yesterday he wouldn't have executed Lewis for being a murderer and a coward. Today he carried a different law.

He walked round to the driver's door and opened it. He laid the Benelli between the front seats, the barrel resting on the rear. He put the Steyr in the door pocket and rearranged his holstered Glock on his belt. He got in and sat the water bottle between his thighs. The keys were still in the ignition. He started the engine and closed the windows and turned up the air con.

"Give me my phone," said Turner.

Hennie didn't move but he was fully conscious, taking shallow breaths. A waxy pallor. The bullets appeared to have missed the major vessels. Multiple slow leaks of blood and intestinal fluids. Depending on how slow, he might last hours, or be dead within minutes.

"You were going to leave it on my body," said Turner. "Give it to me."

Hennie looked at him. Then he dug the phone out of his bloody pants and handed it over. Turner switched it on and entered his PIN. Forty percent battery. He checked the log. Among various others were two missed calls from Iminathi and five from Mrs. Dandala. Not a single call or message from Captain Venter.

Turner's mind crawled toward the truth. Not because of the dehydration, the headache, the residue of madness, but because he didn't want to get there and see it. He remembered his walking dream in the desert. The dust, the rhino whips, the blood. The bland, efficient face. The face he had forgotten and whose blandness he had thirty years later come to trust. The dream that had been no dream but a lost memory, recovered on the verge of death.

"Eric Venter."

"What?" gasped Hennie.

"Venter turned me in. At the bookie's."

"Who the fuck else would it have been?"

Turner thought about it. The timing.

"You couldn't have got to him that quickly."

"He got to us," said Hennie. "Put you up for auction."

"How much?"

"Two hundred Krugerrands. Paid in advance. Three million rand."

Solid gold coins. Paid in advance. Turner said, "He's here in Langkopf?"

"While you were slogging through the sand, he was drinking prosecco with me and Margot."

Turner put the phone in his shirt pocket. He pushed the gear stick into drive and pulled clear of the corpses. He swung a U and headed for the road.

"Where are we going?" said Hennie.

Turner didn't give him an answer. He didn't have one. He had no plan. The shape he was in, he knew he couldn't get far. His thoughts labored to reach beyond each passing moment. Margot. Simon Dube. Venter. They had no reason to give up now. The best he could do was whatever came next, even if he didn't know what that might be.

"You won't get into the compound," said Hennie. "Not with Simon holding the fort."

"If Simon's holding the fort, who's up in the plane?"

"Dirk," said Hennie. "And Iminathi. On a mission of mercy. If I wasn't leaking shit into my own guts, I'd laugh. They went to protect you from me."

So Imi was the woman he'd hoped she was after all. He had misjudged her. But she hadn't misjudged Dirk. The entire sequence of events unrolled in front of his mind, like a tapestry depicting an allegory of folly. One call, two nights ago, and only the nameless girl would be dead. They had all played their parts—the vain, the vicious, the stupid, and the scared—he as much as any of them. Eight dead men on his back; Hennie would be the ninth. And it wasn't over. He recalled something Hennie had said in the bookie's.

"Ride it till it crashes."

"What else can you do?" said Hennie.

"How many men has Simon got working for him?"

"If he called in all the shifts at once, about a dozen."

Hennie groaned as the wheels mounted the tarmac. Turner drove toward town.

"Is this vehicle on a tracking network?"

Hennie nodded. "Standard security practice."

"Good," said Turner. "They'll come to me."

FORTY

On the tarmac the Range Rover was astoundingly smooth. He felt better than he had an hour ago, but now that his body sensed safety—the coolness and luxury, the immense comfort of the seat, his sudden return to a world where speed and distance cost nothing—he felt closer to collapse than ever. His exhaustion insisted on rest, but if he rested he would die.

He found that he had no strong feelings about dying, or anything else. He was too depleted for fear or anger. He was hollowed out. Numbed. Yet survival had become a relentless drive within him, as if it were a force independent of his will, as if it were not him. If it had been up to him he would have pulled over and gone to sleep, but it wasn't. He had to obey. He had to go on.

"How did you do it?" asked Hennie.

Turner didn't answer him. He swallowed a mouthful from the bottle.

"Call it a last request," said Hennie.

Turner remembered Rudy's last request.

"For fuck's sake you beat me," said Hennie. "You put me on my knees, my mouth's full of dirt. Be fucking gracious."

"I took two and a half liters of water out of Rudy."

Hennie blinked and stared and thought about it. "His blood?"

"Blood, heart, lungs, guts. Brains."

"Jesus Christ." Hennie thought further. "The plastic bags. The shovel." Hennie laughed and pain lanced through him. He fought it off. "Fuck me. They should put you on TV."

"When you left him, he was still alive. We talked. He knew what was coming."

He felt Hennie's eyes on him. Turner glanced at him. Hennie was not horrified. He seemed in awe.

"The law of the land," said Turner.

Hennie stiffened with another spasm as his entrails leaked enzymes and filth into his peritoneal cavity. His fists clenched and his back arched and he bared his teeth. It passed.

"Out, out, damned candle."

"Brief," said Turner.

"What?"

"Out, out, *brief* candle."

"Right. Right," said Hennie. His eyes gleamed with unspilt tears. His voice was hoarse with emotion. "And all our yesterdays have lighted fools the way to dusty death."

The power of the words, their beauty, struck them both silent, and for a while an unspoken communion reigned between them, which seemed like peace. Or something more mysterious and precious.

Hennie went rigid again and against his will he cried out. He reached instinctively toward Turner and Turner grabbed the big man's hand and met the awful strength of its grip with his own. It was a long time before the wave of agony crashed and ebbed. When it did, Hennie still kept hold of Turner's hand.

Hennie's phone rang in his shirt pocket and activated the Bluetooth device. Turner saw the caller ID on the instrument-panel message center.

"It's Margot. Do you want to take it?"

"I won't get another chance."

Turner thumbed the control on the steering wheel and accepted the call.

"Hennie?"

"Hello, love." Hennie tried but failed to conceal his torment.

"Hennie, what's wrong?"

"I'm with Turner."

A fraught silence. Then: "Where?"

"In the Range Rover. He put three nine-by-nineteens through what feels like my colon. Not up to his usual standard, but it did the job."

Something like a strangled sob came through the speakers.

"Will he get you to the hospital?"

"Only in his dreams."

"Turner?"

"You've got lawyers," said Turner. "Call them."

"If Hennie dies, you die. As God is my witness."

"Forget it, love," said Hennie. "Walk away."

"I can't walk away from you. I'd have nowhere to walk to."

Hennie ground his teeth, grunting with the effort to conceal another swell of pain. He failed and let out a terrible childlike cry.

"Hennie, tell me where you are, I'm on my way." Margot's attempt to convey calm revealed only the depths of her desperation.

"You can both hear me," rasped Hennie. "You're my witnesses. On my soul. Deathbed statement, right? That counts for something, right, Turner? It carries more weight, legally."

Turner saw the despair in his eyes. He saw no reason for cruelty. He nodded.

"I killed the girl in Cape Town," said Hennie. "I killed Rudy Britz. Everything that's happened—trying to kill you, Turner—it was all my idea and my doing. Margot Le Roux had nothing to do with it. Any of it. She's innocent. She's clean—"

Hennie broke off and twisted in his seat and gargled. He squeezed Turner's hand.

"Save your strength," begged Margot.

"I love you," said Hennie.

Some thread inside him tightened to and beyond its limit.

"Don't let go," pleaded Margot.

"Time to hit the road to dreamland."

The thread snapped and Hennie's thick fingers relaxed and his racked body went slack. Whoever he had been had flown. Turner felt the instant of his leaving, his spirit passing by. It was unmistakable. The love, the hatred, strength, the pain; the Shakespeare. It was there and then it was not. He wondered how all that could vanish so quickly. He let go of Hennie's hand.

"Hennie? Hennie!"

"He's gone," said Turner.

This time her sob wasn't strangled. It was a lamentation, tailing off as if she'd fallen into somewhere dark and infinitely deep. Then silence. When her voice returned, it was even.

"I'm going to have you eaten alive."

Turner felt an ache of sadness. For all that they had done to him, he couldn't find it in himself to see Margot, or Hennie, or the rest of them, as evil. They had done evil things. But so had he. They were all of them more than their deeds. Weren't they? They could rise above them if they chose to. He tried to find the energy to explain this. But he was too weary, and he knew he would not succeed. He could only join her on the road to catastrophe.

"Simon will tell you where to find me," he said.

Turner cut the call off.

The road became the main street of Langkopf.

No sanctuary here. No one who could help him. Or no one who would. Winston Mokoena. Eric Venter. The young doctor from Bloemfontein.

He could call Colonel Nyathi in Cape Town. Nyathi would call Venter. Venter would fold his hand and call Mokoena. Between them, they might well hold Margot off. Then the lice would scuttle away from the light. Turner saw nothing he could prove against Venter or Mokoena or Margot. And Nyathi, and his superiors, would not want such proof. Venter would be forced into quiet retirement. Turner would be commended, and if necessary threatened—hadn't he murdered Sergeant Britz and eaten his liver?—then gently shunted off. A promotion … to the suburbs. The machinery of justice would grind on.

And no one else would die.

There it was: the correct thing to do. The right thing to do. The good thing.

Yesterday, perhaps, he would have swallowed it. Swallowing went with the job. But that was the man who had been driven into the desert. The man who had walked out would not hide behind the lice who had betrayed him. He would rather have not walked out at all.

Turner drove straight through town. As he reached the curve that swept around the hill he made a right. He headed back to Jason's farm to make his last stand.

FORTY-ONE

Margot beckoned Simon into the kitchen through the glass. She had left him at the table outside when she realized Hennie was hurt. She didn't know why she had bothered. Pride. A sense of decorum. Simon knew everything. His delicacy was superb. She had long admired and appreciated him without ever feeling or showing any warmth toward him. Now he was the only person alive that she trusted.

"Hennie's dead. Turner—"

She didn't finish. She didn't want Turner's face in her mind. She couldn't remember the last time she had told Hennie that she loved him. He had told her every day. She wanted to fall against Simon and weep but couldn't allow herself such weakness. It wasn't a decision or a choice, just something she could not do despite wanting it. The very thought turned her mind into ice. The only place she could go was into the hardness of heart that had always been her final refuge.

"I'm sorry," said Simon. "Neither Mark nor Khosi is answering his phone. We have to assume they're dead too."

"How did that bastard survive?"

"I have no idea."

"I want every man on our payroll armed and ready to move in twenty minutes. Pull them off the mine, get them out of bed, whatever you have to do. And find Turner. He's driving the Range Rover."

She left Simon working his phone and walked through the house to Hennie's den.

It had the atmosphere of what she imagined a traditional British club to be. A snooker table. Vintage leather armchairs. Big game trophies mounted on the walls. Bookshelves filled for the most part with military histories. Memories flooded into her and she pushed them away as tears slid down her cheeks. Time for all that later. She took a key from a silver cup she had won in a skeet competition and opened the gun case. She took out her Mossberg 930 autoloader and a box of double-zero shells. She set the box on the snooker table and opened it and slotted nine rounds into the shotgun.

All her life she had been enraged by inferior people. Or rather, inferior people telling her what she could or couldn't do. Her parents. Her teachers. Willem. Any number of bankers, lawyers, and engineers. People who could not see who she was, who could not see beyond their own narrow minds and limitations and projected these onto her. She had proved them all wrong. Now a ghetto cop had shoved his precious integrity down her throat, turned her son against her, killed the only man she had ever loved. She had offered him every concession, tried to make peace. He had brought death. He had made the house that she and Hennie had built into a mausoleum. How could she live here knowing she'd let Turner walk away? How could she live on at all?

She carried the Mossberg through the house toward the front door. She didn't take spare shells. If nine wasn't enough, she'd be dead. The thought did not cause her any fear. Everything she most feared had already happened.

She doubted she could ever forgive Dirk. If Hennie had been

in that plane, as he'd intended, he would still be alive. He died to save Dirk's integrity. And what was all this integrity? Blind obedience to the rules of someone else's rigged game. A game designed to keep the sheep in their pens. Power subverted it, exploited it, and pissed on the sheep, at every moment of every day and without a twinge of conscience. Dirk should have known that, but the truth was she hadn't taught him. She had shielded him from dark doings. The bribery and violence. The murder of his girlfriend's father. She'd fed him a fairy-tale version of her success. The one in the magazines. She should have taken him in, dirtied his hands, tainted his soul. Too late now. He had tainted hers.

As she reached the front door her phone rang. It was Dirk. She stared at the name on the screen as the ringtone chimed. She didn't want to hear what he had to say. He wouldn't want to hear what she had to say to him. He was out. She'd kept him out. Let him stay there. She thumbed the red icon. The chimes stopped. She opened the door and stepped onto the porch.

Simon's white Toyota 4Runner TRD Pro was parked down the driveway. Two security guards stood waiting. Simon, dressed in combat fatigues, was loading guns into the back. His phone rang and he answered it, exchanged a few words. As he saw her he hung up and walked toward her, his expression troubled. He looked pointedly at the Mossberg in her hands.

"What's the problem?" she said.

"With respect, you should stay here."

"That's not up for discussion. Are we ready?"

"I've got eight more men on the road. They'll meet us in town."

"Where's Turner?"

"The tracker in the Range Rover says he's at Jason's farm."

"Why there?"

"He must be in bad condition. On the open road he's a rabbit. In town he exposes civilians. At Jason's he's got food, water, a good place for a siege. It's what I'd do." He pointed at the guards and the Toyota. "This isn't what I'd do."

"What do you mean?" she said.

"My duty is to protect you. My advice is to back off. As far as I can see, you haven't done anything yet that you can be charged with."

"You have."

"Let me take my chances. Mokoena and Venter won't want a circus. Turner's made his point. Maybe he's had enough."

"He's killed nine men. He won't stop now. Neither will I. Hennie's death changes everything. There's only one way to finish this, and I'm going to be there."

"Let me take him alone."

"That makes no sense. This isn't a matter of honor. I want him killed like a rabid dog."

"Our men are trained to protect your property and your personal safety. They're not trained for tactical combat. In a big city the police would give this to the Special Task Force. Full armor, headset communications, snipers, gas, stun grenades, drone surveillance. Teamwork like clockwork, massive support, medical backup. We've got bunch of amateurs and we're two hours from the nearest trauma surgeon. We'll have a high risk of casualties."

"I'll take that risk. We're twelve against one and he must be more than half-dead already."

"He was outnumbered and more than half-dead when he shot Hennie."

"Hennie must have been careless."

"Please, let me go alone."

"No."

"What if I refuse to go through with this?"

"Then I'll go alone."

Simon looked at the shotgun again. She backed two steps away.

"The only way you'll stop me is if you and your men tie me down. Try that, and casualties are guaranteed."

She was never more serious in her life. Simon knew it. He also knew he could disarm her in less than a second. So did she. The threat was stupid. She let go of the handgrip and let the stock of the shotgun swing to the ground, holding the barrel with her left. The threat was withdrawn. But she didn't surrender.

"I apologize. But, Simon, you're the only person left I can depend on. Hennie depended on you. You were the only real friend he had out here. The only man he regarded as his equal. He would never have put it this way—you know what he was like—but he loved you."

Something shifted in Simon's eyes. She was making no secret of bending him to her will, yet she had spoken no less than the truth.

"I need you."

He considered her for what seemed like a long time. Weighing his heart—his loyalty, his pride, his honor—against his head. She didn't feel that she was being manipulative. She had heard him. She appreciated his advice. But she had weighed her own balance and made her choice. He was a free man, so could he. Simon nodded.

"You give the orders, Mrs. Le Roux."

FORTY-TWO

Mokoena had just finished a large breakfast when Iminathi rang.

It promised to be another long day. Heat, dust, corpses. The amassing of sufficient evidence to support the telling of a tall tale.

The writing of that tale, in a way that would satisfy curious and powerful readers in two separate administrative judicial regions, would occupy several days more.

And all of it in the company of Eric Venter, whom he had loathed from the moment he had shaken his limp, moist hand. Of one thing Mokoena was certain: Margot didn't pay him enough. A bonus would be forthcoming, but what would he spend it on? The prospect of a word with Iminathi, whose assistance in these tasks he would sorely miss, was therefore more than welcome. He accepted the call.

"Imi, how is Kimberley?"

As he spoke he identified the drone of a propeller.

"I'm not in Kimberley. I'm in a plane with Dirk."

Mokoena instantly canceled his schedule. The fact that Imi had evidently deceived him altered his fond feelings for her not one whit. He was many species of villain but not a hypocrite. Her news might even be welcome. He was a reluctant participant in Margot's latest scheme and had always thought it folly. That Imi could be back in league with Dirk pleased him; he had rarely seen a more harmonious match. He had been disgusted by the way it had ended and moved by Imi's grief and shame. If he felt any anxiety, it was only for Imi's safety.

"Congratulations, my dear. Tell me what I can do for you."

"Hennie's dead. Turner's on the run, to Jason's farm. We think Margot will go after him."

"How do you know all this?"

"Dirk called Simon and asked him to stop her. Simon said he would try, but we just saw his truck on the road from the compound."

Mokoena computed the possibilities, as much with his gut as his mind. Like a conductor who could comprehend the meaning of entire operas in a flash of perception. The many operas in which Mokoena had played were, on the whole though with noble exceptions, tragicomedies of suffering and the struggle for power. He had latterly confined his own roles to modest portraits of greed, a much-maligned vice which he considered a virtue next to anger, pride, vanity, envy, and other flagrant invitations to self-destruction.

That Simon had failed to dissuade Margot from her course was a given. Only desperation could have led Dirk to believe that any other result was possible.

Meanwhile, if Turner managed to survive, Mokoena believed that he himself could walk the resulting tightrope without falling off. He had been wise to play as small a role as possible in recent events.

If Turner was killed, which Mokoena had been ready to accept, albeit with regret, that puzzle would now be complicated by Dirk's lust and pride, not to mention whatever supposed virtues he was currently high on. Few impulses were more dangerous to the general good than heroism, particularly when the audience was the woman you loved. Unlike Margot, Mokoena had always sensed Dirk's essential strength of character. She had mistaken that strength for weakness because it had failed to reflect her own combative and quasi-paranoiac personality. Dirk's knowledge of the legal system was now sufficient to cause very great complications, should he so choose. And God only knew what Oedipal factors were in play; a province beyond Mokoena's expertise.

So Turner's death represented a slacker, thinner, longer tightrope, strung a good deal higher above the ground.

To his knowledge six armed men had died at Turner's hands in the last twenty-four hours, and he doubted poor Hennie had died alone. The mighty and stone-hearted desert itself had failed to dispatch the intrepid lawman. He wouldn't let a gang of glorified janitors take him down without a fight. More bodies. More paperwork. Even taller tales to tell.

"I'm on my way to Jason's," said Mokoena. "Reassure Dirk that I support his sentiments and tell him to take you home."

He listened to her speaking but her voice was now distant, the words made inaudible by the propeller. He collected his car keys and headed for the door, his phone still to his ear. He thought of digging out his gun but remembered Gaston Boykin. He was going to talk, not shoot. The gun could only increase his chances of getting killed. It was a mystery to him that so many were unable to appreciate this simple fact.

"We're on our way to Jason's now," said Imi.

"Tell Dirk that's a very bad idea. Even better, tell him you think it's a very bad idea."

"But I don't," said Imi. "We're going to do what's right. We're going to stand up to her. That's why all this has happened, because we were all too scared."

"Imi, listen to me. I appreciate his intentions but believe me, at this point Dirk can only make things worse—"

She hung up. Mokoena blundered through the front door without stopping to set the alarm and clambered into his Cherokee.

FORTY-THREE

When Turner returned to the red Range Rover with his jug of eggs and fruit, a fly had entered with him. He wondered if its buzzing could be heard on his memo.

He realized he was glad of its company. The fly was alive and it didn't want to kill him. As time passed the air con slowed it down until all it could do was scuttle around on Hennie's face. Now it sat unmoving on his right cheekbone, just above his beard. Turner hoped it wasn't dead.

He reactivated the recorder to finish the memo to Venter.

"So I'm sitting in a car with a dead man who died with poetry on his lips.

"I expect to die, but that doesn't bother me. I'll tell you what does.

"I came here to arrest a drunken driver.

"Not just because it was the law but because it was right.

"For no good reason I gave them, nine men tried to murder me.

"I killed them all.

"And that was right, too.

"So why does all this right feel wrong?"

Turner paused to drink the egg concoction in the jug. He'd swallowed nearly a liter, and it had worked. He felt half human. He set the jug back in the footwell.

"Maybe you can tell me, Captain. I remember the expression on your face when you saw Margot's photo in the magazine. I didn't know what it meant then, but I know now. It meant you saw your chance from the beginning. You saw it all. That's why you agreed to send me up here. You knew how hard I would push. You knew I would never let it go. You used me like an enforcer in a cheap protection racket, except this racket wasn't so cheap. They stuffed your mouth with gold. But you're going to choke on it.

"Because this case is still mine.

"It's always been mine.

"And I am going to break your heart with it.

"Yours etcetera,

Warrant Officer Turner."

He saved the memo and started the upload to the cloud.

He put the phone in his pocket.

He felt as if his body had melted into the seat. To get out of the car seemed a greater challenge than crossing the desert. More guns. More killing. More right that felt wrong. He looked at the fly. He knew how it felt.

He heard the whine of the Cessna in the distance.

Dirk and Imi. They were still looking for him. Maybe they knew where he was. Jason's hardworking ancestors had cleared the surrounding fields of stones. Just yellow grass. The plane could land here if they wanted to.

If Margot didn't get here first. If she was coming.

He remembered her anguish.

She was coming.

Time to move.

He opened the glove box and found a pair of binoculars. He

slung them round his neck. He opened the door and recoiled from the heat. The fly buzzed to life and swooped past his face to freedom.

Turner set the jug in the footwell and heaved his legs out one by one. He pulled himself to his feet and leaned one hand on the roof and pulled it back. The metal was burning. He took the Steyr from the door pocket and stuck it in the back of his pants. He closed the door. He opened the trunk and found a carton of shotgun shells. He put a half-liter bottle of water in his thigh pocket. All his movements slow, his joints unsteady, his muscles threatening to cramp. He opened the rear passenger door and reloaded the Benelli and extended the stock. He propped the shotgun against the door. He raised the binoculars and glassed the length of the road.

Three white vehicles in convoy.

The plane droned directly overhead.

He took the UMP9 submachine gun from the rear seat and checked the chamber. He slung it across his back and stuck the spare magazine beside the Steyr. He closed the car door. He had chosen his death ground. He had cover most of the way there. Truck, shearing shed, tractor: to the redoubt of rolled silage. They wouldn't see him but he would see them.

He glassed the road.

The convoy was a kilometer from the gate.

Turner felt sick. They didn't need to be here. Most of the men in those cars could have no idea of who he was or why they were coming to kill him. All they had to do was turn around. They were free to do so. They had the power. But they wouldn't. They would do as they were told. Anger stirred in his chest. He had come here to do an honest job. He had played it straight. They had forced him to become a monster.

Turner picked up the shotgun and limped across the yard.

He would show them a monster.

FORTY-FOUR

Margot bent her head to peer upward out of the window. The Cessna had circled the farm and she couldn't see it but the noise of its propeller was getting louder. The convoy had just passed through the gate and was driving slowly toward the farmhouse. Margot was in the second vehicle. Simon sat next to her in the back seat, behind the driver.

"What does Dirk think he's doing?"

"He's going to land," said Simon. "My advice is to turn back. Forget this."

"We've been through that."

"This operation is dangerous enough. With noncombatants in the field it becomes even worse."

"Nobody asked them to be here," said Margot. "Move in now and they won't be able to interfere."

"This could take hours," said Simon. "We can't just drive up to the door."

His caution infuriated her. Panic and rage pounded through her heart. He wasn't even looking at her, he was studying the terrain ahead. He's doing his job, she told herself, but she could hardly hear herself. She was going to lose. Even Pyrrhic victory was going to be snatched from her hands. She was going to lose it all. Total humiliation.

"Stop. Let me out of the car," she said.

Simon spoke into his phone. "All units stop now. If you come under fire, head back to the road at maximum speed." He turned on her. "Margot, stay here."

He always called her Mrs. Le Roux; his patience was at breaking point.

"Turner could be anywhere. I have to assess the ground. We need to make a methodical sweep. Let me do what you pay me for."

He stared at her until she nodded. He took his assault rifle in his left hand and opened the car door and stood up and out smoothly. She heard a hollow thump then a distant double crack.

Simon grunted and dropped from her sight.

Margot stared out of the open door as the double cracks continued and the men in the front seat shouted and the car lurched and swerved forward to clear the car ahead.

The car ahead wasn't moving.

Sudden deafening bangs stunned her. A constellation of holes appeared in the windshield and blood splattered the steering wheel and dashboard, the roof. Her face. The 4Runner slowed to a crawl. The driver swayed in his seat. He mumbled in Xhosa and the car lurched forward again in a curve and the open rear door swung shut and she saw the driver's hands slip from the wheel. His companion, yelling, reached across to grab the wheel and again the car slowed into a creeping semicircle.

All the time the double pops in her ears, the slam of bullets through glass and sheet metal. Distant yells of agony and panic from the other cars, the first car now behind them to their left and still not moving.

She twisted to look through her window and saw the third car, its windshield opaque with bullet holes and sprayed blood, also trying to turn. Its side window shattered and she saw the driver's head burst open and suddenly the car lunged straight toward her. She threw herself across the seat as the third car hit her door broadside with another shocking bang and the window collapsed and showered the seat with glass. The 4Runner rocked violently and tilted, then groaned back down, metal on metal, to sit at a shallow angle.

All three cars were now motionless.

In a few seconds her perception had been swamped with absolute chaos. She found herself gasping for breath. *Get out. Get out.* But she saw the passenger door open and the guard lunge out, his head down, plunging for the ground, crawling on his hands; watched him skitter across the grass, then fall on his face as a pair of bloody holes erupted from his side. He tried to get up and crawl on but two more slugs thudded into him and he went back down.

She crammed herself down into the footwell and clasped her elbows to her ears and panted in terror. Terror such as she had never known. The short pops continued—spaced, methodical, pitiless. Then they stopped.

The engine of the stranded 4Runner droned quietly. From outside she heard a man crying out in pain. Shouts in a language she had never learned, yet their meaning was clear enough. Shouts of fear; surrender. Shouts for mercy. More gunshots began, louder, closer; twelve-gauge shotgun rounds. More shattering glass. The shouts abruptly cut off by the blunt, ugly blasts.

A sudden silence.

She sensed—perhaps saw, she couldn't tell what she knew anymore—a figure loom at the window. She closed her eyes. She tried to think but no thoughts came. The silence seemed unbearably long. Its unknowable meaning invaded and amplified her fears. She sensed the figure move on but dared not look.

She started at three rapid shotgun blasts, almost right above her head. She forced herself not to scream.

A pause, then another blast.

The awful silence returned.

The shotgun boomed again.

Margot lay there and waited to be killed like a sheep. The Mossberg was still propped upright in the angle of the door by her head but her limbs were paralyzed, her insides liquid and melting. She could neither fight nor fly. No memories, good or bad, flashed through her mind. No images of her Dirk. Or of Hennie. Her whole life was erased. All she had been. All she had thought herself to be. Her identity. She could only imagine the car door opening, the muzzle of a gun pointing at her head. She was a dumb beast waiting to slaughtered. She had once seen a goat standing motionless, frozen, as a lion padded casually toward it. Now she understood why. It was easy. It was natural. It was wise. Just let it happen and be done. The experience, the pain, the horror of fear vanished from her awareness, leaving a blissful void as her reward for utter acceptance. She was face-to-face with death, and she felt freed.

She heard the door open. *Let it happen.*

But nothing happened. She waited. And nothing happened.

She lowered her arms and opened her eyes and looked up.

A man stood watching her, framed by the doorway. He held a Benelli shotgun, muzzle pointed at the ground, in his right hand. She knew it was Turner—who else could it be?—yet for a moment, despite that certainty, she did not recognize him. He was as gaunt as a ghost. His skin hung slack from the bones of his face. His shoulders, his upper body seemed to teeter on his hips, seemed to sag as if a fair breeze would topple him over. But that wasn't so.

As if from nowhere Simon Dube lunged into view, his shirt gleaming red, no weapons but his hands, fingers clawing for Turner's throat as if only bare hands could settle the issue between them. Turner warded him off with a backhanded blow to the chest and Simon hurtled back down. Turner pointed the shotgun beyond her field of vision. His face twisted with despair as he fired. Blood spray darkened his pants. He turned back toward her.

He reached up and took his shades off. His eyes were dark tunnels drilled into a vein of some unspeakable ore. In her state of naked being she could see everything as it was, without fear, without hatred, uncontaminated by any emotion at all, and what she saw was the immensity of his suffering. The suffering she had inflicted upon him. She felt a strange compassion. Not for him but for the pain he embodied. And yet perhaps that was all he now was. Perhaps that was all that she had left him. That and the right to kill her. The blood debt she owed him could only be paid in blood.

But he didn't collect it.

Instead he held her eyes for longer than she thought she could endure. His gaze the most awful sight she had ever encountered. But she did endure it. She was obliged to. All this horror was hers. No, it was his, too. It was theirs. It connected them as deeply as anything had ever connected her to anyone, except perhaps her son. But that bond was broken. For a moment they shared the immense weight of what they had done. And in that moment she loved him. She loved Turner. The contradiction was more than she believed she could bear. Yet bearing it was the only future she had.

If she wanted one.

If she reached for the Mossberg he'd shoot her and she'd be at peace. She wouldn't have to mourn Hennie. She wouldn't have to face Dirk. Or the triumph of his girl, who would probably become her daughter-in-law. She wouldn't have to face the families of the dead. She wouldn't have to help Mokoena shovel up the mess. She wouldn't have to avoid prison. She wouldn't have to live with total humiliation and defeat.

She could do all that. She could pay those debts and more.

All she had to do was open her mouth and admit to them, admit them to him. To tell him the war was over. To surrender.

She opened her mouth but no words came out. She couldn't speak. Some physical force squeezed her throat shut, she could feel it. That force was herself. Her truest self. Her. The self beneath all the other selves, who had driven her so far and who knew the taste of surrender and defeat, who had choked on it half her life and who had sworn never to swallow it again. She took a deep breath to try again, to try to conquer that self. Then Turner spoke and her choices were snatched away.

"Go home," said Turner.

Turner threw his shotgun aside put his shades back on and walked away.

Margot took the breath and clambered up onto the seat.

Go home?

She was calm now, calm with an ice-cold rage. Glass fragments clung to her hair and she shook her head to get rid of them. Her shirt was stained with blood. It was the driver's; she wasn't hurt. Turner was hurt. He could hardly stand up straight. One on one. Simon had been right. She could take down a wild rock dove on the wing, with a throat shot so as not to damage the meat. Jackals on the run by night.

Go home?

He hadn't meant it unkindly, she knew. It was the best advice she'd had in days. Maybe she just needed a reason to do what she wanted to do, to follow her gut and her heart. But no one spoke to her like that. No one.

FORTY-FIVE

Turner watched the Cessna taxi across the grass toward the farm buildings.

The battle—they would call it a massacre, but only because he'd survived—had lasted less than two minutes. The convoy had halted sixty meters short of the silage rolls where Turner had taken cover. When Simon had stepped from the car it had been as good as over.

Two-round bursts. Two bursts for each driver. Front car, rear car, middle car. Copper fragments and lead cores tumbling through flesh-filled boxes, the doors and glass offering no more protection from the H&K rounds than a shirt. Within ten seconds he was shooting at three beached whales. He gunned down the escapees as they fled. Not a single round was fired in return. When the magazine was empty, he moved in with the Benelli and mopped up the survivors.

He had offered no personal threat to any one of these would-be assassins. For whatever reason—their pitiful wages, the thrill of the chase, blind obedience—they had traveled here to hunt him down. And he was weaker than any of them. He owed them no more mercy than they would have given him.

Even so.

An eerie quiet now lay across the farm. The firework tang of powder smoke tainted the air. He saw a black Jeep Grand Cherokee turn through the gate and drive slowly up the track. Mokoena leaned out of the window with his right arm raised and his palm open in a gesture of peace.

The Cessna trundled toward the windmill pump and stopped. The doors opened. He saw Dirk and Imi climb out. They stood in postures of shock and stared at the carnage. Imi turned her head and stared at him.

Turner walked toward the red Range Rover.

He wanted to be done with this madness. He wanted to forget it all. But the look on Margot's face hung in his mind and he knew she wouldn't let him go.

FORTY-SIX

Mokoena absorbed the sight of the bloodbath without surprise or any other emotion. He would dwell on its tragic dimensions and the role that he had played later on. Now he had to prevent those dimensions from getting any larger. There were enough players left on the field to do more damage and two of them at least were far from their right minds.

Turner was shambling toward the Range Rover with the gait of someone suffering from some obscure neurological disease.

Margot emerged from the wreckage of one of the white vehicles and started after him in a daze. She was carrying a long black Mossberg shotgun. Mokoena had seen her use it and Turner's head was considerably bigger than a skeet. Switch on the siren? It was as likely to provoke her as bring her to her senses. Her senses were beyond prediction.

Imi and Dirk were running from the Cessna toward the farm buildings. More fuel to the fire. They no doubt meant well but they were the worst people in the world to try to cool this down.

Mokoena swerved toward them and put his foot down. His Cherokee sped across the grass and the couple saw him coming and stopped by the wind pump's water tank. He braked hard and skidded to a halt just in front of them. As he got out he grabbed a pair of handcuffs from the door pocket.

Margot was still walking after Turner, her intent unclear. Mokoena circled the Cherokee to Dirk and Imi. They both appeared bewildered and horrified.

"Dirk, show me your right hand," said Mokoena.

"Why?" said Dirk, confused, while automatically extending his arm.

Mokoena snapped the bracelet around his wrist before Dirk even saw it. With another expert maneuver he locked the second bracelet to the handle of the Cherokee's passenger door. Dirk made to protest.

"You've done your best," said Mokoena. "Let me do mine." He looked at Imi. "Stay here with him. Not a word from either of you. If shooting starts, kneel here behind the engine."

Mokoena hurried toward the yard. He drew level with Margot. She was still walking, the Mossberg canted across her chest, her finger on the trigger.

Turner reached the Range Rover. He must have been aware that she had followed him and now he turned to wait for her. He looked like a man who had just walked across hell but was still standing on the wrong side of its gates. His Glock was on his right hip. His gaze and Margot's seemed locked in some unfathomable communion. Margot stopped five meters away from him.

Mokoena stopped, too. "Margot?" he said, gently.

She looked at him. He saw a terrible self-knowledge in her eyes, painful to witness. He felt a deep sadness. He felt ashamed.

"I could have stopped this," she said.

"Any one of us could have stopped it," said Mokoena.

"Why didn't we?"

"We can talk about that later. As long as we stop it now."

"I don't know if I want to."

"The rest of us do." Mokoena glanced at Turner, an appeal for support.

"No charges will be brought against you," said Turner. "Or against Dirk."

"Why not?" she asked.

"Because enough's enough."

Margot's mouth curled. "Are you telling me I've won?"

"You can look at it any way you want," said Turner. "We just have to carry it."

Her expression seemed to clear and for a moment Mokoena thought she would let it go. Then something caught her eye and she stared at the red Range Rover. Her shoulders trembled with a shuddering intake of breath. She held the breath as tears rolled from her eyes. Mokoena looked at the car.

Hennie sat dead in the passenger seat, his face pressed against the glass.

"Oh, Hennie."

Mokoena saw the final collision, as he had seen it from the beginning. He struggled for the right platitude. "Margot, please. You know Hennie wouldn't want this—"

"Mother?"

Dirk. Mokoena cringed inwardly.

Margot looked beyond his shoulder at her son. The clarity returned to her eyes. She smiled as if at some secret only she possessed; as if she suddenly knew how to restore order to the world she had built and then destroyed.

"Mother died today," she said.

"Margot, I beg you," said Mokoena.

Margot swung back to face Turner.

"Time to hit the road to dreamland."

She snapped the Mossberg to her shoulder with perfect form.

Turner pulled his left foot back like a duelist as he drew his pistol.

The slam of the pistol shot blurred into the shotgun blast.

Blood flew from Turner's left arm.

His bullet took Margot through the heart. A single-shot kill.

The secret smile was still on her face as she dropped.

"Margot gets what Margot wants," said Mokoena.

Turner holstered his gun and walked to the Range Rover. He opened the passenger door and Hennie tumbled out to lie in the dust, his arm stretched out toward Margot. Turner closed the door. He looked at Mokoena.

"Where's Venter?"

Mokoena could see no personal advantage in Venter's survival, only even more difficulties than those he already faced. A dead Venter could shoulder the blame for what had passed. After all, he was the only one placed to orchestrate the conspiracy from the beginning.

"At the hotel," said Mokoena. "Waiting for my call."

"Tell him to be outside in twenty minutes."

"What happened to you out there?"

"It's better no one knows."

Turner walked around the Range Rover and opened the driver's door.

"Turner?"

Turner stopped.

"Life moves on," said Mokoena.

Turner looked at Dirk and Imi. His thoughts and feelings, if any, were inscrutable. He turned to Mokoena.

"Make sure we have no reason to meet again."

Mokoena accepted the threat in good grace. "Sound advice."

Turner got into the Range Rover and drove away.

Imi and Dirk watched him go. Dirk was in shock. Imi had her

arms around him. She was strong. The sight of them, at least, gave Mokoena hope. If anyone could make water flow uphill, Iminathi could. He took the keys to the handcuffs from his pockets and sighed. There was much to do. But if Winston Mokoena was anything, he was a man who got things done.

FORTY-SEVEN

Turner stood in the shade cast by the hotel's yellow canvas veranda. He drained the last of the smoothie and put the jug on the ground. As he straightened up Venter came through the glass doors and saw him and stopped.

He was dressed in a lightweight tan suit and carried a stainless steel security case. A variety of emotions struggled for control of his face, none pleasant. He fashioned something that was supposed to be a smile.

"Turner. Thank God." He saw the blood soaking the arm of Turner's shirt. "You're wounded."

"Did you get my memo?"

Venter frowned, puzzled. "No, I—when did you send it?"

Turner took his phone out. He checked the upload to the cloud. It wasn't a big file, but at local speeds it still hadn't completed. He thought about it. Then he canceled the transfer. He returned the phone to his shirt.

"What did you have to tell me?" asked Venter.

"Let's go."

Venter tried the smile again. "I'm here to organize the search and rescue for you. As soon as I heard you'd disappeared I got on a plane."

"Get in the car."

"Where's Mokoena?" asked Venter.

"Mokoena's busy."

"Where are we going?"

"We're going to examine a crime scene."

They got in the car and Turner sat holding the wheel, staring through the windshield.

"You sure you don't need a doctor?" asked Venter.

"Nineteen eighty-seven," said Turner. "A street protest in Khayelitsha. Do you remember it?"

"There were dozens of minor riots in the eighties."

"You were involved in this one."

"I was involved in many."

"A young woman was whipped to death."

"Thousands died in the State of Emergency. I witnessed tragedies every day. That went with the job. It still does, doesn't it?"

Turner looked at him. Venter held his eyes, with difficulty.

"If you're talking about your sister," said Venter, "I don't know if I was there. It's possible, but I don't remember. Even if the police did kill her, I didn't. I would remember that. You know me, I haven't got the stomach for doing that kind of thing."

"Only for watching it."

"What could I do?"

Turner didn't know how much it mattered. It didn't matter at all to his plans. He had a path to follow, the only path he could see, and there was no stopping. He wouldn't find another until he got to the end. What that other path would be, and where it would take him, was the work of tomorrow.

He put the car in drive and pulled away.

He drove north from Langkopf. When he reached the pickax

memorial he turned off the road and followed the tracks, past the bodies of Lewis and Khosi, drying in the blackened dust, and out into the desert.

He drove in silence. Venter, clutching the suitcase to his chest, did not speak either. He seemed to understand that there was nothing he could say that Turner would hear. Perhaps he too knew that the path he had chosen could only be followed to its end.

In Turner's mind—in every cell of his body—the distance to be traveled was immense. The Range Rover consumed it in twenty minutes. The salt pan opened before him. The heat quavered at the limit of his vision. A tall, black obelisk appeared, shimmering, floating above the ground. It's form shifted and danced. For a moment it disappeared. When it reappeared, it gradually resolved into his Land Cruiser.

As they got closer, a flock of vultures took wing and soared away beneath the noontide sun. Turner drove past the stranded vehicle and swung in a wide circle. He pulled up beside the Cruiser and turned off the engine. He opened the door and got out. Venter stayed inside.

Turner went to the Cruiser and opened the trunk. He took out his trumpet case and his laptop and carried them to the Range Rover.

He studied the scene of yesterday's events. His atrocity.

Already the desert was reclaiming itself. The solar stills were black pits, empty except for Rudy's boot. The carrion birds had helped themselves to the organs conveniently provided and then stripped the remaining carcass to sinew and bone. Only the one booted foot remained, and even that bore the marks of their appetites. What remained of the shattered skull had been picked as clean as stone.

Turner opened the passenger door and looked at Venter.

"Get out."

Venter got out.

Turner stowed his laptop and his trumpet case inside. He closed the door.

"Open your jacket," he said.

"What? What do you mean?"

"Open your jacket."

Venter put the case down by his feet and held his jacket open. He had a regulation Glock 17 on his right hip and a nylon handcuff pouch on his left.

"You can draw the gun and shoot," said Turner. "Or you can give it to me, in the holster. Your best choice is to draw."

"Have you lost your mind?"

"We've both lost more than that."

Venter's face writhed as he struggled to come to terms with reality. Turner felt no satisfaction in his panic, no pleasure, no victory. Venter reached across with his left hand and unclipped the holster and gave the gun to Turner. Turner tossed it across the pan. Venter glanced after it and saw the headless skeleton in its shredded uniform. The vacant blood holes. The eyeless skull.

Sweat poured down his face, provoked as much by fear as by the blinding heat. His defeat was plain to him, yet he went through the following motions as if in a trance. He grabbed his steel security case and laid it on the hood of the Range Rover. He appeared to hope that the case and its contents would save him. He produced a ring of keys and selected one and held it between finger and thumb.

"Do you know what's in this case?"

Turner held out his hand. Venter gave him the keys.

"Take a look for yourself," said Venter.

Turner checked the keys on the ring. He put them in his pocket.

"What can I say?" said Venter. "I saw my chance and I took it. I missed. I set you up, yes, I betrayed everything I stood for. Everything we both stood for. I'm sorry. But here we are. We both know the reality. The force contains over fourteen hundred officers with criminal convictions. Convictions, not allegations, including murder and rape, including brigadiers and colonels. Your crusade won't change that. So let's be grown-up about it. What's in that case is six kilos of twenty-two karat gold. With you alive, I guarantee we can get more, much more. Margot's more exposed than ever."

"Margot's dead."

Venter took that in. He licked his drying lips.

"So are fourteen others."

"Jesus."

"If you hadn't made that call, I wouldn't have had to kill any of them. I had to kill them all."

"You take the gold. Take it all." Venter started panting. "What happened here isn't in our jurisdiction. Cape Town doesn't need to know, Christ, they won't even want to know. Neither will anyone else. Let Mokoena bury it. There's nothing I can hold over you without hanging myself. I'll retire. I'll be out of your life. I'll be gone and you'll be compensated for—well, for what you've been through. For you it's a win-win."

"You mean, 'be reasonable.'"

"Right. It's the only intelligent thing to do. Now let's go back."

Turner reached under Venter's jacket and took the handcuffs from their pouch. The keys to the cuffs were on the ring in his pocket.

"You're taking me in?" said Venter. "What's the point? You'll only damage the service. You think they'll thank you for that? They'll have you directing traffic."

Turner locked one bracelet around Venter's right wrist. Venter, resigned, offered his left. Turner ignored it.

"A million years ago this was a sea," said Turner. "When they brought me out here yesterday, I was probably the first man ever to set foot on it. I doubt anyone will ever set foot on it again. That makes you the last."

Turner snapped the second bracelet around the steel handle of the security case.

Venter gaped at the case of gold chained to his arm. He stared out at the quavering veil that barricaded the salt pan from the rest of creation. He swung on Turner.

"I know you, Turner. You're not going to do this. This isn't you."

"You should have listened to my memo."

"I didn't get your bloody memo."

"You've got it now."

Turner opened the door of the Range Rover and climbed in and closed the door and started the engine. Venter grabbed the case and staggered round to the passenger door and lunged for the handle. Turner pressed the central locking switch and the locks clunked. He saw Venter's face through the window. He pitied him. But not enough to reopen the door.

Let justice be done.

Turner drove away.

He didn't look back.

As he crossed the pan he saw his own footprints in the salt. Wherever he went he would carry this desert with him for the rest of his life. It was worth carrying. He thought of the nameless girl who had saved him from its timeless embrace. He would carry her too. Much had been taken from him and he'd never get it back. But much endured.

What had Mokoena said? *Life moves on.*

Turner took the bottle of water from his pocket and poured a mouthful down his throat. It tasted good. When he got within range of a signal, he made a call.

"Mrs. Dandala? It's Turner. How are you?"

"You didn't answer my messages." Her voice was as irritable as ever.

Turner smiled. "I apologize. Work got on top of me for a while."

"No one will thank you for it."

"That's okay."

"Well? So where are you now?"

Turner said, "I'm on my way home."

THE END

I want to thank Albert Zuckerman, founder of Writers House, New York, whose creative expertise helped me knock this novel into shape. No author has a greater friend.

—TW